XU XI was born in Hong Kong to a Chinese-Indonesian family. The city was home to her until her mid-twenties, after which she led a peripatetic existence around Europe, America and Asia. For eighteen non-consecutive years, the author held a second career in international marketing and management with various multinationals. At the end of 1997, she finally surrendered completely to fiction. She now inhabits the flight path connecting New York, Hong Kong and New Zealand.

The New York Times named her a pioneer writer from Asia in English. "In the 1970's and 1980's, when she was developing her fictional voice, Xu Xi felt alone in her homeland. Unlike most Asian writers here, she wrote in English. Twice, for long periods, her antidote for isolation was to live in the United States." She is an active champion of literature from Asia, and compiled the first comprehensive anthology of Hong Kong writing in English covering prose and poetry from 1945 to the present. There is no question, as *Asiaweek* once said of her work, "that she gets to the heart of the matter." In addition to writing, she also teaches at the MFA program of Vermont College in Montpelier.

Awards include a New York State Arts Foundation fiction fellowship and the *South China Morning Post* story contest winner. She has been a resident writer at the Jack Kerouac Project of Orlando, Florida, Kulturhuset in Bergen, Norway, and the Anderson Center in Red Wing, Minnesota. Her fiction, essays, book reviews and op-eds have been published and broadcast internationally. She holds a MFA in fiction from the University of Massachusetts at Amherst.

Hong Kong Rose is her second novel. Published in 1997, it was an instant bestseller but lapsed out of print. This new edition re-introduces readers to an important work that boldly tackles courage, cowardice and compromise in modern Asian society. Visit *www.xuxiwriter.com* for more information on her work, interviews and appearances.

XU XI's books from Chameleon Press

Overleaf Hong Kong: Stories & Essays of the Chinese, Overseas (2004)

Chinese Walls & Daughters of Hui (2nd ed 2002)

History's Fiction (2001)

The Unwalled City (2001)

Other books

City Voices: Hong Kong Writing in English 1945 to the Present, ed. Xu/Ingham
(Hong Kong University Press, 2003)

HONG KONG ROSE

(2nd Edition)

A Chameleon Press book

HONG KONG ROSE

ISBN 988-97060-5-9

© 2004 Xu Xi (*a.k.a.* S. Komala)

Published by Chameleon Press
23rd Floor, 245-251 Hennessy Road, Hong Kong
www.chameleonpress.com

Distributed in North America by WEATHERHILL
41 Monroe Turnpike, Trumbull, CT 06611
tel 800.437.7840 • *fax* 800.557.5601 • *www.weatherhill.com*

Agent for all rights HAROLD MATSON COMPANY
276 Fifth Avenue, New York, NY 10001 • *hmatsco@aol.com*

Typeset in Adobe Garamond and Optima

Cover design by Image Alpha (Holdings) Ltd.

Printed and bound in Hong Kong by Regal Printing

HONG KONG ROSE

A Novel

by

XU XI

Chameleon Press

For the sibs, Wilma, Merly, Felix and Mary,
and now also Greg and Lee.

With thanks to Liz Gay and Scott Jones, who read,
and to Steve Black, for Liberty.

The Sick Rose

Oh Rose thou are sick.
The invisible worm,
That flies through the night
In the howling storm

Has found out thy bed
Of crimson joy:
And thy dark secret love
Does thy love destroy

Songs of Experience
William Blake

What is that which the breeze, o'er the towering steep,
as it fitfully blows, half conceals, half discloses?

Now it catches the gleam of the morning's first beam
in full glory reflected now shines on the stream

The Star Spangled Banner
Lyrics by Francis Scott Key

October, 1987

Guess I'm not going to become an American after all.

Regina will. Tomorrow. She's ecstatic. Now she'll be able to come out of "concealment" as an illegal alien, and go back to Hong Kong for the first time in sixteen years. Amnesty. From the US Government and our mother. She'll also register to vote and apply for a passport.

While I'll be facing deportation, if I'm lucky.

Poor Mum. What will she do when she finds out? How can I expect her to understand that one day I'm earning over six figures, boosted by an expense account plus enormous bonuses, and the next day, nothing? Or that the last five years spent legalizing my alien status are now classified as allegedly criminal activity? All I've got to show for my American exile is an extravagant co-op mortgage, non-existent savings, endless rows of dresses, shoes to rival Imelda's and a speedboat on Long Island. It would have taken her years as a secretary back home to earn what I did in one year here on Wall Street.

It's a good thing Dad's not exactly around to see this.

But Dad would have been kind. With his usual resignation, he'd consider my company's misfortune nothing more than the exigencies of life. I wish he were around; at least he'd understand that all this is about more than just losing a green card.

Now why does the East River actually look clean tonight?

I'll miss this view. 5108 Chase Manhattan Plaza. Respectable address, nice office to swan around in, and the Statue of Liberty against the red glare of twilight. Gordie laughs when I say I never intended to live in America, that I didn't want to leave Hong Kong — he thinks I've always been American at heart. Maybe that's why I work for him. He brings out both the yin and yang in me. Besides, I can talk to Gordie about who I really am, and he listens, the way no one else ever has.

So when he told me this morning, too late, to start shredding, a bomb exploded inside me. But I did it. It wasn't because Rent-A-Wing,

Inc. was over. My recent American life has been about more than merely this job. But the Feds showing up here this afternoon unleashed the full horror of my situation. Now here we both are, prisoners in our steel and glass tower, while strangers ransack through files just outside our office doors. They wouldn't even let us sit through this night together. What did they think we'd do? At least we each have our bottles of scotch.

But as Gordie told me only an hour ago, I'm an innocent accessory at worst. He had me managing the legitimate side of the business. I never really believed it though, all his aircraft financing from dubious sources and leasing of suitably equipped private jets to Chinese and Arabic millionaire "entrepreneurs." Gordie was running arms. Just when did I finally figure it out . . .? Doesn't matter now. I supposed I liked the insanity of it all. Besides, Gordie made me laugh. You can get through life around someone with a sense of humor.

I suppose I'll go home in relative disgrace. Gordie's lawyers will keep me out of jail, I hope. He's already figuring out what to do next, and once he's set things up, I'll go work for him again. At least I have a temporary home to go to. Mum may have her peculiarities when it comes to me, but she'd never cut me off completely. She may have trouble understanding why I won't seem to care, but that's another story.

Tonight though, I close this chapter. My story, the one I've told Gordie in bits and pieces over the past six years, is about a perpetually reluctant dance full of unexamined, but highly choreographed, movement. How else did I end up here, in my thirty-third year, staring out of a plate glass window, sipping yet another scotch with the sun in my eyes, talking to Lady Liberty?

In January 1972, I, Rose Kho, went to college in the United States. By May of '74, I came home with my BS in political science and a minor in mathematics. I married my childhood sweetheart Paul Lie in the summer of '77. Gordie says it was those early American years that really changed my life.

1

The first time my boyfriend Paul took me home to meet his parents over dinner, I was in Lower Six and had just turned seventeen. We had been dating six months. It was late January.

"Don't wear a dress that's too brightly colored," he told me when he called. "And don't wear makeup, except for a little lipstick if you insist."

I had been wearing makeup for two years by that time, and was more than a little peeved at his instructions.

"What about high heels?"

"No more than half an inch."

"Paul, I was being facetious."

When he came to pick me up that Saturday, he was dreadfully nervous. I remembered how happy I had been the first time he was invited to dinner at my home, a month after we'd been dating. My mother had gone to the market to find the best crabs available and cooked up a feast for him. I had been so proud, so excited that even Regina's wry remarks did not dampen my enthusiasm. Yet Paul seemed almost afraid to bring me home.

His family lived on Kadoorie Avenue in a spacious flat over twice the size of my home. It was sparse, in quiet colors, and the furniture was Scandinavian. There was a large, and, I supposed, expensive Chinese vase in one corner. Two huge, wooden African masks hung on the center wall of the living room.

Paul's father was one of the few Chinese barristers in Hong Kong, and probably the only Chinese to have practised in Johannesburg. Paul Lie Sr. was a tall and extremely striking man; his high cheekbones and wide face belied his northern heritage. What struck me was his rather brown complexion, which made him look somehow less Chinese. Paul said his father swam and liked being in the sun. He was cordial, but formal.

Mrs. Marion Lie was the most severe woman I'd ever met. Almost as tall as her husband, who was just shy of six feet, she had the palest complexion, undisturbed by makeup. Her dark brown hair was almost black, and her eyes steely grey when the light caught them a certain way. She looked more Chinese than I'd expected; Paul had told me she was Eurasian and quite European looking. But, when she smiled the severity disappeared, and a spark of tenderness underlined her beauty.

She inspected me. At that moment, I was glad of my plain, dark blue dress. When she finally extended her hand, smiling, her long fingers were cool and bony. "Paul has told us a great deal about you. We're very pleased you could come."

At dinner, his parents sat very still and chewed their food slowly. They all spoke softly; they did not interrupt one another. His mother, who had been an English teacher, enunciated her words in the Queen's English. Paul Sr. spoke English with a curious accent, a mixture of Chinese and South African. But when he spoke to Paul or me, he lapsed into Mandarin, which Paul understood but did not speak, at which point Mrs. Lie would politely remind him that not everyone knew what he was saying, because she spoke hardly any Chinese at all.

Dinner was a bland black mushroom soup, rice with an indifferent chicken and overcooked mustard greens. This was followed by a watery custard for dessert. Their Chinese servant, complete with a white and black samfoo and waist length pigtail, served Western style, with an array of silverware too elaborate for the meal. All through dinner, I felt I was moving about too much, eating too quickly. When Mrs. Lie asked me to pass the salt, I was so startled by the sound of her voice that I almost dropped the shaker and barely managed to squeak out "certainly."

After dinner, we moved to the living room where Paul's father poured cognac from a crystal decanter into heavy crystal glasses. I feigned a sophistication I didn't feel as he handed me a glass; whiskey was my father's drink. The only time I'd tasted cognac before was at my father's secretary's wedding banquet, and then only a few sips. Mrs. Lie sat next to me on the sofa while Paul and his father stood by the rosewood bar tray. A sudden image of my mother's living room metal roller tray flashed; she kept on it a hideous, pink, yellow and green floral-patterned Chinese thermos of hot water along with four yellowing tumblers.

Mr. Lie addressed me. "Paul tells us you plan to study mathematics."

"I'm not sure, I think so."

Paul smiled at me from behind his dad, which helped me fight the mounting shyness I felt.

"Tell me, dear, what subjects are you good at?" The affectionate tone in Mrs. Lie's voice surprised me; it was at odds with her imperious manner.

I cleared my throat. "History, math and physics. And music. I play piano." I was unaccustomed to this kind of conversation. My mother's idea of education was that my sister and I must go to university but ended there. That we needed to choose a course of study didn't seem important. Regina sometimes threatened to major in diving, which horrified my mother, who believed this was perhaps possible. As for my father, he rarely spoke about such things, since he considered it my mother's role to look after our education and upbringing.

"Rose is an excellent student," Paul said. "She just doesn't tell anyone."

I reddened as his parents nodded in approval. While it was true I did well, I sometimes doubted my abilities. History, after all, was pure memorization, spitting back on our essay exams the notes our teacher dictated. I didn't necessarily remember anything afterwards. As for math and physics, I simply applied the formulas we'd been taught. Despite my A's, I wasn't sure I actually knew anything. Regina, who flunked anything she didn't like because she didn't attend the exams, grasped the principles of every subject she cared about with a passion. She *understood* things while all I did was pass exams. My sister frequently made this point to me.

"So you're going to matriculate before you go to university abroad?" Mrs. Lie asked. "Will you finish your bachelor's early?"

"Uh, perhaps."

"Ah, perhaps you're not aware, the American system doesn't require upper six. That's equivalent to what they call freshman year." She sensed my uncertainty, and tried to put me at ease.

I knew, of course I knew, but I wasn't sure. Here was an adult confirming it to me at last. It was reassuring.

We chatted a little longer. The cognac made me more talkative,

5

and by the end of the evening, I was feeling far more relaxed. When Paul was preparing to take me home later, I overheard his father say to him, "she's absolutely delightful, and such a pretty girl" and I felt a surge of joyful satisfaction that I'd won some initial approval.

Paul later assured me that I'd passed the parental test with flying colors. Although I hoped he was right, a part of me felt that the reason I'd passed was because I knew which cutlery to use. I was invited back twice before I left for the States a year later.

Paul and his family were on my mind as I flew back home after almost three years in America. Exhausted as I was, I had hardly slept, dozing off in snatches which were interrupted by confusing dreams, startling me into wakefulness. Marion Lie's last letter had been warm and anticipatory — she was looking forward to Paul having "his well-educated and by now much more sophisticated girlfriend accompany him to the social functions a young solicitor ought to attend in Hong Kong." I had definitely been right to discard all my college blue jeans before coming back. Homecoming, as Marion had clearly intimated through her letters, especially in the ones of the past year, was about preparing for life with Paul, an adult life in a bigger world than anything I'd ever experienced.

Yet when I finally walked down the arrival hall ramp at Kai Tak airport, it seemed that the world had shrunk. Dad was waving at the end of the walkway, while Mum kept shouting "Rose! Rose!" as she came to meet me halfway up the ramp. I tried to act grown up, but cried as soon as I felt my mother's arms around me.

And there was Paul, looking radiant.

I was lost in the heady excitement of being the returning graduate. Paul kissed me in front of my parents, that's how pleased he was to see me, while my father smiled indulgently.

Outside, the July air submerged me in its damp heat. I sneezed. Dad disappeared to retrieve the car.

". . . and Auntie Helen and Uncle Chong are looking forward to seeing you, and of course we have to . . . " My mother had been talking non-stop since we got into the car.

Dad was edging his way through the streets of Kowloon City towards Junction Road, a main thoroughfare between the airport district and Kowloon Tong where we lived. Ever a nervous driver, he kept his eyes glued to the road, leaving Mum to jabber away in the front seat. Paul squeezed my hand. I was feeling unbelievably cramped, and said very little. We drove through roads that seemed too narrow for cars, and the sight of all the high rises stacked next to each other made me anxious.

We travelled up Beacon Hill Road towards our flat, which was at the top of that hill. When we moved here the year before I left, I had found the suburban-like surroundings spacious. Mum had been so proud, because we finally could afford our own place in a nice, middle class neighborhood, instead of renting. There were only four flats on each of the twelve stories in our building. We lived on seven, overlooking Lung Cheung Road and a small park ringed by trees. Paul's park, where we used to go to neck.

Now, the area struck me as congested. Living in Plattsburgh, a small city far north upstate almost on the Canadian border in one of New York's poorest counties, made my home pale by comparison.

It was not till we got home that I realized how old my mother looked.

My parents were both in their late fifties. When I had left, Mum already had some white hairs, which she dyed, and the start of a few wrinkles. Dad, on the other hand, could pass for a man in his early to mid forties. Now, Mum seemed to have aged ten years — a welter of wrinkles covered her face — while Dad looked only a little older. I thought of my twin sister Regina, and the shock of first seeing her in Plattsburgh looking older when I arrived the semester after she had.

Once we unloaded all my stuff at home, Dad remarked, "She doesn't look any older, does she Paul?"

"No, uncle, she doesn't."

Paul hovered around me all the while. I hadn't changed much, except for losing a few pounds, because of my anitpathy for Plattsburgh's food. Mum bustled happily, showing me the new curtains and seat covers she'd sewn for my homecoming. I smiled politely, and complimented her choice of fabric. But as I wandered around our home, I felt a strange disquiet, an unease, as if I somehow didn't belong within these walls.

"I'll leave you with your parents, since you have a lot to talk about." Paul, always the gentleman, knew exactly the right thing to do. "Walk me to the bus stop?"

It was already eight in the evening, but the air was still sticky and humid. I suddenly missed the chilly evenings I'd left behind in upstate New York. Paul held my hand tightly, and walked slowly, carefully, as if he were afraid I would run away. We stopped at the park, and sat down on the grass in our old corner hidden by a clump of bushes, where he kissed me awkwardly. Graceful in every other way, Paul was a clumsy lover.

"I'm glad you came back, Rose. I'm sorry, so dreadfully sorry." He repeated this last part twice, as if the words could cleanse him, as if nothing between us had changed.

"I should get back," I said, even though his kisses and touch made me want to stay. He was leaning over me, holding me very tightly now. His body was charged, excited, as he pressed harder against me. I wanted to cling to him, to give way to our passion, the way we used to before I went away. "Just a few more minutes," he whispered. I tried to pull away from him, "Paul, I can't." His grip loosened, reluctantly. "I love you, Rose."

And I left him, abruptly, unable to confront all these confusing and conflicting feelings that churned inside me. I was happy to be back. I was also nauseous.

How badly I wanted to hide away in Paul's arms that night. It was strange, going "home" when being with Paul was what I'd longed for all the time I'd been in the States. Yet this was Hong Kong, and family had to come first. Paul knew that. It was one of the reasons I loved him and knew I belonged to him; he always did the right thing where it mattered most.

Wonder what Gordie's saying to those guys from the Feds. With Gordie, the right thing is whatever he's doing at the time.

"Now, how about Regina?"

We had been talking about everything I'd done, and eating for hours, before Mum finally raised the question. Mum had cooked me a feast of memories, all the food she knew I couldn't get in the States. I could not stop picking at the remnants of our meal. The flavor of shrimp paste and *tong choi*, the hollow-stemmed water spinach of summer, lingered.

"She's well." I found a piece of garlic with my chopsticks. It prickled my tongue, drenched as it was with the sauce from the salted fish and bean sprouts, one of my father's favorite dishes.

"Yes, but why hasn't she graduated?"

"She didn't want to."

My father was silent. I wondered if he felt justified in his non-involvement, because Regina no longer took money from him. I tried to deflect the questioning by shifting the focus elsewhere. "Oh, by the way, Regina knows a friend of Uncle Chong's and Auntie Helen's. Somebody called David Ho. He gave Paul a ride from Montreal to Plattsburgh when he came to see me at school."

My father raised his eyebrows. "Not Ho Yuet Kan's son?"

"Who?" The name sounded vaguely familiar to me.

"The shipping tycoon. Helen and Chong have a friend who is one of his sons, from his first wife. You know, the Malaysian Chinese one? Remember the society scandal when she left him suddenly and went back to Penang?"

"Is Regina dating him?" My mother's voice was hopeful in light of this new information, despite his questionable heritage.

"I don't think so, Mum." I reluctantly put down my chopsticks, now that every last dish had been emptied, and caught my father's indulgent grin.

"Too bad." She was lost in thought for a moment, but soon launched back into more immediate matters. "What I don't understand — she said something in her letter about going to the University of Eeowa . . ."

"It's I-owa, Ma, not Ee-owa."

"Oh yes, okay, but anyway she said she wanted to go there to a," she pulled out a crumpled aerogram from her handbag and searched for the right words, "a 'MFA in creative arts'. What's that, Rose?"

"It's some kind of graduate program, so that she can combine poetry and painting."

"In Iowa," Dad interjected, "she will write poems about corn and paint pictures of hay."

"Oh what do you know? Your dad always thinks he knows it all, even though he hardly knows America."

"Hawaii is America. New York is America. We were there."

"Not the same. Your father always has to argue. He never changes, Rose. Never changes."

I felt myself cringe. It was exactly as it had been before I left, only now, there was no Regina to intercede. I thought enviously of the quiet calm at Paul's home. "We can talk in the morning," I said. "I'm tired." I stood up and began clearing the table.

"Go to bed, Rose." Dad was conciliatory, almost apologetic. "I'll help your mother with the dishes. You've had such a long flight."

I tossed around all night. Being with Paul, having my fiancé again, feeling his desire, stirred me in a way I had not expected. Yet between my legs, the memory of Andrew still lingered. I dreamt that I was walking out of a warm house into a downpour. The house was in Plattsburgh, on the banks of the Saranac River. A lighthouse in the distance beamed. I saw Andrew's face in the window, looking sad, as he waved goodbye to me.

Then, Regina appeared naked in the window, smiling cruelly and laughing. Andrew began to laugh with her, and I was more lost in the downpour while they laughed and caroused and smoked pot together.

I awoke, my hair damp with sweat. The air conditioner was off, since I'd grown used to not needing one at all in Plattsburgh, even in the dead of summer. And this was only my first night home.

In the beginning, the excitement of being back overtook my discomfort at having to live with my parents again. It was, in a way, a pleasure not to worry about meals, and to simply have money doled out to me as and when I needed it.

Dad set me straight about the financial situation within days of my return.

"Mum likes to work now," he said one evening, as we drank scotch together on the veranda. Dad had always been liberal about alcohol consumption, contending that all civilized persons needed to imbibe for pleasure. "She doesn't need to, because I'm making enough at Golden Phoenix to support her."

My father used to work for their parent company, Pacific American Airways, as their technical purchasing manager. A lot longer ago, he was a fighter pilot in China and later flew for China Air Transport, the CAT of the Flying Tigers. He doesn't say much about those days. Twilight years in a regional cargo airline as the general manager was his retirement gift for loyal service.

"But she says she wants to keep working," he continued, "because she wouldn't know what to do with herself if she didn't."

"Don't you send Regina money?"

"Your Mum does. Regina won't take the money I send her. She's a stubborn girl, your sister."

In the distance, the lights of the airport runway flickered as one aircraft after another landed on the narrow strip of land jutting out to the sea.

"Regina said things were still tight because you and Mum couldn't afford to come for my graduation."

"Your mother was working!" Dad's tone was almost angry. "I asked her to take a holiday and go, but she said she had to work because she couldn't find a replacement, and the company was busy."

I wanted to ask him why he hadn't come, but that wasn't the kind of question I asked my father. It would have been too much of a challenge, too much of a questioning of his authority. Was he proud of me in some small way for my intelligence, or did he only love me because I was his "perfect" daughter?

"So, Dad, what kind of work do you think I ought to do? I mean until I get married." I startled myself when I said that. But being around Dad again, the world as it used to be fell back into place. I was once again the five year old who could make her father smile simply by saying that I was going to marry him when I grew up, to which he'd reply, laughing, that then, I would have to become his concubine since he was already married to my mother.

His face sparkled with pleasure that I had asked his advice. "Now let's see, it would be best if you tried to work for one of the foreign companies. What are you interested in?"

I felt confident and brave in the light of that question. One thing college in America had taught me, which I hadn't learnt in my Hong Kong school, was to research my options, make my decision, express my opinion clearly, and back it up with a strong argument. A year of speech classes and the debate team hadn't hurt. I had been waiting to tell my father the ideas I had for my life, and now, I could.

"I want something to do in marketing, preferably something international. One of my professors suggested I get an MBA."

He looked slightly displeased.

Marion's advice rang in my head — that it would take time for my father to appreciate the real meaning of my education, because in his world, women didn't have careers, only jobs. I had to be tactful. "But of course," I added quickly, "there's nothing like experience, is there?"

My comment mollified him. "Ah well, nowadays you young people all believe in MBA's. Probably there's something there — in my day, we just worked. But it's different for a girl because your husband will take care of you. I can ask Peterson if there's anything at Pacific American if you'd like."

I had been expecting that. "You don't need to, Dad. I've already started to see what possibilities there are. I'd rather do this myself, not that I don't appreciate your help. I can always send in an application to the British hongs and the American companies."

He seemed pleased by what I said, because I was showing him that I was independent and able to fend for myself. Regina and her feminist friends wouldn't have been impressed by Dad's attitude. But despite his sometimes old-fashioned ideas about women, he really did want me to break away from depending on family, even if it meant working. I think he was simply a pragmatist: as long as a wife could work and still be a mother and homemaker, the way Mum was, it meant extra income. I was glad Regina hadn't come home. She meant well when she argued with Dad, but it created such unnecessary tensions. My sister could benefit from Marion's diplomatic style, but she had no time for Paul and his family. Being in her shadow for too long, it was a welcome change to find myself on my own and able to cope.

"It's Paul." My mother handed me the phone, her face beaming with complicity.

Although he had called every day since I returned, he tactfully waited a week before asking to meet, knowing it was what my parents expected. When he came by that evening to take me out, I wished I hadn't agreed to the date. But with Paul, it wasn't like "dating" anymore.

"You're still so beautiful, Rose," he said, as soon as we were alone in the lift. "I've missed you." He put his arm around my shoulders.

Unaccountably, I tensed up.

He pulled his arm away. "What's the matter?" His voice was concerned, kind.

"Nothing. Just not used to being back, I guess." I managed a smile.

"Of course."

But his solicitude strangely irritated me.

We went to the Scene, the disco at the Peninsula which had been our hangout. I had expected it to be different, changed, but it was much the same as before. "*Wei!* Rose Kho!" people from our old crowd called out, surprised to see me back in Hong Kong so soon.

All night long, I felt the tension of being around Paul. On the surface, things seemed just the way they used to be. We chatted with friends who were happy to see me back home. We gossiped about the ones who had hung on in America, joking that they would turn into ABC's. I found out there was a club of American college graduates from Hong Kong who met regularly, although it was dominated by West Coast graduates. Still, I agreed to go to one of their functions in a couple of weeks, and Paul was game enough to say he'd come along.

On the dance floor, I relaxed, knowing that conversation was impossible. Paul had already taught me the steps to the hustle, the latest dance craze. I was happy. Dancing meant an easy oblivion. We were once again the most popular and admired couple. Paul always shone when he danced. He was handsome and taller than the average Hong Kong guy, and had an elegance and grace that made him the most sought after dance partner. But what delighted me most was that he was mine again, to the obvious envy of several of the girls in our circle who, in my absence, had probably made an unsuccessful play for Paul. This, I knew, was why I had come back. Paul had waited, true to his promise. He smiled at me across the space that separated us, and my earlier nervousness disappeared. He wasn't just a teenage Prince Charming anymore, but my Paul, my fiance.

That night, when he took me home, we stopped at the park. As I sat down on a bench, I tugged at my skirt, which was short.

I caught Paul staring at my thighs for just a second before he sat down. "You really don't have to worry, Rose. There'll be plenty of jobs. What about government?"

I wondered why he was being so serious. On the ride back in the taxi, he had barely touched me except to hold my hand. Still a bit high from the alcohol and dancing, I edged closer to him. "I can't see myself as a civil servant, can you Paul?"

His body wouldn't relent. "Hey Paul, it isn't that late yet." Unbuttoning my blouse so that the top of my bra showed, I whispered, "I'm not that civil, am I?" I wanted him to touch me, to be as hot and bothered as I was.

"Rose, please."

My hand slid onto his thigh. I felt the bulge in his pants. "Rose, let's not take any more chances." He removed my hand.

"Paul," I put both arms around his neck, pushing my body closer to his. "Don't you want to? You did the first night."

"That was different. I couldn't help myself. Besides, you're not in America anymore."

"But I feel the same, don't I? Isn't this what you wanted?"

He stood up. "You're just over excited from seeing everyone tonight. I'm taking you home before we get into trouble."

My body remained a mass of nervous energy in bed that night. But he was right, of course he was right. Things were different here. For a moment, I wished I were back in my own place in America, away from the restrictions of living at home. It seemed absurd that we should have to neck in a park, as if we were still teenagers, as if we were still virgins, especially when we had known each other as long as we had.

The first time Paul had called to take me out, I was sixteen.

"Do you remember me?" he asked.

I hadn't thought about anything else after we met. That he thought I could possibly forget who he was astounded me. "Yes," was all I could manage. Mum was watching me from the dining table where she was sewing. I turned my face towards the veranda and tried to keep my voice low. Even with my back to her, I knew she was straining to hear every word. Paul asked me out to a party the following week. I mumbled thanks and hung up as quickly as possible.

"Who was that?" She stopped the escape to my bedroom

"Just a friend."

"It was a boy."

"I know." I wanted to add that she did too since she answered the phone, but thought better of it.

"Did he ask you for a date?"

Regina would have told her it was none of her business, and had in fact been telling Mum to mind her own business since the first time a boy asked her out at thirteen. Paul was the first boy ever to call me. I didn't reply right away.

"Rose, look at me when I'm talking to you."

I turned around. "Yes, he did."

"I hope it's not to a tea dance?" The afternoon tea dances at dimly lit nightclubs where "boys and girls cuddle each other" were, to Mum, the epitome of the sordid. Regina had been going since she was fourteen without Mum's knowledge.

"No, to a party."

"Whose?"

"One of his classmates at La Salle."

"Oh, so he attends La Salle. That's good. Catholic?"

I nodded, wishing the inquisition would end.

"Is he Chinese?" She had been warming up to this all important question.

"Yes." I omitted the fact of his Eurasian heritage, because Paul looked almost completely Chinese. Since she didn't ask, I also didn't tell her that the classmate having the party was Portuguese.

"Well I hope he comes to the house to pick you up. You know I prefer boys to do that."

I breathed a sigh of relief and rushed back into the bedroom.

The week flew by.

"Auntie, Uncle, I'm very pleased to meet you."

From Mum's face, I knew she was delighted with Paul at first sight. She gushed over him, asking him all about his future study plans, until I wanted to hide from embarrassment.

Dad was far more reasonable. "Don't keep these two with all your chatter. They want to go out."

Paul smiled. "That's quite all right uncle. I arrived early because

15

I wanted to meet you and not rush out straight away. It seems so rude to be at a friend's house, and not even have the courtesy to speak to their parents."

Dad's right eyebrow rose slightly, unimpressed by Paul's speech. Mum beamed a huge smile at him.

"That's very true, Paul, " Mum began. "It is important for young people to have manners. Rose, you can learn something from Paul."

I cringed, and glimpsed Dad's amusement at the situation. He caught my eye and his smile reassured me. It let me know that nothing mattered more than my own mastery of the situation.

I found my tongue. "We should go now Paul, shouldn't we?" The authority in my voice surprised me.

"Yes." He answered with a rapid smile. "We should."

That first date resides in my memory with a startling clarity. Paul told me then that when we met, which was at a barbecue Regina dragged me along to, he knew he wanted to be with me. I wondered how he knew, but all of me fluttered with a strange nervousness that night, and I never asked. I felt adult with Paul. And then, when he brought me home, he kissed me very lightly on the lips, and I knew, with absolute certainty, that I would see him again.

Mum, and even Regina, didn't believe Paul would continue to see me. But I knew. Somehow, he made me know, right from the beginning, that I was special. By simply being me, from the very first time, he made me feel loved.

So what infuriated me most of all now was that Paul could, and wanted to, maintain such control, that he accepted the absurdity of our situation, even though he claimed to love and want me. He hadn't even suggested a motel. Yet I knew he just wanted the best for me, so I forgave him. He understood something about me, the way his mother did, and helped me to grow up, although I wouldn't admit that to him. And perhaps, after all was said and done, I remained in love with Paul because he reassured me over and over and over again that he thought me the most attractive girl in the world, and because of my mother's parting words as I packed for college, "don't worry, maybe one of the Chinese boys will ask you out over there if the American boys won't, because there won't be many Chinese girls and they can't be choosy," words for which Paul said she deserved to be forever condemned.

I had been back almost a month, and living at home was becoming claustrophobic. It was hard to say this to my parents, however, because they both did so much for me, and did what they could to help me succeed. For example, to avoid the weekend crowds, Mum took time off work to help shop for clothes for my interviews. We went to a store in Tung Ying Building on Nathan Road, which she liked because of the bargains. As we rummaged through the racks, my mother suddenly said, "it's very expensive to live on your own, so you better live with us for now."

My living situation was not exactly what I wanted to discuss at the moment, because I didn't quite trust my feelings. "Well, it depends what I can make," I ventured cautiously. "I wouldn't mind sharing with some other girls."

"Here, try this one on," she held up a hideous pink dress which was too girlish. I grimaced. "Really, Rose, you've become so fussy." She hung it back on the rack. "Your father would never agree to your moving out, you know. Anyway, only the English *gwai muis* live on their own. None of the local girls do that."

"Ma, that's such a racist expression."

"Why do you keep calling me 'ma'? You never called me that before. Sounds so lazy."

"Mum, I just want to get a job first.

"Why don't you teach? Good money, teaching."

For all her emphasis on education, Mum was completely unimaginative and ignorant when it came to how that education should be applied. "I don't want to teach. I want to work in business."

"It's really too bad you didn't stick to the sciences, Rose. I would have been happy to foot the bill for medical school. You're a good enough student."

It was a familiar plea. The fact that biology bored me fell on deaf ears. "I thought money was still tight. Besides, I don't want to be a doctor."

"Hmmm. Maybe not," she held up a dress covered with flounces and lace. "Too fancy for work. Oh, we're okay now that Dad's working again and there's more money. And I got a raise recently and make almost $1,600 a month."

I was still on US currency. That converted to $320 American. Regina told me she could bring home more than $100 a night in tips alone as a cocktail waitress in New York.

"Here, Mum, how about this one?" I held up an off white, two-piece skirt set, which had pearly grey buttons. It was a straight skirt — not the wider A-lines or pleated skirts my mother favored — and looked chic and adult to me. I remembered the French designer clothes I had seen in Montreal. They were classically cut, simple and elegant.

"Like a Chinese funeral."

"Come on, Mum. Everyone wears white now."

"Well, try it on."

We ended up getting that outfit and two others, plus a black cocktail dress I could wear to a dinner Paul had to attend. My choice was influenced by Marion's advice on evening dresses — when in doubt, go for the classic black dress — although I would never say it to my mother. Mum had balked at the black, which, she said, made me look like an English widow. But she gave in, because I badgered her for long enough, because it was cut low in the back and was terribly sexy, which, for all my mother's nagging, was something she liked her daughters to be, at least in the evenings.

I was glad I had badgered my mother about that black dress. The evening I wore it to the Law Society dinner with Paul, his boss complimented me, and I saw the look of pride on Paul's face. My search for a job was helped by Paul's social and professional network; from that dinner alone I got several more introductions for interviews.

However, a nagging anxiety had begun to take hold over the length of time it was taking to find a job. I couldn't hide this from Paul.

"Don't get discouraged, Rose," he reassured me on the way home in the taxi that night. "It's only been two months. You just need to be patient, that's all. "

To me, it was already too long, but Paul was so good to me over all this. "I'm trying to be," I replied, smiling. But I was tired of offers for jobs in sales, which seemed to be the only position available at entry level or what interviewers appeared to think I was suited for. Paul wanted me to be a management trainee at one of the British hongs or a bank, which he said would be the best job for me, although sometimes, I wondered if he were right about that.

"Sometimes, I wish I didn't have to bother working. It's ridiculous really, since in the end, as a woman, I'm only going so far and no further."

"Come on, Rose, we've been through all that. You need to talk to my mother soon, I can see."

I lapsed into silence. I desperately wanted to settle into a job first, so that Marion would see I wasn't wasting my education. Yet I knew that, within limits, she considered it inconsequential what I did, and would think it perfectly fine if I gave up my job once I had children, and engaged in activities befitting a society wife the way she had.

Most of all, I wanted her to feel proud of me, and be truly happy about my marrying Paul. Her approval had become more important to me than that of my own mother.

Marion's first letter to me in Plattsburgh had been a pleasant surprise. "Rose dear, forgive me for taking the liberty of writing to you, but I know you are important to Paul and I would like to get to know you better while you're away. I don't mean to interfere, but if you would care to write me, I would be pleased to maintain a correspondence. With kind regards, Mrs. Marion Lie." My heart had leapt with joy at that short note, the contents of which I memorized and carried inside me. In the months that followed, she became "Marion," the woman to whom I could write about my intellectual development. She asked me questions that made me think, and always made me feel important. In fact, she sometimes called me her most precious and beautiful flower. I craved her intelligence and wonderful use of language; in time, I came to look forward to her letters even more than to those from Paul or my mother.

We arrived at my home. As we came out of the taxi, I took his hand and led him away from the entrance to my building and headed towards the park.

"Rose . . ." His voice held a warning ring.

I let out a slightly impatient sigh. Paul's good behavior was beginning to annoy me. "There's something I want to tell you, that's all."

He gripped my hand and followed me, somewhat reluctantly, to the park where we sat on a bench. "So what is it?"

"Don't be mad, but I interviewed at an ad agency for an assistant account executive position."

"Rose!"

I had waited a week to tell him, knowing his disdain for advertising. "It's a small office, about thirty people." I began speaking quickly into his silence, trying to get in all the important details. "They recently became affiliated with one of the Madison Avenue agencies. You know, what they call a 4A? So they're expanding. They've got some reputable accounts."

"How did you find out about it?"

"I answered a classifed."

Paul didn't speak for awhile. He was clearly keeping his temper. Sometimes, such silly things got him angry, like answering classifieds, of which he totally disapproved, believing in introductions and personal recommendations. But then, it was different for him in law, especially for a graduate out of Hong Kong University's first law class. Every one of his classmates had jobs ready for them when they graduated. Paul simply didn't understand. The world he came from called the shots; I wasn't from that stratosphere.

He never let go of my hand. Finally, "It's sort of like sales, isn't it?"

I could tell he wasn't pleased. "Not exactly, it's client servicing. Uncle Chong explained the difference, and said it was probably better suited to me than sales."

It was the wrong thing to say. Paul didn't have much time for either my uncle or aunt, although he would never admit it outright.

"Come on, Paul, it's been almost two months. I want to start earning some money. It's only a first job."

"Rose, you're just not serious enough."

I sighed, exasperated. Ever since we were teenagers Paul hadn't thought I was serious enough about education, my future, my family or anything else. He could be so tiresomely perfectionist that sometimes he had me running scared of my own shadow.

"Besides," he continued, ignoring my annoyance, "why are you so worried about money? Has Regina written another of her money letters to you again?"

Now, I was really irritated. I got up from the park bench and picked up my purse.

"Where are you going? It's only ten." He rubbed his hand against the small of my back, suddenly sliding his fingers under my blouse. "Come on, Rose, don't go yet."

In a sharp swift movement, he stood up, clutched me tightly to him, and kissed me even more passionately than the first night I returned. All my pent up frustrations released themselves at that moment. He led me, his arm firmly around my waist, to our corner of the park, under the tree where we'd spent hours when we first started dating. As we lay down together on the grassy slope, his desire hard against me, all the earlier confusion ebbed away, and the world Paul presented made such complete sense that I wondered why I ever questioned it. I loved him unconditionally, with the same pleasure that had first drawn me to him. It was something I didn't understand, but knew was right.

Then, as abruptly as he had started, he pushed me away and sat up. "The trouble with you, Rose, is that you never can wait for anything." And with that he got up and left, while I sat there, stunned, my desire in shock, feeling like Paul had just slapped me soundly across the face.

2

A few days later, the ad agency called late in the afternoon and offered me the job. I almost said yes right away, but checked myself. They could wait. Paul would have said the same had I told him, and on that point, I was inclined to agree.

I didn't tell him or my parents. Mum's opinion of ad agencies was highly colored by what Paul thought. As for my father, he didn't express much opinion at all. What I really wanted to do was call Marion and ask her advice. But I couldn't do that to Paul; it would have hurt and embarrassed him if his mother knew before he did. Besides, he had called and apologized profusely for the other night, saying that he didn't know what had come over him and that he had no right to speak that way to me. While I was feeling somewhat more kindly towards him, I didn't want to let him know I'd fully forgiven him for what was, after all, pretty awful behavior on his part.

In this state of flux, I headed for my aunt Helen's where I was expected for the weekend. Visiting my aunt and uncle was one way to escape the sometime uneasy atmosphere of living at home.

Helen was dad's older sister and only sibling. She had met Uncle Chong, who was a *wah kiu* from Kuala Lumpur, when he was a student at St. John's in Shanghai. They had eloped, since my grandparents disapproved entirely of the match, taken off to Malaysia, where they lived for some years, and only later come to Hong Kong.

Regina worshipped Helen, while I had always been a little in awe of my aunt. But it was easy being around her and Uncle Chong. Having no children of their own, they treated Regina and me like adults even when we were children, and never made us do anything we didn't want to.

In her usual manner of launching straight into whatever was on her mind at the time, Helen greeted me with, "We have a guest coming to dinner tonight. An American." She made him sound slightly disabled, but that was the tone she used for everyone. "He prints magazines in Asia."

I tried to imagine an American in Hong Kong running a printing plant. Somehow, it didn't register.

"By the way, do you want to invite Paul along to dinner?"

Uncle Chong went into an erratic coughing fit from his armchair perch, where he was buried in the *China Mail*, one of the two English afternoon dailies. It sounded suspiciously like a guffaw disguised as throat clearing.

"That's sweet of you Auntie, but Paul's going out with some friends." I thought I had already told her that, but perhaps I was mistaken.

"Oh, what a pity." And she bustled off to get on with preparations for dinner.

Staying with my aunt was like bunking with friends in the States. Uncle Chong worked for the Sheraton Hotel as a sales manager, and had talked the company into giving him housing, which was one of the hotel suites that was designed in a very American style. He called himself their "expat gook," ever since some manager at corporate headquarters had said at a meeting once, too loudly, what's the gook doing here? "He could be forgiven," Chong had said good humoredly in recounting the incident, "since his only time in Asia was Vietnam, and he was one of those military operation types who don't know their ass from their mouth, or one end of Asia from the other." But even though our family laughed at the stupidity of Chong's colleague, what stuck with me most out of all this was my aunt's final judgment in the matter. "You watch," she had declared, "it won't be long before these so-called 'senior' foreign expats will be working for Asians all over Asia, expats or otherwise, and then these arrogant *gwailos* better watch out!"

"So, Rose," my uncle said, "how's the job search? Did you try some of the advertising agencies like I suggested?"

Uncle Chong asked questions that made me get right to the point. "I did, but Mum says that people work very long hours at ad agencies, which she didn't think was good for me. Other than suggesting I teach, she told me to work in a bank, just like Paul did. But the personnel manager at the Hong Kong Shanghai Bank was quite dismissive."

He grinned. "Rose, do you really want to be a banker?"

"No." I felt instantly better when I said it. What I did like about Chong and Helen was that I could say what I thought when my parents weren't around. "But, well, I still am a university graduate, even if I didn't go to a top school. You know we couldn't afford to."

"Silly girl! What has the school you went to got to do with anything? Are you or aren't you educated?" His annoyance startled me. "Besides, so what if you are a graduate? How much do you think you know about running a business? Or managing people? Building a career isn't about face — oh, admit it, Rose, you just want an important enough sounding job for face, like all Hong Kong people. There's nothing wrong with wanting it, you understand. But you have to earn it. The company you work for or the title you have doesn't make you a better person. For example, do you know what my first job was when I entered the hotel industry? A bellhop, and then manning the reception desk. The industry's about service. How can you know about service if you've never served in your life? The trouble with these British hongs is that they revere degrees, and forget that business is about customers."

He sounded remarkably like some of my American professors. Back in the States, it had been easy to agree with all that. But knowing what my mother, and Paul, and all my friends expected me to do, and were themselves doing, I was wary of making the wrong first move.

My aunt bustled into the living room. "Rose, be a good girl and help me set the table. Now Chong, stop lecturing her. She has to figure out what she wants to do for herself."

I set about as my aunt asked. Dinner at my relatives generally meant bland Western food. As a girl, I didn't particularly like eating with them because of that. Helen wasn't much of a cook, and hotel life suited her perfectly as she could order room service any time she wanted. My mother was a wonderful Chinese cook, and since Dad also loved to eat, meals at home were varied and appetizing. These past two months had, however, been such an orgy of eating everything I'd missed while in the States, that I was grateful to be facing nothing more exciting than tossed salad and a nondescript chicken tonight, which was about as much as auntie normally could muster.

So I was surprised when the bell rang, and a waiter and assistant chef rolled in a tray piled with smoked salmon, Caesar salad, mushroom soup and steaks. Plus what looked like an expensive bottle of red wine, a Cabernet, I think. The arrival drama was heightened by the simultaneous appearance of my uncle's and aunt's dinner guest.

In the confusion that followed amid greetings interspersed with directions to the kitchen staff, I caught sight of a slender Caucasian man, whose most noticeable feature was his dark, wavy hair, almost black, who hugged my aunt effusively. In the background, my uncle's voice was saying, "by the way, Elliot, this is our niece, Rose."

Calm returned. We sipped champagne and nibbled the salmon. I wondered what the occasion was. Elliot was a sociable and lively man. He had known both Chong and Helen for a long time, from Malaysia. He told stories about night life adventures with models and actresses in Singapore and Kuala Lumpur, about waterskiing on water "smooth and clear as crystal silence" off the East Coast of Malaysia. He painted a vivid picture of an Indonesian waterfall, high up in the hills, where he was surrounded by hundreds of shades of green, where the foliage created a warm, humid wrap — "like a verdant womb" — in the spray under the waterfall. A photographic image appeared in my mind, drawing me into this magical universe he embraced.

"So what do you do, Rose?" he asked.

I had just popped a piece of salmon in my mouth, and chewed quickly, embarrassed.

"My apologies," he continued. "I didn't mean to catch you off guard."

"That's okay," I replied, swallowing, my hand over my mouth. "I just graduated. Came back July fourth." It came out, that unintended American coincidence, before I could stop myself.

Elliot smiled slightly. "How auspicious of you. You've just been let loose into a whole life ahead of you, while the rest of us have to fix the pieces behind us that didn't go right."

His comment disappointed me. It was a letdown compared to the beautiful images he'd conjured previously.

"Now Elliot," my uncle chided, "stop feeling sorry for yourself. You see Rose, we're celebrating his new business venture."

"Venture's too grand a description," but he was smiling.

"Come, let's have dinner," my aunt interjected.

Dinner was delicious, since it wasn't auntie's cooking. I devoured the steak. Life at college had been starved of any kind of luxury, given Regina's and my shoe string budget, which was why I raced through four years in two and a half, so that I could get back, make money and indulge a little again.

Elliot sat beside me, and watched, amused. "Carnivorous, aren't you?"

"Man wasn't made to subsist on *dou fu* and gluten," I remarked, referring to Buddhist vegetarian fare.

He chuckled. "I wouldn't want to meet you in the jungle."

"Listen," Uncle Chong broke in, "tell this niece of mine that it won't hurt to do some hard work at the start of her career. I think she'd learn a lot and have fun in an ad agency, but she's being too conservative too soon. You know what Elliot did when he first came to Asia? Go on, tell her."

He squirmed a little under my uncle's rhetoric, but gave in. "I was a clerical assistant and proofreader for a printing company in Singapore."

"And, and . . . ," Chong's face was slightly flushed from the wine. "You know where he went to university? Columbia. Right, Elliot?" Helen had raised a finger to shush him.

Elliot smiled through his embarrassment. Under the table, I felt his foot tap my ankle, once, very lightly, and was grateful for his complicity in my waywardness.

It was an enjoyable evening. Elliot made me wish I was older, already working, and less of a "kid," which was what he called me when he said goodbye. When he departed that night, he kissed me the way Americans did, a light peck on my cheek, and said he hoped he would see me again. I took it for politeness. With Americans, I had discovered, the warmth and sincerity they injected into casual encounters could be misleading if you didn't understand their signals. Hong Kong people were just the opposite — misleadingly formal when extending friendship. I liked Elliot, and his open attitude to the world I came from. He was a far cry from my uncle's colleague, who didn't know one end of Asia from another.

Yet what lingered about him for months afterwards was that

single tap of his foot against my ankle. His secret communication meant he understood something about me, without his having to say a word.

I took that ad agency job. Didn't tell anyone, not even Paul, until after I'd accepted the position. Such nerve. Was that really the way I was back then, what was it, thirteen years ago? When Paul found out he was amazed into speechlessness, a rare thing for him. Paul always cared, perhaps too much, about what he thought was right for me.

Funny how the Statue of Liberty's discolors in the evening light. It's as if the sun rays peel off her robe.

The day Regina and I started primary one, my mother had tied a red ribbon in my hair and sent us off to school. Regina refused to use anything more than a rubber band, because even at six, she didn't like looking like me. Our teacher pulled me aside at assembly and removed the ribbon, explaining that pupils weren't allowed to wear red with our uniform. My sister gleefully told my mother later, delighted that I had been "made fun of" in front of everyone. Mum cut my hair short right away. As she cut it, she said, "Why do you always play so long in the sun, Rose? I keep warning you you'll get too dark. It makes you ugly, which is why the teacher picked on you out of all the other girls." I tried to object, to say that it had nothing to do with being dark, that I hadn't been picked on at all, that I just hadn't followed the rules, but Mum wouldn't listen and Regina kept laughing and teasing me. At night, I cried myself to sleep, although I did it softly, quietly, so that no one would know.

I remembered that as I dressed for my first morning of work. My new beige suit was smart. My short hair — I'd never grown it long again after that — was neat. And my complexion, having been in nothing warmer than Plattsburgh's tepid summer sunshine, was as pale as its natural coloring allowed, although never as fair as either Regina's or Mum's, no matter how hard I cared to try.

Dad drove me to the bus stop. "You look very grown up, Rose." I tried to smile. The butterflies still fluttered.

"Don't be nervous," he said, because my father had always been able to read me. "You'll do very well because you're a good girl and always have been."

I felt even more like a six-year old than a young adult. I had visions of being asked to do something, and not having any idea of what I was supposed to do.

"All you have to do," my father continued, "is ask if you don't understand something. It's just like being at school."

I stared dubiously at the road ahead. Paul's half-hearted approval and my mother's indifference to this ad agency job made me feel all the more uncertain. All my father had said when I told him of my decision was, "I think you'll do well." But then, Dad was encouraging no matter what I did. When he dropped me off, he told me I looked very adult in my new suit. Then he drove off, and I boarded the number seven bus which would take me to the ferry.

I sat on the top deck. The sky was brightly blue that morning, and the summer air humid. Tiny beads of perspiration wet the back of my neck and forehead as my make up slowly melted. My nylons stuck uncomfortably. The rattan bus seat nicked my skirt. I hoped there weren't any bugs. It was only seven forty five but already the morning overwhelmed me.

The bus stopped on Waterloo Road, just a block away from my old school Maryknoll, to let on a few passengers. The top deck was full except for the seat next to mine.

"Well hi, Rose," Elliot Cohen said as he sat down next to me. "Going to work?"

It took a moment to recognize him, and I managed a stuttering, "Oh, Mr. Cohen, hello."

"No, no, absolutely not. It's Elliot, okay? Don't make me out to be that old. What's your real name, by the way?"

"What do you mean? My name's Rose."

"Your Chinese name."

I was surprised by his question, especially coming from a *gwailo*. "No one really calls me by my Chinese name, not even my family."

"Oh, I see." He pulled out a handkerchief and wiped his temples. "So, would you rather be on the beach?"

I began to laugh, and immediately, my body relaxed and the heat faded into the background. "Actually, I didn't want to get out of bed this morning," and I started telling him about my first day and the nervousness I felt. It was easy, talking to him. He listened patiently, without comment.

"You know what happened my first day of work?" He rearranged his jacket, which was draped untidily over the back of the seat ahead. "I spilt tea right on my lap, in the most embarrassing place, first thing in the morning, and in trying to catch the cup, sent it flying right down the front of my boss' shirt. It was a new shirt too, which he'd just picked up from the tailor's the day before. He wasn't amused."

He spoke seriously, with a perfectly straight face. I couldn't stop giggling.

"And then, while trying to change a typewriter ribbon, I pulled the desk drawer completely out and it landed on the office manager's foot. She was furious. I learnt my first Cantonese swear words that day."

I still don't know whether those stories were true, but the more he talked, the more he made me laugh, and the less nervous I felt. The double decker trundled on its way — past the Red Ruby restaurant, which was Mum's favorite Sunday *dim sum* place, Kwong Wah Hospital, where Regina and I'd been born, and Wah Yan Secondary, Paul's former rival school whose debate team he worked hardest to beat — until it reached the junction of Nathan Road. Several junks, full sails unfurled, appeared momentarily on the horizon ahead and then disappeared from sight as the bus turned onto Nathan. Time seemed to vanish. Elliot Cohen asked me more about my job, and I found myself telling him all about the interview as well as my family's mixed reactions to advertising and my own suspicions that perhaps I wasn't doing the right thing. Before I knew it, we had already passed the train station. Our bus halted at the terminus, where we alighted and walked together towards the pier to board the Star Ferry. The morning sun radiated the skies over the harbor but my body cooled as if an internal air conditioner had been switched on.

On the island after disembarking, we stopped by the concession stand to say goodbye. He startled me by taking my hand. His palm was cool and dry. "Don't worry, Rose. You'll be fine," he said, squeezing gently. "Just do what I suggested, and take things a step at a time, okay?" And with that, he was gone.

"But my dear, surely you can accept a graduation present. Or think of it as a token for the start of your professional life." Marion smiled, almost indulgently, at me.

I gazed at the Girard Peregaux watch I'd been given, almost afraid to take it out of its velvet cushion. It was ladylike and delicate, tastefully expensive, with a thin gold metal band that was as elegant as a bracelet. The Lies had insisted, less than a fortnight after I started my job, on taking both Paul and me out to dinner at Hugo's in the Hyatt, where they presented me with their gift. The restaurant was much fancier than anything my family went to. Paul smiled at me; it was the happiest I'd seen him since I began work. If nothing else, his parents general acceptance of me seemed to somehow reassure him that my whole future hadn't disintegrated because of my choice of job.

After dinner, Marion offered coffee at home. We stepped out to the Hyatt's driveway. Down the slope below us, the streets of Tsimshatsui hummed. It was a Saturday night. Paul Sr. glanced around restlessly, and quite to my surprise said, "Come on Paul, let's you and I allow the women some time alone together tonight. What do you say?"

Paul glanced uneasily at me. "Well, if Rose doesn't mind . . ." but it was obvious he couldn't offend his father.

"Of course she won't, will you, dear?" With that, Paul Sr. leaned over and kissed my cheek. "You be a good girl and run home with Marion. She'll send you back in the car."

Marion gave her husband a thin-lipped smile, but didn't seem particularly upset. "Rose will be fine with me," she said. And then, rolling her eyes in an amused manner, she added, "men."

The Lies' Mercedes arrived. Marion and I stepped in. Paul Sr. leaned over and kissed her. "Goodnight, Darling." Paul signalled an unobtrusive and apologetic wave. I waved back with a smile, to reassure him that everything was just fine.

The car pulled away, and, as it did, I watched Paul and his father walk downhill to Peking Road in the direction of the nightclubs and girlie bars, wondering where they would end up, wondering what they would do together.

"You mustn't mind my husband," Marion began. "He's the most faithful of men. But he does like a bit of nightlife now and then, something outside the society circuit, if you know what I mean.

Don't worry. You'll learn."

It was friendly, the way she said that, and it made me feel as if she were speaking to an equal. While I would never have dared respond in kind, I appreciated the way she brought me into their family, making me feel like I was already a part of their world. She told me about their life in Johannesburg, about Paul's Aunt Fay and Uncle Alex, his father's brother, of whom I knew Paul was extremely fond. As she described life of a marooned Chinese society in this far flung and exotic world, I tried to picture it all, cocktails against an almost surreal sunset, the spacious homes, the empty wilderness that surrounded them, the isolation that brought them together, so closely together, in a fashion not unlike the *wah kiu* world of my own family. I listened to her willingly, fascinated by her immersion in a life that seemed to stir her to a strange kind of passion.

And as she spoke, a strange confidence took hold of me. I could imagine myself in her world. It was the reason Paul first took to me, because he recognized me for one of them. After all, I was not like Mum, and, as much as I loved my father, he simply wasn't ambitious, not the way I was. As for Regina, she may have been more than me of everything — beautiful, intelligent, courageous, outspoken — but she couldn't come home and make it here. Her opinions from a distance counted for less, had, in fact, begun to matter less even when we were in university together. With Paul, I could excel in the Lies' social sphere, despite my less privileged background. I wasn't an intruder, or merely a social climber, not as long as I could capture and retain Marion's affection and approval. Paul could have had any girl in our circle he wanted, but he chose me because I could stand his mother's scrutiny, and in Marion's eyes, that was the most important thing. And so it was becoming in my eyes too.

"She got a raise after only two and a half months!" My mother's delight at this turn of events contrasted sharply against her initial lack of enthusiasm at my taking the job. "And look, her photo was in the papers, see, at a cocktail with the TV station!"

Mum waved the news clipping across the dinner table. We were at home having Chinese hot pot. Paul nodded politely. Uncle Chong stretched his arm out over the plates of raw meats to take the clipping, and smiled at me. Dad was grinning happily.

"It was just luck," I said. "The company changed bonus payments to year end instead of at Chinese New Year, so my boss let accounting give me my end of probation raise half a month earlier to simplify administration. It really wasn't a big deal."

"But your boss must think you're good, because he was confident enough to give it to you early," Dad asserted.

There seemed to be no way to downplay the event with my family. Even Aunt Helen, who didn't believe in making a fuss over monetary matters, was impressed by the news photo, although Mum, surprisingly, was exceptionally proud. That had been, as Paul pointed out privately to me, one of those "fortuitous" situations that could have happened to anyone who was there.

Mum spooned more shrimp into my bowl from the hot pot, saying, "Here Rose, have more. That's your favorite." I expected her to give Paul some as well, but for the moment, she seemed to have forgotten his existence.

Chong scooped more spinach and *hong ho* leaves into the stock. "So tell us, Rose, do you like the work you're doing?"

"It's a lot of fun. I get to meet clients and work with the creative personnel in the agency. We have one copywriter who's really good. He won an award for his commercial."

Paul interjected, "But it was only a local award, right?"

I nodded, "That's right."

"It's a big American company, isn't it?" Helen asked. "Will they send you to the States for training? Some companies do that, you know. Like your dad. He was sent by Pacific American to the States, and even by the American Air Corp when he was in China."

I looked at my father in surprise. He'd never mentioned training in the US. "Where did you go, Dad?"

My father poured more sake for everyone. "Arizona, but forget about it. Such a long time ago. Here, let's toast your good work, Rose."

I turned to Paul, but could not catch his eye.

After dinner, Paul and I went for a walk, leaving the others to chat in the living room. He was quiet as we went down in the lift, and didn't take my hand. Outside, the cool, evening air refreshed me. Late autumn was the best time of year. The typhoon season had passed, days were warm, nights cool, and the air far less humid than in the summer. It was weather I liked.

We walked in silence towards the park. I was beginning to feel uncomfortable. Paul seemed angry at something, but I couldn't be sure what was bothering him.

"It's indecent how much time it takes to prepare hot pot," he said suddenly. "Why does your family do it?"

It was such an unexpected question, that I couldn't respond to it right away.

"Rose, didn't you hear me?"

"I'm sorry, Paul, of course I did. Well, it's just that we've always done it. Mum and Helen enjoy cutting up the meats together, and Dad likes going with Mum to the market to get all the fresh meat and seafood. When Regina and I were children, it was our job to wash the vegetables. I still do that. It's sort of fun."

We stopped at the staircase to the park, and leaned against the railing. My cardigan, which was slung over my shoulders, slid down my right arm. Paul stretched out his hand to put it back in place. "I guess one could call that fun," he said, and then, "Why was your father in America, Rose?"

His tone was abrupt, almost suspicious. I shrugged. "I'm not sure. Perhaps he did his pilot training there. He doesn't talk much about those days."

"I've never understood why your family's so friendly towards Americans."

"Don't say things like that. It's insulting." I was hurt by his manner, by his demeanor the entire evening.

"Oh?" He smiled sarcastically. "Would poor Rose prefer it if all I confined myself to talking about was to priase her for making more money the way her family did at dinner?"

That hit home, and I reddened. It embarrassed me the way money preoccupied my mother. But he was being unfair. Mum seldom fussed over me the way she'd done tonight, and I craved that praise, even luxuriated in it, because coming from her, it made me feel good to know she could sometimes be proud of me, the way she was of Regina's beauty and creative talents.

My voice was low, even. "We can't all be wealthy like your family, Paul."

"Are you trying to start a fight?"

"No, but you're being awfully unreasonable tonight."

"Am I? Well then, perhaps I'd better leave you to that family of yours, and take my 'unreasonableness' elsewhere." He straightened up and began to walk away. "Goodnight, Rose."

If only we could talk about what had happened between us! Perhaps it was all too difficult, too much for us to put behind, and had permanently upset our balance. Paul's face, the first night of my return in this same park, haunted me. His whispered apology still rung in my ears now, months later, and, for the first time, I wondered whether or not I'd ever really forgiven him, despite my insistence that I had.

How I hated those evenings in the park. We had no privacy; everything had to be polite and unsullied in front of my parents. I know that's how it was for any other young Hong Kong couple, but I wanted more, wanted something better. Elliot Cohen made me laugh back then, the way Gordie does now and always has done. I need that laughter, that lightness. Being back in Hong Kong was too much about what ought to be, despite what really was.

Two weeks passed and Paul didn't call. My pride prevented me from calling him, but every time my mother's slightly needling voice asked how Paul was, and why weren't we going out, the knot in my stomach tugged just that little bit tighter.

It was early Saturday afternoon. I had just washed my hair and sat down to open a letter from Regina. My sister rarely wrote, but, when she did it would be at least a dozen pages long.

Paul rang. "What are you doing today?"

"My aunt invited me to the opening of an art gallery later this afternoon. It belongs to a friend of hers." I could feel my guard going up. He should at least apologize for his last, abrupt departure and unaccountable silence.

"Would you like to come over to my house for dinner afterwards?"

Dinner invitations to the Lies were never a last minute thing, what with his father's social calendar. "Won't your parents mind?" I asked.

He heard the caustic tone in my voice. "Listen, Rose, I'm awfully sorry for the way I behaved last time. It was uncalled for." He paused. I could picture him chewing his thumb, which he did whenever he was nervous or unsure of himself. "We need to talk about a few things, I guess."

It was hard to stay mad when he was sensible and gentle. "I guess so."

"Then you'll come?"

"Okay."

Before he rang off, he added that I should come around six thirty for drinks and wear my pale green dress.

Having first pointedly told my mother not to expect me home to dinner because of the Lies' invitation, I slit open Regina's letter, and counted twenty pages. She was in top form, excited about her painting and making strides towards a first poetry chapbook. It was a wonderful letter, full of energy and joy that leapt off the pages. I loved my sister's letters. Despite the fact that she never said anything that most people would want to know, like what she was up to or going to do in the near future, she always managed, at least in the letters she wrote to me, to pour out heart and soul in the most beautiful language. Even when we were children, I adored her compositions and admired her drawings and calligraphy. Regina was talented, and, despite whatever rivalry existed between us, I had always been proud of her for that.

Towards the end, she told me what I had suspected was the case for some time.

"Don't tell M&D, whatever you do, that I'm not really graduating in December. It's the only way I know of to extend my student visa. Dr. Ong and Dr. Polk both gave me independent studies so that I'll still be registered as a student at P'burgh. I'm going to New York in the winter where I'll be able to work illegally. I need to save more money in case I decide to go to grad school. You know, the U.S. government isn't giving out vacation time work visas for foreign students anymore. It's a hassle. But, anyway, I'll get around it somehow.

"I don't know if I want to come back to Hong Kong for a visit, even though Mum expects me to. It's expensive. Sometimes, I think I never want to go back, that everything will be just fine if I stay in

America. I'm not sure about grad school. It'll solve the visa situation for a few more years, but I don't really give a shit about a degree. It's tiresome enough getting a bachelors. All I want is to do what matters to me, in or out of school.

"Well, as you're still going out with that stuffed penguin, don't send him my regards. You can tell him if I ever see him again, I'll go after his cock with a cleaver for what he did to you. Thai women do that, you know, when their husbands are unfaithful, although I guess that wasn't exactly Paul's crime. Find yourself another boyfriend, Rose, or you'll end up married to that excuse of a man. Love, Regina."

I contemplated my sister's life. It was completely different from mine. As a child, I had worshipped her daring, and desperately wanted to be like her. Not now, though. Not anymore.

I hid away the letter in my dresser, so that Mum wouldn't happen accidentally on it. It would hurt her if she knew how Regina really felt about things. I pulled out my pale green dress to see if it needed pressing. Rather elegant for dinner at home. But I didn't give it too much thought.

"You frequent all the right places, don't you?"

I had been lost in a painting of the hills of Guilin rendered in oil on a tiny canvas, wondering what Regina would say about it.

Elliot indicated the painting, "Not bad, but a little pretentious, don't you think?"

He looked extremely smart, almost dapper. It was not the way I remembered him on board the bus. I was about to ask him why he was here when my aunt walked over.

"Ah, I see you found each other. How nice. Well Rose, what do you think of the gallery?"

I didn't really have an opinion, but with Aunt Helen that would have been unforgivable. "It's, how shall I put it, adventurous? I mean, I can't see your friend doing much business if she only exhibits local painters."

"What's life without a little adventure, right?" Elliot winked at my aunt. "Your niece is a rather self assured young lady."

"Oh, excuse me, there's someone I have to talk to . . ." and off went my aunt.

"So local art doesn't sell, eh?" Elliot remarked.

I gestured towards the small crowd of invitees, mostly Chinese businessmen and their wives. "Oh, it sells," I said. "As long as you can get them to buy."

"How would you do it?"

"I'd double the price of all these paintings. They're marked way too low. That's the only way anything sells in Hong Kong, if people think it's expensive, exclusive, when it's actually just ridiculously overpriced."

He chuckled. "You don't think much of the Hong Kong buying public, then?"

"I'm not referring to the public. Just people with too much money to spare."

Elliot burst out laughing. I suddenly felt rather silly. Here I was, expressing opinions on something about which I knew nothing. He probably thought me a bit much. But, then again, I was getting away with it.

"Go on," he said. "Your view of Hong Kong is . . . refreshingly unusual."

"Or naive."

"I'm not sure I'd want to meet you across a negotiating table."

I couldn't imagine doing any such thing. Elliot had to be at least ten years my senior, and was in business in Asia regionally. It would be a long time before I'd catch up to the likes of him. But the one thing that struck me was how differently from other older people he behaved, especially expatriates. I encountered mostly Australians, Europeans and British *gwailos* in my work, and a few Americans. They all drew clear divisions between themselves and locals, and could even be quite snobbish and overbearing. Elliot talked to me as if I were his equal.

He led me over to that drinks table and ordered me one. "Were you born in Indonesia too?"

"Oh no. You're thinking of Helen." It was an explanation I had become used to giving about my family's history. Helen, who was several years older than my father, had been born in Central Java, but then my grandparents moved back to Fujian province where dad was born. Mum had been born in Indonesia and had lived there until after the war. My parents met and married in Hong

Kong. He already knew Helen and Chong's background.

"Your typical w*ah kiu* family history," he remarked. "Bits and branches all over the place."

He appeared to be waiting for me to speak. When I didn't offer anything further, he continued, "So, why do you look so elegant this afternoon? Are you going somewhere special?"

I was back on familiar ground now. "No, only to my boyfriend's home for dinner. His parents are quite formal though." And, before I knew it, I was telling him all about Paul, how we had dated since high school and that he had even come to see me in college in the States once, and how we were going to get married when we were both better established in our careers.

"Lucky man," he remarked when I'd concluded my speech. He glanced at his watch. "Well, I have to be off. I was going to invite you for a drink, as your aunt suggested, but I guess you have other plans." He gave me an amused look. "Hope I see you again soon."

He held out his hand. I reached out to shake it, and, as I did, he leaned over and kissed my cheek. I wanted to ask what he meant about my aunt, but he took off rather too quickly for me to say anything else.

I wandered around the gallery for a few more minutes after that and then bade Helen goodbye. She mumbled something vague about Elliot, but her comment escaped me.

I had a little more than an hour to get across the harbor back to Kowloon. By the time I got the bus to Paul's place, it would be six thirty. The Lies were exceptionally prompt people. They weren't terribly Chinese that way, because when they specified a time, they meant it exactly, instead of the approximate timing most Hong Kong people meant. But it was easy for them to control time. They had a private car and driver who ferried them at their beck and call. Paul's father had just purchased a new Mercedes. My father was lucky his old Skoda still ran, and Mum and I travelled at the mercy of the wholly unreliable public bus system and some of the equally uncertain minibus routes.

It was not till I was on board the number one bus to Prince Edward Road that it dawned on me what Aunt Helen was up to. Elliot. She wanted me to go out with Elliot Cohen. I suddenly burst out giggling, and covered my mouth with my hand when I realized the other passengers were staring at me. I imagined my mother's fury, my father's utter amazement, and Paul, dear Paul would only be further confirmed in his belief that my aunt was slightly nutty. It was even harder to suppress my giggles after that.

But when I finally got off the bus, I caught myself thinking that although Helen's idea was quite hysterically funny, it wasn't without its own brand of appeal.

The party of people in the living room took me aback. Marion greeted me with her enigmatically cool smile. "My dear Rose, how lovely you could make it."

I didn't want to let on that I had no idea this was an occasion, but, inwardly, I was fuming that Paul hadn't given me fair warning. She glanced at my dress approvingly before floating back to her guests. Paul Sr. came towards me, an unusually ebullient air about him.

"Rose dear, how sweet of you to come help me celebrate. Most kind of you."

I glanced around, a little desperately, looking for Paul.

"Your boyfriend will be here momentarily," his father said. "He was delayed with some friends. In the meantime, come keep an old man company." Paul Sr. took my elbow and escorted me towards the crowd.

It took awhile to sink in that Paul's father was now a judge, and that this was the reason for the party. The place was filled with solicitors and barristers and a few government officials. I felt lost, wishing Paul would show up. Time crawled. Dinner was announced and people lined up for the buffet. I found myself seated between an English woman on my right who was deaf in her left ear, and a Chinese gentleman who kept "accidentally" touching me, either with his knee or hand, after which he would always apologize. My anger simmered. Tonight wasn't a sudden thing — it had to have been planned for weeks. Paul simply hadn't bothered to invite me properly. I ate with little appetite, wondering when he would show up. My only consolation was that Marion would smile at me reassuringly from time to time, making me feel like it was okay for me to be here alone.

Guests were already leaving when he finally sauntered in. His mother glared at him silently. Paul Sr. glanced at him. I absorbed his slightly dishevelled state. When the last guest had left, his father said, "You owe us, and Rose, an explanation."

Paul Sr.'s inclusive remark helped steady me. Paul barely looked at me.

"I had to work." And then after a pause, "I'm sorry."

"Indeed." His father turned his back on him and began walking away, adding, "You'd better escort Rose home."

As soon as we were alone, he spoke quickly, before I could say anything, "Please don't ask, Rose. I'm sorry. I can't explain." He led me into the taxi where he held me tightly all the way home. "But Paul," I demanded, "why didn't you tell me about tonight, about the reason for the dinner? Aren't you proud of your father?" He did not reply, and kissed me instead, tenderly, gently. As he laid his cheek against mine, I could have sworn he was crying.

That night, I tossed around for hours, unable to sleep. My body wanted Andrew, wanted some kind of relief from what I couldn't understand. When he left me that night, Paul had hugged me so tightly and had such a sad look on his face that I couldn't think about him without crying. He was working and lost track of time, he insisted over and over again in the taxi. It was all so insane; I knew he was lying. But why? As the onslaught of desire took hold in bed that night, I tried to conjure up Paul's face, Paul's hand on mine, Paul's lips against my cheek. But, instead, I saw Andrew's broad grin, felt him enter me slowly, pleasurably torturing me, making me enjoy every moment of our heightened physical state.

On the January day I first arrived in Plattsburgh, Regina had asked Andrew Chiang to pick me up from the bus station there. She had collected me at Kennedy, put me on board the right Greyhound at Port Authority, and then disappeared back into the city to finish working for the winter. I was, she blithely informed me, to stay with him for a week until she got back, because her place was filled with a bunch of theatre friends building a set.

"I recognize you," I said, as soon as I saw him at the station.

Regina had told me that he used to live across the road from us.

Andrew smiled at me. "You must be exhausted. Come on, I'll take you to my apartment."

I had had eight hours on the bus to digest this concept, but my expression must have given away how perturbed I still felt about it.

"I don't bite," he said, as he helped me with his bags. "Besides, my roommate's still away."

The idea that I was really away from home, and would spend the night alone in some strange guy's apartment suddenly seemed more grown up than I wanted to be. I was annoyed at Regina's act of desertion, but I didn't want to appear ungrateful to him. I forced a smile.

Andrew's apartment was on the second floor of a large old house near campus. I gazed at the space around me. It was like Kowloon Tong, except that the roads were wider, the houses larger and the landscape piled with snow. The searingly cold air I encountered as I stepped out of the car made my eyelashes freeze.

"Cold, isn't it?" he said. "Don't worry, it's a lot warmer indoors."

We climbed up a wide staircase — "Look," he indicated the ground level where his landlady lived, "the fireplace is lit. Pretty, huh?"

I was still feeling jet lag and fatigue from my thirty-eight hour trip. Everything looked old and new at the same time. What struck me was how quiet everything was. At home, the sound of planes and cars never stopped. But then, I didn't imagine anyone would want to spend much time outdoors in such weather.

"You need some gloves." Andrew picked up my bare hands and rubbed them vigorously. "Here, stand by the radiator. You'll thaw."

"Is it always this cold? What's the temperature?"

"A few degrees below."

"Below what?"

"Zero, of course. What did you think?"

There is something dumbfounding about the silence of falling snow. That first night in America, I stared at the never ending shower of flakes. Andrew's car slowly disappeared under the white layers.

He sat next to me on the window sill. "*Maan maan wui gwan.* You'll get used to it slowly." He handed me a cup of hot chocolate. "Here, welcome to America."

His kind air reassured me. A wiry, slender guy, he had a shock of *laan jai* "teddy boy" hair and unusually large eyes. "You're indoors

41

half the year. But indoor life has its advantages." He smiled at me. "How's the chocolate?"

"Good."

"You're not like Regina, are you?"

I peered at him over the rim of my cup. "What do you mean?"

"Not so noisy."

I smiled. "No."

He was silent a moment. There was something un-Chinese about Andrew that I couldn't figure out. He spoke good English, and was quite Westernized. But the most Westernized Chinese friends I had, even Paul, would always have something about them that made me feel, this is a Chinese person.

Andrew got up suddenly. "Everyone's been wondering."

"Who's everyone?"

"The *kung fu* brigade. The other Chinese students, especially the guys. It's a small community here." He straightened up a pile of books on a table next to the window.

I stared at him. He seemed the antithesis of a martial arts type. "What do you think of the *kung fu* brigade?"

"I didn't do *kung fu* back home."

"But you do now?"

"Only when I have to."

"Which is . . . ?"

"When I get homesick."

Andrew was a lifetime ago. Whatever's happened to him?

They search thoroughly, those bastards from the Feds. Hell, I sound like Gordie these days. What'll happen to him? I hate to admit it but I worry about the man. He'll probably survive this debacle too, somehow, the way he's survived the entire escapade that has been his life.

I may not do so well.

Regina did not come home that winter after my return to Hong Kong. Mum was a little concerned at first, but she was caught up in the hectic routine of her work days and church activities, into which she squeezed Dad and me when she had time. Besides, what with Christmas and Chinese New Year coming up, life at home acquired an air of anticipatory flurry.

My mother worked for a small Chinese Indonesian trading company as a secretary cum office manager. Most of her own family was still in Indonesia, in Jakarta where she'd grown up, and the company was as close to a "home" as she'd ever known since arriving in Hong Kong after the war. She complained about her boss and gossiped about all her colleagues. Yet every Chinese New Year, she made her boss' family a large turnip cake, packed full of dried shrimp and sausage, protesting that it was nothing when Mrs. Chee, the boss' wife, praised her cooking and thanked her profusely. The annual ritual was not complete until she had doled out generous *laisee* money packets to all the other staff, partly out of tradition, and, more importantly, to show them she really didn't need the money they paid her.

Dad, in the meantime, had taken up a new hobby while I'd been away in the States. Since joining Golden Phoenix, his workload had become much lighter, and he often came home earlier than Mum. This was how he started experimenting in the kitchen, and he was, like Regina, a natural cook.

"He burned the bottom of my pressure cooker!" Mum recalled, laughing. "What a mess that time — you'd just left for America, Rose. But now he makes good *bami goreng* and *chow ho fun*, you know, the dry kind, with sliced beef. Oh, and linguini with white clam sauce." Noodles of every kind — Indonesian, Chinese, Italian — had always been his favorite food.

So life back home was a constant feast. "Rose, you want some lumpia? With fresh chilli?" Dad liked everything *laat,* spicy hot, especially his Indonesian spring rolls in plain, unfried pancakes, packed full of meat and vegetables, which absorbed the stinging bite of the tiny red and green chilli. The bigger the bite, the greater the pleasure of consumption. When it came to food, Dad had an international, not Chinese, palate.

It took me aback how comfortable he was in the kitchen. From what Mum told me, he even went to the track less as a result of his new interest.

"Make her fried noodles, with plenty of bean sprouts and pork strips," Mum would command him. "You like that best, right Rose?"

When it came to food, my parents never fought, which was why

43

I loved eating with them. I still didn't cook. After I moved out on my own in college, fed up as I was of living with Regina's messy habits, I survived on peanut butter and jelly sandwiches, lots of salads and Domino's, either plain or with mushrooms. Regina brought food over weekly out of pity for me.

But what was missing these days was Dad's former interest in model car building.

He first took it up in the fall of '71, after leaving Pacific American and before he'd decided to work for Golden Phoenix. It was just after Regina had left for college, while I was still hanging out at home for a semester, trying to decide whether or not to go to the States. I spent quite a lot of time around my father during those months, and he seemed pleased by my company, both of us being in a similar state of transitional uncertainty.

"Too much of my life," Dad used to tell me, "I've been stuck behind a desk pushing piles of paper from one end to the other. Out of the in-tray and into the out-tray, day in, day out. If I have to sit behind a desk, I would rather make something."

My father's flying days had ended when he left China. After the Communists drove Chiang Kai Shek out of the mainland to Taiwan, he had headed south to Hong Kong, where Helen was already living. He found a job with Pacific American Airways in their purchasing department; there he remained for over twenty years until he decided on early retirement.

"American cars," he said, as he delicately held an engine piece of his current auto, a T-bird, between tweezers, "were the sleekest, finest machines in the world. Just like their aircraft. But that's changing now."

The dining table, which he had appropriated as his work table, was covered with numerous plastic parts. It was early afternoon and Mum was still at work, which was why he could get away with this. He inserted the engine part into position. The front end of the car was coming together nicely.

I watched, fascinated by his meticulous exactitude. "How do you mean, Dad?"

He laid down the tweezers.

"Twenty years ago, I would have given up everything to go to America. That was the country with everything, while China was one big mess. But all through the sixties, the country went a little crazy. In another twenty years, say by the beginning of the nineties, America is going to be one big mess just like China today. You wait and see."

I picked up a tire and turned it round in my palm. Watching my father peer at these pieces through his spectacles, I remembered trying to imagine this country he spoke of, to which I might be going in a few months. Go to America, go to America. That was all I ever heard from Regina, my mother, aunt Helen and uncle Chong. My father however, the longest standing American company employee, seldom added his voice to the chorus.

"Don't you like America, Dad?" I could hear Regina's admonishing in my brain — Dad's advice is not advice; he hasn't time for anyone except himself!

"I didn't say that. Haven't I worked for the Americans all my life? Didn't I agree that you and your sister should go there?" And he turned back to his model and continued his painstaking labor, squeezing a dot of glue onto the tip of a toothpick to apply it to the piece at hand.

It wasn't worth pursuing. He was a funny man who could go along in the same routine for a long time, and then suddenly change course without warning. For years, he had never said a word while Mum pushed Regina and I to do well in school so that we could go to America. When he left Pacific American, he had done so without any previous discussion with Mum. She fought with him for weeks after that over the loss of income, accusing him of sabotaging his daughters' future because he was an old fashioned man who didn't want women to do well. All he ever replied was to say that things were not the way she thought. It was the same thing he said whenever I asked about pre-Communist China, adding that life simply had a way of going on.

So perhaps now, the time for building models had passed, and life had moved on to a culinary domesticity. It wasn't such a bad thing, I thought, as I bit into the lumpia he dished out to me.

Christmas my first year back was one social whirl. Paul sparkled at all these events where people knew him, admired him, and sought him out. So you're Paul's girlfriend, I heard one person after another say to me at dinner parties, balls, cocktail receptions. It made me proud to hear that, and to know that the firm he worked at, Auden, Rose & Wang, was solid, and more important, eminently respectable. Three times that season, Paul and I made the social pages of the *South China Morning Post,* a feat my mother looked upon with pride and joy. My father was more begrudging in his praise, but even he couldn't resist showing those clippings to his staff.

With the slowing of the social season, and the approach of Chinese New Year, Paul began spending many of his weekend days and evenings at our home. I sometimes wished we could do the same at his home, but he rarely suggested it, in fact, only invited me over when there was an occasion, usually a dinner with his father's associates and friends. It bothered me a little, but I didn't say anything. Perhaps I should have, for it was destined to end badly a few days before the actual new year. My mother was busy making her annual turnip cake for her boss. Paul stood around the kitchen, watching her.

"Auntie, you do such a good job," he told her.

"Oh it's nothing. You get used to it when you've done it as long as I have."

"But you make it look so easy."

My mother giggled like a happy schoolgirl.

"Paul," my father called out to him, "come over here and join me. Maybe you can pick a horse for me."

"Don't get him started on your habits." There was venom in Mum's voice.

"Oh Mum, Dad's only having fun."

"You're always defending your father."

"Paul," I linked my arm through his, "tell my mother it's not all that terrible. Everyone in Hong Kong gambles. Why even your firm entertains at the Jockey Club."

He extracted his arm abruptly. "No, Rose, your mother is right. Gambling is a bad habit. It's like drug addiction."

"Paul!" I looked at him and then at my father in horror. "That's not true."

"Oh, you modern young people," my father declared, "you're all too influenced by Western psychology and such sort of rubbish. So,

46

Rose, it seems Paul thinks I'm a gambler too."

I went to my dad and sat down next to him. He appeared quite nonchalant, even amused by Paul's statement. But I felt hurt for him. "Of course you're not, dad," I reassured in Chinese. He's *luan shuo*." I often spoke to my father in Mandarin, since he disliked Cantonese and claimed he already spoke too much English at work. Regina and Mum wouldn't speak Mandarin, mostly because Mum spoke it with an embarassingly pronounced accent; they almost always spoke English at home, mixed with a little Cantonese, although my mother sometimes lapsed into Indonesian.

My father laughed and turned to his magazine. I quelched the upset I felt.

Later, when Paul and I were alone in the park downstairs, I turned on him. "How could you?! How dare you talk to my father like that."

"Oh, calm down, Rose. I didn't mean anything by it, and your dad wasn't upset. Come on, kiss me. If you're very good, I'll even go further the way you like it."

I pushed him away. "Oh, so now you want to shut me up? Yet other times you treat me like some kind of untouchable! What is it with you anyway?"

"Rose, what is it? Are we talking about your father or you?"

"Dad's right, you do twist things around."

"Oh, is that what he's been saying about me? How nice of him."

We were glaring at each other, oblivious to the night wind, caught up in the biggest fight since my return.

"Well you do!"

He pulled me roughly towards him. "I've always been so good to you, and yet you get mad at me over some silly thing and pick a fight. I don't understand."

"You don't understand anything!" I could feel tears, and blinked them away angrily.

He cradled my head and began kissing me, walking me to a corner of the park where he sat me down on a bench. He began touching me all over, and I could feel myself relenting, growing in desire, thinking it's really all right, I was just being silly, it's really all right and he does love me; then he slid his hand under my skirt and into my panties, which startled me so much I bit his neck, harder

47

than I intended but he seemed not to notice. I could feel myself getting wet, and then, suddenly, he withdrew his hand, pulled away from me and stood over me in my now dishevelled state.

"You're as bad as he is, except you're addicted to sex. That's why you got pregnant in the first place."

And he got up, straightened his clothes, and, like the time before, left me there.

I sat for a long while, too numb to cry. He'd finally said it. Despite his apologies over the last year and a half, he believed it was my fault I got pregnant. Did he really think that just because I had the abortion that it was something I was pleased about? He hadn't asked, hadn't even tried to find out how I felt. He was just relieved that I had taken care of things, not told either of our parents, and carried on living. On top of it all, I'd even come back to him after the whole messy business was over, because he'd begged me, swearing his love for me.

And now sex was my "problem" not his.

It got late. The winter air chilled me, but I was too disturbed to go home. Finally, afraid my parents would be concerned, I headed back. But they were already asleep.

Paul did not return my calls to his office all the next week. Eventually, I called him at home, which I rarely did. His father answered.

"My dear Rose," he liked to address me this way, "you've just missed him. He's gone out with the boys. For the weekend, you know."

"Oh, of course, how silly of me. I should have called earlier." I tried to sound breezy and casual, but I felt my heart sink. I had no idea who he could possibly be with, and it dawned on me then that I really knew very few of his friends, the "boys" his father referred to. The people we knew in our social circle were only acquaintances or business contacts, and we rarely went out with other couples. For a moment, I thought it was all over between us.

"But he said to tell you he'd see you Sunday night when he got back, in case you called. According to plan."

"Y-yes. That's fine."

There was a pause. "Is everything all right, dear?"

"Certainly, why wouldn't it be?" A little too hurried and anxious.

"I thought perhaps . . . well never mind. See you again, soon, I hope? We like you to visit."

I wanted to say that if Paul would invite me I would most happily come, but held my tongue. "For sure. My regards to Marion."

I stood by the phone, puzzled and worried.

"Who was that?"

I jumped. "Mum! You startled me."

"I didn't mean to. Who was that?"

"No one. Just Paul's father." I suspected she'd been listening to the entire conversation. She did that sometimes.

"Now, you know Rose, sometimes you aren't very diplomatic. You shouldn't be talking to his parents when he's not around. I mean it's okay if he brings you there. But since he's away with his friends anyway, you should know better than to be bothering his family."

The shock must have showed, but it was more than I could hide.

My mother rolled on. "Oh yes, Paul called me and said you two weren't getting along terribly well. I told him I understood. After all, you're young and not as sophisticated as he is. It's only natural that he'd get tired of you."

"He is *not* tired of me!"

"Rose, don't shout. I'm not deaf. Sometimes, you're as bad as Regina. I've warned you time and time again about your aspirations with Paul. He's wonderful, but he needs someone very attractive who has social graces to partner him. You know how you are . . ."

"Shut up. You don't know what you're talking about. Stop it!"

"Oh Rose, poor Rose. I've always been afraid of Paul jilting you."

"Mum!" My voice was pitched almost to a scream now. "Stop it!" I was crying uncontrollably, the tension of the past week unleashing itself.

"Your father's to blame too. Stuffing your head full of ideas about yourself, spoiling you. He just . . ."

My father's voice rang loudly through the living room. "Leave her alone!"

It was as if he'd slapped her mouth. Dad hardly ever raised his voice. She went silent. Then, she turned away and walked out, murmuring something about church and letting the heavy wooden door slam as she left.

I sat down in the armchair and calmed myself.

"I'm sorry if I've caused any problem," my father began.

"You didn't cause any problem, Dad. I shouldn't have shouted like that. Mum's just exaggerating." A pause. "He is going to marry me, you know," I gazed at my father, a little defiantly, trying to get a grip on myself.

Dad nodded reassuringly "Yes, Rose, of course he will. Of course he will."

But it was the sadness in his voice I couldn't dispel for a long time afterwards.

3

It always surprises me when an elastic band, stretched taut beyond endurance, snaps back whole. My relationship with Paul was like that. When we were teenagers, he was the only person in the world who understood me, and I clung willingly to him for that. But as we ventured into adult life, it seemed as if we constantly wanted to test the limits of the bond that connected us.

The first time I told Gordie this, he said that elastic lost its pull with time. And then he snapped one at me, hitting my cheek, hard. I struck out at him. He grabbed my hand and kissed it. "Doll," he said, "a real bond doesn't need to be tested."

He's raising his scotch in a toast from his glass-windowed office. Damn Gordie, how can he be so cheerful, even now? Never says die, does he?

A couple of weeks passed, and Paul behaved as if we'd never fought, as if he'd forgotten everything that happened. I kept wanting to say something, but it felt quite pointless since everything seemed perfectly normal. Then, out of the blue, he completely shocked me by suggesting we go to a motel.

"Well, you know I want you," he said, not looking at me.

We were in the park after our weekly date. Paul had been unusually amorous. He alternated between complete lack of control and almost monastic tendencies.

"I am sorry about what happened, you know," he continued. "And I was wrong to blame you. After all, I wanted you and you didn't get pregnant on your own."

There it was, just like that. He would apologize and I could trust him again. He still wasn't looking at me. I took his face in my hand and turned it towards me. "Paul, it's all right, really it is. I survived."

"Oh Rose, you understand." He buried his face against my neck and I held him close to me. Strangely enough, in the face of his emotion, I was unmoved. We sat together in each other's arms in silence for several minutes.

Finally I spoke. "It just seems so, well . . ."

"Dirty?"

I nodded.

"And what do you call making a public spectacle of ourselves in the park?"

There wasn't a soul around. "It's not as if anyone's watching."

"I still feel funny."

He had a point. I missed the privacy of having my own place. Besides, it wasn't as if we had anywhere we could go unless we wanted to take a chance when either of our parents were out. He suggested going a few weeks later. I made a quick mental calculation about my period cycle and told him when the best time would be. But he told me to start taking the pill to be safe. I wondered how difficult that would be to arrange, but realized Paul wouldn't be interested. He just expected me to take care of things.

The first time Andrew kissed me, I had been crying in his arms because I was homesick and missed Paul. I had been in Plattsburgh a year. Regina was away in New York. She took off frequently, cutting classes for modelling jobs that paid a fortune.

"Come on, *ah muih,* don't be such a baby." His nickname for me was "little sister." Most of the kung fu brigade also called me that since they'd sort of adopted me. By then, the guys accepted that I was "in love with Paul" and had stopped trying to date me.

"I can't help it," I sniffed. "I don't like being here and want to be with Paul."

That was when he kissed me. It startled me so much I kissed him back. And before I knew it I was caught up in an embrace that I didn't want to get out of.

He finally untangled us. "You're going to get into trouble, you know."

I had been faithful to Paul a whole year, but it wasn't as if I hadn't noticed Andrew and a couple of the other guys either. "Maybe it's time I did."

"You won't blame me?" I thought about Debbie, his girlfriend, a smart, pretty blond who seriously wanted to marry him and was headed to law school. They were both juniors.

"I won't tell." It came out decisively and certain. Dutch courage, perhaps.

And that was how it started, quite accidentally, quite unplanned. I told him I was a virgin, at which point there was no stopping Andrew. He did insist on using condoms, although we took plenty of chances as well in our quickie encounters on stairwells and in library carrels. After that, he came to my place whenever he could get away from Debbie and when Regina wasn't around. I liked it because it kept things simple, and I wasn't in love with him.

Andrew came to mind a lot as I worried all the next week about how to get the pill. There was simply no way I could go to our family doctor, and all my girlfriends were single so I didn't dream of asking them. Finally, I made an appointment with a doctor in Kowloon City whom I was pretty certain would be unlikely to know any of my relatives or friends.

"Why do you want it?" he demanded. He was middle aged, and had a rather nasty manner.

I had prepared a story. "I've heard it regulates your period."

"Are you very irregular?"

"Extremely. Sometimes, I skip a month. I did this past month."

"How do you know you're not pregnant?" He burst out laughing as he said this. I stared at him, stone faced.

The examination took all of a minute and a half, and I left with the necessary prescription.

The taxi dropped us off by a back street entrance to the motel. As well as I knew Kowloon Tong, I didn't at first recognize where we were. I found the convoluted route to allow a discreet entrance amusing.

"I walked around all last week to find this one," Paul said in utter earnestness, as he ushered me hurriedly into the main lobby. "You can't tell it's a motel."

Two months had elapsed since Paul first suggested this, because he wanted to be absolutely sure about the pill being effective. What old house had this been, I wondered, as we entered the lobby with its fake marble floors. Regina and I had bicycled and skateboarded through the back streets of this district as children. There had been trees and big homes surrounded by high concrete walls, many with jagged pieces of colored glass cemented along the top to keep burglars out of the homes of the rich. But there had been other homes, pre-war houses which belonged to ordinary people, like the one we rented. A quiet area, except for the planes — Kowloon Tong was prohibited from building high rises because it was on the flight path to Kai Tak airport.

So whose family home, sold no doubt for a huge profit, had this once been?

A tired looking man emerged and led us silently to our room. It was designed to resemble an ice cave, with white stucco walls. In the centre of the room was a sunken tub. The bed was heart shaped with a red satin cover.

Paul grimaced. I started giggling.

"*You mun tai ah?*" The man gave us a dour look, unable to determine what my problem was.

Paul handed him some money and closed the door. "I didn't expect it to be quite this bad."

"Nothing a little champagne won't cure." I pulled the bottle out of my bag. It was a surprise. I started to pop the cork.

"Rose! Surely we can't finish a whole bottle."

"Why not?"

It took Paul the entire three hours we had purchased to loosen up even a little. First he complained the champagne wasn't cold enough. Then he said the water in the tub wasn't hot enough. When he finally let me take my dress off, he didn't like my choice of black lace underclothing — my "Andrew specials" — another surprise which I thought sexy and he thought vulgar, but I could tell he was getting turned on. But he averted his gaze and fussed with the condom — he had never used one before — even though I'd reassured him about the pill and told him it was a safe time for me anyway. He'd start to kiss me, and as soon as I'd get aroused, he'd stop and find something else to do. I found myself sipping glass after glass after glass of champagne.

In the end, I got drunk, and we never did anything.

On the way out, we passed two Mercedes, an MG and a Rolls in the parking lot. Their license plates were each covered by a sign.

Perhaps if I hadn't gotten pregnant in Plattsburgh, things would have been different. Who knows? Water under the bridge, as Gordie always says about everything he classifies "forgettable ancient history."

Aren't we supposed to learn something from history?

The river's turning murky.

That one guy peering through the files is tall for an Asian. He looks Chinese, ABC. Broad shoulders, probably works out. Reminds me of Paul, the way he scrutinizes each document meticulously. If there's anything incriminating, he'll find it.

Meanwhile, my job was not at all what I'd expected work to be like. Life at the agency was hectic. The boss was an early morning man who liked things organized and systematic. The creative department, on whom we depended for our product, rolled in around ten thirty if they hadn't been gambling and drinking too late the night before. If we were lucky, they might remember what client we needed an ad for that week. As for the media folks, who were also the accountants, we got our numbers but no rationale.

Client presentations became my job.

"You studied in America," the creative director told me, "so your English is good. Write up something, anything, so long as we have a few overheads to present, and a document to leave behind. We'll talk our way through the rest."

The first time I tried it, I was extremely dubious. The job was a launch campaign for a new orange juice in a tetra pack, which the creatives tossed around like a basketball as a way of "experiencing" the product. The truth of the matter was that it was the most vile tasting stuff we'd ever come across. I agonized over what to put down on paper, desperately trying to find some rational connection between an undrinkable juice and basketball.

The client barely glanced at the presentation, but was thrilled by our basketball idea. After that, I wasn't nearly as worried about presentations again.

Paul didn't share my perspective about the job.

"It's frivolous, Rose," he told me on one of our weekly dates.

I was beginning to dread these dates. About the first clumsy motel attempt he never said a word. But he had retreated to being much more cautious, containing himself to kissing me goodnight at my doorstep instead of stopping at the park. Work was a great relief:

it kept my mind off sex.

"Oh, you just don't have any sense of humor," I retorted. "It's not like everything I do is as silly as the orange juice affair."

We were at the top of the Empress Hotel on Salisbury Road, which commanded an excellent harbor view. I sipped my scotch and soda. Paul frowned upon my choice of drink, saying it was unladylike, but didn't try too hard to change it.

Paul took my hand. He had a way of holding it that I could feel even in his absence, that I had felt all the time we had been apart during my years in the States. It was a gentle, caressing hold, possessive yet unassuming, as if it simply belonged there. It was like the way he held me when we danced.

"I just want what's best for you Rose," he said.

I heard the sincerity in his voice. It was hard not to love Paul when he was kind to me.

"Rose Kho?"

I looked up into Elliot Cohen's face. He was with a Chinese man.

I made introductions. Elliot introduced Albert Ho. Paul and he seemed to recognize each other, and after a brief conversation, it became clear that this was David Ho's brother, or, rather, his half brother. Paul and he then launched into a long discussion about their respective families and mutual friends.

Elliot crouched by my chair. "So this is where you hang out."

"Only sometimes," I replied. "I prefer the Sheraton, but don't like to go there in case I run into Uncle Chong, and, well, he'd insist on buying our drinks and Paul doesn't like that."

"I know. *Mm ho yee see,*" he said, indicating he understood it was bad form, a "disturbance of meaning."

"Oh, you speak Cantonese?"

"Siu siu."

"I've never met a *gwailo* who does." I covered my mouth in embarrassment as soon as I'd said it, exclaiming, "oh, I didn't mean to be rude . . ."

He waved it away. "You're not. We're all racists here."

I smiled. Once again, I was struck by how comfortable Elliot made me feel.

Paul took my hand. "We should be going. It's late and your

parents will be worried."

I frowned. It was unnerving the way Paul treated me around other people. When we were alone in the park, he never worried about the time. I disliked his manner.

But these thoughts passed quickly, and the social situation asserted itself and I simply smiled nicely and agreed that, yes, it was time to go.

"So good to meet you," Albert said, holding out his hand to me. I stared at him. He was extremely well groomed, quite unlike David, who was a photographer and rather casual, which was why he got on well with Regina.

Elliot leaned towards me and kissed my cheek. "My regards to your aunt and uncle, if you see them before I do." I caught Paul's disapproving frown, and retreated as quickly as I could.

David had given Paul a ride to Plattsburgh to see me. They had arrived, on three days notice, from Montreal. Regina and David took to each other instantly and went out for a long walk, my sister contending that Paul and I needed to be alone.

"Well, Regina hasn't changed," Paul said as soon as they'd left the house. I didn't respond, but was embarrassed for Regina's blatant behavior.

"So this is where you live," he continued.

I was a mass of nerves. The night before, Andrew had made love to me and said I should relax about seeing Paul again.

"There's some tea ready, Would you like some?" I offered. He nodded and continued to look around the room while I disappeared into the kitchen.

"It's terribly cluttered in here," he said, as I poured the steaming liquid into his cup. "I wouldn't have expected it of you."

"They're mostly Regina's things in the living room." I felt awkward in my dress, having gotten used to wearing jeans on campus. I'd worn it especially for him, along with the gold bracelet, a going away-to-college present from Marion. I'd remembered to put on the bracelet just minutes before he arrived. Jewellery seemed out of place in this casual college environment.

Regina and her friends had built ceiling-to-floor bookshelves and painted them scarlet. They then hung spray painted grey sheets on the windows as curtains. The sofa was purple, something Regina had scrounged off her air force host family before I arrived. On it, her friends had draped green velvet cushions which they'd filched from the theatre department's prop room. And the armchair was upholstered in a yellow fabric with huge white daisies. The room was not improved by Regina's things strewn all over the place — at the moment, a pile of notebooks sat in one corner; a bag of clean laundry from two days ago sat in another; three used cups lined one bookshelf.

"I'm sorry to stop in so suddenly. Are you sure you have room for me? I can stay in a motel."

"Of course there is." I almost said, you can sleep with me, but bit my tongue. My newly developed sexual familiarity was the last thing I wanted Paul to discover. To cover my almost faux pas I continued without pausing, "who were these relatives you went to see?"

"My uncle and his family. My cousin was killed in an accident. We went to the funeral."

We sipped our tea. I had no idea what to say next. I had not known Paul had an uncle in Montreal.

There was a long silence. "My cousin was the same age as me."

"Which cousin, Paul?"

"You know, Robert. We grew up together in South Africa."

He lapsed into silence again. He looked so sad and lost, like he didn't know why he was here or why I should matter to him.

My heart melted. Robert had been his comrade and ally, and they had been inseparable as children. Whenever Paul spoke of him, it was as if Robert were right there in the room. He never mentioned that his cousin's family had moved to Canada, and I had assumed Robert remained in South Africa after Paul left. I think in that moment, out of all the years I had with Paul, I loved him more than at any other time.

"You've changed," he said suddenly. "You're even prettier than I remember. I like your dress."

We were sitting opposite each other, and he smiled for the first time since his arrival.

"You sound more American, though," he said in a tone that implied I had contracted some mildly infectious disease.

58

"And you act like a *gwailo*," I retorted. He wasn't pleased I called him that.

He stood up. "Can I see the rest of your flat?"

I walked him through. He frowned a little at the sight of the cracked bathtub. "This *is* college life," I reminded. Regina's room we didn't stop at very long — it was in an even worst state than the living room. When I opened the door to my bedroom, he looked around approvingly.

I've always been something of an ascetic when it comes to interior decor. Back then, my room consisted of a mattress on the floor, a wooden table and chair which I used for a desk, my suitcase which I used as a dresser, and a clothes rack to hang clothes which I curtained off with a spotless, starched and ironed, white cloth. All my books were lined up on three shelves of bricks and unfinished pine boards. The only hangings on my wall were a poster of the unicorn trapped in the garden, a reproduction of the tapestry at the Cloisters in the Bronx, and a piece of blue, gold and brown batik which I had brought from home.

There was very little dust anywhere.

And then Paul put his arm around me and kissed my cheek. "I've missed you, Rose."

It was as strong a gesture of approval as he'd give. "I've missed you too."

Paul ran his fingers through my hair. He had always liked my soft, limp hair, and thought it looked good as short as it was. He kept one arm around me and lovingly fingered the bracelet, playing with the intricate lace work design over its clasp. Around the band were roses, etched in careful detail in the gold. It was certainly much nicer and more expensive than anything my parents could afford to give me.

The front door opened and Regina and David returned. Regina headed for her room and emerged with an overnight bag, declaring that they were taking off to New York for the weekend. I was at a loss for words, but Paul gave her a friendly enough smile, and as soon as they were gone, he looked at me and said, "I want you Rose" and all my trepidation, prior to his arrival, disappeared, and I leaned forward to kiss him and he took me in his arms, as if we'd never been apart.

That first time in Plattsburgh, Paul made love to me for hours on the mattress on my bedroom floor, and I comforted him in my arms afterwards while he cried over the death of his cousin Robert.

So, perhaps if Regina hadn't left us alone that weekend he wouldn't have dared make love to me, and I wouldn't have gotten pregnant and had to have the abortion. Paul offered to marry me right away once I told him, promising to tell his parents and telegram me with the date. I believed him, although in retrospect I can't imagine why. My rational side told me there was no way a marriage at this time could work, but, even so, I left the abortion almost too late. Regina urged me to do it at the last possible moment which was the same day the telegram arrived from Paul saying, "I'm sorry, I love you but I can't." We never told any of our parents.

In late spring, Paul's parents planned to go away most of the month of April and the early part of May.

I was at his family's for dinner and whispered to him in the hallway near his bedroom that maybe I could spend the night. He shushed me, horrified his mother would hear.

"What are you two lurking around here for?" Paul Sr.'s voice made us both jump.

"Nothing Dad. Just showing Rose the rhythm stomper." He hastily turned me in the direction of the thin wooden figurine of an African warrior. "See the flat base, Rose? And the skinny waist? People used to hold these statues by the waist and stomp them up and down to drumbeats. It's a kind of percussive musical instrument."

I pretended to be highly absorbed in everything he was saying, and suppressed my giggles.

Paul Sr. suddenly tickled me in the ribs, making me squirm. "Go on Rose, you don't have to pretend not to laugh."

"Paul." Marion's voice, icy cold, addressed her husband. "The coffee's ready."

We all sauntered into the living room.

"So, are you both looking forward to your visit back to South Africa?" I directed my question at Marion.

Paul Sr. responded. "Marion can't wait, can you dear? It'll be a nice change from Hong Kong. My brother will be there at the same time, you see."

"I wish I could go too. I'd like to see Uncle Alex again. Why isn't Aunt Fay going?" It was unusual for Paul to expose his feelings this way in conversation with his parents, but he idolized his uncle, Robert's father. I had seen photos of them together. Alex resembled Paul Sr., except that the former was much more dashing. Paul and Robert could have been brothers, although Robert was pure Chinese.

"Fay can't bear the memories of Robert." Marion remarked. "It's difficult for her."

"I daresay she can't." Paul Sr.'s tone was cutting. I wondered at it. The one photo I remembered of Fay — there were hardly any of her in the family albums — was of a thin, fragile Chinese woman, with a large hat to block out the sun. She was pretty but unsmiling. Paul and Robert were about seven, one on either side holding her hands.

"It's the weather," Marion said quickly. "Fay's always been sensitive to the heat. That's why she prefers Canada so much more. You'll meet both her and Uncle Alex, Rose. At your wedding."

I smiled happily. Among the Lies, I felt I belonged. I wished my mother could hear Mrs. Lie now, the way she accepted me as her future daughter-in-law. Paul and I weren't officially engaged yet, but as far as the Lies were concerned, it was all just a matter of time. Paul put his arm around me, and his mother gave him a bit of a look. But Paul Sr. smiled at us and I saw Marion's expression soften.

When I left that night, Paul Sr. followed us to the door. "Don't you two young people do anything I wouldn't do while we're away, right Paul?" But he winked at his son and laughed as he said this. It was rather ridiculous, especially coming from a judge, but a welcome antidote to what I'd come to expect from Paul.

"Your dad's wonderful," I said as soon as the door's closed. "He's so . . . understanding, and doesn't treat us like children. My mother couldn't imagine us having sex, and my father, well, you know how he is."

"Rose! Don't talk about your parents like that. Or mine."

"Oh Paul, don't be so prudish."

Despite his seriousness, I could tell his mind was on his parents being away and my whispered suggestion. That night, we went to the park where he was extremely passionate, until I felt that finally, we could recapture just a little of that first and only time in Plattsburgh.

Yet it took him a whole week to get up the courage to bring me home once his parents left, and the first time he worried that the maid would catch us, and we ended up not doing anything. The second time, we waited till her day out, but the phone rang just as he was about to enter me that night, and it wouldn't stop ringing until he gave in and answered. It was his mother, making sure he was all right; that dampened both our enthusiasm. By the third time, we finally managed a passable imitation of the act, but we stained the bed sheet and had to wash and dry it right away before the maid came back, terrified as he was of any tell tale signs of my presence. But Paul seemed so happy that he'd finally made love to me again that I couldn't deflate his joy by letting on that the whole thing had been a non-event as far as I was concerned.

By the time his parents came back, things were "dire," as Marion would say.

The Sunday they returned, Andrew Chiang was in Hong Kong and called to say hello. I made a date to meet him the very same evening, knowing Paul would be home with his parents.

We met at the Star Ferry pier on the island. He looked out of place somehow, standing there. Andrew and I had never been public with our affections, since we had kept our affair secret, and we didn't even shake hands by way of greeting.

"Funny to see each other here, isn't it?" He stood there awkwardly. "I feel like I'm meeting you to *pak tor.*"

"In that case, we should be holding hands and walking around on a Sunday afternoon with our cameras in Statue Square."

He laughed, and became just Andrew again, and I realized how much I'd missed his easy, undemanding companionship.

"So, want to go dancing?"

We headed for the disco at the Hilton. He took my hand and squeezed it, and I was surprised at how natural this felt, as if we were a long time couple. I wonder now that I wasn't more cautious, but that night we didn't run into anyone I knew. On the way, he caught me up with his life. Debbie and he had split after graduation, because she wanted to get married, which he readily agreed to, but when she wanted to meet his parents, he refused, and then she accused him of only wanting to marry her so that he could stay in the U.S., and he had replied, "something like that" in his typically laconic manner, and that had been a bit more than Debbie could take. Andrew being Andrew, he took off to Montreal and wound up with a professor of anthropology at McGill who liked the idea of marrying him to help him stay in Canada because it suited her liberal beliefs, although it probably had more to do with how much she liked his lovemaking. Now, his return to Hong Kong was precipitated by a fight with his "wife," because she'd caught him screwing one of her students, and had threatened to turn him into Canadian immigration for fraudulently establishing his residency.

He had told me the whole saga in his irrepressible manner, making me laugh, but I knew how desperately much Andrew wanted to remain in North America, how he dreaded the idea of living and working in Hong Kong. "What are you going to do?"

"Oh, she probably won't do anything. She is, unfortunately, rather fond of me, which is why she keeps delaying the final paperwork for citizenship with some trumped up excuse or other. Of course, she didn't expect me to actually take off for Hong Kong. Time I visited the folks anyway."

"Are they pleased to see you?"

"I guess."

I knew very little about his family, except that they were "very Chinese," and didn't understand why he wanted to go to America in the first place. He carried on as if his life was completely separate from theirs. In a way, I understood how he felt. As Westernized as my own parents were, they hadn't a clue about my life in the West.

"So is lover boy still in the picture?"

"Paul? We're going to get married, eventually."

He stopped short and let go of my hand. "You, married? Why?"

We were at the Hilton. I pushed open the glass door and led him into the lobby. "Why not? Don't look so shocked, Andrew. You make it sound like a terminal disease."

"It will be, for you." He suddenly put his arms around my waist from behind and gently bit my ear the way he used to in bed.

"You're not the marrying type," he said as he let me go.

I laughed and ran down the steps to the disco.

Dancing with Andrew was like a throwback to my teenage life, when parties and discos were The Thing To Do, when Regina and I used to laugh over guys. When he took me in his arms to slow dance, he pulled me close and whispered in my ear, "so are you getting enough?" I felt him press up against me and I went hot inside.

We ended up in another Kowloon Tong motel because that was the only place to go. We didn't emerge till just before dawn. I had to sneak back home as quietly as possible, because my parents thought I was out with a girlfriend. Andrew went back to Canada a couple of days later and I didn't see him again before he left.

But the point of all this is that I skipped my period in May after that incident. At first, I felt a tremendous joy at the thought that I was pregnant with Andrew's child. But the joy competed with panic. This time, there was no Regina to look after me, no one to rely on who would understand enough to simply take care of things. I didn't even dare go to a doctor since I couldn't deal with the raised eyebrows that would ensue once I said I wasn't married.

I waited, hoping that perhaps it was all a mistake, and that my period was delayed. When the end of June rolled round, and it didn't arrive again, I did the only thing I could — I told Paul I thought I was pregnant, but left out the part about Andrew. Paul never missed a beat. We announced to the family that we wanted to get married in August, although he didn't say anything to friends. He promised me over and over that this time he wouldn't let me down. "Our little secret," he called it. I had never known him to be so excited or happy about anything as the prospect then of being a father. And I believed that it never once occurred to him that I wasn't carrying his child.

But in late July I discovered I really wasn't pregnant after all.

Disappointment hovered around me for weeks afterwards like a slightly grey cloud, forever threatening to burst into a downpour, but never quite doing so. Paul said it was simply not meant to be, but that our marriage was. He was so patient, kind and understanding. Unconditional love has such irresistible appeal.

We were young. I was only twenty two. But I should have known better than to believe in such unconditional love. I should have.

The sun's almost all gone now. Night time in New York is soothing, more comforting than nights in Hong Kong.

"A bit rushed, isn't it?" Paul's father said to me. "After all, you're still very young. Is everything all right, dear?"

It was the second time he'd asked me in private since Paul and I announced our plans. By now, I already knew I wasn't pregnant, and it was hard pretending we really preferred a small and private wedding because we were impatient to get married. I didn't think we sounded very convincing.

"After all," he continued, "you're both adults. And it's not as if you have to wait for marriage, if you know what I mean."

We were sitting across from each other in the Lies' living room just before dinner. Paul was helping his mother get something out of their storage cupboard. Looking at my future father-in-law, trying not to meet his eyes, I wondered why, of all the parents, he was the only one who even raised the subject, and then, only with me and not Paul. After all, the possibility of pregnancy must have occurred to everyone.

He seemed concerned and kind, and I was tempted to blurt out the whole story, everything, but that would have been impossible. Instead, I nodded and smiled politely, and murmured something about how we were just impatient.

"Well it's all just a question of time before you do become my daughter-in-law. If it means anything, Rose, I already consider you part of our family. But I still think you need wait. One can, uh, take care of 'accidents' you know."

And then, I understood. He thought it was all my doing. He guessed I was pregnant, but probably thought it was deliberate to make Paul marry me quickly. A frustrated anger welled up inside. I wanted to say — your son should have had more courage the first time I really got pregnant — but of course I held my tongue. "Perhaps you're right," I replied, smiling as if I really meant it.

Paul and his mother returned to the living room, and my conversation with Paul Sr. ceased. All through dinner, I wondered why his mother seemed so pleased about the sudden marriage, because she, unlike her husband, talked incessantly about it and where Paul and I should live.

That night, when I got home, my mother was still up. I mumbled some response to her question about whether or not I'd had a nice evening and was heading to the bedroom when she startled me by saying, "You shouldn't be so jealous of your sister, you know."

"What do you mean?"

"You're in such a rush to get married, just to prove that you can do it faster than her. It's silly. You shouldn't have pushed Paul so hard. He's just too much of gentleman to say no."

She was irritating me, but I held my tongue.

"After all, he's from a much more sophisticated background than you. If you rush into this, you may be sorry later. I know you probably think you're being very clever, but don't be too clever for your own good, Rose."

In that instant, I decided to postpone the wedding. But all I said to my mother was, "Well, we'll see." I went to my room and closed the door.

When, I wondered, as I brushed my hair, would she ever understand?

Once, when Regina and I were nine, my father had given me a new dress for bringing home a great report card. Regina, who hadn't done badly either but not as well as me, got nothing. Mum was furious, and complained that Dad wasn't being fair. I cried when we were in bed that night and told Regina I wouldn't wear the stupid dress. She climbed into my bed, hugged me and said it didn't matter, it was just a dress, and that she knew I loved her which was all that mattered. But I had woken up in the middle of the night and seen her standing by the closet door looking at the dress, her fingers crushing the corner of the skirt. Her features were twisted, angry and horrible, and I was so frightened I hid under my covers. When I told her the next morning, she said I must have been dreaming and didn't seem to remember anything. But I checked the dress and saw the crumpled hem. I never told Mum.

Since the day I met Paul, I hadn't been jealous of Regina.

A week later, I told Paul I wanted to postpone the wedding at least a year, because I wasn't sure I was ready for marriage. He protested at first, but gave in easily, almost too easily. What he did say was that he admired me for my maturity, and realized that I was rather more serious than he'd thought. We announced this together to our parents, and I said it was my choice. My mother started to say she didn't believe me, but Dad defended my decision, drowning out comment from Mum. Marion was sad but accepting, and Paul Sr. seemed, strangely enough, almost relieved. The summer of '75 was a turbulent one.

4

Daylight fades out and a red sky caresses.

I am in debt to too many credit cards, not to mention the mortgage on my Brooklyn Heights co-op. I haven't saved much money; despite my large salary and generous expense account, I spent what I earned as quickly as I earned it on expensive vacations, dinners at restaurants almost every night, and clothes. Life around Gordie has been like that, and, truthfully, I liked the abandonment of responsibilities. It was better than sex. I've simply done what my father did, gambling on the present outlasting the future. But Dad had Mum to shelter him against his gambling debts. I don't really even have Paul any longer.

I held my head up like Lady Liberty out there with her goddamned eternal light. Stiff and unyielding, foolishly proud. At thirty, as Confucius taught, I took my stand.

Red skies at night.

October arrived.

It had been an air conditioned summer. All through the hottest months of the year, I had hardly noticed the heat and humidity. Most of my days were spent in the indoor air at the agency, or at our various clients' offices. Evenings at work-related functions also took place indoors, as did social functions Paul and I went to. And dinners at my future in-laws had become more frequent, sometimes as often as twice a week. The Lies invariably had their air conditioner on, as they found the heat unbearable.

About the only relief I had from all this indoor air was at home, because Dad hated air conditioning and wouldn't install it in our living cum dining room, although he gave in to Mum who insisted on having it in the bedrooms. I hardly turned mine on at all now that Regina wasn't around.

October and cooler weather brought a welcome change as the indoor and outdoor climate finally converged again.

"Can you go on a boat?" My boss, the Australian who ran the

agency, stuck his head into my cubicle late one Thursday afternoon.

By now, I was used to his elliptical style. "As in ferry?"

"No, boat. You know, out."

"As in row?"

"Only if you want. When they anchor."

I still had no idea what he was talking about, and smiled patiently.

"Sunday," he continued. "No, wait I think he said Saturday. Queen's Pier. Your Dutchman will be there."

"Flying or pouring?" I worked on both KLM and Dutch Lady condensed milk.

"Oh, flying of course. Regional media. Not for the pouring. Ask Sally," he meant his secretary. With that he disappeared.

As I dutifully headed over to Sally's desk, I imagined trying to describe that exchange to Paul. It would have been hopeless.

What transpired was that we had gotten an invitation from *AsiaMonth* magazine to a launch party Saturday, but my boss and his wife couldn't go. Our client, however, was going, so someone from the agency had to be there. Apparently, all the other Western staff were busy, and, naturally, none of the Chinese staff would go since they saw the event as a *gwailo* affair. Which left me. I was used to my role as intermediary between foreign and local employees. Speaking good English as well as Chinese and having a Eurasian boyfriend had something to do with it. But I didn't like being so acutely aware of the racial division.

Still, it sounded like fun, because Sally said they were planning to stop and swim as well, so I agreed.

I called Paul right away, because my boss said I could bring him if I wanted. "Why would you want to work on a Saturday?" he asked.

"It's not exactly work," I replied, feeling a little put off. I thought he would have appreciated this invitation, since it wasn't as if he got to go out on launch parties either.

"What time again?"

I told him for the third time.

"The Law Society's annual cocktail and dinner is that evening. We're going to that. I don't want to be stuck on a boat all day."

"But I told my boss I'd go!" I hadn't meant to sound quite so querulous but Paul, typically, hadn't told me about this other event. Besides, I'd been to more than my share of Law Society functions, all of which were deadly dull.

"Well, you shouldn't have without checking with me." There was a finality in his tone that brooked no argument.

Any other time, I would have reasoned with him, pointing out that we would still have plenty time to make the dinner, since the boat was scheduled to be back no later than five. It was just that Paul avoided accompanying me to anything that had to do with my job — neither the dinners and *mahjeuk* cum card parties with my Chinese colleagues, nor the drinks parties among the Westerners. It wasn't even that I minded going alone, but what irked me was that Paul didn't want to be a part of my life.

I knew all his arguments. Law was a serious career, advertising was not. It wouldn't do for him to be at parties where such a lot of drinking and gambling occurred. Life was too short to waste on unimportant social obligations. One had to remain focused to get ahead. It was irksomely familiar.

He had just begun to launch into his arguments when I interrupted him. "Forget it. If you don't want to go, I'll go alone. And I'll give the Law Society thing a miss this time." I surprised myself by the finality of my tone.

Paul went deathly quiet on the other end of the line. "Very well, suit yourself," he said as he hung up.

For a moment, I wanted to ring back and say it was all a mistake, that of course I'd accompany him to the Law Society thing and tell my boss I couldn't go on the boat. My boss wouldn't care particularly; it was relaxed that way at the agency, which made working there easy. But Paul just seemed unreasonable. I knew he was furious at me.

Then I heard Sally calling across the office, asking if my boyfriend was going since she was on the phone with *AsiaMonth,* and I said, no, just me and she said okay and that was that.

Saturday came, and Paul hadn't spoken to me at all. I should have been worried, but an irreverent unconcern prevailed.

The weather cooperated for a boat outing. I was excited. The only time I had ever been on a launch was in school, when a classmate had invited Regina and me along with her family. Her father worked for a bank, and the local managers were allowed to draw lots for the boat when the expatriates didn't want to use it. It had been the end of October, but a glorious day, warm enough to swim. We had gone far out to a bay off one of the outlying islands, Lantau I think. Hardly anyone else was around. Regina dove off the side of the boat, a graceful swallow, her long hair flying behind her in a ponytail. Our friend's father snapped a photo just at that moment. It was one of the few photographs I kept of my sister.

So I buried Paul in my conscience, promising myself I'd ring him and apologize on Sunday.

At the pier, I greeted my client and his wife. The rest of the party of a dozen or so was an assortment of agency people and client types, some of whom I knew or at least recognized. Just as I realized I was the only Chinese in the group, I felt a hand on my shoulder.

"Hi, glad you could make it." It was Elliot Cohen.

Of course I knew he was *AsiaMonth* but, for some reason hadn't fully registered that fact when the invite came up at the office. I stared at him stupidly for a second before finding my manners. "Oh hi. Nice to see you again."

We started out at ten thirty. I made a concerted effort to chat with my client William about business just long enough so that I'd have something to say to my boss on Monday. By noon, the sun's bristling warmth made my skin tingle pleasantly. We dropped anchor in an isolated bay somewhere out near Sai Kung, where clean, crystal blue water surrounded us. I overheard someone remark what a shame it was the beaches were getting so crowded and dirty, but that at least most of the water around Hong Kong was still clean. I leaned against the railing and luxuriated in the peaceful scenery.

"Not like riding the bus every day, is it?" Elliot had sidled up next to me.

His evenly tanned complexion made him look slightly Mediterranean. "How come I haven't run into you again?" I asked.

"Probably because I don't live in Kowloon anymore."

There was a loud splash. My client's wife Moira was in the water. "It's lovely," she called back to us. I admired her unconcern, her willingness to plunge in first, before any of the others had even

71

changed. I had to go in as well. Soon, we all did.

Around one thirty, Elliot offered us waterskiing. Again, Moira was the first to do so. I watched her ski a loop out on the open seas, her crimson swimsuit and blond hair a bright blur against the horizon, swerving gracefully behind the speedboat's wake. Where had she learned to waterski like that, I wondered. Surely not in Holland. There was something surreal about this alien world of foreigners, far apart from the core of my city which could be so hellishly crowded, so unpleasantly claustrophobic. Was I privileged or damned to witness this occidental paradise?

My musings were interrupted by both William and Elliot exhorting me to try my turn. "But I've never been on waterskis in my life," I protested.

"It's easy," Moira said, as she unstrapped the skis. "Lean forward and hang on. You're small. You'll pop right up."

I continued to protest, my Hong Kong reserve getting the better of me.

"What are you afraid of?" William asked, smiling. "If you fall in, all you have to do is hang onto the skis and swim back to the boat."

Elliot looked slyly at me. *"Mm gou dahm,"* he said quickly, almost under his breath, but loud enough for me to hear. Then, in his normal voice he said in English, "She's just shy."

That did it. I wasn't going to let Elliot call me a chicken, even if no one else understood what he'd said. "I'll have a go."

And I did, with no trouble at all. It was as Moira predicted: I popped right up the first time I tried. What I hadn't expected was the wild sense of freedom all that speed brought. It was magically powerful. When I returned to the main boat, because it was time to head back, I had turned several shades darker. My mother would criticize my complexion for sure, repeating that only fair skin was beautiful on Chinese, forgetting the Indonesian blood mixed in there. But I didn't care, because nothing mattered when I flew over the water's surface, gliding with an ease I'd never known before.

Back at the pier, I was the last to disembark. The party scattered. William and Moira waved, and Elliot promised another boat party soon before it got too cold. I was about to thank him and head for the Star Ferry, but before I could do so he said, "Can I offer you a lift home?"

"I thought you didn't live in Kowloon anymore."

He was facing west. Squinting, he shielded his eyes with his hands. "You look good dark. Brings out the Indonesian in you. It's quite sexy."

He said it in the same low tone he'd used earlier, when he made that crack in Cantonese. I recalled a passing comment I'd once overheard my boss make about "that Cohen character, he's a *hahm sap lo*," meaning a sex maniac. I felt myself blushing but knew it probably wouldn't show and didn't respond.

My silence didn't faze him. "I have my friend's car. He's out of town. Be happy to run you back."

I could feel him daring me again. "Thanks. But you're being too nice to Helen's niece." He would, I was sure, understand my Cantonese meaning, placing him at the same level as my aunt.

"That way," he pointed in the direction of the car park opposite the taxi stand.

Riding with Elliot was a little like waterskiing. He drove smoothly, but fast. Elliot liked to drive. His whole attention was given over to the road, and he didn't speak the entire time. The way he manipulated the stick shift, confidently and in full control, reminded me of Andrew, who used to drive us when we wanted to sneak off together. The traffic in the cross harbor tunnel was light, and we were back in Kowloon Tong in less than fifteen minutes.

"Here you go, Cinderella," he said when we arrived. "Don't keep Prince Charming waiting." He kissed my cheek as he leaned over to open the door. The hairs on his arm brushed my arm in the process, and I felt goose bumps. "See you soon, okay?"

I slid out. "Okay." As he drove off, I suddenly felt very happy, and realized with a start that I hadn't given Paul a thought all afternoon.

Early winter brought the onset of the social season.

"Quality. Look for quality. Even if all you own are two skirts and three blouses, they should each be chosen to outlast fashion trends."

Shopping with Marion was distinctly different from shopping experiences with Mum. We were in Lane Crawford's on Nathan Road in Tsimshatsui, one of the few department stores she would deign to enter. Half an hour of browsing through evening dresses hadn't yielded much.

"Perhaps I should make something," I ventured, thinking I could sew something simple and elegant easily enough for much less money.

"It won't be worth it. There isn't a single tailor in Hong Kong who knows how to turn out anything but the most conservative dresses."

I glanced at her own conservative dark grey suit. Just like something the queen would wear. All she lacked was a hat.

"Wait, I think I see . . ." she motioned me towards a rack, and held up a deep crimson cocktail dress. It was gathered up on one side by a rose of the same fabric. I stared at it doubtfully. It was revealing.

"Try it on. Go on."

Inside the fitting room, I wondered at her insistence. It was an expensive sheath of a dress, and looked it, but revealed what even I thought was more than I dared of back and leg. I imagined she might not approve once she saw it on me. I slipped it on in the changing room. It felt like I was wearing nothing at all.

"Perfect," she said, as I slid gingerly out. "Here, put these shoes on with it."

I slid on the pair of very high heeled, delicate evening shoes. Marion sighed audibly, exclaiming "If only I were still your age!" And then she added, almost under her breath, "they'll adore you now."

She paid for the dress, which was outrageously priced, despite my protests. Secretly, I was relieved not to have to pay for it, although I was embarrassed by her generosity. I pictured Mum's eyes popping out of her head. Mum and I only shopped at sales. Yet here was Marion, right before Christmas, buying a current season's dress at full price in the most expensive department store in town.

This was only the second or third time I'd ever been shopping with my future mother-in-law. I had been surprised when she offered, no insisted, that we do this for the upcoming charity ball at which Paul Sr. was hosting a table. Paul had been encouraging, assuring me that if his mother chose the dress, it would be perfect. Knowing how puritanical he could be about my clothes, I wondered at her choice.

"It would have been perfect for Johannesburg," was the last thing she said when she dropped me off at home.

The evening of the ball, I waited nervously at home for Paul to pick me up. Dad had glanced at my outfit, nodded a vague approval, and buried himself in his newspaper.

Mum hadn't gotten over the price of the dress. "It's a little bit short, isn't it Rose? You didn't shorten it did you?"

"No." I tugged at the skirt, feeling undressed, wishing Paul would hurry up.

"So Mr. Lie is inviting . . . how many people did you say would be at his table?"

It was at least the tenth time that week she had asked me the same thing, and I had to restrain myself from a curt reply. "Ten, plus himself and Marion. You know, the standard twelve-person setting?"

"Now, you're sure the Lies really want you to go? By the way Rose, you shouldn't really call Mrs. Lie Marion. It isn't nice. They weren't just being polite, were they? After all, Paul's father is quite an important man, and . . ."

My father interrupted her. "For goodness sake, why shouldn't they invite Rose? She is Paul's fiancée."

"Yes but I just hope it wasn't because Rose suggested it. You didn't do that, did you?"

Mum was just being Mum, but something inside me snapped. "Why do you always talk as if I were stupid? I know better than that. Besides, Marion . . . Mrs Lie, told me how glad they were that Paul and I would join them, because she knew young people didn't always like to be stuck with their parents. I mean, she even bought me this dress." I wanted to say that Marion had written to me all through college, and that now, she was preparing me for a life in their family as Paul's wife, which was why we had this familiarity. But such a notion would have shocked Mum, who would have denied it, who wouldn't have understood why people who didn't have to should concern themselves with me. She'd been that way all through school about the teachers who tried to tell her I was a good student. I wasn't Regina, and as far as she was concerned, only

Regina could shine.

"Now calm down Rose. You just don't understand Hong Kong society. People don't always say what they mean — you know, *hak hai*, "manners for guests" — so you have to learn to understand their real intention. It is a little strange that she'd buy you such an expensive dress when you're only a friend of Paul's . . ."

"He's going to marry me!" I couldn't refrain from shouting. "What is it going to take before you'll believe he loves me?"

The doorbell rang. I rushed back to my room, afraid of the tears that had begun to well up. I got my evening bag and dabbed a tissue to my eyes, careful not to smear my mascara. Paul was talking to my mother in the living room. I stepped out to meet him. As soon as he saw me, I could tell that he knew something was wrong.

"You look wonderful, Rose. My mother always has such good taste." He pinned a corsage of white orchids with a single red rose to my dress. And then he led me out of my home.

In the lift, he put his arm around me. "She's been at you again, hasn't she?"

I leaned close to him and nodded.

He held me more firmly and stroked my cheek with his finger. "It's okay, Rose. You're with me now. And you are beautiful tonight, just like you always are."

That night Paul pulled me aside after dinner and gave me an engagement ring. The size of the diamond made my mother's eyes bulge when she saw it later. That night, I knew with absolute certainty that the Lies finally approved and that Paul now had their blessing to marry me at the proper time. I believed Paul when he reaffirmed his love for me, and all the uncertainties I felt about the strange way he behaved at times dissolved into a sea of forgetfulness.

Perhaps it was the social season, but life with Paul rolled smoothly on. He was at his best in this milieu. I was privileged to accompany him and was myself becoming increasingly comfortable there. Although I revelled in this public spotlight, in private moments, the ring felt weighty on my finger and I wondered if, in fact, it really belonged there.

Early the next year, just before Chinese New Year, Paul asked when we should schedule the wedding. It was shortly after Regina had finally graduated from Plattsburgh State and enrolled in a masters program at the University of Iowa. I didn't understand how she could stand going to school forever instead of pursuing a real career and marriage.

When we had gotten engaged, I had wanted to be married quickly. Now, just a few months later, I wasn't as sure. "What about summer next year?"

"A whole year? Why Rose? Mother's getting quite anxious."

It wasn't as if he'd been eagerly or even regularly discussing marriage. In fact, this was maybe only the second or third time he'd mentioned it since we'd gotten engaged. Pointing this out wouldn't have been any use though. He would have looked askance at me and said something like, "but Rose, what on earth do you mean? You know it's always uppermost in my mind." Paul and I simply didn't talk. Things were supposed to be understood between us, at least, that's how he liked it to be.

"Besides, you'll be getting too old," he continued. "You're going to be twenty three in April. Isn't that a perfect age to get married?"

I shrugged and continued to flip through the magazine I was reading. It was after dinner at his home. His parents were out and the servants had all retired to their quarters. He leaned across the sofa and put his hand across my page.

"Come here, Rose." He pulled me towards him and started to kiss me. Sliding his arm under my knees, he lifted my legs onto the sofa until I lay under him.

"Paul, please. Not here."

"They won't be back for ages."

He continued to kiss me and hold onto me tightly, one arm around my waist, the other braced across my shoulder. I felt engulfed by him. I wanted to escape, yet knew my own growing desire. There was a feverishness about Paul that he hadn't displayed in months. All through dinner he had talked about work. The politics among the partners. His problem case. The new clerk who kept coming to him with too many questions. He said he found him distracting. And, now, this unexpected passion.

Suddenly, he undid my skirt and pulled at my panties. I pushed his hand roughly away. "Paul, stop it. What if they come back early?"

He began to unbutton my blouse. "I don't care. I want them to see us like this."

With great effort I pushed him off me. He stood up, unzipped his pants, and thrust his penis towards my face. "Please Rose, take care of me."

I rearranged my clothes hurriedly. "Paul, I'm going home."

He hardly heard me. As he began to take care of himself, there in the middle of his living room, I ran out the door.

All the way home in the taxi my body wouldn't stop trembling. My desire was knotted in my stomach. Could this really be the man I was going to marry? I didn't understand him at all. Something separated us, something I couldn't articulate. I wanted him, felt passion for him, passion that I usually had to keep buried. These frenzied outbursts of his seemed to come from nowhere, and caught me unawares each time. They were few and far between, but, with each incident, I had to acknowledge this gulf between us. It was like his anger, rapid and irrational, ignored completely afterwards, as if it had never happened.

Fortunately, my parents were out when I got back.

The phone rang. I let it ring six times, afraid it was Paul. But he never called immediately after these incidents, preferring an unrestrained silence instead. On the eighth ring, I finally answered.

"Rose! I'm so glad someone's home. Listen, Regina's going to stage her first art exhibit at Easter. Isn't that wonderful?!" Aunt Helen shouted when she was excited. "Chong and I are supposed to go to the Caribbean then, but maybe we can squeeze in one day to stop in Iowa. Why your sister had to plant herself in the middle of nowhere is beyond me! There isn't even a direct flight there."

Regina sometimes called my aunt collect with her latest news, which Helen would then try to convey through me, so as not to hurt my mother's feelings. It could get complicated, but things always did with my sister. Helen didn't stop until she elicited my promise that I would try to go even if my parents wouldn't.

Lying in bed later I began crying silently, uncontrollably. I willed myself to stop, feeling childish and somewhat selfish. It seemed to me that Regina's whole life was opening up in front of her, while I was at the mouth of a gaping abyss into which I couldn't stop from plunging. Did I love Paul? Of course I did, with a fierce clinging desire that I wasn't permitted to exhibit. I never said such things, not to friends or family or even Regina, whom I loved despite everything about her. The trouble was, both Paul and Regina commanded all the space around me. Now that I was no longer Regina's slave, I was freed to be entirely enslaved to Paul.

Back in college when I was living with Regina, I once woke from a dream in the middle of the night. It was a kind of dream-memory about the time a torrential typhoon rain soaked us at camp on Fei Ngo Shan — Flying Goose Hill — when we were fourteen.

I got up to get a glass of water. As I passed Regina's room on the way to the kitchen, I heard her moaning loudly. Regina was a noisy sleeper. Even when we were children, she used to toss around, making low, groaning sounds. Sometimes, she seemed to be carrying on a conversation, but I seldom could make out what she was saying.

I stood in the kitchen, sipping my water. At that camp, Regina and I had sat up all the first night and whispered to each other about boys. She had her eye on someone in tent number three, while I was still in too much ecstasy over being allowed to go to a co-ed camp to really focus on anyone in particular. The second night, when the typhoon hit, we were both drenched completely, and the rest of the week of camp was cancelled. Regina cried all the way home because, she said, she was in love and would never see him again.

A loud crash emitted from Regina's room.

My sister was banging one arm wildly against the wall when I entered. She was asleep. In this turmoil, she had knocked over a ceramic pot next to her bed which had smashed into pieces.

"Enough, Miguel," I heard her moaning. "Please Miguel. Please Miguel." She kept repeating this. I tried to wake her. Then, her eyelids fluttered, she sat up and surveyed the mess.

"What happened?"

I tried to explain.

She rubbed her nose. "Oh well," was all she said, and then, she lay down and prepared to go back to sleep.

"Regina, who's Miguel?"

Her eyes were closing as she mumbled, "Don't have any idea

what you're talking about," and in a few minutes she was sound asleep again.

I dismissed the incident as another typically incomprehensible Regina thing. But a couple of weeks later, just before she was to leave for New York, she announced, "a friend of mine needs to crash for a night."

I had washed my hair and was bent over in a chair towelling it dry. Her tone of voice made me look up.

"He really wants to meet you."

"Why?" I had little patience for most of Regina's friends. None of them ever looked like they washed, and all they talked about were Big Ideas, having little interest in ordinary, everyday human existence. The current lot of friends were all existentialists who spoke endlessly about absurd drama. It struck me that life was sufficiently absurd without having to watch the same thing on stage.

"He thinks you're interesting."

"Have I met him?"

"No, never. He's from New York."

"Then how does he know I'm interesting?"

"By what I've told him."

I didn't think much of it until he showed up an hour later. He was a painter from Bolivia who had dark skin, longish brown-black hair covering his neck, and the most wickedly sensual eyes.

Regina seemed happy to see him. She flung her arms around his neck and kissed him on the mouth. Clutching his arm, her head leaning on his shoulder, she steered him towards me in our living room. "This is Miguel. Miguel, my twin sister Rose."

He took my hand and kissed my wrist. The sensation was peculiarly pleasurable. "How charmingly different you are." His voice was rich and soothing, like Chinese peanut soup that warmed your tongue before sliding down your throat. "Why won't you come to New York with your sister?"

The question took me aback. I wondered what Regina had said about me. "I'm in summer school."

"Ahh too bad," he murmured, letting go my hand. "Such smooth skin."

I was both repelled and fascinated by him.

The moment I could pull Regina aside, I demanded, "Why on earth did you deny knowing a Miguel that night?"

She was distracted and made me repeat the question, which I did. Miguel was outside on the porch smoking a cigarette. She kept glancing down at him from the window. "What night?"

"You know perfectly well which night, when you broke the pot."

At that point, Regina looked me square in the face with vacant, unblinking eyes. "Rose, I don't have any idea what you mean." And with that she went downstairs and out to join Miguel.

I was at a complete loss. Although by now I had come to accept that there would always be something a bit strange about Regina — most of which I put down to artistic temperament — this seemingly wilful amnesia was new. I could understand her not remembering some of the things she said or did in the middle of the night, but the broken pot was right there the next day, and we even had had a conversation about it. She had laughed and said she was probably trying to crack someone's skull.

From below, their voices drifted up to me. It sounded like an argument. Miguel appeared to be trying to persuade Regina of something, and she was adamantly refusing. I moved away from the window, not wanting to pry. After a few minutes, I heard the sound of his car driving away, and when I looked, I saw Regina sitting next to him, her face buried against his shoulder. I couldn't be sure, but it looked like she was crying.

That evening, Regina cooked a wonderful meal for all three of us. Miguel provided a bottle of expensive wine. Any trace of an earlier argument was gone.

Over dinner, Miguel spoke about his life in Bolivia, about the palatial home his family had, about sipping drinks on the veranda while watching magnificent sunsets. His voice embraced beauty, and his face seemed pained by the memory. I was wary of him but he struck me as very sophisticated, full of savoir-faire as he told me about the club he owned in New York where Regina worked the previous summer.

"I thought you were a painter," I said.

"That too. But I must make a living. Won't you come work for me in the city?"

He smiled at me, and I was aware of the sensation of being made love to. I blushed uncontrollably. It was as if a firecracker had gone off inside.

Regina said, "Miguel's driving me to New York. Why not at least come along for a few days before school starts?"

"I would be delighted to have you along."

Something in the way he said that put me on my guard. "Why?" I demanded.

"Why, for the pleasure of your company." He rolled the word "pleasure" around his tongue, thrusting it out as he spoke. "You will have a marvellous time with me, I assure you. I promise to look after you while your sister is at work. Do you like beautiful things?" His eyes bored into me as he spoke. "I will give you many many beautiful things for your company."

Regina whispered softly, "What price a pound of flesh?"

Their combined voices were simultaneously seductive and frightening. I felt as if I was being hypnotized. Miguel leaned over and brushed a hair out of my eyes, and held my cheek against his palm. "You could make lots of money at my club. My clientele like Oriental girls. They all adore Regina." The touch of his fingers on my face gave me goose bumps.

The harsh note in Regina's voice cut through the air. "She won't come. She wants to hurry up, graduate and go home to work and marry her sweetheart Paul. Besides, Daddy takes care of her."

"Regina, . . ."

"Oh shut up, Rose. It's no secret Dad likes you better. Why pretend it's not the case? I don't care. I can earn my own way."

"Ah, sibling rivalry." Miguel's voice, soothing, liquid, nullified my will to reply. He ran his hand down Regina's back and kissed the air towards her.

Regina calmed down and the rest of the dinner went smoothly enough.

"Early night," Regina declared shortly after dinner. "We're leaving first thing in the morning."

Miguel followed Regina to her room. I dismissed my unease at the evening's events and went to my room.

I had been reading for over two hours when someone knocked at my door. Thinking that Regina had perhaps been unable to sleep, and now wanted to natter a bit — she usually liked to the night before she went away anywhere — I opened the door. Miguel stood there, leaning against the door frame.

"I'm sorry to disturb you. Do you have a match?"

He had on slacks and no shirt and held an unlit cigarette in one hand. His chest was lean and muscular, as evenly brown as his face. That sensation of being made love to overcame me again.

"Sure." I moved forward towards the kitchen. He placed one hand on the small of my back as I passed him, and I felt his palm slide rapidly down. I walked away hurriedly, pretending not to notice.

"There's no fire," he said, lightly touching my elbow. "Come here."

And before I knew it, I was caught in an embrace, and his lips glided over my neck and breasts as he opened my robe. One half of my brain told me — this is rape. The other half wanted to give in to him. He whispered, don't be afraid, I wouldn't do anything you wouldn't want me to. But I felt him hard against me as he edged me backwards into my room towards my mattress. A powerful desire raged through me. By the time he entered me, I wanted him dreadfully, with complete unconcern. The warning signal flickered and died in my brain.

As my climax subsided, I felt a hand on my buttocks. I opened my eyes and saw Regina. She was naked and smiling, deliriously happy. I saw Miguel's hands on her breasts. She slid her other hand between my legs, with Miguel still in me. I was too confused, too surprised to say anything, and I heard Regina say, "it's okay Rose, he's had a vasectomy."

And, then, the warning signal erupted into a screaming siren, and I pushed both of them off me. I wanted to shout: I trusted you, Regina, how could you do this to me? Miguel left the room, and there was only Regina holding me, comforting me, while I shook, trembling with a fear I didn't understand. "Who is he?" I demanded, wanting to know. All she would say was "Shh, quiet now. It was nothing. It's over." I eventually calmed down and drifted to sleep.

The next morning, I awoke as if from a nightmare, and then, I remembered and began to cry. I showered for a long time until there was no hot water left. And then, I got dressed and went to find my sister.

Regina behaved as if nothing had happened. She had packed her things for summer and was getting ready to leave. Miguel lounged around outside by his car. He hardly said two words to me.

"What's going on? Who is he?"

"Oh Rose, leave me alone. I'm trying to get ready."

"But Regina, last night . . ."

"Don't be a baby, Rose?"

"But what do you mean?"

"Oh Rose, for heaven's sake. Don't you see? He's my pimp."

My face must have frozen. I couldn't say a word. Regina looked at me and then began to laugh. The more she laughed, the more frightened I became. Some strange, crazy thing was happening between my sister and me, something I couldn't fathom, couldn't make any sense of then or for a long time after that.

"Rose, Rose. You're so gullible. Will you always believe everything I say?" With that, she kissed me and left for New York.

That was all so long ago. I buried it and refused to confront it, because, well, what good would confrontation have done? I had life to get on with. But Regina hovered, even after Paul failed to disturb, like an Indonesian mosquito disrupting my Chinese sleep, encircling my dream-memories of our mother's ancestry, hinting at the threat of malaria to throw me into a delirium. Like Paul's malaria, a mild version he contracted as a child in South Africa, into which he occasionally relapsed. Yet whenever he awoke from his feverish sleep, everything was normal again, as if the illness had never overtaken him.

One evening last year over scotch I told Gordie about Miguel. I talk to Gordie a lot over scotch. I'd never told anyone until then. He was quiet, one of the rare times he didn't make a wise-ass comeback remark. Finally, he took me in his arms and held me for a long time. "You were right to bury it," he told me. "There wasn't anything else to do." When he said that, I was finally freed of Regina's strange hold over me, and I could continue to love her because she was my sister, despite her cruelty. I cried for a long time in Gordie's arms, and he let me cry, never saying a word. Gordie has a kindness that doesn't require gratitude or acknowledgement. He never brought it up again. He is a truly generous spirit.

The beginning of night. I still don't always like the dark, even now. Dad told me once when I was a girl that real fighter pilots don't mind the dark, because it's easier to navigate when the sun's not in your eyes. I tried to believe him, because I wanted to be a fighter pilot too, wanted to be brave the way I imagined he had been.

But in the darkness now the world's a blur. I'm losing sight of Lady Liberty.

A week after his feverish outburst Paul announced we were getting married that summer. The occasion he chose was a dinner with his family when several of his father's most socially important friends were present. He named the date in July and the church, Saint Teresa's, which was my mother's church, adding that my mother was already planning the ceremony with the priest. And he said that the wedding banquet would be at the Jockey Club, where his father was a member, and that the menu was selected. His mother looked like she was ready to cry, that's how happy she was. Paul Sr. came over and kissed my cheek, saying what a sly dog his son was. Everybody congratulated us.

I only wished Paul had told me first. I froze a polite smile on my face and accepted all the good wishes.

As soon as we were alone, he talked non-stop about the wedding arrangements, silencing me with a kiss or embrace whenever I tried to interrupt. When we reached my home, he apologized for his behavior the previous week, which he said was far less circumspect than I deserved. Then he kissed me, lovingly, fondly, for a long while, displaying a tenderness that reminded me of that most gentle manner with which he treated me when we first met. Then he left, abruptly. I never managed to object.

Dad was up when I got in. He was standing on the veranda, watching the last plane taking off. It was close to midnight.

"One day," he declared as I headed towards him, "there'll be too many flights to keep up this night time curfew. War brought changes, you know, but peace created a whole new world. It used to be easy to fly, when all you did was rely on instinct. Nowadays, control towers are noisy babblers. We all speak English, but there are too many accents."

I liked listening to my father talk about flying, and would

encourage him to say more on the rare occasions he chose to talk. He had flown for awhile under Chennault, and I loved the stories about those days, stories he told only me, never Regina. But tonight, he could tell from my manner something was wrong because he cut short his reflections as soon as he saw my face. "Was dinner okay?"

"I found out I'm getting married." It slipped out before I could stop myself. I leaned against the veranda railings and didn't look him in the face.

My father looked curiously at me. "Didn't you know?"

I knew he thought I was joking. "No. Paul announced it tonight. Everything's arranged, everything. You know Paul. It'll be perfect. His parents were delighted." I began to cry silently. "Mum knew," I finally managed to add.

We faced the night sky together. In the distance, the lights of the runway flickered into blackness. My father handed me his handkerchief. I wiped my tears away. We stood in silence for half an hour. Finally, I handed him back his handkerchief.

"You don't have to cry, Rose. And you don't have to marry Paul unless you want to, do you understand?" There was a cold anger in his voice that I'd never heard before.

I nodded. In my heart, I knew he was right. "Paul overwhelms me, just like his whole family does. But I love him. I can't help it."

My father looked at me with such sad eyes that I wanted to exclaim, Dad, please don't, because for a moment, I thought he would cry. Instead, he remained silent, and I knew that what he wanted to say, but wouldn't, was that he didn't want me to marry Paul.

I finally broke the silence. "Mum wouldn't be happy if I . . ." My words trailed off, unfinished.

"She should have talked to you first." His tone was angry, abrupt.

"But she didn't. You know she wouldn't. This is exactly the way she'll accept it, if she's in control and I'm not. You know that. If I say anything to her, she'll gloat over my admission that I didn't even know!" I could feel the turmoil rising.

"Calm down, Rose."

"And you know if I try to cancel, she'll say it was Paul who called it off. She'll tell everyone. She'll make me look like a fool."

He hesitated before saying, "Be reasonable, Rose. You know we love you."

I looked him squarely in the face. I wasn't upset anymore. "I've always been reasonable. You know that."

He looked away, knowing I was right.

What more could I have asked of him? My father loved me and always had, but it precluded crossing my mother, except on rare occasions. It also precluded any discussion of life over the edge that both Regina and my mother could venture with impunity, at least within our family's walls. But did my mother really love me? My unasked question hung in the air, silently suspended between us.

Finally, his face averted, my father said, "It'll all be clearer in the morning."

And our conversation, I knew, was over.

I slept very little that night. Around five, it began to rain lightly. An unseasonal rain. It had rained like this one winter day when I was around nine or ten. Regina had been grumpy all morning because she couldn't go out to play.

We used to live in an old, two-storey, pre-war house on Somerset Road. My parents rented the furnished downstairs flat which opened out to an untamed garden lined with jasmine bushes. A bamboo grove graced the back garden, where I'd sometimes catch sight of a snake or two slithering. We'd find the occasional snake skin at the edge of the grove; Regina and I would bring these indoors, frightening Mum out of her wits. Mum hated the house because the pipes were old, the electrical wiring primitive and the fixtures old fashioned. She detested the landlord who lived upstairs. He was a Chinese painter friend of Helen's who, Mum claimed, "spied" on her. Most of all, my mother hated renting, because it meant people knew we couldn't afford our own modern flat and furniture.

Regina called our home the ancient dungeon. I loved that old place with its creaky doors, drafty rooms and old Chinese wooden beds, and was sorry when we moved to Beacon Hill Road.

Anyway, that day, a Saturday, Regina was running around the house, something my parents prohibited, but they were both out. Her incessant pounding on the wood floors made the two-tiered metal trolley rattle. Mum kept glasses and a thermos of water on it, because she believed in drinking only warm water. Two of the glasses toppled off the trolley and shattered on the floor.

"Look what you've done, Regina. Mum will be mad." I surveyed the mess.

"Clean it up," she said.

"You clean it up."

"I'm the princess and you're my servant, so you have to do it."

The sun had come out and the rain slowed to a drizzle. Regina grabbed her skateboard and raced out of the house. I knew she wouldn't be back for hours.

I began to clean up the broken glass. There was never any arguing back with my sister. Just as I'd finished sweeping up the last few shards, I heard my mother's raised voice behind me, "how could you be so clumsy?"

Startled, I dropped the dustpan, scattering the glass pieces.

"Now see what you've done!" My mother looked very angry. It was so unlike her to get this upset over a couple of broken glasses that I was stunned into silence.

"You must have been running around the house to knock those glasses over. Were you? What have I always said about doing that?"

"It wasn't me," I managed to squeak out.

"What was that?"

"Regina broke the glasses."

Without warning, she began slapping my face. "Stop lying Rose. Don't blame your sister. You're such a little liar! How could I raise such a liar!"

I backed away, terrified. "I'm not lying, Mum, I wouldn't do that."

She continued to hit me until I began to cry. My father walked in and called out to Mum to stop, pulling her arm away, saying it didn't matter.

And then my mother began to cry. I ran away into a corner, frightened by this turn of events. I had never seen her cry before. My mother nagged, complained, grumbled and moaned, driving everyone crazy. But she didn't cry.

"I have to work so hard, take care of our girls, and you gamble away our money." She had slumped into an armchair, her body sagged as if drained of everything.

"Shh, don't say anymore." Dad motioned me to go to my room and sat on the arm next to Mum.

I sauntered off obediently, just as she was saying, "You've got to stop, you've got to stop. What about your children, what about me? How can you risk our safety like this, how can you?" I wanted to hear more, but Dad shut my door. The last thing I heard was "I'm going to get the money from Helen, no matter what you say. I don't ever want to see those men again."

5

In April, right after her exhibition, Regina tried to kill herself.

When we were teenagers, Regina often said to me that if she couldn't get away to the States, she would commit suicide rather than live in Hong Kong. I never paid any attention. She did try once, locking herself in the bathroom and slitting her wrist with a razor blade, having first announced to me that she was going to do so. I got the spare key and unlocked the door, only to find her busily binding up her wrist. She made me promise not to tell anyone. I never did.

Regina called me at work with the news.

"I'm okay, really I am. It was just that I saw myself rotting away here in Iowa. But now Tristan, I mean Dr. Clarke has promised to let me do my thesis away from this place, and he's even going to help me get to New York. Isn't that wonderful?"

Months without a word, and now this. I didn't know how to react.

"Come help me move to New York," she barrelled on. "I'm getting out of here in May. We can drive there together. Please say you'll come. Please."

I was still feeling guilty about not going to her exhibit, although Regina didn't seem to mind, saying it was just a stupid student thing. "I'm getting married in July," I told her. It was the first time I'd actually said it, even though Paul had made it public by now to everyone we knew.

There was a deafening silence. "Oh Rose," was all she said.

I promised Regina that of course I wouldn't tell anyone about what she referred to as her "botched" suicide. She never did tell me any real details, having spent the rest of the phone conversation carrying on about Tristan Clarke, who moved heaven and earth as far she was concerned. Even though she hadn't said so, I sensed she was having an affair with him, or, at least, yearned to have one. Regina had a way of obsessing about specific members of the opposite sex. Perhaps it was her reference to his "bitch of a wife" that triggered the thought. Who would name their son Tristan, I wondered, when she finally hung up.

I made plans to go to the States after that.

"But there's still so much organizing to be done," Paul objected when I first told him. "You haven't arranged for your wedding dress, or the evening gown. And the invitation. You promised you'd get it done — after all, you know so many graphic designers — and you haven't done a thing about that. And we haven't even begun to find a place to live."

We were driving along Clearwater Bay Road late one Sunday afternoon. Paul had recently bought a brand new car, a Toyota Corolla. But he was a nervous driver, constantly worried about scratching the car, and clumsy in manoeuvring. He was scared if he went even half a mile over the speed limit. Watching him drive made me impatient.

"We have months. Besides, I haven't seen Regina in years."

"That's her problem. She should have come home to visit. You're working. It isn't easy for you to go all the way there. Why isn't she coming to the wedding, anyway? Your sister's the most selfish . . ."

"Paul, let's stop here, okay?" I indicated a parking bay overlooking the valley.

He pulled over, almost hitting a lamp post. I cringed. We stepped out, and stood at the edge of the precipice. No one else was there, and most of the traffic was headed back into town. Paul was fussing with his keys, trying to fasten the key case. For a moment, I imagined pushing him over the edge. I recoiled, horrified by my thought.

"Isn't this nice, Rose? Aren't we lucky we can go for a drive like this?"

"Yes."

He put his arm around me. It felt strangely avuncular. "Poor Rose, I'm being too selfish, aren't I? You can go visit Regina, as long as it isn't more than ten days or so. All these wedding preparations are rather stressful, I know. Don't worry, I'll take care of things."

I wanted to say, Paul this is crazy, we can't get married. I don't know you. But the very idea seemed insane. Of course I knew Paul! Sometimes, it felt like I'd known him all my life.

"Come here," he said, pulling me closer and kissing my cheek. "I love you, Rose. I'll always love you. You belong to me and I belong to you. Remember when we made that promise?"

I buried my face into his shoulder, memories returning uncontrollably. I wanted to say, we were just teenagers, what did we know? But he held me more tightly, as if his grasp could bind me to him.

"Remember how you first started talking to me, telling me everything that was in your heart?"

He wasn't going to let me forget. I had no secrets from Paul.

The sun was going down. Its red rays blinded me momentarily, and I turned my face away from the glare. At the end of July, I was going to marry Paul. Nothing else seemed certain except that.

The week before I left for the States, Aunt Helen insisted I come over for dinner so that she could give me all kinds of things to bring to Regina. Paul declined the invitation, as usual. By now I'd given up expectations that he'd ever join me with my uncle and aunt. It was only my parents to whom he would *bei mihn,* because "face" was important, but only up to a point. When I arrived, Elliot was there. Helen was in a flap.

"Oh Rose, Rose, you can't imagine . . . anyway, I absolutely have to run out to get the painting . . . lovely frame but that man's so slow. He'll be furious if I don't give it to you to bring to his "darling Regina," but things have been so hectic. Here, Elliot, entertain my niece until I get back. Oh, Chong will be back soon. He had an emergency also — some guest had a heart attack in his room while being, uh, 'amused' by a prostitute or something like that." And she raced out the door.

"Looks like it's you and me," he said. "Want a drink?"

I was still deciphering what Helen had said. "Oh, what? Yes thanks."

He poured me a scotch on ice. I sipped it absently. As the scotch stung my tongue, I suddenly realized, "How did you know I drank scotch?"

Elliot smiled, and motioned me to a seat. "The time I saw you with your friend, you were drinking scotch. You also asked for it late in the afternoon on the boat."

"That's awfully observant."

He shrugged. "It isn't hard."

I had just untangled in my head that Helen meant our former landlord, who was very fond of Regina and made special paintings for her.

"I hear you're off to the States."

"Yes, to see my sister."

"Your twin sister, right? You two don't look alike."

"How do you know what she looks like?"

He gestured towards a photograph of Regina and me on my aunt's sideboard. "Isn't that her?"

"Yes. We're fraternal twins. She's the pretty one."

"You're not so bad yourself."

I smiled, embarrassed. "I wasn't fishing for compliments."

"Just telling the truth."

We lapsed into an awkward silence. Elliot was wearing a batik shirt. He looked remarkably at home in it. Every time I saw him, it was like meeting a different person. This time, I thought him handsome; I hadn't before. His dark hair, which was naturally quite wavy, was combed neatly back. This made all his features — the intelligent blue eyes, thin lips, flat ears and high cheekbones — stand out in rather prominent relief. As he stood there, I was struck by how perfectly proportioned he was. Only his feet were slightly too big for someone of his height and size. They looked about a nine, the same as Paul who, at five eleven, was at least over two inches taller than Elliot.

"How's *AsiaMonth* doing these days?"

He seemed to appreciate the question. "Pretty well. Tough business though."

"I'm getting married in July." I hadn't meant to say that, but it popped out.

"Are you?"

"You sound surprised."

"I wouldn't have thought you the marrying kind."

Troublesome refrain. "Why not?"

"Too independent."

"Really?"

"Really."

We lapsed into a longer, more awkward silence. I didn't understand the direction of this conversation. Each time I saw Elliot, I had the feeling that he knew more about me than I expected, and it made me uncomfortable.

He broke it first. "You look good on the dance floor, by the way."

"When did you see me . . ." I thought it must have been one of the social functions Paul and I found ourselves at.

"At the Hilton, oh a couple of years ago." And then he grinned wickedly, "your date was a good looking guy. I would have said hi but you two seemed rather, uh, immersed in each other?"

He knew it wasn't Paul. I looked away.

"Sorry, I'm being nosy. It's none of my business."

Had it really been two years since all that with Andrew, and the wedding that didn't happen. It didn't seem possible. I was about to say something, but Uncle Chong came in at that moment. Aunt Helen followed five minutes later, and the mood changed entirely.

Before I left that night, Helen pulled me aside. "Make sure she's okay, will you Rose? Your sister's fragile."

I digested that thought. Regina wasn't what I'd describe as "fragile."

Sensing my uncertainty, Helen continued, "Oh I know she's a tomboy and seemingly independent and all that, but you're the strong one Rose and always have been. I know about the suicide attempt."

"She told you?"

"Yes. Regina always tells me things. She needs to, you understand? It's sort of like getting attention. That's the way Regina is. I'm very glad you're going to be with her, even for just a short while. She needs her family more than she admits."

I wanted to say, so why doesn't she talk to us, but I knew the answer to that. Regina had long ago separated herself from us, even from me, because, I suppose, we chose to let her go.

We returned to the others. Chong was saying something to Elliot about Kuala Lumpur.

"So Rose," my uncle said, "have a safe trip and give my love to your sister."

I was struggling with the package of foodstuffs and presents that Helen had loaded on me for Regina. "I will."

"You'll be busy when you get back, preparing for the wedding."

I nodded, hoping he wouldn't say much more.

"Say hello to Paul also," he added, "and that we're sorry he couldn't make it tonight. By the way Elliot, would you be so kind as to see my niece home."

I started to protest, but was drowned out by solicitude.

Elliot relieved me of some of my packages. The lift doors closed on my relatives' good wishes and farewells.

"You really don't have to see me back," I began.

"Nonsense. I have to do the right thing by Helen's niece." There was an unmistakable barb in his voice.

"You use Cantonese to your advantage, don't you?"

"I use everything to my advantage, if necessary."

He bundled us into a taxi, and directed the driver. There was something extremely Hong Kong — I had thought it was Chinese — about Elliot.

He switched back to English. "I apologize, by the way, for being rude earlier."

"It's all right. I deserved it."

He put his hand on my arm. "No you didn't. But I will be bold and say that you deserve more than merely marriage."

"And what would that be?"

He leaned towards me, and I felt he wanted to kiss me. I almost pulled away, but didn't. He sat back suddenly. "I'll tell you someday."

"Regina, how can you stand to live like this?" I was standing in the middle of her living room in front of a heater, trying to keep warm while I dried my hair. May in Iowa was like winter in Hong Kong. Since I arrived at my sister's apartment the day before, all we'd done was pack up her stuff. I was taking a break in between bundling up her boxes of books. She had an incredible amount of things, in rampant disorder. My sinuses were going haywire from the dust.

"Like what?"

"With all this dirt, with dishes piled up in the sink, with your clothes thrown in a heap on the floor out of which you try to fish a pair of clean panties. I mean, how can you live like this?"

"Oh that." She gestured absently at a stack of books by my feet. "Hand me those, would you? I've got to get this packing done."

Back in Plattsburgh, she would have flown off the handle at me. But Regina seemed remarkably calm. Now, amid the remnants of her graduate school life packed in boxes, she seemed to have been mellowed by the whole exercise.

"God, I hate packing." She flopped on the floor, having thrown the final stack of books into what she called her last minute box.

I looked around at the rubbish still strewn around the apartment. "Don't we have to clean up?"

"This dump? Nah. The beauty of living like 'this' as you describe it, Rose, is that you never have to worry about things like keeping landlords happy. Mine will be only too glad to get rid of me. He thought he was getting a nice, quiet China doll when I first rented this place. Hah."

"You just don't care, do you?"

"No. I'm happy, you see."

There was something refreshingly simple about life with Regina. I spent all my time caring about doing what everyone else would approve of as the right thing, while Regina laughed all that in the face. Of course, I realized, she was happy at the moment, but there was no guarantee how long this would last.

"You don't understand," she continued. "I'm really in love. I've never been in love like this. Mum's hopeless. She lectured me about carrying on with a married man. I told her she should talk, considering how many years she put up with Dad spending all their money, and how good was her marriage? Then she started crying and yelling at me saying how could I cheapen myself this way. Cheap! Hah! It's her own loveless marriage that's cheap. God I'm glad you're here, Rose. I've missed you so much."

"You told Mum?" I was incredulous. Regina was quite open about all the wrong things, and hid away what we did need to know.

"It came out when I was talking about Tristan. I couldn't help it."

Mum hadn't said anything to me before I left, but that wasn't surprising. Despite everything, Regina would always be her favorite, and she couldn't stand anything that marred that picture.

"So do I get to meet him?"

"He'll be over tonight. Oh Rose, he has the most incredible mind. He's doing so much for me, you know. Giving me money to get the apartment, and he'll be out when the semester's over. He'll leave his wife for me. He will."

There was an edgy fanaticism in her voice. I dared not contradict her. What could I say? This was Regina, and all I could do was give Tristan the benefit of the doubt until I met him. I started sweeping up the mess, unable to stand the debris around us. Regina went off to prepare dinner.

Tristan arrived.

He was an ebullient man, armed with three bottles of wine. From the moment he walked in he had his hands all over Regina and kept making sexual remarks. Regina was starry eyed and silly and she drank too quickly and giggled too much. I didn't understand her behavior. But what struck me most was how dreadfully unattractive he was.

He was rude, overweight, balding and untidy. During the course of the evening, he belched several times, which Regina thought was funny. And he was ugly, with a crooked mouth, pockmarked face and ears that stuck out. This, I wondered, was the man who inspired such a sense of beauty in my sister?

"You don't look like twins," he said after the first bottle, most of which he'd drunk. "In fact, you barely look like sisters." He stuck his hand up Regina's shirt. "In fact, I'd love to screw both of you together. Christ, I get hard just thinking about it."

I blushed, but felt a mounting anger.

Regina laughed. "Don't. You'll embarrass Rose. She's proper you know."

"Best type. I'll bet she's hot in bed."

I stood up, furious. I wanted to shout at him, at Regina, to say that he should stop making a fool of my sister, and that Regina should stop being such a fool. Instead, I told them I needed to get some air, because I couldn't take the cigarette smoke. When I came back fifteen minutes later, they were naked and fucking on the living room floor. I closed the door and left, revolted by the sight. I did not return again until Tristan had departed.

"So wasn't he wonderful?"

We were driving out of Iowa at three the next morning when Regina asked me this.

"Honestly?"

"Of course, honestly."

"He's awful. He's got no intention of coming to New York. Regina, he treats you like a whore."

"You're jealous."

"Of him? Don't make me laugh."

"No, you're jealous because I'm happy and you're not. At least Tristan can't wait to get into my pants, which is a damn sight better than Paul."

We drove in silence for hours, stopping to check into a motel in the middle of nowhere in Indiana. I hadn't told Regina everything, but I had said that Paul sometimes acted like he didn't want me.

The next day, while crossing the Ohio state line, Regina suddenly said, "He is coming to New York, you know. He must. His wife doesn't mean anything to him at all."

Perhaps it was the rhythm of the ride, the empty highways ahead, but Regina began talking and didn't stop. She told me all about her painting, which was probably the most important thing in her life besides Tristan. He had kept her going, she said, and stopped her from going under, encouraging her to write more poetry that helped keep her balance. When I asked her what she meant, she admitted that Tristan had pulled her back in time from her suicide attempt.

"I'm a coward, Rose, you know that? I want to give up because I don't believe I can make it. I want to go home but I daren't, because everything inside me would go to pieces again. I'm a coward."

I sat close to her and leaned my head on her shoulder. "You'll always be my warrior maiden."

She shook me gently away. "It's not like that anymore. You don't really know me now, just like I don't know you. It'll never be the same."

We drove on, taking turns so that the other could rest. More than halfway through Pennsylvania, I insisted on stopping again at a motel. Regina's original idea had been to drive non-stop and sleep in the car. I drew a line at that, because I wanted a shower.

The highway appeared to be a trucker's route, and I hesitated at the sight of the dubious motel we finally found.

"Relax," Regina assured me. "At least we'll be guaranteed good coffee."

The water was hot and I luxuriated under the spray as fatigue washed itself off me. When I emerged, Regina was sitting at the desk rolling a joint. Spread out in front of her were several snapshots of paintings. Coming up behind, I put a hand on her shoulder. "You shouldn't smoke so much pot," I remonstrated.

She shrugged away my hand.

"Are all those yours?" I asked, indicating the photos.

"Yeah."

Without warning, she spun around and exclaimed, "I hate not knowing who I am."

I didn't respond, not sure of what she meant.

She had lit the joint. "This," she said, holding it up between her fingers, "keeps me level, you know? Around all the white bread."

"You're exaggerating."

"How would you know?" she snapped. "You haven't been there. Haven't been through it."

"Calm down, Regina. What did you expect, in the middle of Iowa? Why did you think I went home? You could have too, you know."

Her face changed, and she looked almost ready to cry. "It's not the same for me. I had such a dream of freedom in America." She held up the photos, fanned out like a deck of cards. A jumble of colors on her large canvases. "Do you think I could have done these back home?"

"So there's a price for freedom."

"You saying I don't deserve it? That being free means not knowing, never knowing who I really am?"

"It's not that. It's just that, well, freedom's kind of a luxury I think. Americans are born with a bit more of it than the rest of us. That's all. Come on, take a shower and get some sleep. You'll feel better."

While my sister showered, I lay between the sheets and thought about her lack of emotional fortitude. Was I the stronger because I still persisted despite Mum, Paul, his family and Hong Kong?

Perhaps my survival instincts were better, or perhaps I was simply more pragmatic. I couldn't be sure. All I knew was I wouldn't give in to the demons that gripped Regina.

"Rose! Rose! Look! It's New York."

It was about five thirty in the morning. I snapped out of sleep. Regina's ridiculously early morning starts made it hard for me to stay awake when we first got on the road.

"There's Manhattan."

To my left in the distance, I caught my first glimpse of the skyline of lower Manhattan. It was crisply cold. There was something infectious about Regina's excitement that made me forget how lousy I felt after nights and days on the road, prolonged by the rest stops in cheap motels.

I sat up properly in the back seat.

"This city now doth like a garment wear / The beauty of the morning, silent, bare. Wrong city, same feeling. Rose, I can't believe I'm finally going to live here for real."

"It is beautiful." I gazed at the onset of dawn, a scarlet glimmer over a clean, grey landscape. And suddenly I felt the beginning of tears in my heart. Here was that other half of me which seldom found expression, in the bond that tied me to Regina, to a sense of awe, to something greater than the cynical present tense of my existence. All my pain shrank to the tiniest speck inside me. What mattered except this, this moment of nature against the man made landscape that excited such joy in my sister? For a second, I experienced a flash of *déjà* — not *vu* but *senti* — recalling the feelings of my first sight of snow in Plattsburgh.

"Oh go on, Rose, cry. You don't have to be grown up like Mum says. There's no cowardice in tears," and I wept, like a child, now that brave Regina was there to protect me again.

The next few days were another whirlwind of moving into Regina's new apartment. She had found a place on the upper West side near Columbia which was a tiny box of a studio. I couldn't see how all her stuff would fit, but Regina carried on with vigorous optimism. By the time of my departure, we still hadn't figured it out. Half her boxes remained locked in the car. Given the relative precariousness of the neighborhood, I worried each night that her station wagon would be broken into. But Regina was quite relaxed. I envied her lightness, her ability to divorce herself from material concerns.

On my last night, we sat on Regina's threadbare futon after a wonderful meal of noodles she'd made me.

"Is Miguel still around?"

She didn't answer at first, and I thought she was going to deny all knowledge of him. "Poor Rose," she said at last. "I owe you for that, don't I? He's back in Bolivia. Deported."

"What for?"

"Drugs."

This chain that connected yet separated us. I tried to picture Regina at my wedding. Even without discussing it, I knew she wouldn't be there.

"Poor Rose," she repeated. And then, as if she had read my mind, "You don't really want to get married, do you? Why don't you dump the stuffed penguin and live with me and Tristan in New York?"

Suddenly, the mental weight I'd been carrying floated away like a giant helium balloon. I started to laugh, and grabbed Regina's arms like I used to when we were children so that she could swing me off the ground. A madcap whirl engulfed me. I fell on top of her and absorbed her laughter, which made the absurdity and isolation of our lives seem bearable again, if only for a short while.

Paul met me at the airport. He handed me a bouquet of white orchids with a single red rose in the centre.

"I'm glad you're back," he said, as he walked me and my bags to his car. "I've really missed you, Rose."

"Why?" I was surprised by my own curt response.

"I've thought a lot about us. About how I've hurt you. I never meant to."

I had pulled out the rose and was curling my fingers around its stem, unable to respond. I hadn't expected to see Paul at the airport. I hadn't expected this show of kindness and concern.

"I don't deserve you," he said.

On the way back to my home, he told me that he knew he was wrong to be so snobbish towards my family, that in marrying me, he was marrying where I came from.

"You make it sound like an affliction."

"We're all afflicted. You know that."

He was concentrating on driving, but I could see the pain in his face. There was something in my destiny that tied me to Paul. If I asked myself too many questions, the answers weren't there. If I tried to talk to Paul, his presence would dominate, and I could not argue back. I suddenly thought: unless I ran away from him, I would be his forever.

"Aunt Fay and Uncle Alex can't make it to the wedding. I'm sorry you won't be able to meet them."

"Why not?"

"Uncle has a contract starting a week before the date. In Libya. He tried to change it, but couldn't." Paul's uncle was an engineer.

"Can't your aunt come?"

"She won't go anywhere without him. Who would take care of him, she'd say. It's a great love between them."

So it was a pattern in his family, this incessant closeness. Perhaps one day I'd understand. We arrived at my home.

"I won't see you up. I'm sure you have plenty to talk to your parents about in private. Oh Rose, I'm so ashamed of how I've behaved towards you."

There it was again, that anguish which I found unbearable. I held the power to soothe him, protect him. Pyrrhic knowledge. I embraced him, kissed his pain. Yet as I left, I realized that I still had no idea what he believed his transgression to be.

A month before the wedding, I was offered a new job. It was with Pan Asian Airways as their marketing manager. An inflated title, because the airline was small and only two years old, flew to a handful of Asian destinations, but in their own way gave the likes of Cathay Pacific and other regional carriers a run for their money. They did package holidays to offbeat places.

The head guy was an Australian, and an old friend of my boss at the agency.

"Take it," my boss told me.

"But I've been here less than two years. Are you trying to get rid of me?"

"It's an opportunity, Rose. You don't like FMCG's, so an agency

102

is kind of the wrong place for you. Look, I don't want you to leave us but Colin Kenton's a good man. You'll like working for him."

"But what's the job, really, I mean?"

"It's up to you, isn't it. You cut deals with travel agents, run a few ads which you'll of course place through us, and travel a lot. Remember, you get all the airline benefits."

"Sounds difficult."

"Rose, Rose, don't be such a coward!" Seeing how piqued I looked, he added gently, "look, you know you're welcome to stay on here. Just think of what's coming up — advertising for milk powder. Baby nappies next. Fun fun fun!"

I rolled my eyes, but knew he was right.

Paul freaked. "Pan Asian?! Rose, you must be joking. They'll be bankrupt before you know it. They're only in business because Kenton's a distant cousin of the Swires." He was referring to the British family that owned Cathay Pacific. "Why won't you interview at the bank? You know my dad could introduce you."

We'd been over that *ad nauseam*. "As long as they can fill the planes, isn't that what counts? After all, some people want to go to Kota Kinabalu." It was the first destination they had won air rights for.

"Would you?"

I had, naturally, never been there, and could barely place it on the map. "I might," I responded defiantly.

My family wasn't much more help. Mum hadn't even heard of them. Dad muttered something about how difficult the airline business was and that there really wasn't room in Asia for a small regional carrier, although he did add that, in the beginning, Cathay Pacific wasn't much more than a cargo airline for smugglers, so there might be hope for Pan Asian yet. Uncle Chong scratched his head and said that travel agents might expect bigger commissions since Pan Asian wasn't a major player, and would unlikely be for years to come which meant they couldn't make money.

In desperation, I asked Aunt Helen out for *yam chah*.

We went to the huge place in the Ocean Terminal, where Helen knew three of the captains and could be guaranteed a table. I'd come to appreciate how well my aunt had adapted to Hong Kong and had, in fact, entrenched herself into local society the way neither of my parents had. *Yum chah* with her was fun; with my parents I had to endure my mother's complaints about how rude Hong Kong people were, how lacking in systems the restaurants were while my father pretended an indifference he didn't feel.

So at peak time on a Saturday, we were directed to a perfect table where Lie *tai tai* was seated and poured her customary choice of *seui sin,* water daffodil tea.

"You're the only person I know who can get a table for two in this place on a Saturday," I told her as we sipped our tea. "How do you do it?" When Helen and I were alone, we always spoke in Cantonese.

She laughed. "People. Everything comes down to whom you know. One of the captains here is the brother of the front desk receptionist at the Sheraton. Chong hired her recently into the sales department, which was a big promotion for her. So her brother is eternally grateful. The other two captains I got to know by chatting with them every time I come here, asking them questions about themselves. Now, they take care of me when Ah Wing isn't here."

"But never mind all that. Tell me about this job."

It was easy talking to Helen about work. She didn't grill me the way Uncle Chong did, nor was she as unaware as Mum was about the world I worked in. She also had the patience to listen, like Dad. The difference was, my aunt would offer an opinion that centred around me, instead of around the big picture of history, society and politics the way my father's opinions did.

I spelled out the situation at Pan Asian.

She waved at the trolley lady with the *sin juk gyun,* which she knew I liked, and motioned me to eat. I bit into the steamed bamboo skin roll, savoring its delicate blend of sauce covered vegetables and meat.

"It seems to me," she began in between bites, "that you want this job."

I hadn't stopped to examine this rather fundamental issue, caught up as I was in whether or not this was a good company, and what its future potential was.

"I suppose I do. But how could you tell."

"By the amount of enthusiasm in your voice when you talk about it. What's the boss like?"

"Less elliptical than my current one — they're both Australians, by the way. More direct. A bit of a wild man."

"Wild man? You mean, flashy, crazy?"

"No. He actually acts and looks quite conservative. You know, standard business suit and tie. It's the way he thinks. Nothing's impossible to him."

Helen weighed this. Meanwhile, she signalled for a bowl of tripe. Its rich, earthy smells tickled my nostrils. *Laahpsaap* food, all junk, Mum would have said.

"Do you think you can work for him?"

"Oh yes." I was certain, unhesitant.

"Then you have your answer."

I nibbled thoughtfully at the tripe. A shred of ginger skittered across my tongue, its tangy flavor mingling pleasantly with the tripe. "Is it that simple? What about Pan Asian? The industry? The pay package, which Mum says may sound good but what if their cash flow's a problem?"

"Rose, it's excellent you're cautious, but aren't you too young for that?" Seeing my quizzical look, she continued. "When I married your uncle, I had no idea what I was getting into. Here was this man who spoke lousy Chinese — you know even his Hokkien is barely passable — telling me he was a real Chinese."

I laughed. Uncle Chong was actually quite literate in Chinese. The problem was that he was tone deaf, and he mixed up Mandarin tones with Cantonese and Hokkien, in between speaking a heavily American accented English peppered with Malay. The running joke in our family was that Chong was fluent in three languages, but didn't have a mother tongue.

"And he wanted to take me to Kuala Lumpur, which your grandparents said was the other side of the world. Your grandmother was terrified that I'd become a slave on a rubber plantation, because she'd heard the only thing that grew in Malaysia was rubber trees. She wasn't educated, you know. Old folks don't believe in looking at the full set of facts, just those that suit them. But Chong was smart, and more importantly, *ying jan*. I could tell he was sincere. So, when I eloped I knew I was taking a big gamble with my life. High risk high return. You're your father's daughter. You should understand that."

I gave her a wan smile. Even though she never referred to it, I knew Helen bailed Dad out of gambling debts. Mum both appreciated and resented her for it.

"I was older than you are now when I ran off with Chong. Consider that."

It was a new perspective on my family's history. Mum's version was that Helen was an old maid by then and Chong her last chance.

"But don't listen to me, or anyone else for that matter. Make up your own mind. If Pan Asian crashes, figuratively I mean, you find another job. How bad can it be? Remember, in any company, your job's only as good as the boss you have, unless it's your own business. *Da gung jai!*" She mimicked Sam Hui's current hit about the working man.

I wondered how Helen knew the pop tune. My parents certainly didn't.

A waitress pushing a cart with my favorite egg custard tarts came down the aisle next to our table. Helen saw me eyeing them and ordered a dish.

"You don't change, do you Rose?" she remarked as I devoured my second one.

"What do you mean?"

"When you were a girl, your mother kept wanting to make you try some other sweets. But you insisted on only eating egg custard tarts." She laughed heartily. "Your father would tell your mother to leave you alone, and then they'd start bickering, because your mum thought it was bad for a child not to appreciate variety in life. In the meantime, you'd eat the whole plate of tarts, and then your mother would exclaim Rose, how can you be so greedy, and order another plate for the table!"

"I didn't know I was quite so stubborn," I said, laughing.

"You were determined, and sure of what you wanted and liked, although most people thought you rather timid. You ought to remember that about yourself, Rose."

I finished the rest of the tarts.

6

When I came to see Colin Kenton to further discuss the job, I said he'd have to wait until after my wedding and honeymoon.

Kenton was a tall, gaunt man, with a middle-aged fleshiness around his jowls and middle. He growled, rather than spoke. "Why?"

I contemplated my future employer, mildly livid on his side of the desk. It was, I would discover, his normal state. The glaringly obvious answer to most people was clearly what he didn't want to hear. "Because you wanted me, and I'm taking the job."

It was hard to tell whether he was smiling or frowning. He uttered something that sounded like "unnhh," adding, "my condolences." With that, he dismissed me to his secretary cum office manager Teresa Chan, who handled all the administrative paperwork for new employees.

She was a thin woman about six or seven years my senior. I could tell she wasn't about to approve of me if she didn't have to. "Speak Cantonese?" My too-fluent English was already a problem, again.

"Yes, of course. I'm a Hong Kong yan."

She looked at me doubtfully as she handed me a form. "Here, fill this out and return it to me." I rummaged in my bag for a pen. She handed me one, which just confirmed to her, no doubt, my state as *yat gauh wahn,* a hopeless "cloud lump." I glanced around for a space to sit, and headed towards the reception area.

"No, sit at that desk." She pointed in the opposite direction. I obeyed. This was going to be an uphill manoeuvre.

When I handed back the form, she glanced at it. "Oh, so you're one of the smart girls who went to the States for university."

"Only because I wasn't smart enough for Hong Kong U."

It was the first time she smiled. "But then maybe one is less stuck up that way."

We spoke a little longer, and her demeanor became chattier, friendlier. Before I left, she offered to usher me back to Kenton to say goodbye. After that, she walked me to the reception area, saying she'd see me in mid August. It was her preliminary stamp of approval, and for that I was grateful.

The first day Paul and I saw our new home, it was early July, on what had to be the most sweltering day of that year. We were a little snappish at each other, what with all the wedding plans, and the seemingly endless search for the right home. My mother wanted us to buy a flat, and had dragged us to several modern, dinky flats in high rises. I balked at the expense, as did Paul. Dad suggested we should get a house in the country, meaning far out in the New Territories where houses were available, so that he could visit on weekends. I balked at the distance. Paul hated driving and liked working late, which was why we ate out most nights. Convenience mattered more to him than pastoral surroundings. Marion was more absorbed with wresting control over the wedding plans away from my mother than with our future housing concerns.

Only Paul's Dad had the sense to stay out of the fray. I had gone to see him over lunch a week before we actually found our home.

"A home," he said, "has to reflect both of you. Otherwise, you won't want to be in it together."

I thought about my parent's chaotic flat, with its mixture of Indonesian, Chinese and European decor, all jumbled together, some piece always threatening to topple over. There was an incongruity about a Chinese goldfish painting hanging above the dark wooden native Indonesian statues of a half naked couple next to an ornate Italian ceramic floral arrangement on top of a Korean sideboard. And that was only one tiny corner of the living room. I shuddered.

"You're both quiet people, with lots going on in both your heads."

I glanced appreciatively across the table at my future father-in-law. He had an ease of manner I liked, a command of himself that drew your focus towards him whenever he spoke. He was one of the most intelligent men I knew. Yet he had a subtle charm that made me feel feminine, ladylike, without taking away any of my accomplishments as an educated professional.

His characterization of Paul and myself was the most accurate I'd ever heard.

He continued. "That's why your home must be quiet, but with enough space for the interior noise. You are not modern people, by which I mean you're not in a rush to change the world, are you?"

He looked hard at me. It was disconcerting. Paul Sr. had the kind of eyes that reflected the annals of history. I felt like a hundred ancient imperials were commanding me to heed their words, to meet my destiny. But then he smiled and became just Paul's dad again.

"I suppose not. I'd like an older flat really, something with high ceilings and cool breezes in the summer."

"Then call Dr. Ng."

So there we were, in Dr. Ng's huge old flat on Nga Tsz Wai Road, on the border of Kowloon Tong and Kowloon City. The building, a square, concrete block, was only three stories high. A two-bedroom ground floor flat with trees right outside the window. Paul and I looked at the living room, which was spacious for a Hong Kong place, and then at each other, and we both knew, right away, that we could live there and call it home.

A week before the wedding, Paul disappeared.

His father joked about the last wild bachelor's fling, because the previous night had been his bachelors' party. Marion was put out because Paul failed to show for dinner at his home to which both my parents and I had been invited to. Dad adopted a Buddha-like calm, saying we should eat before the food got cold. After putting up with months of Paul being tiresomely responsible over arrangements, I thought the whole thing hilarious and privately rejoiced at his performance.

Mum panicked.

All through dinner, she fretted and worried so much until even Marion, normally the most unruffled person I know, tersely remarked that Paul was quite old enough to take care of himself. When even that remark did not shut her up, Marion actually raised her tone slightly, saying, "Honestly, it's not a major crisis."

On the way home, Mum looked so miserable I thought she was going to cry. It was all Dad could do to stop her from calling the Lies the minute we got home.

"It's too late. We'll disturb them. Besides, Paul will call Rose when he's done with his carousing."

I tried to picture Paul passed out drunk at a friend's flat, and started giggling hysterically.

"It's not funny," Mum retorted. "For all you know, he may be hurt or in an accident, or maybe some bad men have done something to him."

Dad mimicked Mum's "bad men" which made me laugh even more.

"It's not funny, " she repeated.

"Oh Mum, go to bed. I'm sure he's all right." I began to wonder why she seemed so worried, but put it down to her way of turning ordinary happenings into melodrama.

It must have been around three in the morning when I woke up to the sound of Mum's crying.

My bedroom was right off the living room, and the telephone was in the hallway between the living room and my room. Mum was trying to talk softly, but I could hear her sobbing and talking. I opened my door as quietly as I could and listened.

"He's not going to show up for the wedding, Regina, I know it. Rose is going to be humiliated in front of all her friends. I always knew Paul was too good for Rose, but she's so proud, just like her Dad, can't see the first thing in front of her. You try to talk to her Regina, before she makes a fool of herself. Please talk to her.

"Ridiculous. I know my own daughter better than that. Rose is smart, but she's not pretty. Paul's handsome; he must have lots of girls chasing after him. He probably felt sorry for Rose when he first took her out. You see, no Chinese boy would find her beautiful. She isn't like you, Regina. I thought that because Paul was only half Chinese, well, anyway, I've tried hard to be nice to him to help Rose, you see . . ."

I closed my door and stopped listening. I wanted to scream. A part of me wanted to rush out, confront her, rip the phone away from her and say to Regina, "tell her to shut up, tell her to shut up." I told myself that she was just being her usual melodramatic self, that she was just talking without thinking, something Dad often accused her of doing. But this time, I couldn't make myself believe that anymore.

If I confronted her, she would simply say she was only trying to do what was best for me, and that I didn't understand how cruel men could be.

At that moment, I sealed off the part of my heart that gave my mother complete, unconditional, filial love.

But Paul, darling Paul, showed up right on time and was a radiantly handsome groom. He apologized profusely for his no show, which was, he said, a last bachelor's thing. Our wedding made the social pages. When Paul Sr. danced with me at the banquet cum reception — we had decided on a cross-cultural affair — he was a little flushed from too much champagne, but told me that he was honored to call me daughter, something that pleased me to no end. Marion smiled a lot that day, and told me how lovely I looked. I thanked her for helping me choose my dress, which she'd done with her usual good taste and elegance. Dad was in rare form, and he and Paul toasted each other so many times I was sure Dad would be ill before the night was over. Even though Dad pretended to be above the snob value of the whole affair, I could see how pleased he was that his daughter had married into the "right" society in Hong Kong.

Only Mum looked a little crestfallen and out of place. Near the end of the evening, when I had become just a little tipsy, I whirled round to Mum, smiled as sweetly as I could and said, "Pity Regina couldn't be here, but then, this is all a bit too elegant for her, isn't it?" And from her look, I could tell I'd hit where it hurt because no matter how beautiful Mum thought Regina was, neither she nor Regina had a hope in heaven of pulling off what I'd just done by marrying Paul. The truth of the matter was, although neither would probably admit it, they both did want a little of what I had that day.

Twenty three. A society bride in white and red, because I wore tulle and lace for Church and the traditional Chinese po for the first part of the evening reception. The green silk evening dress I wore for the latter part was classic Marion, who had it specially designed and tailored. And the glitter of glamor and jewellery. A perfect night where darkness never came, already embalmed in memory. Saturday, July 10, 1976.

Looks like my ABC Fed man's found something out there in the files.

What was it Paul used to say? Amassing the facts discloses the truth.

"Honeymoon" is a misnomer. What takes place in the bright glare of sunlight comprises the honeymoon photos we keep. I amassed numerous photos for my wedding album, including shots from our Hawaiian honeymoon which I proudly showed off to colleagues, friends and relatives.

We went for two weeks, to a lovely hotel on the North Shore, and also for a side trip to Kauai. His parents gave us the trip. I kept thinking during the flight, this is it, now he won't be afraid anymore because even if I do get pregnant, it'll be all right.

The night we arrived, he was exhausted. Truthfully, so was I, because the tension and excitement of a huge wedding had been a mounting frenzy, and this aftermath felt like a chance at last to rest. Despite my fatigue, I anticipated the first night, because . . . well, because I suppose I'm not a woman of much imagination.

We were showered, relaxing in our bridal suite. I was sipping a glass of champagne. "I'm sorry your Uncle Alex couldn't make it. I wanted to meet him." His uncle and aunt had sent an extremely generous *laisee* as our wedding gift.

"I wish you wouldn't keep bringing it up."

I was taken aback by his curt tone. It was only the second time I'd mentioned it in the past two months.

Paul sat in the chair opposite me, glaring at me in the strangest way. "I wish we'd waited."

His statement numbed me.

"We could have waited," he continued. "And you should have waited."

"Paul, we shouldn't have to talk about that anymore, should we?" I put down my glass and headed towards him.

"Please, stay where you are." He must have seen my shocked look, because he added gently, "Let me see you."

I stood there, midway between our two chairs.

"Take off your robe," he said.

"Paul, I . . ."

"Please, don't say anything. Just let me look at you."

I obliged, and stood there naked while he continued to stare at me in that strange way. And then he suddenly got up, pulled on a pair of pants and a shirt, and left me alone in the room for the rest of the night.

I cried all that first night, wondering what had happened to my life. Paul turned up again round about dawn, and never said a word about it. The rest of the honeymoon, we spent together like any other newlywed couple. Everything else was normal except for that one night for which he apologized. I didn't demand an explanation from him. We were married now, and as long as he wanted me for his wife, any explanation would have been meaningless. After all, this was the life we both were committed to. If there were things we couldn't explain, perhaps life could still go on. Perhaps one day the reason for his strange behavior would become clear. At least, that was my hope.

The Monday morning I started at Pan Asian, Elliot delivered a congratulatory tree to my office. It arrived around eleven amid much ceremony and giggling from the secretarial and clerical pool who were sizing up their new way-too-young-and-inexperienced-to-be-a- manager colleague. Teresa, as queen hen, supervised the proceedings.

"Where do you want this thing?" The two men holding the pot were put out by what they clearly considered a ridiculous delivery.

I pointed to the brightest corner, presently occupied by a large filing cabinet.

"If you don't mind, could you just move that cabinet aside to make room for it? It's the only part that gets direct sunlight." I flashed my most charming, imperial smile at them.

"Wei! Lady, *yau mouh gaau cho* — have you 'mixed up some madness'? That cabinet's damn heavy."

"*Mhouyisi, cheang yam chah.*" I knew the "tea money" would persuade them. Sure enough, they moved around the furniture to accommodate my tree, albeit amid much grumbling. But I was still enjoying the humor of his gift, this less-than-subtle statement that Cohen wanted my business.

The same morning, my ex-boss sent over a flower basket on behalf of the agency.

Paul didn't send anything.

Granted he was in the middle of a major case, but up till then, he had never really forgotten any important occasion. The comfort of seeing his customary dozen white orchids with the single crimson rose in the middle would have been fine with me.

I suppose that was why the notion of Elliot flitted in and out of my thoughts for a greater part of that first day at Pan Asian. At around five thirty that afternoon, I finally managed to reach him to say thank you.

"Have you named it yet? All trees have names, you know." His voice had a softness that travelled well over the phone.

"I could name it after you."

"Absolutely not. It's a female tree."

"It is?"

"Most definitely."

I thought for a moment. "Olivia."

"Why?"

"I've never met anyone with that name."

Kenton stuck his head in. Aside from five minutes in the morning when he told me to figure out what my job was, I hadn't seen him again all day. I asked Elliot to hold a moment.

"I'm off to KL for two weeks, by the way." He was about to leave when he saw the tree. "Insect bait," he declared, as he took off.

"Mr. Kenton says Olivia's insect bait."

Elliot guffawed. "Don't call him that. It'll go to his head!"

"What?"

"Mr. Kenton. Listen, I've know Col for years. He's more than bearable once you get a couple of drinks in him."

I listened to him carry on for a bit. Elliot was definitely going to be an asset.

On Friday, Marion was giving a dinner at her home in honor of my new job. Our flat was mid way between Paul's parents and mine. When I arrived home, Paul wasn't back, but he rang to say that I should go on first because he had some work to finish and would go straight there. I protested, because I didn't want him to be late, but he promised he'd be quick and I knew Paul well enough to know that he could move very fast when he wanted to.

I arrived at around seven. It was quite an affair. Marion, knowing better than to command the kitchen for anything really special, had a catered dinner preceded by cocktails to which my parents and several friends of the Lies showed up. I loved Marion for the pride she took in my accomplishments. My mother would never have thought to make this kind of a fuss over my new position, only over money. The job paid well enough, but was only a twenty percent increase over my current salary. Mum thought I should have asked for more.

By seven thirty, most of the guests had arrived. Paul Sr. was especially sweet to me, praising me to all his friends. My mother kept saying, too loudly, that Paul was really very late, and she hoped he hadn't met with an accident. I felt a panic creeping in, and glared angrily at my mother whom my father tried to shush.

By eight Marion asked, "what do you want me to tell the others?"

"I don't know." Could he be in an accident? But what I really felt was hurt and embarrassed. It was as if the truth of my honeymoon was on stage for everyone to see.

She placed her arm around my shoulder. "Don't worry, I'll say he called and something dreadfully important came up and told us to go ahead first. Okay dear?"

I smiled weakly at her. She was helping me remain strong, and I privately thanked her for that. But I wondered why she seemed so calm, so able to take this in as if it was all perfectly normal. Most of all I wondered why she didn't worry, as any mother would, that her son might be in an accident and hurt.

It was the longest dinner I ever sat through. I was sure all wondered and pitied me, although everyone was too polite to say so. In fact, people had a terrific time, and possibly all I felt was a function of my own unhappiness. I can't remember that dinner without cringing, without feeling that my mother could confirm her belief that I had been jilted. I sometimes think now that I've imagined Mum's unfair feelings towards me, that it was all my own construction, that all memory was a fictional invention to make living bearable. But I doubt if I really felt all those things at that moment. Only in retrospect, because hindsight is all I have left.

Marion and Paul Sr. stopped me from leaving with my parents that night.

"A nightcap, dear?" Marion always called me "dear" these days.

It was so rare of her to offer a drink that I knew she wanted me to stay for a reason.

So I obeyed.

They waited till I'd settled in an armchair and had taken a sip of my drink.

"Paul did call," Marion began.

I felt a huge sense of relief. "Where is he? Is he all right?"

Paul Sr. came around and sat on the arm of my chair. "No, nothing like that."

"You must understand, dear," she continued, "he's not like other men."

I stared blankly at her.

"He's different. It doesn't mean he can't love you, or be married to you. You just have to learn to understand."

Paul Sr. laid his arm on mine. "Haven't you noticed that my son has many male friends."

And then, slowly, slowly, the dimmer nudged the light up in my consciousness. Those strange disappearances. The absence of couples as our friends. His refusal to join the social milieu of my advertising crowd, where tolerance of what was different would have threatened his mask. The amount of time he spent hanging out with male friends in bars, when he was not even a drinker. Our strange, sexual encounters. How could I not have known? How long had his parents known, and accepted?

"You must understand," Marion was almost babbling now, rushing through her words as if talk could counter the shock she knew I felt. "He's always been this way. But he's also always cared very much for you. There's nothing to stop you from having children and leading a perfectly normal life."

I stared at Marion. Had all that concern for me only been a ploy to hold me for Paul? She was still going on about Paul's "condition," one he couldn't help. As if she sensed my thoughts, she suddenly stopped talking.

"I didn't plan this," she said abruptly. Her voice was clear and steady. "Life doesn't always work out the way you expect. But you've got a whole life ahead of you, Rose, in a world where you can belong. With us. With Paul. Don't let it go. Be sensible and try to understand."

I started to cry. Marion left the room. She hated displays of emotion. Paul Sr. put his arm around me. "It's all right, we're here for you. One day, you and he will work it out. Really." A part of me raged against this argument, but his father's gentleness, so much like Paul's, made me cling to his arm and pour out the pain through my tears.

"It'll be okay Rose. You have us now. We're your family too, you know."

"Why couldn't he have told me himself?"

"He will one day. You know it's not that he isn't in love with you, don't you? Or that he's not a man? He's just a little different."

I nodded vigorously, as if my assent could make it real. Yet I wondered what he'd say if I told him about what really transpired between Paul and me.

"After all," he continued, "you know he's very attracted to you, and always has been." He stood up and pulled me out of the chair. A strong man, he made me feel weightless. I got a grip on myself, and dried my eyes.

"I can't tell my parents."

He held my face in his hands. "I understand, Rose. It's our secret. Anytime you need me, us, we're here. Do you understand?" He said this in such a resolute, commanding tone. Once more, the power Paul Sr. exuded encased me. It was safe here, in this world, with these people who could live dual lives. They were asking me to be a part of it. Marion had given me more than I ever expected; she loved and approved of me, unconditionally. What more perfect husband could I want? What more acceptance did I need? Was this any worse than the family I came from, with Regina and her suicides. We were all part of the mongrel caste who belonged together, who found a sheltered haven in our tiny city where the proper face was all that counted. In this time and space, it was a home that embraced us all.

Night time soothes.

So perhaps I should have left Paul right then? Yet I remained married to him. It was my choice, just as it was my choice to ignore the realities of working for Gordie. I have no illusions about Paul's cowardice, or mine.

Besides, it hasn't been bad in New York. At least here I'm sheltered from the glare of the public life I felt compelled to lead back home. Resignation to destiny is simply another path to tread. As my father would say, life has a way of going on, no matter what you try to do, no matter how trying the moment may be.

Even the Feds have to quit eventually.

"So what happened to Paul?" My mother was on the phone the next morning.

"He can't talk about it. A senior government person's involved, and Paul simply had to make a choice." I knew she liked to hear how important he was, and besides, this was the story my parents-in-law and I agreed on. "He was sad to miss the dinner, but sometimes, these things can't be helped."

She babbled on about some new curtains she was sewing, and asked if we needed any. I didn't want to say that we'd already had the windows measured by Marion's curtain maker. Then she offered to give me some of her vases, because "you always need different sizes to fit a variety of flowers." I thought about the two crystal vases we had received as wedding gifts by friends of the Lies. The more my mother offered to help with the household, the more I realized how different my life was going to be from hers.

Finally, just before she rang off, she added, "You come home for dinner anytime you want, Rose. I know Paul has to work very hard, and socialize for business reasons. If you're alone and don't feel like cooking, you're not very far away. You're still our daughter."

What prompted her to say that? The aftershock of yesterday evening's events imploded. For a second, I wanted to blurt everything out, to say she was right that Paul couldn't really love me, even if for reasons other than she thought. But then, the remembered pain at hearing her words to Regina stopped me, and I thanked her, saying I was lucky to have such a good mother.

That weekend, Paul didn't come home at all. Yet I knew before Monday morning dawned that I didn't need to confront him. He never came to me, never said a word. He returned from work Monday evening and acted as if nothing had transpired, greeting me with a kiss like a husband should. That night as we fell asleep he stretched his arm across our new, queen size bed, and pulled me close to him. "I need you, Rose," he whispered. And then he made love to me, as he had done after the first night of our honeymoon. I slept dreamlessly in his arms.

So, married at last, we continued our weird and familiar private life that even I now sort of understood. Paul came home after that every night, although where he spent the evenings without me I never really knew. Life went on. It seemed natural not to ask.

7

Elliot invited me to lunch three weeks after my new job started.

"So have you settled in at Pan Asian, Mrs. Rose Lie?" he asked, having given the waiter his order for an impressively Cantonese lunch. We were at Jade Garden, which had recently opened in Swire House, and I was still marvelling at his ease with local culture.

"You make me feel old," I said in English.

"Okay, I won't remind you of the ageing effect of matrimony. And English it is."

"I *am* impressed, by the way, especially since you're not a police inspector, and an American."

"Amazing what we mere *gwailos* are capable of, if we put our minds to it."

We both laughed.

The waiter hovered round and poured us more tea.

"Now," I began, "will you tell me why the tree — you made quite a stir by the way — and all this?" I gestured at our surroundings. "All the other regional publications know I have a minuscule budget and wouldn't give me the time of day. We're not Cathay Pacific or Singapore Airlines, you know."

He leaned back and gazed directly at me. "You don't waste time, do you?"

"Not if I can help it."

"Very well, I'll tell you why you're important to my business. Three reasons. Pan Asian's the only airline in Hong Kong besides Cathay with intra-Asia traffic rights so you have to do well, Kenton's the cleverest deal maker I know, and he knew enough to hire a smart person like you, who just happens to be my favorite lady's attractive niece."

I was about to shoot a comeback, but he spoke first. "Not if I can help it either."

Back in the office after lunch, Teresa said, "*Leang jai,* that Cohen, isn't he?" as I walked into my office.

I was amused she thought him a "beautiful boy." "Yes, I suppose he is."

Teresa followed me into my office with a pile of papers from Kenton. "His Cantonese is very good. He's lived in Hong Kong a long time. You know, he speaks Mandarin too? Too bad I'm already married, huh?" She grinned at me like a naughty schoolgirl. "I told my husband about him just to make him mad!" Teresa, once she'd relaxed, quite liked confiding in me as an equal, placing herself above all the other women in the office since she could consort with the only female manager. I was grateful for her acceptance.

I spent the afternoon wading through the papers on my desk, and answering too many phone calls. For the second time since I'd arrived at Pan Asian, Elliot was occupying my thoughts during work hours. There was something appealing about him. The glasses made him look serious and intelligent; his dark hair, almost black, and tanned complexion made him "beautiful." But what I found most attractive was his exquisite sense of order.

Elliot had taste. Paul spent lots of money on his appearance, but no matter what he wore, you could see it was only because he spent money. The thing about Elliot was his instinctive knack for the sensual pleasures in life within the boundaries of elegance. Definitely appealing. There was something un-American about him, something I couldn't define. Even his accent sounded faintly European. Other than his apparent interest in Chinese culture, I wondered whatever had really kept Elliot Cohen in Hong Kong.

The phone rang. It was two in the morning.

"Rose! He's coming to New York!" Here was Regina who always claimed she was too poor to call, bellowing long distance at the most expensive time of day for her. I forced myself into wakefulness.

"Don't screech."

"He's leaving his wife, he said so. Even Stan thinks this is for real."

"Who's Stan?" With Regina, I had to interrupt her stream of consciousness with short, simple questions. Otherwise, much of what she said would be incomprehensible. She inhabited an orbit way above the rest of us mere mortals.

"Oh haven't I told you about Stan? He's the sculptor I live with. But listen, I need some money."

No use, don't ask. An echo of our childhood refrain about Aunt Helen when she barrelled on a mile a minute.

"I'll pay you back, promise. It's just that I'm a little short right now for the abortion."

I suppressed my rising anxiety. "Regina, whose . . . ?"

"The poor girl simply can't have the child. She's way too weak, and only sixteen."

It transpired that she was talking about Stan's model, a Vietnamese boat girl, "but Chinese of course," she added as if that explained everything. Over the years, Regina would rescue many strays. I admired her generosity.

"Do you mind?" she continued. "Problem is I need the money rather quickly. Can you TT it?"

"TT?"

"Telegraphic transfer, of course. Rose, Rose, don't you know anything?"

I agreed because with Regina it still would be ridiculous to disagree. She would have dismissed any argument or question I raised with "but what's to question, it simply has to be done." Besides, I wouldn't begrudge her money, ever. What she did with it was her business.

She continued at fire engine speed. "Anyway, he's coming."

"Do you mean Tristan?" I was fully awake, now that the matter of international financing was under control.

"Of course. Who did you think I meant?"

I wondered about the mysterious Stan, but thought it prudent not to interrupt her romantic narrative.

"I can't wait. He's been calling me almost everyday. It's expensive, I know, but I don't mind. I love hearing from him. After all, I can earn money. Anyway, he's going into partnership with a gallery owner in Soho, so I'll have a place to exhibit. Isn't that simply amazing?"

"Regina, quit gushing. Do you mean to tell me you're paying for the calls?" That would explain why she was short of cash. Regina was capable of hoarding huge sums of money, spending hardly anything on what most people would consider the bare necessities.

I had been startled by her request for a loan.

"Well, his bitch of a wife . . . but never mind, he'll be solvent easily enough. He's lining up possible teaching jobs here."

So, the man my sister loved was a leech. After the call. I considered again the situation about Miguel. She had probably been funding him in some fashion too, whether or not there was any truth in her remark about his being her pimp.

It was now almost three thirty in the morning. Paul hadn't come home yet, and I had no idea where he was. I had a seven thirty breakfast appointment, another of Kenton's last minute directives the day before. I went back to sleep. Even if life was momentarily insane, at least I had the rhythm of work to sustain me.

Paul kissed my neck when he came in at five.

"Wake up sleeping beauty," he whispered to me.

I looked up at his radiant face. His eyes gleamed as if he were high, but I knew better.

"I'm sorry, Rose. I didn't mean to stay out all night." But he was smiling as he said that, hardly contrite.

I waited.

"I know I owe you an explanation," he began. "Rose, I think I've found my twin. You know how you and Regina are, soul mates and all? Last night, I finally understood what you meant. I've never felt that way about anyone since Robert, my cousin, died. It's strange, and marvellous, and frightening all at once. Is that how you've felt? What you've meant about Regina?"

I remained silent, not wanting to break his train of thought, also not knowing what to say.

"He's someone I've known for years, but not well. You know, someone I could say hello to. But last night, something happened, and we talked for hours. He's never made love to a woman, and doesn't think it matters. He sent his date home care of his chauffeur. Imagine."

First Regina, now Paul. I felt a little overwhelmed by this great surge of emotions around me of which I wasn't a part. "Who are you talking about?"

"Robert." And then, seeing the shock on my face, he corrected himself, "Oh, I mean Albert. Albert Ho. You know, Ho Yuet Kan's son. We were in school together, at La Salle. But he left before Form 5 and finished out in the States. Only he came back, not like his brother, I mean half brother, David. You remember David, don't you? The one who drove me to Plattsburgh?"

I recalled the slightly built, rather effeminate man we met with Elliot. Albert had a reputation as a playboy, which I wondered at when I'd met him that time.

Paul continued in the same vein for the next two hours, until finally I had to get ready for work. He held me in his arms as he spoke, and I felt a little like we were teenagers again, when he used to tell me all his dreams about following in his father's footsteps in law. "I'm happy," he kept saying. "I'm beginning to understand more about my life." But even as he raved on, I knew he was leaving me cold, creating an even greater gulf between us. Each time I told him I didn't know what he meant, he would say, "trust me Rose, you will one day" and then he'd add, "you're my wife and I love you and that's how it's always going to be. I want you to be the mother of my children." Most of all, I wished he could acknowledge the emotional and sexual distance between us, since that had to be at the root of what was wrong about our life together. But that seemed the furthest thing from his mind.

How I wanted to make sense of this too! No matter what I felt about Paul, he was still the only man I'd ever loved. Yet he appeared oblivious to the pain he was causing me. Here he was, telling me that he had a "soul mate" who chaperoned some of the most eligible and beautiful society women, yet thought women dispensable in the greater scheme of things. It was hardly reassuring. But what I did understand was that my husband had found someone who inspired him, someone who opened him up and excited him emotionally, which was something it seemed I couldn't do no matter how hard I tried.

Less than two months after I'd been on the job Kenton asked if I'd ever lived in Kuala Lumpur.

"What gave you that idea?" I had discovered by now it was simpler to say what I thought, in most instances, instead of trying to figure out his meaning or please him as a boss. It worked better that way. Teresa, who had worked for him for four years, was still too Hong Kong reserved for that. From time to time, I'd find her sniffling in the ladies' room over some imagined slight or brusque remark of his.

"Aren't you Malaysian?"

"I'm sort of part Indonesian, but not really, because I grew up here in Hong Kong."

We were standing in his office. With Kenton, staff meetings, such as they were, mostly took place standing up. This way, no meeting ever lasted more than five minutes. He was slightly more cordial with visitors. This irritated Teresa who wanted to serve visitors tea to show that staff at Pan Asian knew proper office etiquette, and she complained that his meetings were always over before the tea could be poured.

He cleared his throat. Kenton smoked heavily and his deep, hacking cough often echoed down the corridor. "So would you like to live there?"

I hesitated.

"Well?"

"I'm married," I finally replied.

"I hired you, not your husband. Think about it." Our meeting was over.

He had to be testing me, and seemed only half serious. I told Teresa over lunch.

"He's *chisin,* 'stuck wire crazy'!" she exclaimed. "What if you have children?" Teresa had one girl already and was trying for a second child.

We were at the new Vietnamese restaurant, one of the first in Hong Kong, which was hidden away on a side street off D'Aigular. Despite its awkward location, and the three storey walk up, it had become popular with the lunch time crowd in Central. Pan Asian's office, in Holland House on Ice House Street, was a short walk away. I especially like the spring rolls, eaten with raw lettuce wrapped around them. They reminded me of my mother's lumpia.

"I like Kuala Lumpur," I said.

"*Ai ya.* You're just as *chisin* as him. No wonder he hired you."

"And what about you?"

She sniffed. "We put up with each other."

In the afternoon, Kenton made things marginally clearer. "Go to

125

KL. We're doing a deal with MAS to hook into their domestic network. Ask Teresa for the details. You wouldn't have to live there till next year at the earliest."

That night, Paul called me shortly after eleven.

"I'm moving out for awhile."

"What do you mean?"

"Well not exactly moving out, just setting up another home. But not exactly."

"And what do you expect me to say?"

"Nothing has to change, Rose. Talking to Albert has helped me so much, you can't imagine. It's like Robert's come back to life again."

No, I wanted to scream. I have a right to participate in our life. You can't keep stage managing me. But I remained dumb.

I finally said, "I have to go to KL. I'll see you when I get back." With that I hung up, and passed another dreamless night.

He wasn't home when I left for the airport in the morning. Somehow, I was relieved.

Kai Tak International seemed unusually crowded as I headed towards immigration around eleven. I was agitated and nervous. Someone accidentally jostled me in line and I turned on him, startling the elderly gentleman into profuse apologies. By the time I reached my gate, it was clear something was wrong. And then the announcement — no takeoffs until further notice because of the typhoon.

A typhoon in October? I peered out of the window. The sky was an indeterminate grey, and the wind gusty. Had it been like this when I left home? I couldn't remember. In fact, I couldn't even remember whether or not I had heard the news on radio, or what I'd had for breakfast, or . . .

A hand on my back and a voice in my ear. "We're both stuck, aren't we?"

I jumped. Turning around, I came face to face with Elliot Cohen.

His arm was still around my waist. He didn't remove it. "Dance?"

Leaang jai — Teresa's voice whispered. He was close to me and

126

invitingly real. Crumbling precipice. "Long lunch," I replied.

He led me towards the exit. "There's Suzanna's in Sai Kung."

I thought about Elliot seeing me with Andrew, and, adopting a composure I didn't at all feel, said, "I guess that's far away enough, don't you think?"

He ran his hand down my back. "You do have a way of getting right to the point, don't you, Mrs. Rose Lie?"

Lunch till dusk. The food was indifferent, but it didn't matter. Suzanna's, a pub-like restaurant on the main road in the village, was dark and deserted. We sat in the booth furthest away from the bar where Suzanna sat, immersed in a woman's magazine. She was a buxom Chinese girl from a nearby village whose family owned the place. I wondered how Elliot knew her.

I drank almost a whole bottle of wine, and it didn't strike me till much later that Elliot only had had one glass, which he left unfinished. We sat across from each other at first, while our legs kept getting tangled. Finally he got up and came round my side of the booth, so that we could hear each other better of course, and I twisted round to face him and our hands kept accidentally-on-purpose touching. But when he leaned forward to say something — I can't remember what we talked about that day except that I know I laughed a lot — one hand brushed my leg and rested there for a moment. I felt my whole body go hot and between my legs I was damp.

"It was a false alarm," he was saying.

"What?"

"The weather."

I glanced out the window. The sky was still grey but the wind had subsided. "We've both missed our flights."

"I'm not sorry."

"Neither am I."

"So," he looked away uneasily. "My place?"

Were we both equally as uncomfortable? If only I could be as urgent as I had been with Andrew, or even Paul when I first came back from college. I hesitated.

"I'm out of line, aren't I?" he said, eyes still averted.

"No!" I hadn't meant to be quite so abrupt, but Elliot must have heard what I really meant correctly because that was when he kissed me, and that wonderful, youthful, awakening urgency I'd forgotten returned and engulfed me completely.

He pulled away first. "I've been waiting to do that for a long time."

I shifted uneasily. "It's not a good idea, is it?"

"You tell me." He didn't look at me.

"I'm in this funny marriage," I began.

"I can tell."

"How?"

"I've been there before."

He paid the bill and we stepped out into the remnant shreds of daylight.

Sai Kung village centre was quiet. A single decker bus lolled at the terminus. It was an old one that still had the manual bar gate, the kind, my mother used to say, which should be abolished because small children could fall out too easily.

"Come on." Elliot directed me onto the bus. "Let's go to the end of the road."

I didn't know Sai Kung well and had no idea where he meant, but followed him willingly. I didn't want to go home, didn't want to face the empty flat. He took my hand to help me up the steps, and didn't let go of it when we sat down.

It was about a forty-five minute ride down a winding two lane road, past villages on the left and the sea on the right. The occasional house presented itself along the way. I had forgotten how rural the New Territories still were, since I seldom came out here.

I talked to Elliot. Pieces of my life with Paul tumbled out. I told him about the abortion, the false pregnancy with Andrew, the distance between Paul and me. I couldn't tell him about the pact I'd made with my in-laws, or the details of my strange sexual life with Paul. But I did say that Paul appeared to be struggling with his homosexual nature. It was the first time I'd said it to anyone. Elliot put his arm around me and listened quietly. A couple of the other passengers, all Chinese, turned hostile stares at us which Elliot pointedly ignored. *Mhao lei keui dei*, he told me, because I tried to pull away from him.

We rode to the "end of the road," which was actually the beginning of the closed-to-public-access road of the High Island

Water Scheme. "You're allowed to walk, but you need a permit to drive," Elliot said, and we slipped past the barrier and started down the road. But it was much darker now, and the bus was getting ready to turn around, so I asked to go back. "Okay," he said, but before that he embraced and kissed me, there in the middle of the path, ignoring all the villagers on their homeward trek.

Our taxi stopped along College Road, about a block away from Nga Tsz Wai. I had directed the driver there, not wanting to stop directly in front of my home, not wanting Elliot to see exactly where I lived, not wanting to run into Paul. Noisy thoughts. Elliot scribbled his home number and address on a card which he slid into my bra. I revelled in his touch, his urgency. Each time he bit my earlobe and whispered, "come on, my place," he wore my resistance down just a little further.

He got out of the taxi with me.

"I'm not letting you go yet." Taking my hand, he led me down Sau Chuk Wan, a side street off College where high walls hid us from pedestrians and passing cars. "Here," he said, leaning me against the wall. And then, he kissed me.

It was like simultaneously being with Andrew and Paul. The long bus ride, during which he listened, bringing out something in me that had remain buried too long, felt like the comfort of my relationship with Paul. Yet I felt his pressing desire, which brought back those snatched moments with Andrew, in the back seat of cars, in stairwells and broom closets, anywhere he could.

Finally we parted, and I walked back home, wondering why I had resisted his whispered entreaties to go home with him, wondering how, under such circumstances, life could go on.

Paul was home. He sat in the living room facing the front door. I tried to disguise my shock at seeing him.

"Where were you?" he asked. It was past midnight.

"Airport."

"Your flight didn't take off."

"That's evident."

He was white with anger. I thought he would rise and strike me. I remained standing, my flight bag still in my hand.

"You can't do this to me."

"Do what? Last I heard you were moving out." I was pretending a bravado I didn't feel. Surely he could tell: my creased clothes, the smell of Elliot on me, the desire between my legs that had threatened me all day. It was a good thing I'd taken the card out of my bra before I walked in.

His expression softened. "I want you, Rose."

It was then I realized he was again exhibiting himself. My body trembled, aching for relief. I went to him, gave myself completely to him. He tumbled over me, dragging us both to the floor, tearing my blouse, and we made love like that for hours, until there was nothing left, and fell asleep, half clothed, on our living room floor. It was the best sexual experience I'd ever had with Paul.

Elliot called the next morning. It was Friday.

"So you've cancelled your trip too," he said.

I was trying to be organized and efficient. It was impossible. "Postponed."

"Too hard to sleep." That wicked urgency in his voice. "What are you doing tonight?"

The problem was, I didn't know. When Paul and I awoke, he looked at our disarray as if he didn't remember what had happened. I had expected tenderness, perhaps even to make love again. But he jumped up, exclaimed he was late, showered and disappeared in fifteen minutes.

Taking advantage of my silence, he added, "come on, my place?"

"No, I can't." Which was truth and which the lie? I didn't know, perhaps didn't want to know. Then added, "not yet."

"Then I'll call you every day until you say yes."

"Elliot, I'm married."

Teresa appeared. "Kenton's looking for you." I nodded, signalling I'd be right there. I wondered how much she'd heard.

The day slipped away from me before I knew it. A weekend ahead to sort out the turmoil. When I got home, a dozen orchids with a single red rose awaited me, accompanied by a note from Paul. It said he'd be back soon. The table was set for a candlelight dinner. The bath was filled. On the bed was a pale rose colored silk robe, another present from him. I luxuriated in my home, and slipped into the bath. Twenty minutes later, I got out, dried myself and put on the robe. It felt smooth against my skin. I sprayed myself with Rive Gauche, his favorite perfume, and waited for my husband to return.

He didn't come home that night.

By mid Saturday morning, I rang his office. No one answered. In the afternoon I went to the hairdresser's. In the evening, I made dinner for us and waited.

He finally called Sunday morning. I began to cry when I heard his voice.

"I'm sorry, Rose."

"I don't want your apologies. Please Paul, just tell me."

"I can't."

"What do you want from me?"

"I don't know."

It was the most honest he'd ever been. I was about to say that I'd wait until he was ready, but to please give me a chance when he said, "Just make sure you give me a son, Rose."

His voice had turned cold. I froze.

"Did you hear me, Rose?"

I held the receiver away from me, gingerly, like a bloodied knife. I could hear him calling my name. In the background, a man's voice, not Paul's, rang out in laughter. I hung up. The phone did not ring again.

"What's the matter with you?" Teresa stood by my office door Monday morning, watching me day dream into space.

I busied myself, embarrassed.

"You're not pregnant, are you?" She winked suggestively, as if to say, of course she knew we Westernized young people did have sex before marriage.

I knew I couldn't be. "No," I responded curtly.

"Perhaps you should go see a Chinese doctor and get something to fortify you." With that she walked away.

Elliot called. "I promised, didn't I? Happy Monday."

I tried to sound serious and annoyed, but my heart danced at the sound of his voice. "You shouldn't do this, you know. Someone will catch on."

"Would you rather I sent flowers every week?"

"Oh please don't do that!"

He laughed at my alarm. "I will unless you see me." His voice dropped. "You kept me awake all weekend, you know."

"Stop that." I felt my body blush. I tried to turn my attention to something, anything on my desktop to distract me. It didn't work.

"You know, Rose, you don't have anything to worry about with me."

"What do you mean?"

"I've had a vasectomy. Call me when you're ready, okay? I can wait." And he rang off.

Miguel flashed and I blanched. I had to get a grip on myself. My world had just gone mad, and here I was, thinking about having an affair with a man ten years my senior, and a *gwailo* to boot. I saw Andrew's grin, heard the laugh in the background of Paul's phone call. Teresa's question loomed.

And then, a gong sounded in my head.

That time in college, I hadn't been pregnant by Paul. It had been Andrew's child, and somehow, Paul knew. It wasn't that he specifically knew about Andrew, but he knew there had been someone else. How stupid of me not to have realized. Paul and I only had sex in college that one time, and then I got pregnant so quickly afterwards. It must have been Andrew's. I counted off the timing. Yes, it had to have been Andrew's. Pretty dumb for a math minor not to have figured it out, but then emotions didn't always have a lot to do with reality. I believed it was Paul's child because that's what I wanted to believe.

Which also meant Paul knew I wasn't a virgin when we first made love.

His peculiar behavior began to make a little more sense now. If I'd stopped to think about things properly, I would have realized that my marriage was all about having children, because in Paul's world, the public image of a happy family life was paramount. Paul Sr.'s words about my husband's manhood took on a whole new meaning. And, if after the requisite time passed, and I didn't get pregnant, it meant . . .

The irony of all this of course was that when I had almost been pregnant with Andrew's child the second time, I had lied to Paul to make him marry me because I didn't want another abortion, and yet that time he never knew the difference.

How naive I was then.

Look at these boys from the Feds. There's a naiveté in their methodical investigation. Do they really think we'd leave anything truly incriminating in our files? Gordie's a scam artist extraordinaire; he could have been a lawyer. We started out legally as a DISC, a domestic international sales corporation, although since '85 after the tax laws changed, we've been a "FSC," a foreign sales corporation. All his doing. Gordie figured out that by incorporating abroad, we'd not only benefit tax-wise in the aircraft financing and leasing business, but Rent-A-Wing, Inc. became just that bit harder to trace. He's a bit like Colin Kenton, only worse, or perhaps more honest about his lack of scruples. But I'm being unfair. Kenton had scruples. His greatest sin was being a maverick in a straight laced world.

Gordie is all about bravado, but he has heart. If he weren't Gordie, I'd be in love with him. He makes me feel like I can do anything in the world, that the life I had wasn't my fault. In that, he's like Dad. He simply takes what life dishes out, sweeping away what he doesn't like, moving on with a hint of a smile on his face.

That's real freedom.

Look at Lady Liberty. Lady L, dressed to kill. Home of the brave. A little bravado took me a long way, didn't it?

Work was the one thing in my life I could be sure of. I went to KL several times over the next few months. It was a marvellous city, just as Aunt Helen had said, languid and peaceful yet seething with a kind of underground energy. The greenery there was wild and untamed, even in the city centre, such as it was. I liked the rawness of the place, so unlike Hong Kong, which was sometimes too civilized even for me. It was easier to relax in KL. Paul didn't seem to mind my travel; he encouraged it. And Marion said to all her friends that her daughter-in-law was exceptionally talented because at such a young age, she already had great responsibilities.

A half year passed. Paul did spend some time away from home, but never for more than one night at a time. We had sex regularly, at least four or five times a month. I still wasn't pregnant.

One evening at home, I got a call from a vaguely familiar voice.

"Mrs. Lie," he began in Cantonese. "Do you remember Cheung Man Yee? From your agency days?"

A minor kung fu and soap opera star who modelled for the orange drink commercial I handled. The teenage girl's heart throb. I wondered how he got my home number. "Yes, what can I do for you?"

"Has your husband been home much lately?"

I felt like he had broken into my home. Paul had recently removed some of his clothes; previously, he always came home to change. "What business is it of yours?"

"Don't need to get so testy. I'm just trying to do you a favor, you know, so that you won't have to worry about your husband. You know your duty as the first wife, don't you?" And then he laughed, a harsh laugh I recognized from the time before when Paul had called. He hung up before I could.

And that was the real beginning of my marriage, a good old fashioned Chinese marriage, complete with concubine. Paul lived in two homes now, and yet treated me as well as, if not better than before. Married in Hong Kong! To the world around me I should have been in heaven. Just before Christmas that year, Paul became a partner at Auden, Rose & Wang. From that time on, I got flowers once a month at my office, my white bouquet of orchids with the single red rose. And then slowly, the jewellery began to appear. If he spent an unduly long time away from me, I could count on an even more expensive piece.

Things were going along swimmingly, as Paul liked to say. My in-laws treated me well. Marion never undermined my position as mistress of my home. Yet she did nice things to make domestic life easier, like lending me her amah once a week to clean our flat. Oh, and our social calendar! Paul was a solicitor on the rise, and he socialized to ensure the continuation of that rise. We joined the right clubs, attended the right balls, worked for the right charities. My mother treated me with a new respect.

Elliot circled my orbit, waiting for me to relent, wooing me with his persistent but subtle charm, while I continued to hold my desire for him at bay.

And Paul even made love to me from time to time.

If I only had a part time husband, did it matter? After all, my feet were unbound, and I wasn't the concubine. An admirer in the background assured me I hadn't lost my feminine and sexual charms. And the possibility of a son still loomed — I didn't have to compete with the "concubine" on that score. In the history of Chinese womanhood, I already had it made.

Tell me Lady L, should I have asked for anything more? I never even got AIDS.

8

In April, Paul had to go to Singapore for two months to organize the opening of a new office for his firm. It was the first time he'd travelled anywhere else in Asia. As a child, he had been all over Europe with his family, but the Lies saw the rest of Asia as somewhat "primitive," as Marion would say.

We were at my parents for dinner. I hardly saw Paul at all during these days before he left, busy as he was with all his preparations, at least that was the way he put it. But he'd managed to come for one last visit with my parents. We were having hot pot, but I simply had no appetite.

"It's the only way to learn anything about a place," Paul was saying. "I've never understood how one can travel on business for only a few days at a time. What can you possibly accomplish?" It was a stab at me, although he would have denied it. I wondered what he'd say if I had to go away for as long.

Uncle Chong was not pleased. "You can't just go off and leave Rose alone! What kind of husband does that?"

"Now calm down, Chong," Helen began. "These two young people have their own lives to lead, and things are different these days. What's the matter, Rose? Why aren't you eating?"

Paul dropped a shrimp out of his wire net into my bowl. "Come on, Rose, have some shrimp."

I nibbled at it, politely protesting that I had had too large a lunch. Sensing my unease, my father turned the conversation to Paul's work, and I could eat in silence.

Earlier that day, a Saturday, Man Yee had called.

"You needn't think he's leaving me, you know. In fact, he's paid the rent for our flat for the next three months so that I wouldn't have to worry." He laughed harshly. "In fact, if things were different, he wouldn't be with you at all."

"I don't have anything to say to you. Don't call me."

"Don't call me," he mimicked. "Your *Heung Kong siuje,* 'little

136

Miss Hong Kong' attitude doesn't change the fact that you're nothing but a social climber. You better get pregnant soon, if you know what's good for you."

I slammed the receiver on him.

How his taunts upset me! They were usually late at night when Paul wasn't home. I assumed Paul was with him, and perhaps asleep, because Man Yee would whisper, his voice a nasty hiss. I dreaded his calls, each one of them taunting and spiteful. They were too insistent a reminder of my double life. But I'd never said a word about them to Paul.

". . . so Rose will come visit towards the end of my stay. It'll be better that way." Paul's voice brought me back to the dinner table.

I took my cue. "Yes, of course. That way he'll have completed his work, and we'll be able to have a bit of a holiday."

"You ought to go to Malaysia," Chong began.

Out of the blue, my mother suddenly asked, "Rose, are you sure you're not barren?"

At least, I thought, after the initial shock had subsided and the deafening silence around the dinner table was noticeable even to Mum, at least she hadn't asked if we were having intercourse.

Helen piped up quickly a minute later. "Is it true Regina's coming home to visit this year? That would be wonderful."

Paul was gripping my hand under the table, willing my self control in front of my relatives, reassuring me once again of his ability to extricate me from the crazy world of my mother.

"She hopes to," my father responded, deftly steering the conversation firmly in that direction.

For the rest of the evening, there was no repeat performance from Mum. Paul and I left early that night, and he was tender and full of sympathy. But the anger I felt was not just towards Mum, although a big part of it was directed towards her. I was angry too at Paul, at the fact that he escaped all censure even though the "fault" was more his than mine.

I made love to Paul that night, and he was strangely passionate. Our lovemaking lasted a long time. I remember that night because it was one of the rare times sex seemed something more than just a physical act which my husband also truly enjoyed. It was like the first time, in Plattsburgh, and it made me cry.

"She doesn't love me," I said, as we lay in bed holding hands.

He leaned over and wiped away my tears. "Don't cry anymore, Rose. Forget about her. You have me now."

I imagined him smiling in the dark as he repeated, "you have me now." Were we both remembering the first time he said that, when we were teenagers, and I'd told him how distant I felt from my mother? Mum and Regina had been all I talked about with him when we started dating. And Paul had counselled me, had comforted me as I cried about a pain I never knew I felt until I met him. Now, my unhappiness at the state of our marriage seemed trivial by comparison.

"I'll miss you, you know. This is it, Rose." He began our refrain from years ago, repeated often during our late night partings in the park by my home.

"This is it," I echoed.

"It's the real thing, isn't it?"

"No one else but you, Paul."

"We belong together, forever."

I wanted to hold on, wanted to believe. That night, I think he did too.

The next morning, I demanded Dad meet me.

"Please do something, Dad. She's really gone too far this time."

"It was wrong of her," he agreed.

My father and I were having coffee and breakfast at the Hong Kong Hotel coffee shop. He generally preferred eating Western food at restaurants, reserving his consumption of Asian foods for home. I watched him unravel his croissant, buttering small portions of it at a time and popping those into his mouth. There was a precision and meticulousness in everything he did, except when it came to my mother.

"She humiliated and hurt me. Why did she do that?"

"Calm down, Rose. You know she has no idea how much that affected you."

I knew. Of course I knew. My mother never knew what made a difference in my life. Why should now be any different? But that day, I wanted it to be different. I wanted to be able to show her how badly I felt.

So why was I talking to my father instead?

"Do you want to have children?"

"Of course!"

I was immediately sorry I snapped at him. My father looked at me in surprise. There was an awkward pause.

"Rose, are you happy? Is everything all right with Paul?"

"Yes." Too quickly.

He must have guessed I didn't want to discuss it, because he returned to the issue of my mother, "Rose, Rose. You've always been smart and level headed. Don't pay any attention to her. You know how she is."

I remained silent, tired as I was from crying for the greater part of the night before finally falling asleep. Even Paul's kindness hadn't been enough.

"You're upset, Rose. You're taking everything too personally. I know she was wrong, but you know she doesn't think before she talks. Regina takes after her."

"But Regina loves me." I surprised myself with that utterance. How could I imagine my mother not loving me?

This time, my father did not have anything to say. We finished breakfast in silence.

It was no use, I thought, as my father and I parted ways. I had declined his offer of a lift home, preferring to take the bus. How could I explain? What indeed was there to explain? Dad probably thought I wanted to wait to have children which should have been a reasonable enough excuse. But, on this score, Paul made it clear to everyone that "we" were ready to be parents. I wasn't nearly as sure.

I sat on the top deck of the bus as it rumbled along the streets of Tsimshatsui. Perhaps there was something wrong with me. But the abortion! That had been real. Regina holding me while I cried after it was over, that had been only too real. I was pregnant once, I wanted to yell at my parents, Paul's parents, everyone. It had to be Paul, possibly a low sperm count or some readily understandable explanation. He wouldn't even entertain the thought, not given his tendencies. He couldn't face himself, or me, if he proved to be even mildly infertile. So, no one would ever be sure, but the blame could fall on me, the woman, the way it did in all Chinese life. And who could argue with that?

But Andrew's child! It would have been a happy child, one who wouldn't be afraid of its life or feelings. A child who, like Andrew, could have shed its Hong Kong past for a life in America, the only place I could have raised it, where the pursuit of happiness was an inalienable, undeniable right. No love child perhaps, but a child of the easy joy I shared with Andrew. This realization made me simultaneously happy and sad. Was I happy, my father had asked. My life, the life I chose, the life I wanted, didn't have space for the idea of happiness. Its space was reserved for loving Paul.

That afternoon, Paul left for Singapore. I was a little sad to see him go. But what I mostly felt was relief that at least for awhile, I would have a reprieve from our life together.

"You've been avoiding me."

Elliot had cornered me at a Friday evening gallery opening of another of my aunt's friends. I had tried to get out of attending, knowing that Elliot would more than likely be there, knowing that the crowd would not be the usual advertising and media lot I knew so that I couldn't count on mingling as easily. But Helen had been especially insistent, because her friend desperately needed a crowd for the opening. So I consented.

"At least have dinner with me. We still can be friends, right?"

I was about to reply when Helen swooped down on us. "Come on you two, join us for dinner. We're headed down to the American in Wanchai." I must have made a face because she added, "Now Rose, it won't hurt to eat *gwailo* Chinese once in awhile. It's no worse than Chinese *gwailo* food after all. Besides, it's better than eating alone."

Elliot gave me a look that said, let's see you get out of this, knowing full well I couldn't say no to my aunt. He was right. Having commandeered travel arrangements — I was to go in the same taxi as Elliot and an American couple who didn't know the way — she sallied forth to usher everyone out.

As we shuffled along with the rest, he asked "Why were you going to be eating alone?"

"Paul's away."

"Oh, for how long?"

It was three weeks since he'd left for Singapore. "Originally for two months, although now it might be three."

He tugged gently at my arm, moving us apart momentarily from the exiting stream. The couple we were supposed to be taking waved at someone else they knew and the wife said they would go with them. I was going to try to find someone else to join us, but Elliot held me back and before I could stop him, he'd bundled us into a taxi by ourselves.

"You didn't tell me."

"It wasn't your business."

"Wasn't it, now?" He ran a finger down my arm, squeezed my hand and let it go. Sliding closer to me, he ran his lips lightly against my cheek and neck. I trembled and pulled away.

"Elliot, please don't."

He did not relinquish his position. "Don't you like it, Rose?"

Of course I did, but the noise in my head was too much to bear. Man Yee had called four times since Paul left, each time to gloat over the fact that Paul had called or sent him something. Paul had only called once, a few days ago, to say that he now might be staying another month.

I tensed up. Elliot pulled back.

"Okay, sorry. I know I shouldn't. Just friends?" He squeezed my hand with a smile. "Okay," I replied.

Dinner was sociable and light. There were about fifteen in our party. Elliot the raconteur entertained everyone with stories about disastrous gallery openings, including one in Kuala Lumpur where a careless guest set the prize painting, which was on rice paper, on fire while lighting his cigarette. As he talked, I was struck again by his familiarity with Asia. His experiences seemed to have taken him everywhere. He was sitting next to me and would try to catch my eye as he spoke. I could feel him drawing me back into his orbit. He kept my wine glass filled, and I found myself sipping more than I intended.

He was right: I had been avoiding him. Since the time in Sai Kung, I had turned down all offers to meet privately and took pains not to run into him accidentally at business cum social affairs I knew he'd be likely to attend. And any time I had, I'd quickly manoeuvred myself into a crowd to avoid being alone with him.

"So what's your connection to all this?" The wife of the

American couple next to me asked. They were the ones Helen had asked me to share a cab with.

"*Helen ge jahtneui,*" Elliot said, under his breath, just loud enough for me to hear.

"I'm Helen's niece," I replied.

"Oh, how nice." And then, indicating Elliot. "So are you two a couple?"

Helen heard her from across the table and laughed merrily. A hyena's laugh, as Mum described it. "Oh goodness no! My niece is a married lady."

Elliot grinned. Under the table, I felt his light tap against my foot. The conversation drifted to another topic.

After dinner, Elliot offered The Front Page, which was just down the road. The band was playing tonight, he said. I grimaced. It was a popular hangout for the expat crowd, just as the American Restaurant was.

"You young people go." My aunt gesticulated to about a third of the group who fell into that category. "It's time for this old lady to go home."

The farewell exodus took place on the street outside the restaurant. Tonight was all getting just a bit too *gwai* for me. This mixed crowd of *wah kiu* and westerners, a sort of *demi monde* of which I was a part, made me uncomfortable tonight. I wanted Paul back, and the safety of our almost-Chinese life, our acceptably Hong Kong life. As if he read my mind, Elliot said in a low voice, in Cantonese, "life has to have sour and sweet, yin and yang, right?" and I smiled, knowing again how comfortable he made me feel in my Hong Kong skin.

"You will come, won't you?" Elliot asked. The party had dwindled down to half a dozen or so, all westerners except for myself and Abdul, a Malaysian painter friend of Elliot's.

"Night's still young, lah." Abdul said. He spoke rapidly, like machine gun fire.

I was more relaxed now, the wine having taken effect. That morning, Teresa had announced she was pregnant with her second child. Shortly after that, Kenton popped by to ask what I thought the potential of Port Moresby was as a destination, to which I'd replied, "only if one wanted to be dinner," to which he'd shot back,

"Rose, don't be so narrow minded, headhunting's an old and respected tradition." In the afternoon, my ex- boss rang to say if ever I wanted my job at the agency back I could have it because he'd decided I was working for a madman, and didn't want my career to suffer. I gathered he and Kenton had had another of their disagreements, probably about money, despite their long and inextricable business relationship, the details of which it was better not to know.

"It's Friday night. Let's go, let's go." Abdul began down the road. Elliot looked at me. I followed.

The music was loud and the dance floor crowded. The raucous rock and blues sounds helped drown out the noise in my head. We danced. Elliot kept feeding me scotch. Again I was aware how little he himself drank, although he bought rounds for everyone. The band struck up a slow number, and Elliot pulled me close to him on the dance floor. I didn't resist.

"I still want you, Rose," he said into my ear. "I can't help it."

In answer, I rested my head on his shoulder. His arms around me were sensual, comforting. He danced us to a corner of the club, out of sight of our party. By the time we returned to our table, everyone else had left.

"Come on, I'm taking you home." I objected weakly, but was more than glad to slide into a taxi with him, into his arms, where his kisses and touch aroused me. We ended up against the wall on Sau Chuk Wan, although I resisted his attempt to walk me back. Before we parted, he slid two fingers into my bra, like he had the first time. "Remember. Anytime." By the time I arrived back home, it was past one in the morning.

The phone was ringing as I walked in.

"Oh Rose, thank goodness you're back." My father-in-law's voice snapped me out of my sensory daze. "It's Paul. I know it's late dear, but may I come over? Marion's dreadfully distraught."

"But . . ."

"I'll explain." And he rang off.

He arrived fifteen minutes later.

"Paul was almost arrested in Singapore."

I stared at him in shock.

"I've taken care of it. An old friend of mine at the British

Consulate intervened."

"What . . ."

"A minor. They found him with a boy last night in a brothel not far from Bugis Street. Marion's been absolutely ill. She had to take a pill to sleep tonight." And then, as I paled, he put his arm around me. "Poor Rose. You mustn't blame yourself. I know it's dreadfully rough on you, but there you are, it's just the way things are. It's the first time, though. With a boy, I mean."

I stood very still for a few minutes, and then I began to feel my body tremble, as if it were not my own physical self but something outside of me over which my control was limited. The whole evening with Elliot seemed like an awful cosmic joke. Paul Sr. held me in both his arms, hugging me while I felt myself convulsing, trying hard not to cry, but the tears came because nothing made sense anymore, and I felt like a pawn in some awful chess game played by Paul and his mother, with my mother cheering in the sidelines.

As my tears subsided, I was aware that my father-in-law was leading me to the sofa to sit down and calm myself. At first, I thought I was imagining things when I felt pressure on my breast and before I knew it Paul Sr. was pushing me down on the sofa and sliding his hand under my blouse and bra.

My father-in-law is a tall man. He is also a handsome man, with fine youthful features. His body is in excellent shape because he swims thirty Olympic laps every morning. And he has presence. No one would dare cross him.

Which is just my way of saying that he was quite a bit stronger than me. I bit his hand in anger.

He recoiled.

I slid off the sofa onto the floor. "I'll scream. Loud enough for your friend Dr. Ng next door to hear." I was shaking with anger, trying to control myself.

He became immediately contrite. "I'm sorry Rose. I couldn't help myself."

I stood up. He remained on the sofa, his head bowed. "You're a beautiful woman, Rose. I wish Paul appreciated you more. Please . . ."

"Please leave."

He got up and barely looked at me. "I'm sorry," he repeated. And then, "It would kill Marion." He waited, as if expecting my complicity.

I turned away. "Get out. Please."

He left, shutting the door quietly behind him.

I sat on the sofa and wept in shame.

The phone rang.

"You do make it hard for a man to sleep."

"Oh Elliot," and my tears were audible over the phone.

"Rose, what is it . . ."

"Please wait for me. I'll be right over."

That night, I became Elliot's lover. We made love till dawn. I told him about Paul's arrest, although I couldn't bring myself to tell him about what my father-in-law had done. In the morning, I finally fell asleep in his arms.

How pretty the lights over the East River are. Everything's so serene in the darkness. It's been over eight years since the first time Elliot and I made love. Women keep track of silly things like that. I wish he were here tonight, to listen to me, to love me the way he used to. Where are you now, Elliot Cohen?

But even Elliot's too long ago. What is it Gordie keeps telling me? That you can mistake neuroses for love? Looking back at my life, and the paths of love in my life, perhaps he's got something there.

"So what happens next?"

The reality of work on Monday made Elliot's late afternoon question seem almost incongruous. It was, as he'd said when I finally left his home on Saturday night, the only question we needed to answer. On Sunday, Marion rang to tell me to remain brave in the face of Paul's latest lapse. She was planning to speak to Paul, she said, because this time he'd gone too far. At the end of that call, she said I was a good daughter-in-law and was happy to know I was there for Paul. I contemplated the insanity of my life. Marion's steadfast resolve struck me as comical.

Teresa was signalling that Kenton wanted to see me.

"I have to go," I told him. "Can I answer that later?"

"Just as long as you do."

Work, I thought as I headed for Kenton's office, was infinitely easier to deal with than the people in my life.

My boss was more than mildly livid. Our chief pilot and financial man were also there. "They're trying to squeeze us out with their fucking fifth freedom argument," he was saying.

When I'd first come to work for him, Kenton kept his language clean. That lapsed quickly. His current irritation was the saga of cargo between Bangkok and Kuala Lumpur. Pacific American was giving us a hard time, because as an American carrier, their subsidiary Golden Phoenix didn't have the same rights. I had mixed feelings about it all, naturally, because Golden Phoenix was my father's livelihood.

"We're not talking about a lot of cargo," I offered.

"But it's the principle!" Kenton bellowed. "We got those rights from the Thais and Malaysians. What business is it of those goddamned Americans?"

Our chief pilot, an exceptionally calm American, took a deep breath. "Rose can put out a press release, boss. Make them look stupid. You know how to do that, right Rose?"

I nodded.

"Better yet, just spread the word around the agents that Pacific's about to lose their cargo rights. See how much they support Golden Phoenix then." Our finance man was a young, aggressive Hong Kong Cantonese who'd gone to the London School of Economics, and believed in fighting dirty.

Kenton had begun to calm down. The whole situation struck me as little more than a storm in a teacup. I'd learned, however, not to belittle these disturbances of men who seemed bent on giving themselves ulcers and high blood pressure, both of which Kenton had. We discussed the matter a few more minutes, and the meeting dispersed.

"Hold on a second, Rose," Kenton called after me. He shut the door and offered me a seat.

"Your dad's at Golden Phoenix, isn't he?"

"Yes he is." I wondered if he was questioning my loyalties. "We don't talk about these things, by the way."

He waved my comment aside. "I wasn't asking. He used to fly for CAT, didn't he, and before that the AVG?"

I nodded. "Yes, he did with CAT, and I've heard him mention the American Volunteer Group, but I don't really know much about it."

"Your father was in the Chinese-American Composite wing. We both flew under Claire Chennault."

"Chennault?" I felt ashamed of my ignorance, and wondered where this conversation was leading to.

"General Chennault. He's famous." Kenton looked at me with that slightly sympathetic air older people used to make the young feel even younger. My thoughts flew suddenly to Regina. How little she knew or cared about the world I inhabited, with all its crooked paths.

"He was part of the group that went to Arizona," Kenton continued.

"Arizona?"

"Yes, for pilot training. At Luke Airfield. With the original Flying Tigers, not the Civil Air Transport but China Air Transport. Did you know that?"

I shook my head. CAT was just CAT. I had never questioned the acronynm. Bits and pieces of conversations among my family surfaced in my brain. Kenton went on to tell me about the special breed of pilots who had trained at Luke, a mixed one of English, South Americans, Indians, even some Russians as well as Chinese. I tried to picture this life of my father's, the one he seldom talked about, but which I knew he cherished. A sudden recognition dawned — I now understood why my father kept that Flying Tigers model aircraft, which he'd been given by the marketing manager at the present day cargo airline, the one my mother called an ugly dust collecting "souvenir."

It was already past six. Kenton seldom stayed late, being an exceptionally early morning man. He was often in the office by seven or even six on occasions. But he seemed inclined to talk for some reason, so I sat there and continued to listen. He rambled on about the "Two Airlines Uprising" in Hong Kong in 1949 — "November I think it was, either the seventh or ninth. Quite a time, Rose. Thirteen planes flew back to China, and the rest went to Taiwan, to CAT's headquarters. Was your father one of those pilots?"

"I don't know." It bothered me that I knew so little about his life. In fact, as I thought about it, I realized I didn't even know what year my father had come to Hong Kong, or when he actually stopped flying, or, for that matter, who he would have been flying for around '49 if in fact he was still flying. It was all just family history, stuff I half knew because I'd heard it all my life, but hadn't questioned in any depth. Paul's comment about my family's friendliness towards Americans came back to me. A little nasty, perhaps, but at least Paul wondered, which was more than I or Regina or even my mother had done. Mum was equally ignorant, because whenever I asked her, she dismissed my questions with, "oh you know how your father is, never tells anyone anything." We did take Dad for granted, with Mum's main grumble being his gambling habit which, she claimed, kept our family short of funds.

"Well," he looked at his watch, "mustn't keep you. Give your father my regards the next time you talk to him."

Whether our private conference had anything to do with work, I couldn't fathom, but it had certainly calmed Kenton. Now, I was curious. "How well do you know him?"

Kenton smiled. "We were on the same mission to Burma. Ask him about the C-47 that almost crashed. He'll remember. By the way, you're a lot like him."

As I left his office, I thought about the ten thousand things that clamoured for attention in my head. If only the right pieces would fit. If only.

A couple weeks passed and I heard nothing from Paul. Man Yee hadn't called either. A kind of peace settled over me. Elliot called several times, asking to meet. I finally agreed, naming the piano bar at the Peninsula. It was unlikely we'd run into anyone I knew there on a Sunday night.

He was seated in a corner booth when I arrived. Elliot rose, and kissed my proffered cheek. I was about to sit opposite him, but he set me next to him in the booth.

"It's awfully good to see you," he said. "Scotch?"

I shook my head. "Lime soda. I think I ought to be around you sober for a change."

"So, you think me the result of over indulgence?" He put his arm round my shoulder. I shifted uneasily away.

"Don't. Someone might see us."

"Sorry."

We sat quietly until our drinks arrived.

"Well cheers." He raised his glass of red wine.

"What to?"

"Over indulgence."

I laughed. It was too easy being with Elliot.

"You haven't answered my question."

"Could be because I still don't know what's next."

He sighed. "You certainly know how to test my, uh, patience."

"I'm not trying to."

"Guess I know that too."

We lapsed into silence again.

"Elliot, I . . ."

"Rose, I . . ."

He kissed my lips, lightly, quickly. "Come on, my place. It'll be easier to talk there."

We left. My heart, I knew, had already begun to embrace him.

Now, I even had my lover. In Paul's absence, it would have been easy to over indulge. But it made more sense in my mind to discover Elliot slowly. Once he knew I would continue to see him again, he was in less of a hurry to arrange each meeting, although each time we made love, I knew he reached deeper inside me. Our relationship made me a little afraid, because it sometimes resembled the intimacy I had with Paul.

A month passed. Paul still hadn't made contact, except to send a message through his office confirming he was definitely staying a full three months. I never called his parents because I didn't want to speak to his father. Marion called several times; each call was friendly and inconsequential. We even had tea together once. She behaved as if nothing were wrong, as if her presence in my life could assure the continued reality of my marriage. I did not disabuse her of that notion.

Elliot and I met about five or six times. I made it a rule always to go home, no matter how long I'd stayed — we often made love till the early hours in those days. The comfort of sleeping in my own bed, even if only for an hour or so, was a necessary act. After all, my marriage wasn't quite two years old. I wasn't ready to give up on it yet.

I returned home one morning at five. There was an envelope under my door addressed in Chinese to "Paul's wife." The handwriting was unfamiliar.

"You shouldn't stay out so late. He'll find out you know, and then where would you be? We can't hurt Paul. He needs us."

I tore it up.

The next day, Paul called me at work. "Why don't you come to Singapore week after next? I'll take a few days off. Stay the weekend as well if you like." He was so ludicrously matter of fact that I found myself accepting what he said at face value.

"I'll try."

"Don't try, Rose. Come. I've missed you so much. Why didn't you call?"

He was turning things around on me again. Even after all that had happened, he still managed to make our life seem normal. Perhaps he was right; perhaps things were better this way.

"I'll be there," I said.

I saw Elliot a few nights later and told him. We had just sat down to a dinner he prepared at his place.

"You're going to go, just like that? On the strength of a two minute phone call?"

"I am married to him."

"But some explanation, Rose. Or at least an acknowledgement, if not an apology. My god, the man was almost arrested."

"He doesn't know I know."

He shook his head. "You're in a most bewildering marriage. I don't understand any of this at all."

"It's just the way things are." I continued to eat calmly. Somehow, his disbelief only served to reassure me that what I experienced was perfectly normal. There were pieces of my life I deliberately left out, like about Man Yee. "Besides, you're going to Kuala Lumpur, so what difference does it make?"

"You make our relationship sound dispensable."

It is, I almost said, but held my words in check. I was feeling callous; the sting of Man Yee's note made me cruel.

150

"Don't do this, Rose."

"Do what?"

"Shut me out."

"We hardly really know each other, Elliot."

He got up and put on Chopin's nocturne in E flat major. Its gentle beauty softened me, forced me to recall his words the last time we made love. This isn't just sex, you know, he'd told me. Words which made me cry, because I knew he meant it. We ate our dinner without speaking until the music ended.

"Don't I know you at least a little, Rose?"

I felt ashamed of my earlier manner. Elliot was kind. He really wasn't demanding anything of me except an acknowledgement of what we'd shared. "Yes, Elliot. You do." He kissed me then, and made love to me. With Elliot, I had no choice except to acknowledge the truth of my feelings.

When I landed in Singapore, it was pouring. The thunder and lightning overwhelmed my senses, putting to rest momentarily the confusion that plagued me all the way there. Paul looked calm, even happy. Who was he, I asked myself, as he kissed me in greeting.

As we stepped out of the airport, the rain stopped. "This happens a lot," he told me. "You get used to it. I guess you get used to anything." We got into a taxi and headed for his place.

Although I'd travelled to several places in Asia previously on account of my work, this was the first time I'd been to Singapore. The city's flat landscape reminded me a little of the long drive from Iowa to New York with Regina. The sea breezes cooled the otherwise sultry heat, as had the rains. I found the climate pleasant, less stifling than Hong Kong, which was at the onset of summer.

"How have you been, Rose?" There was real concern in his voice.

"Not great."

"It's been difficult, I know. I'm sorry about that. But it's almost over. I'll be back home soon."

"And you?"

"I get a little bored. There's not much to do after work."

So there would be no acknowledgement, that much was clear. How much or little did Paul think I knew? Being around him again, however, I slid back into the patterns that were familiar, comfortable. There didn't seem to be reason for too many words.

The next few days passed easily, in the fluid routine of our marital dance. We did not talk about his other home in Hong Kong, which I had by now worked out was somewhere in Kowloon City, near the airport. Whatever I felt about my relationship with Elliot was safely locked away, and there was no danger of my disclosing that secret. In retrospect now, I can't remember anything that happened during my visit to Singapore that was disruptive or difficult. Paul even was relaxed about lovemaking, being neither urgent nor furtive. If anything, I remember the sensation of being happily married, like any other normal couple, when the passage of days merged into a tableau of predictability.

The night before I was due to return, Paul asked if I'd ever heard of Bugis Street.

Here we go, I thought. "Isn't that the after hours night life street?" I feigned an innocence he expected of me.

"Sort of."

"What about it?"

"We can go there if you like."

I knew where he was headed. "Do you think I'll like it?"

"It might be good for your education."

Education be damned. Of course I was curious, and if my husband had been a different man, I would have readily agreed, would even have suggested it. Bugis Street set Singapore apart from Hong Kong, being an anomalous expression of another kind of life. It was a life I once would have thought had nothing to do with me.

So we went, and from our assumed perch as tourists we could gawk and pretend the parade of transvestites was all just an oddity to view for amusement. Certainly, the other tourists around us carried on that way. But as we sat there sipping our drinks, I was keenly aware that Paul was trying to speak to me, and that this was the only way he knew how. Taking me to Bugis Street was to expose me to another side of humanity, a side to which I believe he felt he belonged. He could not admit to me he was different — abnormal I think he would have called himself back then. Yet he wanted me to understand that whatever that difference was was normal for him, and that loving him as I did meant coming to terms with that difference. It was what he was trying to do, and he wanted me to be a part of it. Of that I was sure.

The array of colorful costumes and artful makeup of the men assailed me. They pranced, they posed, they pouted and simpered. A part of me wanted to revile them, or laugh at them. Anything to separate myself from that which I couldn't understand, because I could not accept what was happening to my marriage and life. Yet was it really so difficult to accept that this was when these men came alive, when they really became who they were born to be? And, suddenly, my heart wept and smiled for them. My connection to Paul was a bit like the connection to Kenton that I'd recently discovered — somewhat inevitable and not entirely within my control. And that in time, perhaps, the meaning of these destinies would emerge.

I would remember the night on Bugis Street for a long time to come. It was how we celebrated our second wedding anniversary.

9

August. Paul's impending return loomed. His stay in Singapore had extended over three months.

"Summer's lease." Elliot mixed me my second Long Island iced tea.

"What was that?"

"Shakespeare. And summer's lease hath all too short a date."

He recited the complete sonnet, rubbing a cube of ice gently round my stomach as he spoke. The words floated towards me from a long time ago, a vague recollection of literature class in secondary school when I had to memorize the sonnet. Now, as he spoke the lines, "eternal lines," their meaning penetrated in a way they never had done during my school days.

We were on a borrowed boat, late on a Friday afternoon, the eve of Paul's return. Elliot had an endless source of friends and acquaintances who were good for access to free transport and lodging of one sort or another. Plane tickets and hotel rooms, flats and houses all over Asia, cars, motorcycles, boats of every size and description, with or without crew. This was the latter, a mid sized one he could operate himself. This occasionally struck me as rather odd, and I wondered what he'd done either to ingratiate himself with or impose himself on all these people.

Out of sight from anyone — the sea around us was deserted — I experienced an exhilarating sense of freedom.

"So you're saying it's over?" I asked when he'd finished his recitation.

"Is it?"

"I hadn't thought about it."

He shoved the ice cube into my bikini bottom. "There. See how you like that."

I jumped up from where I was lying, knocking over my drink in the process. "Hey! Cut that out."

He pulled out the cube, which was already half its original size.

"You deserved it."

It was true that I'd avoided thinking about Elliot and me since returning from Singapore. A seemingly insatiable appetite for him consumed me, and we spent many nights together. My notion of discovering him slowly had vanished. Around Elliot, I sometimes felt afraid he was going to disappear forever.

Earlier that week, after another frantic bout of lovemaking, he had said, "I'm still going to be here for a long time, you know."

Now, lulled by the sun and waves, lightly intoxicated by the mixture of white spirits, I pulled Elliot's arms around me, more from a need for his tangible presence than from desire.

"You're like a Lolita, playing with me."

"I wish you'd quit with all these literary allusions. Save them for someone like Regina. They're lost on me."

He pinched me playfully. "I'm educating you."

I wouldn't admit it to him, but I did learn a lot from Elliot. He knew an incredible amount about music, art and literature, both Chinese and Western. And his library of books astounded me by its variety. Yet it was his photographic memory of everything you ever wanted to know about anything that impressed me most. Elliot could quote whole passages from books or dialogue from movies at any given moment, or sing both melody and harmony from the middle of the second movement of an obscure concerto or symphony. He claimed he couldn't draw, which prevented him from accurately depicting the visual arts. But he could describe in minute detail any painting or statue he'd ever seen until you could visualize it in your mind's eye. He warned me not to be too impressed, calling this ability nothing more than a "party trick" he happened to be born with. But I admired it nonetheless, because it allowed him to remember, and therefore know infinitely more than the average person.

We went below deck to shower and change.

"You're turning black," he said, as he soaped my back.

"Pigmentation."

"What will Paul say?"

"He won't care."

Elliot bit my neck. "What would he say if he knew about me?"

"He'd kill me." It had slipped out.

"Figuratively you mean." He rinsed the soap off.

"Literally."

"You sound serious."

"I am."

Was I, I wondered, as we headed back to the mainland. On the radio, the currently popular tune about summer days and night from "Grease" was playing. There was a suppressed anger in Paul. But, having glimpsed it, its power was ingrained on my consciousness.

We arrived back at the pier in Tsimshatsui. I was glad I lived in Kowloon, because there was less chance of running into people that we mutually knew on that side of the harbor, except perhaps my aunt.

"So when do I see you again?"

"I don't know. I'll call."

"Will you, Rose?"

"Of course I will."

He had helped me onto land, and was preparing to take the boat back to the Yacht Club where his friend kept it. "Truth in lies on a summer's night."

"Where's that from?"

"Nowhere. Just something someone once said. See you, Rose."

I watched him pull away from the pier. "See you."

The boat headed back across the harbor. A few minutes later, I walked over to the terminus and boarded my bus for home.

"See, Mum, I'm not the only one who's got a tan."

My mother examined Paul. He had gotten darker from living in Singapore. It suited him and made me think about his South African origins.

"Oh Auntie, you can't imagine how Singapore . . ." He and my mother were off, jabbering away.

The experience had improved Paul. He was relaxed and happy to be back. He asked to visit my parents, and even wanted to go see Aunt Helen and Uncle Chong. My fears that a new strain would divide us had not proven the case. It was good to have my husband back.

"They sound like Chong." He meant the way Singaporeans

156

spoke. "Even a little bit like you, auntie."

It had been awhile since Paul had quite so much to say to my parents. Now, he appeared to view my family in a new way. He had learned something about South East Asia, which helped him make sense of my family's background. Whenever I tried to explain my ancestry to him before, he would ask me questions about Indonesian and South East Asian history I couldn't answer, and dismiss what I did know, the impressions and pieces gathered in my mind which I'd mentally combine into a whole. His tenure in Singapore apparently had given him at least some of the answers he needed.

Over dinner, Paul remarked, "By the way, that friend of your aunt's, Elliot Cohen who publishes some magazine, is quite well known in Singapore."

I tried to sound casual. "Oh really?"

"Who's this?" My mother wanted to know. "Someone you know, Rose?"

"Business acquaintance. He knows Helen and Chong."

"Actually," Paul continued, "he's better known in Kuala Lumpur. His wife is a famous actress, and he's kind of a patron of the arts, especially music, around those parts."

"Is something wrong, Rose?" My father knew me too well. He could pick up even the most subtle change in me, the slightest nuance of agitation or discomfort.

"Oh, it's nothing. Something's gotten into my eye," I lied. Pretending to rub away a cinder, I carried on talking a little too fast. "How did you hear all this, Paul?"

"Oh, from Albert Ho. He came to visit me several times in Singapore, and knows a lot of people." Paul spoke matter of factly, but I saw his glance and knew that he'd registered the nervousness in my voice.

My mother then began asking whether or not Paul would have to return to Singapore, and the subject was dropped.

Later, back at home, I asked Paul about Albert's visit. All the time, I had worried about Man Yee, that Paul in fact would bring him to Singapore. I had been dead wrong.

"You don't understand, do you?" Paul read my mind.

"Should I?"

157

"It's a friendship, nothing more."

And what about Man Yee, I wanted to ask, but I kept my counsel. I didn't want Paul to recall my manner earlier and ask me about Elliot. He would have; he used weakness and uncertainty in others to his advantage.

But Paul's mind was on Albert. "He helps me, Rose. Trust me when I say that. One day you'll understand. Just understand one thing about us: I love you; Rose, we belong together."

He took me in his arms, and Elliot ceased to exist for the moment. In the weeks that followed, our life seemed normal again, and I found myself talking to Paul, telling him about the little exigencies of life that any wife could share with her husband. It seemed to me he wanted to listen, to know me somehow in a new way, as he had done with my family.

Nothing really changed, though. Except for Thursdays.

Thursday nights, by some tacit arrangement, became Paul's nights with Man Yee. He never admitted this, but I knew. Paul would still go out, usually with Albert, whom I began to realize was nothing more than a platonic friend who shared some of Paul's dilemma, as I came to think of it. Occasionally, he'd disappear on Mondays as well, especially if we'd made love on the weekends.

How easily that pattern asserted itself! It wove its way into our lives like some invisible thread, tightening us into our web. What had changed was that a kind of contentment settled over me that didn't demand or insist on Paul's presence. After all, everything was quiet and discreet. Man Yee's phone calls stopped, which was a relief. Paul did not say or do anything to hurt me. If anything, he became an even more attentive and doting husband, doing family things with me without complaint. And the unexpected disappearances stopped. In this ordered fashion, life could go on.

In the months that followed, I did not call Elliot. At first, he would call, and each time he reached me, I'd cut short the conversation, pretending I had to run into a meeting. After awhile, he'd leave messages with Teresa. I didn't return those calls.

The Feds look like they're maybe about to quit. Gordie's rolling his eyes. No such luck. What is it with these guys? Do they think I'm going to duck, that if I'm in my office they can keep an eye on me?

When I first told Gordie the whole story about Paul, Man Yee, Elliot and me, he didn't roll his eyes. All he did was listen quietly. At the end of it, he started to kiss me but stopped, and said, quite solemnly, I wish you really had been my picture bride.

Time for another scotch.

On New Year's eve, we ran into Man Yee at a party. It was at the home of my ex-boss, a large flat on the south side of the island where many expatriates lived. I had thought about not going, afraid mostly that I'd run into Elliot. Paul happened to see the invitation card, and, to my surprise, offered to go with me. He definitely was trying to fit into my life, and so I said we'd go.

Paul was talking to some people out on the verandah when Man Yee arrived.

It was a grand entrance. He was dressed in half drag, by which I mean he didn't hide the fact of his maleness. His face was made up, and he wore a glittering space-age suit studded with sequins, tightly cut to fit his slender figure. Around his shoulders was slung a fake fur. He tottered on high heeled evening shoes. His hands were covered in white gloves that went up past his elbows, and he waved around a long cigarette holder, its glowing tip like some star on a wand. People applauded.

He sauntered right past me and went straight for Paul.

"You!" He pointed his cigarette holder at him. People turned to stare. Paul's face froze in shock and he went pale. Man Yee began to laugh harshly. Then, he turned his body in a sultry, seductive motion, removing the fur like a stripper, and declared to the crowd, *"Leang jai!"* Everyone laughed. To the party, it was just one big joke.

I was bothered, but remained cool. After all, Man Yee's outrageous behavior was well known. Paul looked so shaken I suspected he didn't know. He saw me coming towards him. There was a guilty, furtive look in his eyes. He broke away from the people he had been talking to and met me halfway.

"Quite funny, wasn't it?" he began. He was going to brazen this out too.

"I suppose."

His eyes darted round the room, in search of Man Yee. His attention was scattered, unfocused.

"So have you had enough of this party?" I asked.

"Oh, would you like to go home?" Solicitous, concerned.

"Perhaps."

"Well, it's all right if you want to go first." His whole person was distracted by Man Yee, who was flirting with several people, men and women alike. His manner irritated me.

The music was loud. I followed Paul's gaze. With a determined movement, I headed straight for Man Yee, took his hand and danced him into the middle of the floor. Once he realized who I was, he threw his head back and laughed stridently. But we danced, performed actually, for the entire party. Paul looked decidedly distraught. But I didn't care. This was my world; I knew what I could get away with. He had controlled me long enough, and this was a small piece of revenge.

Soon, everyone was dancing. In the confusion, Man Yee had whirled away from me. I spun round, wondering if Paul would have the guts to join me. Instead, I found myself dancing with Elliot. He took my hand and wouldn't let go. Paul was nowhere to be seen.

The sound of midnight. Elliot pulled me roughly towards him and kissed me hard on the mouth. His tongue tasted of booze. "See you, stranger," he said as he let me go. I went in search of Paul. In the half darkness, I could make out Man Yee and Paul talking excitedly together near the door. Paul was trying to get Man Yee to leave with him. Man Yee was doing his best to make a scene, which Paul was trying to prevent. I saw my husband open the door and shove his lover roughly out. He never once turned back to look for me.

On the dance floor, I saw Elliot with his arms around a tall blonde, a model. He led her towards the verandah and began kissing her. I felt someone's hand on my waist; it was Abdul, Elliot's friend, and his hand began wandering near my breast. I shoved it roughly away and went out the door. Our car was gone.

I spent New Year's day, 1979, alone. After that, Paul began staying away from home as often as three or four nights a week, and even occasionally on weekends. I started travelling all the time, to Kenton's delight. It was one way to make life bearable.

In spring of that year, Pan Asian opened a new route to Port Moresby — one flight a week. I was finally convinced I worked for a madman.

Dad hadn't been able to stop laughing when I told him about it. "Papua New Guinea? Who's going to fly there?"

"Headhunters?" I ventured, at which he burst out laughing even more.

"Why would headhunters go there?" Mum was still trying to figure out where Papua was.

"To — hunt — heads." Dad and I said together, and carried on laughing.

Paul came to her rescue. "Oh don't mind them, auntie. They like to have their joke. Anyway, Rose won't find it so funny anymore when she has to go there and the cannibals come after her."

"Cannibals?" The look of horror on my mother's face was priceless and I cracked up again.

We were at my parents for dinner, our monthly visit. Paul and I carried on as if our marriage were perfectly fine. And, in some ways, we were fine. We ate breakfast together when our paths crossed, because we were both early morning people. He talked about his work and family, and I did likewise. We still shared a bedroom.

So I was a little surprised later that evening at home when Paul said, "Why do you and your dad always make fun of your mother?"

"Because she's stupid." It slipped out before I could stop myself.

"Such childish hostility, Rose. You surprise me."

"Do I? Perhaps I should, more often."

"Don't I surprise you anymore, Rose?"

I was behind the shoji screen in our bedroom, changing into my nightdress. His tone of voice, especially the way he said my name, was almost affectionate, something I hadn't heard in awhile.

"You needn't always change behind that screen, you know."

I didn't move. "It was your idea." He had brought it home one day, set it up and told me he'd prefer me not to be "prancing around naked."

"Women aren't the only ones allowed to change their minds." He gently pulled aside the screen, revealing me in my half dressed state.

Paul stood there, chest bare, pants unzipped, in a state of arousal, a look of pleading softness on his face. I had instinctively covered myself with my nightdress. He took it away. "You're my wife, Rose. I love you," he whispered, touching my breast.

Miguel and Regina came back in a flash and I pushed Paul away, more roughly than I intended. His face turned cold and angry.

"Damn you, Rose," was the last thing he said as he left that night.

I sat in bed in a cold rage for hours. A wonderful way to spend a Friday night. It had been weeks since we'd made love, longer even since he'd shown me any real kindness. How dare he want me only when it suited him. But my anger at Paul quickly dissipated. This wasn't about him, or what he did to me. It was about who I was, about my own silent anger at Mum and Regina, which I lacked the will to confront. And all because I wanted to maintain the status quo, wanted to go on with life in my cowardly fashion, wanted to avoid consequences of any actions for which I would be held accountable.

The truth of my marriage was that Paul still loved me, regardless of who he was, and this was his way of showing it. Did I love him? Perhaps I did, but I wanted that love on my own terms, or perhaps, unexpectedly, I was beginning to fall out of love with him? The thought frightened me — I couldn't imagine life without loving Paul.

I lay awake for hours until sleep came at last, suspending for a time the unfulfilled desire his brief touch had aroused.

He wasn't there the next morning. I packed quickly and left for Kuala Lumpur, a day earlier than planned. On board my flight, Elliot was assigned to the window seat beside me. He stood in the aisle.

"Do you mind? Or would you rather I switched seats?"

I didn't budge. "That depends."

"On what?"

"On whether or not you set this up."

"What do you think?" He lay his hand on my armrest and leaned towards me. His hand brushed mine. A shot of static. "Of course I did."

"In that case, sit down."

We didn't speak for a long while. Airborne, Elliot finally said, "You're a strange one, Rose."

"Am I?"

He leaned towards me. "What are you afraid of?"

I didn't answer him, didn't even turn to face him.

"I've thought about you, hoping you'd call."

"And when I didn't?"

"I still hoped."

"Optimist."

"No, realist. You know it makes no sense, what you're doing to yourself, that is."

"And what's that?"

"I'm not sure, but it's dreadfully self destructive. Life isn't about appearances."

The flight attendant trundled a drinks tray next to me.

I glanced at him. "Should we get absolutely smashed?"

"You can. I have no intention of doing any such thing."

I asked for a glass of wine and stopped talking to him after that. It had been a shock seeing him, and a part of me wanted to pour out everything to him the way I had the first time. But he was annoyed at me, which I understood. So why had he manoeuvred to sit next to me?

Elliot was reading a book. I sneaked a glance at the cover. Blake. I vaguely remembered seeing a couple of volumes of his poetry in Regina's collection of literature, but couldn't recall any specific poems. I tried to ignore him, pretending I didn't care that he was ignoring me. In truth, I was infuriated. I turned my head away and scanned the cabin pointlessly.

"Okay, you can stop sulking," he said to the back of my head.

I tried to suppress a smile. "You're presumptuous," but I did turn back to face him.

"And you can stop pretending you don't want to . . ." He was leaning over as he spoke.

"Fuck you?"

The friendliness in his expression vanished. "Well if that's the way you want to be." He reopened his book, and didn't say another word the rest of the flight.

I was sorry for my rudeness, but all of me was tightly wound that

163

day. I could have changed the tension with a few simple, civil words, but I was angry at civility, and the way it wreaked havoc in my life. At this very moment, Paul might be buggering some boy for all I knew, or, at any rate, Man Yee. And all it would take was an apology from him for me to love him again.

I closed my eyes and dozed off. In my dream, Paul and I were making love in the rain. In the distance, the lighthouse glowed where Regina watched me through a storm. When I looked at Paul's face after it was over, he turned into Elliot.

"Of course I didn't." Elliot's whisper, as he lightly kissed my earlobe, woke me. "We're almost there."

I rubbed my eyes. "Didn't what?"

"You wake up fast."

I sought my reprieve by going to the toilet. When I returned, Elliot was holding a white rose and staring out the window.

"Didn't set this up," he said as I sat down and buckled my seat belt. "Our seating arrangement was pure coincidence. I didn't know you were going to KL. Here," handing me the rose, "it's the best I could do at short notice."

I took it. "I'm sorry about earlier."

"I don't accept apologies. Just invitations."

"To what?"

"Piano recitals. By a talented Malaysian girl giving a performance tonight, courtesy of her teacher whom I know well. Chopin. And a little Lizst. Want to tag along?"

I didn't reply.

"Come on," he coaxed. "You're not doing anything, anyway."

I was about to protest, but the grin on his face and the mischief in his voice made me smile. His eyes were laughing at my unspoken protest, a pretence in any event, because when Elliot looked at me, he only saw the truth.

In the afternoon, the shadow of the Equatorial Hotel fell over the swimming pool. I lay in its shade, the tropical heat lulling me into the comfort zone. My latest copy of the *Harvard Business Review* sat, unread, on the table beside me. Kenton had objected when I'd asked for a subscription, but agreed in the end, remarking that Harvard wasn't where you learned how to do deals. I retorted that it didn't hurt to raise standards from time to time.

The water in the pool had been surprisingly cool.

Elliot had promised to pick me up "after dinner at 8:30." I had half hoped he would have dinner with me. He had shot out of the airport without telling me where he was staying. But, then, there was no reason he should have.

A little girl with curly blond hair ran around the poolside and stopped next to me.

"Hello," she said. "What's your name?"

"Rose."

She had one of those angelic faces that seemed almost surreal in its sweetness.

"My father's over there." She pointed to the opposite side of the pool. I looked up and saw a tall blond man standing on the diving board. He waved to his daughter.

She pressed her fingernails into my flesh, startling me into sitting up. "I'm going to live in Malaysia, but my mother doesn't want to come." Her English was faintly European. I couldn't place the accent. "Where are you from?"

"Hong Kong."

There was a loud splash, and her father's form emerged, shooting straight out of the water like some violent aquatic creature.

"Goodbye, Hong Kong Rose." She gazed at her father swimming back towards the diving board end. "My father told me not to talk to strangers."

I watched her run away, two of her fingernail marks still visible on my arm.

At dinner in the hotel restaurant that evening, I saw them again. The father stopped at my table and smiled. But the little girl looked blankly at me as if she'd never seen me before.

He prompted his daughter. "Kristin, say hello to your friend."

She turned her face against his leg and hid.

"You must forgive her. She sometimes has attacks of shyness." His accent was distinctly Scandinavian. He glanced at the single setting. "Are you alone? May we join you?"

It was almost eight. "I do have to leave soon, but you're welcome to sit with me for a few minutes if you like."

He was blond in the extreme, much like his daughter, with a tanned, healthy complexion. He looked like an athlete. Kristin, who had just turned five, sat quietly in her chair. His name was Lars, and he was an engineer for an oil company. As I listened to him talk about himself, I couldn't help watching Kristin. There was something beautifully fragile about her. She sipped her Coke and never said a word.

"And do you come to Kuala Lumpur often?" Lars was saying.

"I , oh . . . ." because Elliot was standing at the doorway of the restaurant and had just caught my eye. I looked at my watch. He was five minutes early. I signalled for him to wait and stood up.

Lars turned towards the door. "Is it time for you to leave already? What a pity. Well, perhaps you'll have dinner with us one evening while you're here."

I fumbled in my purse for some money. "I apologize for dashing off, but I do have an appointment."

"Let me," he said, covering my hand over my purse. "I enjoyed talking to you."

I tried to wave goodbye to Kristin, and she gave me a slight nod. Elliot looked amused. "I see you've adopted a family."

"It's a habit I have when I travel. Breaks up the monotony," I retorted, more sharply than I intended. I led the way through the lobby to the taxi rank.

"And are the fathers always candidates for the centrefold of *Playgirl?*"

"Just get a taxi."

"Yessir, I mean, m'am!"

On the way over, Elliot took my hand and squeezed it. I smiled at him. He lip synced — *peng you?* friend? — at me and I felt like embracing his hand with my lips. He drew me closer to him and put his arm around my shoulders. "Okay?" he asked. I leaned my face into his shoulder, my body remembering the times we'd made love.

The music teacher's house had a sprawling living room with a cool marble floor. There was a huge, imposing abstract metal sculpture placed slightly off centre, and several large paintings, which reminded me a little of Regina's, hung on the walls. Trees

166

proliferated in a green jungle outside the French windows at the west end of the room where the piano stood.

There were over fifty people, including a couple of government officials from the ministry of art and culture. Several of the women were in sarong. Elliot tried to find our hostess, but we were ushered to our seats in readiness for the recital before he could. Standing near the piano was a young Malay girl, about thirteen, with a crooked mouth and a scar on her left cheek. As the seated crowd went silent, she walked awkwardly to the piano and sat down. On her skinny, gangling frame, the pretty green dress, no doubt sewn especially for the occasion, did nothing to flatter her.

I felt a little sorry for her as she raised her hands above the keyboard.

And then, for the first time in my life, I witnessed an artistic transformation.

She opened with Chopin's fourth prelude, a haunting minor piece I had studied as a child in the days of forced piano lessons. The steady rhythm of her left hand hypnotized me as she coaxed the melody out of the keys with her right. As I listened and watched her, she seemed to become someone or something excruciatingly beautiful and exalted. It was frightening.

The feeling did not leave me as she continued to play my favorite nocturne, the eerie one in E flat minor. She closed with a short piece by Lizst. When her recital was over, I felt a tug on my hand. Elliot was trying to release his fingers from mine to applaud. It was only then I realized I had been gripping his hand throughout the entire performance.

In the burst of applause that followed, she turned into an ugly duckling again, curtsied and literally ran out of the room.

"Amazing, isn't she?" Elliot's voice brought me out of the clouds. "I've only heard her once before and she almost made me cry."

"Thank you for bringing me."

"Is Regina anything like this?"

His mention of my sister surprised me. "As a poet, you mean, or a painter?"

He escorted me towards a table where a colorful array of fruit juices sat in punch bowls of scooped out watermelon shells. "I mean, is she an artist? Like Leanna's prodigy?"

167

"You must be Rose, I'm so delighted you could come." A striking Chinese woman in a sarong held her hand out to me. I thought she looked vaguely familiar, like a face from a movie or a glossy photograph. "I'm Leanna, the music teacher."

Elliot leaned over and kissed her cheek. "Darling Leanna. You look wonderful. Rose, I'd like you to meet Leanna Ong."

She addressed me. "So what did you think of my pupil?"

"Brilliant."

"Are you very fond of music?"

Her question gave me pause. I rarely thought about music, or any other art form, on its own merits. And yet here I was, in a home that breathed art, confronted by its glare. Elliot, who played Rachmaninoff when we made love, was thrusting me into a new way of looking at the world.

"I suppose," I replied slowly, "that you might say I am becoming increasingly fond of it."

"So is Regina?" he asked as we headed back to the Equatorial.

It was unnerving, the way our conversations stopped and started. What was more unnerving was the way we managed to follow each other's train of thought.

"Yes, I think so."

"At which?"

"Both painting and poetry, I think. Oh I'm not sure. I don't know anything about art!" He had touched a chord the way Regina used to when she exalted.

"Of course you do." He pushed away a strand of hair which I'd been chewing.

"Ouch." I frowned.

"Sorry, but I'll feed you if you're hungry."

The night air was humid but comfortable as we stepped out of the taxi. Elliot had instructed the driver to wait. There was a strange tension between us.

I didn't know what I wanted from him.

"Nightcap?" We both said at once, and then we laughed and the tension eased.

He paid off the taxi and we headed for the lobby bar. It was crowded but we found a corner.

"Do you remember the first time?" He sat opposite me, playing with his stirrer. He didn't look at me.

"Some of it I want to forget."

"I understand."

We both fidgeted with our stirrers.

"Rose, I . . ."

"Elliot, I . . ."

He spoke first. "I'd be patient. I'd wait till you were ready to give him up."

"I don't know if that's possible. I have to admit I've thought about divorce lately. Still, a divorce isn't the same as giving him up." It had slipped out so easily to Elliot, this thought I had harbored for weeks. Till this moment, I hadn't told a soul.

"Then I'd wait a very long time."

"Why though? It's pretty obvious I don't really have the courage for . . . this, whatever 'this' is."

He looked me in the eye. "Simple. You might be love."

"That's almost frightening."

"'And mutual fear brings peace' . . . "

He was about to tell me, but I intercepted with a guess. "Blake?"

"I'm impressed."

"Don't be. I'm uneducated, but good at sneaking peeks at book covers."

He laughed.

"Now will you tell me how you got that rose on the plane?"

"I'm good at sneaking into first class and pinching things off half-finished trays."

It was so easy being with Elliot right then that I wondered how I could have shunted him aside for Paul. The first night, I had shown up on his doorstep after Paul Sr. and literally collapsed into tears in his flat. And he'd been kind and gentle, never passing judgment on my life.

Watching him now, laughing and talking, the earlier tension dissipated, I suddenly understood the bond between us. We both had faith in the possibility of love.

And before I knew it, the night was over and he was walking me to the elevator. My body trembled inside, but I didn't know whether or not I dared restart what we had. He touched my cheek with his finger and lightly kissed my lips. "Good night my love," he said and I shuddered as I entered the elevator, alone, because part of Elliot's appeal was the way he conjured up Paul.

"He wasn't your husband, that man last night?"

Lars and Kristin were next to me by the pool late Sunday morning. I had been sunbathing and sipping a cold mango juice when they came along and joined me. His inquiry was accompanied by a pointed stare at my ring finger.

"No, he wasn't."

"Your husband isn't here with you?"

"No."

He began rubbing sun tan lotion over himself and his daughter. It struck me how gentle he was with her, despite his own strength. I remembered my kung fu friends from college, the way power and energy seemed to ripple through their bodies. Lars' body was like that.

"So was your friend last night from Kuala Lumpur?"

"No he's from Hong Kong too."

He had one of those irritatingly blank expressions, and I couldn't make out his meaning. I felt like telling him he was being too inquisitive, almost rude, but his manner was unnervingly polite.

"So will you meet him today?"

I hesitated. The problem was, I didn't know. A bellhop bearing a ringing placard with my name came by, which spared me from answering. I went to answer my phone call.

"Sun creature. How are you this morning?" Elliot's voice had a reassuring effect on me.

"Basking."

"Is Mr. America around?"

Jealousy definitely had its appeal. "Try Danish."

"No thanks, I've had breakfast."

"Your loss."

"Aha. Maybe it's about time we had lunch again."

"Maybe."

"The problem is, well you see, I'm a guest."

I waited, wondering what this was about.

"Leanna's guest."

"I see."

"It's not what you think. She's a, uh, sort of family friend."

"You don't have to explain anything to me," but it was blurted out rather too hurriedly, my disappointment, I was sure, evident. I remembered Paul's passing comment about Elliot's wife. Surely, he wouldn't have been so crass . . . surely Leanna . . .

"But . . . damnit Rose, you make it hard for a man to sleep."

Now, my voice smiled. "Some like it hard."

There was the briefest pause. "Game plan?"

"Thursday nights in Hong Kong. Perhaps."

"Then I shall call you each and every Thursday morning until you say yes."

I returned to my poolside seat, feeling slightly giddy. Lars was dropping Kristin in the water and catching her as she came up. She was giggling in between her spluttering, and I heard squeals in a foreign language. He left her to paddle around in the shallow end, having firmly tied her buoy wings on.

"It was your friend?"

"Yes."

"You will see him?"

"I really don't understand why you're so interested?"

"Forgive me. I wanted to ask you to join us this afternoon to go around Kuala Lumpur. You see, Kristin keeps talking about her 'Hong Kong lady friend'. I don't mean to impose, but she seems to like you."

Now it was my turn to glance at his ring finger, which was bare. The evenness of the tan told me he either never wore a ring, or had removed it awhile ago. "Isn't your wife with you?"

"Oh no. You see, she died last year of a brain tumor."

And then Kristin's strange behavior began to make sense. Lars smiled into my silence. "It's okay. I've made peace with death. Now, I try to help Kristin understand."

Kristin has grown into a well adjusted teenage girl. She still calls me her Hong Kong Rose. I am fond of her and her father. Lars has since remarried, and remains a good friend. Had things been different, maybe I could have married a man like him instead of making the life I have for myself. At least friends remain, if love does not.

Or perhaps, as Gordie tries to tell me, love can come into my life in a new way now. That the sexual "discoloration" surrounding love in my life no longer needs its intense pigmentation. Funny, but it's the intensity that causes discoloration. Gordie kisses me sometimes, but without the passion and complications I associate with love. Yet in idle moments it crosses my mind that he'd be easy, much easier to love.

I returned from that trip on Friday in a strange and sullen mood. Work had been rough. I was fed up of arguing with the sales manager who was not meeting his targets and spending an ungodly amount of marketing money. And my body wanted Elliot, despite the complications he brought to my life.

Paul was home when I arrived in the late afternoon.

"We have to talk," he said as soon as I walked in.

"So speak."

He forced his words out slowly, painfully, "I — need — to — have my private space."

"And what about me?"

"I still need you, Rose." He was crying noiselessly, tears sliding down his cheeks. "I know it's not fair, but I won't let you go."

I was standing, holding my bags. I walked into the bedroom to put them down and saw his bouquet of orchids with the single red rose on my dressing table. I came back into the living room. My insides felt like a steel girder had wrapped itself around me.

Paul handed me a jewellery box. It contained a necklace with opals that shone like fire. Then he held up a very delicate, deep green lace dress, almost too beautiful to wear. "You see," he looked at me with his sad eyes, "they can't ever wear these the way you can. None of them can."

I stared at these two pretty objects my husband offered.

"Here," he placed the necklace around my neck and fastened it. "And you can wear this dress to Auden's dinner tonight . . . I'm sorry, I should have told you earlier, but well, you know how things were." He drew me towards him, and lifted my cheek to his lips. "I have another surprise for you."

Paul removed a manila envelope from his briefcase, and handed it to me.

I took it, bewildered. "What is it?"

"Open it."

The title deed of our flat had my name on it. I stared at the document, uncomprehending.

"Dad helped me buy it for us, for you." When I began to protest, question, he silenced me. "Our family flat is in my mother's name only. That's the way we do things."

The magnitude of what he had done made me dumb. I wanted to throw it all back at him and tell him to go to hell. But it was all so overwhelming, so strange.

"Yuhnleung ngoh." He suddenly knelt down, and flung his arms tightly around my waist as he asked forgiveness. *"Ngoh kou lei. Mhou leihhoi ngoh.* — I'm begging you. Please don't leave me."

The impact of his Cantonese words pained me, and I pushed him away, horrified. "Oh Paul, please don't do this," my response in Chinese also. I brought him to his feet. I was crying quietly, like him. "You don't have to do this with me, not with me."

"Rose, forgive me," he said in English now. "But you have to believe I still love you. I just have . . . another life."

"Why don't you live it then?"

"Because I can't."

"But you can live half a life with me?"

"Yes. It's worth a lot to me."

I wanted to ask — and does this mean I should lead another life too? — but I already knew the answer. Paul needed to own me. He always did.

He repeated. "It's worth a lot to me, more than you can imagine." His words had an edge to them, like Paul Sr.'s had the night he came to see me. "Rose, you owe me."

I stared at him, uncomprehending.

He continued in an even, composed tone. "You never were pregnant, not even the first time, were you? I knew that. Otherwise we'd have a child by now."

How could he be so wrong, so deluded? I continued to stare at him in a kind of horror.

"I gave you a life here. You couldn't have done it without me."

He was making me both angry and afraid. "And this is why you love me?" I managed to say.

"We need each other."

I left him in the living room, locked my bedroom door, and looked at myself in the mirror for a long time. I had changed. The woman looking back at me was no longer my parents' child. She was elegant, poised, sure of herself. In marrying Paul, I had become more than a Lie; I belonged completely in their society. Did I owe Paul for this metamorphosis? If so, I had paid with my soul.

On my dressing table, the bouquet filled half the table. One by one, I tore off each blossom and meticulously ripped each petal into shreds on the floor. At seven that evening, I was ready in my new green dress and opal necklace. Paul kissed me gently on my lips as he escorted me to the door. He never said a word about the flowers.

10

"It's Thursday."

I held my hand over the receiver and signalled Teresa to close my door. She looked at me quizzically, but did it. My mood since Monday had been peevish, and now, this. "I know," I responded.

"How are you?" There was a worried note in Elliot's voice.

"I've been better."

"No pressure, you know that?"

"Yes."

And I left things in abeyance. The next two Thursdays were the same, and each time, he never insisted, never sounded impatient. It was my prerogative, he told me, to say no, not because I was a woman, but because I had more to lose.

On the morning of the fourth Thursday, Teresa stopped by my office. "He's out of town, you know."

I was preoccupied with my pencil sharpener, which was wedged between a slot in my desk drawer. "Who?"

"*Leang jai* Cohen."

I looked up, startled. "What do you mean?"

"You're playing with fire, Rose. Just some sisterly advice." She closed the door. "Is it worth it? Is Paul so bad?"

I tried to remain composed. "No."

"Paul doesn't come home, right?" When I tried to object, she carried on, "oh, it's okay. Some men need their concubines and mistresses, others their horses, some their work. The point is, they all have something. Mine works all the time and drinks with his customers, even on weekends. You learn. Have children. It helps."

"Teresa, it's not what you think."

"Look, I'm not prying. You don't have to tell me anything. I just know the signs, that's all. Maybe right now, I'm the only one who knows. Later, others will be able to tell. By that time, you won't be able to change course."

Her candor and pragmatism comforted me.

Teresa prepared to exit. "There's always divorce. But no one will help you." From her expression, I realized with a start she'd already been down that path. "At least you don't have children."

I dislodged the pencil sharpener, and accidentally sent it flying across my desk. It landed on the edge. Teresa's "have children, don't have children" mixed message was exactly how I felt. There was no right and wrong here.

At ten, Elliot rang from Manila. "It's Thursday."

"But you're not even in town."

"And I happen to know you're supposed to be in Manila for the weekend for the launch promotion of your twice weekly service. You can always leave this afternoon. I kept an option open on the room next to mine."

The pencil sharpener maintained its precarious balance. "I'm folding a paper plane."

"Why?"

I sent the plane across my desk straight into the sharpener. It toppled. "You wouldn't understand. See you tonight."

My Thursdays quickly became Mondays and Thursdays and as many out-of-town liaisons as we could manoeuvre. He gave me the keys to his flat. It was easy to cheat on Paul. He didn't want to know. Or, perhaps, I mattered only on the surface and not deep inside to him, otherwise, surely, he would have known.

"You're not like anyone I know." I took a sip of the wine by Elliot's bed. Wine and lovemaking made it easier for me to say what I really thought.

He was changing an album. "Why?"

"If it's not Rachmaninoff or Paganini, it's Motown or Tony Bennett or who was that one you played last time? Mason Williams? Ellington? Miles? I mean, I've never listened to so much music in my life."

"I thought you took piano lessons." He climbed back into bed next to me. The wonderful thing about him was that he never got dressed in a hurry afterwards.

"That's not the same. I never listened to anything. You listen to everything. Besides, half my family's tone deaf." Regina and Mum

176

were, as was Paul.

"So when are you going out with me?"

I pretended not to know what he meant. "I am going out with you. Read me some more Blake." I took the dog-eared paperback volume off the bedside table and handed it to him. "Educate me."

He tossed it on the floor. "You're not getting off that easily. You know exactly what I mean. I want to spend time with you the way your husband can, in public, as a couple." He rolled me flat on my back and lay on top of me. "Besides, I think I'm falling in love with you."

"Oh Elliot, it's only been a few months."

"Four months, two weeks, three days and," he glanced at his alarm clock, "twenty hours." He kissed my neck. "Eternity."

"Come with me to Bali next week?"

He got out off bed and pulled on a yukata. "No." He walked to the window and stood by it. "I'm tired of running away with you to never never land. I want to go out with you for a meal or movie or just for a walk right here in Hong Kong. Rose, we can't spend all out time holed up in my bedroom talking about your problems."

That hit home. "So don't ask so many questions. I'm not the one who wants to talk about me, you do. Yet you don't tell me anything about yourself."

He returned and sat on the bed. "Come on, Rose, don't sulk. I hate it when you're that way." He ran his fingers through my hair. I tossed my head away.

"Don't lecture me. You're starting to sound like Paul." I got up and started to get dressed. "I've got to go."

"Why?"

"Because this isn't much fun."

He leaned across the bed and took my arm. I shook it away and continued buttoning my blouse. "Please, Rose, don't be like that. Don't go."

"Then come with me to Bali."

"I can't. I have to go see Leanna."

"Again?"

"It's some family thing."

Up till now, Elliot had never mentioned a wife, and I hadn't asked, though I hadn't forgotten Paul's comment at my parents' home. "That's what you said the last time, and the time before that. You go to KL at least once a month, sometimes more, and you're always going on about her. Who is she anyway?"

"I've told you. A family friend."

He said that every time I asked. And on each occasion, I watched his eyes and expression and knew he was lying. If she wasn't his wife, she was probably his lover. "If you say so."

He seemed startled by my reply. It was the closest I'd ever come to confronting him. "Of course she is. Rose, you don't think . . ."

I slipped on my shoes and picked up my bag. I didn't want to leave, but I couldn't stand it when the reality of our situation got in the way. "It doesn't matter what I think, does it? Have your secrets, Elliot. Paul does."

He didn't try to stop me when I left.

Outside, on Kennedy Road, I hailed a taxi. I was going to tell him to cross the harbor and take me back to Nga Tsz Wai Road. But it was still early, and there was no reason for me to be home. So I directed him to the Star Ferry.

I sat on the ferry, waiting for it to start sailing back to Tsimshatsui, thinking about the new mess I had created in my life, resenting Paul and Elliot for having such power over me. The other day, I had received a letter from Kirstin, with a photograph of Lars' new girlfriend Myrna — the "pretty lady with long hair." Teresa had also brought around recent photos of her two children. Why couldn't I have their lives, instead of this ridiculous excuse of an existence?

"Rose Kho, isn't it?"

I looked up into a face I knew I'd seen before. The camera round his neck jarred my memory. It was David Ho.

He sat down next to me. "We met once, in Plattsburgh. It was a long time ago."

"I remember. You're a friend of my sister's."

His eyes searched my face curiously. "You and Regina really don't look very much alike."

"No, we don't. We're fraternal, not identical. What are you doing here?"

"I'm thinking about moving to Hong Kong."

"Oh."

"I was with Regina just a few days ago, in New York. She and Stan had an opening together."

By now I knew that Stan was a platonic friend and reliable, meaning Regina could talk to him and depend on his support for drugs and other solace. He hadn't been the one to get his Vietnamese model pregnant, and had, in fact, helped her through the abortion. What I still didn't know was whether or not Regina and David were lovers.

"You're fairly good friends with my sister, aren't you?"

"Pretty much." He lapsed into a moody silence.

"You don't look much like Albert."

He grunted something that sounded like "uhhhh." His manner reminded me of Kenton. I was going to give up on much more conversation when he suddenly asked, "Look, have you had dinner?"

I shook my head.

"Why don't you join me? I hate eating alone."

It was such a spontaneous invitation, quite the way Regina would have done it. The company of strangers was preferable tonight over the intimates in my life who were constantly letting me down. "Thank you, I will."

"I know this Chiu Chou place," he began, but then cut himself short. "Oh I'm sorry. Here I am, presuming to teach you about your own city."

I smiled. "That's okay. I'm a good student." I looked out across the water. Wanchai, with its grey, old buildings, looked like a giant anthill as it progressively shrank while the ferry moved closer to Kowloon.

"Terrific."

His place was a restaurant on Granville Road. The proprietor greeted him like an old friend, and gave me a glancing look that said so here was yet another woman.

"They're open late. You know, the entertainment and triad crowd." He said this apologetically as we sat down. "It's probably not your style."

"You've been listening to Regina. She thinks I'm this society lady."

"Aren't you?"

I was spared a reply by the waiter banging two glasses of hot tea on the table and a tray of tiny tea cups filled with the "iron goddess of mercy" tea. *"Sihk matyeh, Ho saang?* What do you want to eat, Mr. Ho?" David ordered a Chui Chou feast of goose and cold crab. He had a confident, easy manner, and seemed an integral part of this Hong Kong world despite having lived half his life in North America. How different he was from Paul, who wanted desperately to belong and who, despite his Chinese heritage, sometimes seemed so out of things. Paul still hadn't learned how to order a Chinese meal properly.

"So, Albert tells me your husband swings both ways. That's very liberal of you."

His forthright declaration startled me so much I almost dropped the tiny porcelain tea cup I was holding.

"Ai ya," he said. "I've put my foot in it, haven't I? You don't talk about those things in this town, do you?"

I looked down into the cup. "Not exactly."

"Sorry 'bout that."

"But since you brought it up, it's got nothing to do with how liberal I am."

The cold crab and thin rice porridge arrived. I realized how hungry I was and dug in. It was a welcome change from my usual, Spartan, Thursday night diet at Elliot's where a light pasta accompanied by raw celery and carrots was the best I could hope for.

"I love food," I said in between digging the meat out of the crab claws. "You know that? It's one thing I can always be sure of."

"Not like a husband, right?" There was a twinkling grin in his eyes.

"You said it."

"So why do you do it, Rose? If you don't mind my asking, that is."

I grimaced. "I don't know. I suppose I don't have the courage it takes to be different. Like Regina."

"It's not courage, Rose, believe me it's not."

"What is it, then?" David probably knew Regina better than I did by now.

"Cowardice. She's afraid to confront life as it is, so she re-invents her existence into life as it should be."

"But doesn't that take courage?"

"If you ask me, it probably takes more courage to remain married the way you are. I don't mean to be quite this personal, but I feel like I know you, because of Regina and Albert I mean."

We continued our meal. I wondered what he would have made of Elliot. I found myself wanting to tell him more, to uncover those secrets I usually struggled to preserve. A private life was almost an oxymoron. In this city, life was conducted on stage for the world to judge.

"Regina thinks the world of you. She's always talking about you."

"She is?"

"Constantly. You remember when we met, and she took off with me to New York? All the way there, she told me stories about when you two were kids. Your sister adores you. You're like this perfect, fragile little girl she can't bear to see hurt."

Was that really how Regina felt? She had always been protective, a chronic worrier about my well being. Yet she was at the same time extremely self absorbed, to the point of being selfish. Rather like Paul.

"Funny," David continued, "but from the first time I met you, I thought of you as something of a pragmatist, tough almost. I mean, you're her sister so I can say this to you, but knowing how Regina can be, I can't picture you feeling sorry for yourself to the point of trying to commit suicide."

"Does she, do you think? Feel sorry for herself, that is."

Before he could answer, a plate of light golden *dou fu* appeared, complete with a bowl of salted water sprinkled with chives. I looked at it, surprised. "I've never had that."

He dipped a piece into the water and set it on my plate with his chopsticks, having first turned them around to use the ends that hadn't touched his mouth. "Taste it. It's almost like Shatin *dou fu*. You remember those, don't you?"

I bit into the delicately fried bean curd. It conjured up flavors and smells of long ago weekends driving to Shatin with my family, a rural village in those days, where rows of hawkers sold their

181

famous *dou fu* of all types. Thinly sliced, thick chunks, the "stinky" ones which were heavenly. And Chinese radish cakes. Everyone bought these deep fried snacks in brown paper bags which soaked up the oil and made a mess. Regina would grab a whole bag for herself, and I'd have to beg her for a few pieces.

He saw the smile on my face. "It is, isn't it? I keep telling Regina this is why she has to come back to Hong Kong, so that she can recapture the sensations of childhood. Isn't that what every artist needs? But she's so stubborn. Wearing her heart, and politics, on her sleeve. The point is, this is still where she came from. She can't change that."

David was refreshing. He was a bridge to my present and past. I took in his casual appearance — quite unlike most Hong Kong people. Elliot, Paul and Albert, who dressed and acted "right," were much more Hong Kong than him. He looked like a teenager or *laan jai*. But he clearly was no *laan jai*. There was something too honest and straight in his manner. I thought suddenly of Andrew.

We finished the rest of the excellent meal. I seldom ate Chiu Chou food, but in summer, its light dishes were perfect for the hot weather.

Afterwards, "Thanks for joining me. I'm headed back to New York in a couple of weeks. Regina will be thrilled I saw you. She had given me your number, and I was going to look you up anyway."

"Thank you," I replied. "More than you realize."

"I know it's impolite of me, but if you don't mind, I'm not going to do the polite Hong Kong thing and offer to escort you home."

I waved aside his apologies. "Forget it."

We shook hands and I hailed a taxi.

Paul was home. "Where were you?" he asked.

"It's Thursday," I said. "What are you doing here?"

"I do live here, don't I?"

"Marginally." I went towards the bedroom.

He barred my way and gripped my arm. "So where were you?"

"Paul, what is this?" I was annoyed in the first instance, but his tone and manner were beginning to frighten me a little.

"You're my wife. I have a right to know."

He had raised his voice and hand as if to slap me. Something

182

snapped inside. Had I come straight from Elliot's, I might have cowered in the face of his anger. But a full stomach, and the levelling effect of talking with David made me want to fight back. I pushed his arm away. His father's face flashed at me for a moment.

"I will scream, Paul. Loud enough for Dr. Ng to hear. And that would get back to your father. You don't want that to happen."

"You little . . ." His voice was low, cold and angry.

"What?" I dared him to say it. I didn't know where this defiance came from.

He was shaking. I was surprised to see tears in his eyes. "You can't do this to me," he shouted. "You're my wife."

"Stop being so melodramatic, Paul. You can't have your cake, as they say." I remained remarkably calm. "You don't have anything to say to me."

He rushed out of the house.

This night was getting too much for me. The phone rang.

"Tell Paul to come to the phone." It was Man Yee, screeching in hysterical Cantonese. "I know he's there."

It had been months since he'd called, but this time his voice did not have its usual hard and cynical edge. The whole world had chosen tonight to teeter on the brink.

Man Yee was wailing. "He's going to leave me. I won't let him. After all this he still wants to go back to you. To a wife! It isn't fair, it isn't fair." And then he began to sob.

I wanted to slam the phone down or gloat in victory. It was likely Man Yee had said something to Paul about my being out all night which was what set him off. What an idiot. I could have told him jealousy would backfire. But his anguish touched me. He loved Paul too. He must. *"Wei, msai gam, mhai mouh dak gau* — come on, you don't have to be like that, things aren't hopeless. Calm yourself. Paul's gone. He's probably headed back to your place."

His sobs subsided. "Really? You think so?"

"Not sure, but he isn't here in any event."

There was a pause. "You, you don't mind sharing him?"

"Do I have a choice?"

I could almost hear the smile in his voice, not sneering the way it used to be, but gentler. "Okay, sorry to bother you."

After he hung up, I did something I rarely did at home, and

poured myself a scotch. We kept a liquor cabinet, "for guests," which was a bit of a joke since we hardly ever entertained at home. Most of the bottles hadn't even been opened. Paul needed to replicate the home he came from, at least on the surface.

I was about to take a sip when the phone rang. Here we go again, I thought.

It was Elliot. "What are you up to?"

I waited a few moments before replying. "I'm about to take a sip of my drink."

"Oh Rose, don't." And then, "I'm sorry to call at home. I know I shouldn't."

For a second I was going to say, why the hell not, everyone else does, but thought better of it.

"I love you, Rose. Really."

"And your wife?" Out before I could stop myself.

"Who told you that?" It was one of the few times I ever caught Elliot off guard. He was invested in being cool. "We're, uh, separated anyway."

"Really?"

"Really."

"Look Elliot, it's been . . . a bit much tonight. I don't feel like explaining right now."

"Don't leave me Rose."

"I won't. Goodnight."

I downed my drink, and poured another. The world, it seemed, wasn't teetering inasmuch as wobbling wholesale. I stared at the golden liquor, glistening against the ice. No answers there. Abandoning the drink, I grabbed my purse and went straight to my parents.

It was late now, past midnight. My mother opened the door.

"Paul's not home." It tumbled out.

"Well, he's probably at a business dinner . . ."

"You don't understand, Mum." I walked into their flat. "He doesn't come home on Thursday nights. But I always see him on Fridays." I hadn't meant to say it, but somehow, it all flew out.

"What do you mean? What are you saying, Rose?"

My dad looked up from his paper. "Rose, are you all right?"

I stood there, staring at both my parents. "I want you to know

I'm not the one who's infertile."

"Now Rose . . ." my father began

Mum cut him off. "Did you get a check up?"

"No."

Dad got up and came over to me, a warning look on his face. "Don't say anything you'll regret Rose."

I pressed my face against his shoulder, the way I used to as a child, when I wanted to shy away from people.

"Come on," he said, leading me towards the armchair, "sit down. You're just tired. You and Paul both have been working too hard, right?" I nodded weakly at him, smiling slightly. "Have a drink and help me pick a winner for tomorrow."

I was beginning to calm down, and everything would have been fine but my mother couldn't leave things alone. "Rose, what are you talking about? You mustn't pretend if you're barren. Go to the doctor and get a check up. That's the only way you can fix it if you know what the problem is. I spoke to Paul last week, and, you know, he's very   concerned about you because it's quite understandable he would want children, and . . ."

"Mum, please stop. You don't understand. Dad, tell her she doesn't know what she's talking about." I remained surprisingly calm, as if all of this made perfect sense.

Dad tried. "Please, Rose knows what she's doing. She's just been working too hard, that's all. So, I like Seven Rainbow Colors. What do you . . ."

"How can you talk about horses at a time like this? Haven't you any sense? Your daughter can't have children, and she's going to lose her husband because she's too stupid to know . . ."

"Mum!" I stood up and faced her. "My husband's homosexual. Do you understand what that means?"

She was dumbfounded. Dad shook his head and glared at me. But I knew I couldn't do this anymore.

My mother started to cry. "Oh, Rose, stop lying. How can you tell me such terrible lies. What kind of daughter treats her parents like this? How can you say such a thing?"

"He rapes young boys because he's afraid of how much he likes to make love to men. He almost got arrested in Singapore."

She cried even louder.

"Stop it, Rose." My father was angry now. "You know this wasn't necessary."

"Why? So she can live her lies?"

"She's your mother! She deserves your respect."

"And what about me? Can she continue to treat me as if I were a complete fool?"

My mother had gone into the bedroom, but her wails were audible. I felt only the cold satisfaction of having finally faced the truth.

"I think," he said quietly, "you'd better leave. You disappoint me, Rose."

I departed, the sting of his censure burning my ears.

My mother called the next morning and demanded I come see her alone without Paul. I went over Sunday afternoon.

"You're mistaken, Rose. Paul is much too handsome to be that way."

I glared coldly at her. "Some of the best looking men are."

She fussed with her plants. My mother has a wonderfully green thumb, although she has absolutely no control over her plant life. The verandah was covered with a wild jungle of green — vines snaking around the metal railings and bursts of colors erupting from the pots.

"He must have a mistress."

"He does. 'She's' a he. He has several. Would you like me to tell you about them?"

She ignored my question. "You have to understand, Rose, when you get married you have a duty to your husband in the bedroom. Whether you like it or not, that's what you have to do."

"That isn't it."

"It has to be."

"You just don't understand. You won't understand anything."

My mother had been kneeling in front of her bauhinias, her back to me. She stopped her fussing for a moment and turned to look at me. "I understand more than you think. You shouldn't have taken Paul away from Regina."

A shock wave raced through me. "What?"

"You know perfectly well what I mean. He had his eye on Regina until you came along and forced yourself on him."

Was my mother mad? Or had I truly missed something way back when? Was it possible I had been so blind to all that going on around me?

She continued. "Regina just let you have him out of pity for you. Your sister loved you so much she always tried to help you, just like she did by paying your way through school. You didn't even have enough sense to work, like Regina."

And then I stood up and picked up my purse. "I'm leaving. And I'm not coming back until you stop lying to me."

She stood up and faced me. Her expression was like Regina's the time she told me Miguel was her pimp — calm, blank, a little over the edge. "I'm not lying to you, Rose. I don't ever lie."

I walked out. My dad was coming into the building just as I was leaving. He looked at me quizzically.

"I'm sorry I made you angry, Dad."

"It's okay. You're just . . . upset."

"I'm so unhappy. I've never been unhappier in my life. Oh Dad, I can't live with Paul." And then, I began to cry.

He soothed me and took me out to dinner that night, just the two of us. We ate at Louis' in Wanchai, a steak house which had been around as long as I could remember. Both of us consumed our shared Caesar's salad in silence.

My father spoke only after our steaks arrived. "You always liked steaks, even as a girl."

I didn't respond.

"It's funny how unlike your Mum and Regina you are. You have patience with traditional things in life, like steaks."

"What do you mean?"

"Well you know how Regina turned vegetarian at sixteen, and how your Mum always wants to eat some place new? But you're like me, you can go back to the same restaurants, like Louis', eat the same old thing, and never get tired of it."

I smiled a little, remembering Regina's dogmatic insistence on not eating meat. It was true that all I ever ordered there was a Caesar's salad and a medium rare steak. "Is that good?"

"I think so."

"But it means I never change."

"You don't have to force change in life. It happens by itself."

He talked a lot that night about how he once thought flying was his whole life. "When I was a fighter pilot, it was the most exciting time of my life. I originally trained in the US. Even your mother doesn't know that. Then in China, I trained under Chennault. He was a wonderful teacher, a brilliant man. He was famous, you know, although you probably hardly know about him. He taught pilots to fly in a loop around the enemy, positioning your plane so that the sun was on your back and staying at a higher altitude than your enemy target. What I most remember him saying was, 'don't do anything stupid just to be brave.' It's how I've tried to live my life, Rose, for better or worse.

"I was thirty five when I left China, older than you are now, and still unmarried. Coming to Hong Kong didn't happen by choice, but because I was afraid of what my future would be like under the Communists. I wanted to be a pilot forever. It didn't matter whether or not I flew real missions, or simply transported cargo like we did at CAT; I just wanted to fly. Perhaps I should have gone to Taiwan — sometimes I think that would have been better for me. But there is a time in life for war to end. Having survived the fighting, I thought it was destiny's way of signalling a different path for me. Maybe that's why I came to Hong Kong, because I knew I'd leave my military life behind me here.

"And then, in Hong Kong, I had to make a new life. I think I've done it quite successfully." He looked wistfully at me. "Of course, it hasn't always been easy."

He was trying to teach me something, but I wasn't sure it was a lesson I wanted to learn. I challenged him. "But why did you marry Mum?"

He smiled sadly. "She was a very beautiful woman, Rose."

I wanted to ask if he regretted it now, if he would do things differently if he could start over. But I couldn't. Conversations with my father were always about what we didn't say. "Is she still beautiful now?"

He sighed. "Some questions are difficult to answer."

My appetite was good. Eating with my father was always a pleasure. It made me wonder why I chose both a husband and lover who ate like birds. "It wasn't very good of me to upset Mum like that the other night. You've only ever asked that I respect her. I should have done. It's just that, sometimes, I can't stand her blindness."

"This is Hong Kong. Chinese fathers don't forgive filial disobedience." But there was a hint of a smile in his voice as he said it.

"Some truths should be told, shouldn't they?"

"What do you think?"

"I don't know." I paused, and then plunged on. "Dad, do you know my boss?"

He didn't even look at me. "Yes."

"Were you a spy of some kind?"

My father speared his last piece of steak and popped it into his mouth. He chewed slowly, carefully. When he'd finished, he touched his napkin to his lips and laid it on the table. Then he took a sip of wine.

"Rose, you tell me. If what you ask were true, do you think I should tell?"

My father had a way about him that defied probing. "I guess not."

"All right then."

"But Dad, your life's been difficult, hasn't it? Are you happy?"

"You young people worry too much about happiness. It's like the American Constitution — 'the pursuit of happiness'. Do you really think people can insist on that pursuit as a right? Writing it down on a piece of paper doesn't make it happen. No matter what all the lawyers in the world try to foist off on their clients, a contract spelling out one's obligations and rights doesn't have anything to do with what's written down. It has to do with what people want and feel and ultimately do. Words alone are meaningless.

"Rose, I'm almost sixty. Do you know what Confucius said about the ages of man?"

I shook my head.

"*Wu shi er zhi tian ming* — at fifty, a man should understand heaven's decree. Which is followed by *liu shi er er shun* — at sixty, my ear is attuned."

I thought about this. "That's terrible. It means your destiny is fated by the gods."

189

"Not really."

"Why not?"

"Well you see, at seventy, according to Confucius, that's when you get to follow your heart's desire, because you'll do it without overstepping the line. Hence, contentment, which is the same as happiness, isn't it?" He was smiling.

"So you have to live to seventy to find out?"

He folded his napkin into a perfect square. "I fully intend to."

I thought a lot that night about everything we did say. He never once told me not to get divorced. Nor would he acknowledge what I had told him about Paul. But what I had to do was clear. I couldn't overturn everything around me. My war, unlike his, hadn't ended yet. In my and my father's worlds, the forces of change were controlled from without, not within, and it was up to us to navigate as best we could, and trust that the winds would favor our path.

After dinner that night, I decided to call Regina. It occurred to me that I never once had.

"I saw David," I began.

"He told me."

Even a friend would call while her own sister was just learning how to. I felt a little ashamed of my ignorance. "It's been a rough few days."

"Poor princess."

Hearing her voice which still sounded the same as when we were girls, I began to pour out to her just about everything I could concerning Paul. About his separate home with Man Yee, even about his father, and the incident in Singapore. She listened sympathetically, injecting responses in between that made me feel better. Then I told her about Mum's reaction, to which she was dismissive. "Mum's a fool sometimes," she actually said, and it was wonderful to have my sister's confirmation, to have her reassure me that, in fact, I wasn't completely off the wall about my mother.

"Leave Paul, Rose. You don't need him."

"But I still love him. I mean, isn't it sort of like you and Tristan, in reverse?"

She didn't respond, and I realized I'd said the wrong thing. After all this time, her beloved Tristan wasn't any nearer a divorce. In fact, he shuttled between Iowa and New York so that he could spend time with his wife and three children.

"Look Regina, I don't mean to be a cry baby. I just needed to talk."

"You call me anytime, okay Rose?"

"Okay, thanks."

When I hung up, I realized I hadn't said a word to her about Elliot.

Strange how the encounters with people around my life created such a crooked path. I'd dart along, changing directions at each twist or turn, trying to look out for the next. And each one made me feel like I was many people, that I wore a different face for each person who touched me — Paul, Elliot, my parents, Paul's parents, Man Yee and even David. Yet who was I? Would Rose be, as Elliot once insisted, as sweet by any other name?

Gordie gave me a snake skin clutch purse as a present a couple of years ago. Said it suited me. Told me it was time I did a little shedding.

Only under cover of darkness.

11

The autumn weather was cool, around 75°F, and not too humid. On my way to work that morning, as the bus drove past my old school Maryknoll, I glimpsed a profusion of yellow flowers covering the slopes by the front gate. It conjured up images of childhood when, during recess, I would play near that gate, climbing up on a ledge among the flowers. In the springtime, I had watched little black worms curl into a ball as I prodded the sandy earth around them with a twig. When they had all curled up, I would scratch holes in the earth with my bare hands into which I buried these round little worm balls. My mother never understood why there was so much dirt under my nails. Nor had I ever told her about my game with the worms.

But Mum simply chose not to understand things. That weekend, Paul and my monthly dinner with my parents had ended on yet another note of non-comprehension. Mum had finally tumbled to the fact that Regina was living illegally in New York, something which everyone else had figured out ages ago. Even Paul, in his diplomatic way, had told her, by way of reassurance, that "lots of people do," to which she retorted that Regina wasn't lots of people, Regina was her daughter, and that if Paul had any sense of his legal responsibilities, he'd write and tell her to get a lawyer. At that point, Dad chimed in and reminded Mum of a certain age falsification which made her explode into pathetic protestations about how my father always twisted things around so that facts got distorted and she launched into her explanation of how she'd come to Hong Kong by herself from Indonesia and was too old to register for Form 6, and that changing her birth date was harmless, because it was just so that she could get an education, and she would have gone on ad nauseum, with that old story, embellishing it with how she's only a secretary and that nowadays girls do many more important things, all to make me feel bad, so I cut her off and said that Paul had heard it a thousand times before. Dad sort of glanced at me and remarked "it was harmless," which made Mum resume a self satisfied air of victory.

On our way home in the car, Paul said, "You cut your mother off."

"Why is everyone making such a fuss about it? Regina used to do it all the time."

He stared straight ahead, never taking his eyes off the road. "It's not like you."

Regina's first poetry chapbook arrived in the mail a couple of weeks later.

"For Rose's invisible worm," the epigraph read. She had sent me a copy, but not my parents. It was strange how Regina seemed not to care about winning their approval. I showed it to Paul who browsed through the pages.

"It's pretentious stuff," he said, handing the book back to me. "And it's not even very good."

"You don't read poetry," I said. "How can you make a judgment like that?"

"No one reads poetry anyway." He went into his study and closed the door.

It was a Wednesday night. I remember the particular day because Elliot was out of town that week. Things had cooled a little between us since the night I walked out, especially when it came to coordinating travel schedules. Paul and my schedules had become fairly routine. He still did his Monday/Thursday thing, but for reasons known only to him, those were the only two nights he didn't come home now. What he did in the evenings when I didn't see him — he often came home late, sometimes past midnight — I didn't know and didn't ask. I used Mondays for myself. But Elliot and I still met Thursdays, if we were both in Hong Kong. In any given week, Wednesdays were always the worst. Paul was impatient, as I was, and we tended to snap at each other. Fridays were the best.

I flipped again to the epigraph page. Regina was enigmatic. When she called to tell me her book was coming out and that she was dedicating it to a part of me, I hadn't known what to make of it. Now, I still didn't know.

The phone rang and I answered it.

"It's Man Yee," a subdued voice said.

"Do you want to talk to him?"

"No. I want to talk to you."

Paul looked out from the door of the study. "Who is it?"

I looked him squarely in the face. "Kenton."

He returned to the study and closed the door.

Man Yee breathed an audible sigh of relief. "Thanks for not telling him. Will you see me?"

"Why should I?"

"It'll be clear when we meet."

I wasn't at all sure I wanted to.

"Please say yes," he said into my silence. "It's as important to you as it is to me. Tomorrow night, okay? I know Paul will be out."

Which meant Paul wasn't spending time with him. But it still didn't mean I wanted to be involved. "How do I know you won't just try to cause me problems? You've been rude and nasty to me, and I haven't done anything to you. What good will my meeting you do?"

Paul came suddenly out of his study.

"That's fine," I said quickly. "We can do that deal with Four Winds. I'll put it together tomorrow. See you when you get back."

Man Yee caught on right away. "Please, at the ABC on Waterloo Road, near Nathan. Around six thirty. I'll be there waiting." And he hung up.

"Your boss shouldn't call you at home," Paul remarked.

"What difference does it make to you?" I retorted.

He glanced at me as if he was going to say something else, thought better of it, shrugged and returned to his study. I wondered why he'd come out in the first place.

All the next day, I debated whether or not to go. Twice, Teresa spoke to me and I was too lost in my own thoughts to reply. "Stop thinking about your *leaang jai*," she said, half teasing, half seriously. If only she knew.

At five forty five, Man Yee called. "Will you meet me? I promise I won't take up too much of your time."

I hesitated. What if he tried blackmail, or something equally as unsavory? But not knowing made it worse.

"Please."

"You realize I'm just going to leave if you give me a hard time."

"I won't. Promise."

I relented in the end, my curiosity getting the better of me.

As a first impression, Man Yee could come across as sophisticated, although he had a rather effete air. He appeared in commercials for luxury products. In the local contemporary soaps, he was cast as a kind of male ingenue. The current role was that of the lover of a beautiful heroine who wept copious amounts and was torn between her husband and him, he being the younger, infinitely more desirable but poorer and powerless choice. Watching him order iced coffees for us, I saw the effect he had on the young waitress, who blushed and giggled before fluttering away with our order. Except in some circles, it wasn't public knowledge that he was homosexual.

"How did you know I'd answer the phone?" I asked.

"Took a chance. Paul wasn't supposed to be home."

I reflected on that a minute. Paul had been scheduled to go to dinner with a client, but it had been cancelled at the last moment. "You know a lot about my husband."

"I ought to." He glanced a little furtively at me. "I used to be, how should I say this, his special friend."

"Used to?"

"We're still . . . friends." He looked at me mournfully.

"So your relationship didn't end?"

"Did your marriage end?" he retorted. "You need to understand," he continued hurriedly, "it's not that I can claim any privilege, because I am only one of his friends. But, for some time now, you could say we haven't had a simple relationship."

"What's not simple about it?"

"His feelings towards me were not the same as mine for him."

He paused. I waited for what he would say.

"I could follow him."

His Cantonese "follow" implied a subordinate's relationship to his or her boss. Man Yee was a slave to Paul, at least emotionally.

"So why tell me?"

"Because your husband is changing. He has a need for much more than you or I have to offer. You need to know. You have a right to know."

He didn't mention Singapore. It made me wonder what he and I did or didn't know. "What about Albert Ho? You do know about him, I'm sure."

He sneered. "The son of Ho Yuet-Kan isn't subject to the same forces of life as ordinary people like us."

The inclusiveness of that remark startled me. I looked into the eyes of this man who apparently loved my husband, hoping to see that which set us apart. Instead, I discovered an unexpected bond. I couldn't dislike him, although I didn't like him either.

"Besides, you have Elliot Cohen."

I stared at him, dumbfounded.

"Don't look so shocked, I won't tell. But I just had to confirm for myself, although Paul, for all his intelligence, can be quite blind sometimes. I mean, he actually wavers between believing and not believing me when I say you're out all night. Never occurs to him to check. It wasn't hard to figure out. I followed you once to his flat. We're all part of the same shit pile, you know." He lit a cigarette. "Do you know where I came from before the talent scouts found me?" he went on. "I used to help my father sell fish balls and pig skin at his hawker stand near the Kowloon City market. Then he died from lung cancer, and I quit school to take over my father's business and support my mother and two sisters. In fact, I can walk to where you live on Nga Tsz Wai Road from where my old spot used to be." He grinned mischievously as he said that. "We keep a Chinese flat in the old neighborhood. You know the kind. High ceilings, no lifts, with stone floors. Paul doesn't even care that there's no air conditioning. He says he's at home there."

I pictured our fully air conditioned place with its Western furniture and Escher print in the living room, our principal asset as we liked to call it. "Why are you telling me all this?"

"Because you ought to know."

Sitting there, sipping tea and conversing in low tones, the absurdity of it all made me want to laugh. My lips must have twitched into a smile, because Man Yee looked quizzically at me and said, "Is the pain of life so amusing?"

I didn't speak for several minutes. An absurd thought ran through my head — laughter is the best medicine. It was something my mother often said, quoting from her favorite magazine, the *Reader's Digest*. I smiled at Man Yee. "So now I know. And what should I do with this knowledge?"

"Whatever you want."

Perhaps, I thought as we parted company, it wasn't so bad to confront that which we most feared. This meeting brought a strange kind of relief. There was something comic about Paul, Man Yee and me. We went through elaborate machinations to hide from each other what we all already knew. Yet knowledge ignited only tiny sparks of understanding; it did not guarantee either progress or change. Was it face? Or a mask? It almost didn't matter which as long as the one we wore allowed life as we wanted it to go on.

Paul didn't come home all weekend. On Sunday Man Yee rang to tell me that Paul hadn't been "home" at all.

Radio's playing "Autumn In New York," same instrumental version Elliot first introduced me to. Reminds me of the trees that used to line Nathan Road, and how the leaves would change colors in the fall. It's a beautiful song. But until Gordie sang the lyrics for me — "in canyons of steel" — I never knew the full power of its beauty.

The Feds are taking a pizza break. Looks like they plan to stay all night. The ABC guy is leaving. No, he's just bringing in the next shift.

So this is how the government spends my tax dollars.

"Do you have much contact with Elliot Cohen, dear?" Aunt Helen asked at lunch a few weeks later.

Coming on top of Man Yee's recent revelation, her question made me spill the tea I was pouring. It soaked into the tablecloth. "A little. He's friendly with my boss."

"I worry about him sometimes," she remarked.

I wasn't sure whether or not to deflect the conversation to another topic. A part of me wanted to know everything about him, to find out what he hadn't told me. It was simple enough; women gossip easily and Helen wouldn't have thought anything if I'd displayed a little curiosity.

Helen continued in the same musing vein. "Uncle Chong's known him for years, from when he first arrived in Hong Kong as a young man. He stayed at the Ambassador, where Chong used to work. He was such a charmingly pleasant young man, in love with

197

Hong Kong and everything about it. Terribly naive though, and got himself married to a beautiful but perfectly miserable woman. All she wanted was a green card and a way out of Asia. Thank goodness that's over."

I couldn't restrain myself. "Was she very beautiful?"

"Oh yes. She's Malaysian Chinese, originally from Kuala Lumpur. One of the Shaw Brothers' starlets and cheap as dirt. She just didn't look cheap."

"Aunt Helen, you're not usually this catty."

"Oh no, dear, I know. It's just that, well, he had this other girlfriend, a fiancée actually, who was also Jewish, an American from New York like him. She was a fashion designer, I think, and such a bright and lovely person. They were perfect together. It broke my heart that he left her for that . . . well, maybe I'm old fashioned, but I don't really think mixed marriages work, do you? Not that I have anything against Paul of course," she added quickly, "because he's mostly Chinese, and his mother adapts well to Hong Kong and she and your father-in-law are wonderful together, the way you and Paul are. The way marriage is meant to be," she finished.

Was I that good a liar, an actress? Surely my aunt sensed some of the problems? Or was her rosy view of life colored by the happiness in her own marriage? Or was she simply mouthing pleasantries to get herself out of a tight situation? But these difficult thoughts dissipated almost as quickly as they arose, and I nodded in agreement at her words. "What was her name?" I continued the conversation. "I mean, is she anyone I'd have heard about?"

"Oh, I doubt it. She isn't anyone famous. Besides, she isn't in Hong Kong anymore. I think she lives in New York now. He visits her still, because of their daughter."

"Daughter?" I had expected anything but this. The idea that he might have been married before didn't shock me, but for some reason, I never pictured him a father.

"Yes, such a sweet girl. Must take after him."

"Oh, so you've met her."

"Yes, in Malaysia actually. She's about six or seven I think."

I desperately wanted to stop myself, because I was afraid she'd wonder why I seemed so interested. But I had to know. "In Malaysia? I thought she was in New York." I tried to sound casual.

"Oh yes, some of the time. But her mother ships her off to her sister whenever she has a modelling assignment or wants to take off with some new boyfriend. Now if you ask me, Elliot would have done better for himself if he'd married Leanna, the sister."

Fuhng jaau! The voice behind me made me jump. Several *dim sum* carts passed by, stacked high with bamboo steamers. "Phoenix claw," the girl pushing the first cart was calling out, advertising the steamed chicken feet in soy sauce. Helen ordered some, and gestured for me to eat. I appreciated the distraction. I didn't want to think about Leanna and his daughter.

"You know," my aunt continued after a short silence of eating, "I do wish Regina and David Ho would get together. It pains me when she tells me about all the men she sleeps with. She even slept with a black man!"

I was incredulous. "She tells you all this?"

Helen nodded. "Your sister is quite impossible, but I do love her."

It was a long lunch.

That same Saturday afternoon, I called Elliot and asked if we could meet.

He was surprised, because we seldom met on weekends, but I assured him it was okay. I went to his flat within the hour.

He was reading when I arrived. Elliot read more than anyone else I knew. He put aside his book and came over to embrace me. I took his arms off me.

"Elliot, why didn't you tell me about your daughter?"

He took my arm and led me over to the sofa. "What's to tell?" He wouldn't look at me.

"Why should it be a secret from me? From anyone?"

"It isn't. I just don't like to talk about it."

"You're the last person who should say that, Mr. Elliot talk-about-it-you'll-feel-better Cohen."

He pulled me gently to him and kissed my temple. "If you must know, I didn't want to seem too old."

"I don't understand, why . . .?"

"Come on, Rose. You're, what, ten years younger than me? There's every reason in the world you'd rather be with someone closer to your own age, someone less encumbered. Even given the way Paul is, you don't want to leave him because, after all, what do I have to offer? That's right, isn't it?"

"But you're not even divorced, are you? Why talk about me leaving Paul if you're still tied to your wife?"

"I'm not really. She's with . . . several other guys. All filthy rich."

I took this in. It was another side of Elliot I simply hadn't seen before. He always seemed in control of his life. Even in our relationship, he seldom made any demands, being willing to work around my schedule. Yet there obviously were many things in his life about which I had no clue.

"And Leanna?"

"She looks after Anita quite often."

"Who?"

"My daughter."

"That's why the trips . . ."

"Yes."

"Leanna's your mistress, isn't she?" I blurted it out unexpectedly, all restraint gone.

Elliot's eyes couldn't lie. They shifted uneasily. He bit his lower lip, curling it upwards. And then, "sometimes."

A slow fury welled up. I tried to quelch it, but it took on its own life, unleashing itself inside me. I was angry at Elliot for lying to me, angry at Paul for only giving me half his love, angry most of all at myself for perpetuating the hypocrisy of my life. And my anger grew at my own feelings of jealousy, at my sense of inadequacy around both these men who professed to love and care about me. Elliot saw my tensed body, and withdrew his arm.

"We all have our crosses, Rose."

I couldn't speak, afraid of what would erupt.

"Please say something."

Standing up, I took the keys to his flat out of my bag and tossed them on the floor in front of him. He scooped them off the ground and pressed them back into my hand. I flung the ring of keys away with such force that they shattered a window pane. I couldn't hold back anymore the anger at this life I couldn't control. Even as I vented this rage on Elliot, who in some ways deserved it least of all, I knew how senseless, how pointless it all was. But I'd been burning on the end of a long fuse, and was now nearing explosion.

"Rose, I love you." His voice barely above a whisper. "Please believe me."

I ran to the door and left, banging it behind me, frightened by the force of my emotions.

Mixed fractions, our primary school Arithmetic teacher used to say, are a nuisance. Which is why you get rid of them and make them proper fractions to solve the problem. Our teacher was an American nun with a moustache and an East Coast accent. The bits of hair that strayed out of her habit were black and grey.

Regina would toss aside her homework angrily when we had mixed fractions, declaring them illogical, saying that if you had to get rid of them, they shouldn't exist in the first place. She was hopeless at math, and simply couldn't be bothered to learn.

I would gaze at my notebook filled with sums of mixed fractions and delight in making them proper fractions, thinking that now, even though they were proper, they were still always more than a whole number, never a whole.

On Tuesday morning, Teresa stalked into my office with a basket of white roses.

"Here," she said, thrusting the flowers at me. "From your American leang jai."

I was going to make a remark, but thought better of it. The card was written in Elliot's handwriting and read, "Truce?" At the bottom of the basket, wrapped in paper covered with pink roses, were the keys to his flat and a tiny piece of broken glass glued to his card. I laughed despite myself, pleased by the manner of his courtship.

"You're not angry anymore?" His voice was tentative when I called.

"No point."

"I can explain if you let me."

I was going to say okay I will, but then realized what I really felt was that there was no point to explanations either.

"There is a point," he said, reading my thoughts.

So, later that night, even though it wasn't either Monday or Thursday, I ended up in Elliot's bed.

"I am going to see you again," I said by way of reassurance after he'd made love to me for the third time.

He poured me more champagne. It was fun being spoiled. "Just making sure."

"I'll have to get angry more often," I said between sips.

"Don't. You're truly frightening."

I laughed. "Regina told me that once, you know. We were about eleven, playing our queen and lady-in-waiting game, me being the latter of course, and she was making me fold up her clothes for the fourth time after she'd messed them up. I told her it was a silly game and that I didn't want to play it anymore. She got angry and said I had to because I was her servant. That was when I took off the sheet draped around me as my 'costume' and glared at her without saying a word. She said 'stop that', but I continued to stare. Finally I said, 'you're just a bully, Regina', and I ripped a button off her favorite shirt, threw shirt and button in a heap at her feet and walked out of our room. As I left I told her, 'you clean up the mess'. She did. We never played that game again. Later she told me I was 'truly frightening'."

He ran his finger down my neck. "*Tit gunyam.* Iron goddess of mercy." Leaning over to kiss me, he whispered, "I told Leanna it's over. I told her about you."

"You what?"

He looked like a boy who'd just brought home a good report card to his mother. "I never was in love with her, Rose."

"What did she say?"

"Not much. You see, she's always had this thing for me, even when I was with her sister. She thought I should have married her. Later, when I broke up with her sister, things were difficult and she was awfully sweet, helping to take care of Anita and everything — my wife officially has custody over her — and making sure I knew when Anita was with her so that I could come see her easily. One thing led to another, and I was lonely . . ."

"You don't have to explain, you know."

"I guess I want to. You don't have to have the same relationship with me like you do with Paul."

As I listened to him talk some more, describing the history of his marriage, I knew how unsure of my own feelings I was. The jealous anger I'd felt had been unexpected. Did I love Elliot? I really didn't know. I couldn't be sure what love was, or what it really meant.

" . . . in the end, she's still family, and she was sweet about it, saying she understood and even asked that we come for dinner, you and I that is, to her place. And she said we were welcome to stay any time."

That last bit took me aback.

"I'd really like you to," he went on. "I want you to meet Anita also."

"Elliot, I'm married."

"So what? So am I."

He wanted me to stay, but I decided it was better to go home that night. Paul was back when I returned.

"You're home early," I remarked, unable to keep the sarcasm out of my voice.

"Rose, it's almost one in the morning."

I strolled nonchalantly towards the bedroom. "You're still home early." I knew he wanted to know where I'd been.

"I kept calling. I wanted to have dinner together."

I was at the door of the bedroom. "You should have made an appointment, the way you do when we have to go to your firm's dinners, and law society functions, and your father's charity balls and Hong Kong U parties. Perhaps I should get an appointment book and keep it by the phone. You can write down the appointments you wish me to keep. Oh, and don't forget to tell me what to wear, so that I won't embarrass you by my bad taste."

It was probably the longest speech I'd ever delivered to Paul. He looked shaken. "Rose, this isn't like you. I didn't realize . . ."

"Oh? What didn't you realize? That I deserve some explanation? That you're not the only one with rights as a spouse? That perhaps I get tired of being 'like me' as you call it? Just what am I to you, Paul?"

He came over and held my face in his hands. "Don't you love me anymore, Rose?"

I was unmoved. "I'm tired. I'm going to bed." I shut and locked the door on him that night. He knocked for awhile, pleading to be let in. I ignored him. After awhile, things went quiet, but I knew he hadn't left. I undressed and went to bed. The next morning, he was gone when I emerged.

Shortly before Christmas, Elliot asked if I would go to Kuala Lumpur with him. What he meant was that he wanted me to spend some non-working days there.

I was going to Kota Kinabalu on business anyway, so I agreed to fly over on Friday and spend the weekend. Paul wasn't pleased that I was staying the weekend. I told him it was work, left my flight itinerary as usual, and let him assume I would be at the Equatorial where I normally stayed. It didn't make any difference. He never called or picked me up.

"I'll pay a share of the hotel room," I told Elliot. I could fly free on my company's flights if I sat in the jump seat, which I often did on short hauls.

"It's all right," he said. "I have some barter left with the Hilton, so it won't cost us to stay there."

He was staying on for Christmas at Leanna's, because Anita was coming out to visit. He'd originally suggested we stay at Leanna's also. I drew the line at that. Meeting her for dinner was one thing, but staying with her seemed a bit much.

I arrived late morning on the Friday as planned. Elliot picked me up from the airport. "Lunch is ready," he said after he kissed me.

And it was. A lovely spread of salad and seafood, beautifully laid out by room service. I was happy. I was determined that nothing was going to bother me this entire weekend.

In the middle of lunch, I remembered something I'd been meaning to ask him.

"Elliot, what's my invisible worm?"

He chuckled. "Who told you that?"

"Regina." I handed him her chapbook. I had wanted to show him Regina's poetry for awhile, but kept forgetting to do so. He dabbed his napkin to his lips, sipped his wine and opened the book. He leafed through it as he ate.

"She's quite good."

"Really?"

"Just my humble opinion, of course."

"But what does her epigraph mean?"

"You might not like it."

"Tell me anyway."

He laid down his cutlery neatly together on his plate, folded the napkin and put it on the side. There was a meticulous precision about everything Elliot did.

He recited the entire poem.

I looked at him, puzzled. "Crimson joy?"

He grinned. "Finish lunch and I'll show you."

It was a long lunch.

In the evening, we were to go to Leanna's for dinner.

Truthfully, I'd been dreading it, but I hadn't said that to Elliot because it seemed small minded. Some instinct told me not to trust Leanna. But I had to be fair, since I didn't really know her yet. I'd never felt like this about Paul when it came to other women. Was jealousy really fundamental to love?

She came by in her car to pick us up around seven. Elliot sat in the front seat.

"You both must be starved," she said. "Elliot never eats."

She was proving her familiarity. Elliot simply laughed. I didn't say anything.

"By the way," she continued, "I invited some friends along and some people I think you might know, Rose. Lars and Myrna?"

There was a distinctly catty tone in her voice. Bitch. She was going to make my relationship with Elliot public and embarrass us. I wanted him to say something, but he remained silent. "Does Elliot know your other guests?" I knew he didn't know Lars.

"Oh yes, they're all our friends."

When we arrived, Elliot held me back a second as Leanna headed towards the front door. "Just relax," he whispered. "I'm sorry about this." I was grateful for that comment and the kiss he planted on my cheek.

Leanna sparkled as a hostess. She wore a tight sarong and a beautiful lace blouse that was cut to fit her rather buxom figure. There was something powerfully sensual about her that emanated in all her movements. I couldn't help noticing again what exquisite taste she had; her home was beautiful, just as she was.

It was an excruciating dinner. All Leanna's friends were Westerners, except for Lars' girlfriend Myrna, who was Malaysian. They were "creative" types, meaning interior designers, ad agency people, and gallery owners. I felt like I was there for the sole purpose of being interrogated, because all through the meal, her friends kept asking me questions about myself, as if they were going to approve or disapprove my having a relationship with Elliot. One woman even said, so how long have you and Elliot been having this affair, you're married, right Rose? Except for Lars and Myrna, it was clear they all knew Elliot and Leanna well, and probably knew them as a couple, because Leanna had invited only couples, creating an odd number at the table.

Lars had been relatively quiet. Finally, he spoke up, "Rose has been a good friend to my daughter, hasn't she Myrna?"

Myrna nodded. "Oh yes, Kristin will be delighted when she hears you're here. This dinner is such a coincidence. It was so nice of you, Leanna, to invite us at the last minute when you found out we knew Rose. Of course, we hadn't met Elliot yet, but now we have, which is nice." She flashed a far-from-naive smile at Leanna.

Allies! I smiled at them. The rest of Leanna's friends went quiet.

"Well," Leanna said, "I'm glad I could invite you both, because Rose doesn't know KL much. So I thought she'd feel more comfortable with some friends."

I spoke up. "Actually, I come here relatively often. In fact, I may have to live here for awhile because of work." From that point on, the conversation turned in my favor. Up till then, no one had asked much about my work, focusing their questions on far too personal things. Once they found out I worked for Pan Asian, and was in fact a client of Elliot's, they seemed to look at me differently. I realized I was one of the youngest at the table, since Leanna was closer in age to Elliot as were all their friends. Thank god for Lars and Myrna, who were my contemporaries.

I was glad when dinner was over.

Back in our hotel room, Elliot said, "Sorry. I didn't know she was going to do that. It wasn't nice of her."

"She's upset at you, isn't she?"

"I guess so."

"I'd never do something like that if the tables were turned."

"I know, Rose. You have more dignity."

I thought about my parents, about the conversations I'd had

with my father concerning Mum.

"That's why I love you Rose, you know that, don't you?"

"So what is it between you and Leanna?"

"I guess the truth is, I've had a hard time since I split up with her sister finding anyone else I wanted to have a relationship with. Until you, that is. Leanna's wanted to marry me for a long time. She also tends to exaggerate my relationship with her into more than it is. I should never have slept with her because I'm not in love with her. But, that's the problem of being a man."

"Is it?"

He wouldn't look at me. "Come on, Rose, you know what I mean."

"Actually, I was thinking it isn't that different from the problem of being a woman."

We made love that night until just before dawn. Elliot whispered, several times, "we're meant for each other Rose, can't you tell?" and I knew, more deeply then than any other time before, that he was right. Around five, Elliot finally fell asleep. I got out of bed and wandered out to the balcony. Humid and hazy air enveloped me, caressed me. I glanced at Elliot's peaceful sleeping form, so unlike Paul's turbulent slumber.

The outdoor table and chair were damp to my touch. I dried off the chair as best I could with my palm and sat down on the still wet seat. No one was about. My solitude wouldn't be disturbed for another hour or so.

I still hadn't told Elliot about Paul's father, or Man Yee. So I didn't have any right getting angry at his secrets from me. But what I knew most about Elliot was how comfortable I could feel with him. Tonight's dinner had been embarrassing, but it would blow over, the way horrible occasions with Paul dissipated. With Elliot, social conventions mattered less, which was refreshing. In a way, Leanna's dramatics had forced my affair out into the open, at least in KL, which wasn't the worst thing that could happen. It was like David's remark, "I hear your husband swings both ways," stated in such a matter-of-fact way, that took away the fear of what I was, what my life was.

Perhaps it was meeting Man Yee, confronting Paul's alter life, that finally did it for me, but I knew that right now, I wanted Elliot in my life. His truce message had helped. He could love me and the anger in me he provoked; there was something real about that. My desire for him, a desire that was more than merely sexual, was something much more palpable and insistent, something that wouldn't go away even after the physical self had been satiated.

I sat till the sun rose, and returned to the bed of my lover.

Paul was at the airport to meet my flight. Stopping on the walkway, I stared at him, stunned. We drove in silence back to our flat.

There was a Christmas tree in the corner of the living room next to a new upright piano. I stared at the re-arranged flat. The piano was where I had dreamed of putting one, but we had agreed to wait till next year to buy, since piano was only a hobby for me.

"Merry Christmas, my love," Paul said, putting his arms around me and kissing me gently on the cheek.

Paul poured me a double scotch with very little water. "Here. We need to talk," he said.

I wasn't at all sure I wanted to talk, but I took a deep swallow of my drink and sank into the armchair. Paul sat on a footstool in front of me, a bottle of wine, a glass and a corkscrew in his hands. He looked so sad and handsome, so finely sculpted in his beauty — I couldn't imagine a more remote lover.

He uncorked the wine and poured himself a drink. I saw that he had one of our best crystal wineglasses. But the Chablis was distinctively ordinary.

"Welcome home." He held his glass up in a toast. "This still can be home, Rose."

"How?"

"We can have a family."

"Just like that?"

"Why not?"

"What about . . . ?"

He placed his hand over my mouth. "Please don't say it. I'm so sorry about everything Rose. I've been stupid and thoughtless. I'm going to change my life. Forgive me?" He gazed at me, his eyes willing my forgiveness.

"Why all of a sudden?"

He took a deep breath. "I don't want to lose you, Rose.

The alcohol was addling my brain and relaxing the tension in my muscles.

"I called the Equatorial," he added.

Perhaps I should have been shocked or scared. But all I felt was a numbness about the whole thing. It was as if I didn't care, but that wasn't really what I felt. "What happens now?"

"I can allow you this, Rose," he said, his head lowered.

As if the permission were his to grant! But Paul had always been the "older and wiser," and his presumption of authority second nature. It was just the way he was, and I hadn't caused him to believe otherwise. Perhaps it was time to start.

"As long as I allow you yours, right?"

He looked up, startled. "I didn't mean it quite that way."

"Didn't you? Do you mean to say you're giving up Man Yee?" There wasn't any point letting on I knew what had been happening there.

"No, I'm not . . ."

I took his face in my hands. Such sad beauty. Sometimes, it wasn't hard to think of him in female terms. "Why don't we leave things the way they are for now, and just let life go on for a bit?" I hardly believed I was saying it.

That was when he put his arms around my waist and buried his head in my lap. "Oh Rose," he whispered, "thank you for loving me."

We sat that way for a long time. I wished so badly to love him, to make my world right again. In the background, I heard Regina's words, "leave him Rose, as soon as you can, you don't need him. That isn't a marriage. There's no shame in making a mistake." I tried to shut her voice out of my head as Paul knelt in front of me to kiss me and before I knew it we were in each others' arms, almost like lovers, and he led me to our bedroom where we made love and he made me feel wanted and desired, a feeling I wanted so badly from Paul, that nothing else mattered, at least not for the moment.

12

"You two should meet," Kenton said, as he introduced me to Gordon Ashberry. "His dad knew your dad. Also flew for Flying Tigers, and later for CAT."

Ashberry shook my hand and said in a soft, American East Coast accent, "It's Gordie, not Gordon, by the way." Gordie was thirtyish, with boyish features and an infectious laugh. I found him good looking in a disarming sort of way. He was tall, over six feet, and well built without being excessively muscular, with dirty blond hair, green eyes and the whitest and most even set of teeth I'd ever seen. No glasses. And he was fair complexioned but not pale. I could picture him sailing or swimming in briskly cold waters; he wasn't the tropical beach type.

"Do you know my father also?" I asked.

"Actually, I do remember him, even though I was only a kid when Dad used to take me to visit. My father later flew for Pacific American, and he'd take me to Hong Kong with him sometimes. We'd visit your father at his office. He gave me a Pacific American model plane once, which I still have. I would like to see him again. I don't know if he'd remember me."

"He will," Kenton said. "Jimmy Kho never forgets a name or face."

Kenton startled me. It was the first time I'd heard anyone outside the family call him Jimmy. I'd always thought it was a joke when Uncle Chong and sometimes Aunt Helen as well used that nickname. Everyone else who used his English name called my father James Kho. Again, I wondered how well Kenton and Dad really knew each other.

Kenton looked at his watch. "Gordie, take Rose to lunch and you two can talk family. I have an appointment."

I was about to demur, because it should have been the other way around since Gordie was the guest. But Kenton, typically, had no time for social niceties.

Gordie asked if I knew a Vietnamese place.

"It's a bit of a hole in the wall," I said, apologetically. "But it's the only one around."

"I belong in holes." He took my elbow to lead me out of Kenton's office. "Come on, let's burrow."

"Watch him," was Kenton's parting shot.

Gordie was the "touchy-feely" type, although at the time, I didn't know the expression. Teresa made a face as we went out — another do sau too many hands gwailo, it said.

We walked over to D'Aigular on Queen's Road Central. It was only twelve thirty, which helped us avoid the one o'clock lunch time crowd. Years later, when I came to work for Gordie in New York, he and I would never eat lunch out till one or later. He would say it was a much more civilized hour the way we did it in Hong Kong.

"I love Hong Kong in winter. It's just like autumn in New York," he declared, and began to sing Autumn In New York. He had a good voice, a resonant baritone, and as I eventually discovered, perfect pitch. People looked at us, but, strangely, around Gordie, I didn't feel either embarrassed or conformist, because he was natural about everything he did. Gordie was a pre-karaoke phenomenon. He just didn't need a video and a club audience to make him sing; life the way it was did the trick.

At the restaurant after we'd ordered, I asked. "How long since you were last here?"

"Eleven years ago, just before I turned eighteen and lost the last of Dad's airline benefits." He looked around the restaurant which was unpretentious and basic. "Mark, my older brother, was killed in Vietnam that year. Dad stopped flying after that and died a year later. Mark flew also."

A lingering pain showed in his eyes.

"So," he said, dismissing the memory abruptly, "do you have a boyfriend?"

"I'm married."

"Pity." He smiled at me. "You're still pretty, you know."

"What do you mean, 'still'?"

He pulled out a photograph. It was creased, an old black and white one of me and my dad when I was about eight or nine. I didn't remember it.

"Why do you have that?" These pieces of my life that other

people held in their hands, in their memories, like Kenton did, were jarring and strange. "We didn't meet when we were children, did we?" I was wracking my brain, but drew a blank.

"No, it's not that." He seemed hesitant to go on. But then, suddenly, "oh what the heck, it's all long enough ago now.

"I spent a lot of time in your father's office when I was a boy. He even used to take me to dinner, or the racecourse. I would ask him to adopt me so that I could stay in Hong Kong, which made him laugh. He was my 'Uncle Jimmy' you know." He stopped to watch my reaction.

"Did you know my mother as well?"

"No." He was clearly having trouble deciding how much or little to say to me.

"Do you want to see my father?"

"I've already called him. We're meeting for dinner tomorrow night. He promised to bring you along so that I could meet you at last. You can imagine my shock when Kenton said you worked for him.

"I was my dad's favorite. He and Mark fought all the time, because they were so much alike, I think. My mother hated Dad coming out this way. You see, he had a 'Chinese wife' here, a sort of concubine. Actually, I think she was a girlfriend from his Flying Tiger days. He never really told me the whole story, but from what I've been able to piece together, they had a daughter. I was kind of his cover, and he'd leave me with your dad while he went to see them.

"Your father was nice to me. I got the feeling he didn't like what my father was doing, but didn't say anything. Anyway, he'd buy me model cars and planes, and we'd build them together in his office at night until my dad showed up to get me."

"How often did you come here?"

"Oh, quite a lot, especially in the summer because of vacation." He looked at me awkwardly, his natural exuberance subdued.

I tried to imagine my father with this American "son" of his. It was unlikely that Mum knew. She would surely have objected.

"So why the photograph?"

"You're your dad's favorite, aren't you?"

I nodded. It was a little like the time I met Man Yee and listened to him talk about my husband — the words of a stranger who knew a private part of me. I felt violated, but couldn't be angry.

"I could tell, because he only had photos of you in his wallet. He'd bring new ones to me every time I came, and tell me about something you'd done at school or home. I became very curious about you, and he was more than happy to talk about you all the time. One day, I told him that when I grew up I was going to marry you and he laughed and laughed. Your dad really has a great laugh. He gave me this photograph saying, 'here, she can be your picture bride', and laughed again."

The plate of spring rolls arrived, along with a generous helping of lettuce. I rolled a crisp, lightly fried roll into the lettuce and dipped it into the clear fish sauce before taking a bite. Gordie watched me eat. It was unnerving. His eyes simply didn't let me go.

"You look like him."

"I know," I replied between bites. "Come on, eat."

"That's what I most remember him saying. He'd take me to eat *char siu* and *siu yuk*. Got so I loved pork, especially the crunchy bits. I think we must've eaten in all the restaurants near the airport, and even some of the *daaih paih dong*. He even taught me to eat, let's see if I remember correctly, *yu daan jyu peih?*"

I laughed. "From the roadside food stalls? Fish balls and pig skin?"

"That's it, yeah." His eyes sparkled with remembered joy. "You wanted to fly," he said, abruptly. "Uncle Jimmy said you'd fly one day. I guess you do now, sort of."

From a long way back, I heard my father's voice telling me about the planes he used to fly. I was quite young. Dad and I were alone because Mum had to bring Regina to the doctor's. Regina was constantly sick as a child, while I hardly ever got ill. Dad took me to the park on Cornwall Street near our house. I made him push my swing. Then he started telling me about flying, about his first training flight and how wonderful it was. I swung higher and higher. I'm going to fly too, like you, but you have to promise not to tell Mum and Regina because they'll laugh at me, I told him. It's our secret he promised me. Our secret.

I felt again that sense of violation. Gordie was rewriting my personal history.

He spoke into my silence. "This must feel strange, Rose. I hope I'm doing the right thing telling you all this. I'm not sure your father would have wanted you to know."

"Probably not. But it's not so bad, is it, that I do know? Anyway, what brought you back here now?"

That's when he told me he was planning to set up a business in aircraft leasing. It transpired he needed a lawyer to handle some initial contracts. I gave him Paul's number.

"So what do you think of Gordon Ashberry?" My father asked after dinner the next evening.

When Dad invited me along, all he had said was that Gordie was the son of a former colleague whom he hadn't seen for many years.

"Nice guy. Quite a *leaang jai,*" I replied. "What was his father like?"

"An excellent man. Never let you down." He said it definitely, almost defiantly. "Some people said he wasn't reliable, but that wasn't true. He was the kind of man who would risk his own life to save yours."

"He was courageous?"

"It was more than just courage. He had a kind of loyalty to people he cared about that was extremely strong. His other son who was killed in Vietnam got a Distinguished Flying Cross, you know."

My father was smiling as he spoke. We arrived at my home where he dropped me off. I was happy for Dad. While I wished he would tell me more, would be less evasive, I was glad that Gordie had returned. They had been so delighted to see each other.

That night, a Thursday, I slept soundly. No Paul, no Elliot. Elliot hadn't been pleased when I cancelled, but I told him I had to do this for my father. I didn't tell him everything about Gordie. There didn't seem any need to.

Right after Chinese New Year, Aunt Helen opened her own shop of Indonesian arts and crafts on Wyndham Street. In the months previous to that, she had talked my ear off about it, mostly because everyone else in the family was sick of listening to her. But I admired her stamina to do something late in life – she was already in her early sixties by then. Aunt Helen would never be too old for anything.

The money for the shop had come from the sale of some property belonging to Dad's family in Indonesia, and Helen had convinced Dad it should be used for the venture. Mum's initial reaction had been hostile.

"And what about our own family?" she'd said to me. "I tried to tell your father that it was crazy for him to do this. But you know how he is. Never listens to me."

Now, on the day of the grand opening, Mum called me at my office and continued her complaints. I listened as patiently as I could, while she berated Dad for wasting money. Finally, I couldn't stand it anymore. "It isn't all that much money, and it's not like you need it right now."

"Oh Rose, you always defend your father. When will you learn . . .?" But this time, I knew she couldn't push her point too far. "And what does Regina think?" I challenged her. It worked. "You know how your sister is when it comes to your aunt. Completely irrational. Can't see for a minute why I should be upset." She eventually hung up, muttering under her breath.

That evening, I went to the opening where I met Paul.

He was being nice to me these days, and particularly good to my family. That was the thing about Paul. He could be so perfect when he wanted to be. He had insisted on sending a huge, beautiful bouquet bedecked with red ribbons and Chinese messages wishing prosperity and good fortune. It stood there now, in the corner of the shop, towering over all the others. Nothing but the best, or at least, the most expensive.

We had been early, because Paul insisted, saying that people in Hong Kong always arrived late to things, and for Helen's sake, it would be good if some of us were there first.

The shop was narrow, its width not much greater than the entrance. It was on the upper part of Wyndham. A mass of colorful batik paintings covered every inch of wall space. It was a narrow and long space, which went back much further than I'd first imagined.

Aunt Helen was radiant. She sparkled with a youthfulness and vigor that made her seem about twenty years younger. She greeted all her friends — and many had shown up — basking in their congratulations and good wishes. Uncle Chong beamed at everyone who came. There was pride in his eyes and joy in his voice as he told everyone about all the last minute things that almost threatened to go wrong, and how Helen had sorted everything out in the end to make the opening a success.

Paul whispered to me, "Doesn't your aunt look wonderful?"

He had his arm around me and was smiling. Actually, I hadn't seen him in two days, but standing there, as our families and friends milled around, no one would ever have guessed.

"How have you been?" I asked him quietly, and he frowned at me. He looked a little fatigued to me these days, as if he hadn't been sleeping properly.

That was when Paul Sr. came up behind me. "Rose dear," he leaned forward to kiss me. "How are you?"

Marion gave her cool smile as she greeted us. "We haven't seen you both in ages. Rose, tell that son of mine he's got to stop working so hard and bring you home for dinner some night."

I chatted with my mother-in-law, studiously trying to avoid catching Paul Sr.'s eye. But he hovered around and I tensed as I felt his hand on my waist.

My father wandered over, giving me a brief respite. He and my mother said hello to my in-laws. They looked so mismatched, such unlikely acquaintances. What did they say about each other in private?

"You look thin, Rose. Are you eating properly?" Dad admonished me.

"She's always working too hard," Paul interjected. "We hardly eat together."

"You modern young women," Dad remarked, "simply don't have time for proper family life anymore."

"Dad, quiet."

"Your mother tells me I'm too quiet and my daughter tells me to be quiet. Women, can't please them, can we Paul?" My father beamed at him, and Paul acknowledged him with a smile.

Out of the corner of my eye, I saw David Ho taking photos to oblige my aunt. His half brother Albert chatted with Paul and myself. Everything seemed so dreadfully normal. I watched David snap away, and thought about our recent dinner conversation. He saw us and waved. Albert was polite, the way he usually was.

Remembering what Man Yee said about the son of Ho Yuet Kan, I pitied more than despised him, because at least Paul had come halfway out of the closet. Albert, a bachelor, should have had less reason for pretence.

My mother was restless and she and Dad left shortly after that. Guests began to disperse. "It's a wonderful place," I remember saying to Paul, and he nodded. Then I heard a familiar voice saying to Helen, "dreadfully sorry to be late," and Helen replying, "nonsense, Elliot, you're never too late." And then, "come over and say hello to my niece and her husband."

I had my back to Elliot, but Paul's eyes locked in his direction. He didn't seem to recognize him as Helen introduced them. It was a little difficult to remain cool. Elliot also appeared perturbed.

"So tell me about your magazine," Paul said.

He registered my husband's face and voice. And then, he collected himself and replied, and he and Paul conversed while my aunt dragged me off to help "direct David with the photography because isn't that what you do at work?"

I was glad for the reprieve, but found myself glancing back time and again at both Paul and Elliot standing there. As David and I picked out items that would photograph nicely, I kept glancing at my husband and lover thinking I simply could not imagine giving up either one of them, because each man had become such a part of me that I had to have both or neither. As we all parted that evening, my aunt said something about having us all over for dinner some night, now that everyone knew each other. I caught Elliot's eye for just a second, thinking he'd be amused, but what I saw instead was a flash of startled horror at my aunt's words.

"Pleasant chap," Paul remarked to me later that night.

I was undressing in my bedroom and was surprised by Paul standing at the doorway. "Who?"

"Elliot Cohen."

I kept my back to Paul. "Oh, him. Yes, I suppose he is."

"What's the name of the magazine he publishes?"

"AsiaMonth."

"Mmmm. Long in Asia?"

"Yes, I believe so."

"Thought he might be. Is he married to a Chinese? Seems the type."

"Don't know for sure. Don't think so."

As he wandered off he said, "We should have him out for dinner some night."

Had it been anyone else, I could have ignored the signals the way I had learned to do by then. Paul was extra sweet to me that night, and even came to my bed. He did that when he met men he was sexually attracted to. How could I not know? I was his wife and friend. There was even something faintly appealing about making love to Paul when he pretended I was Elliot.

"It would have happened sooner or later. Hong Kong's a small place." I could not understand Elliot's distress. He was nervous and skittish when I arrived the following Thursday, and even asked if I was sure Paul didn't know where I went each week.

"And what if your aunt were to know?"

I was washing dinner dishes. "She'd probably congratulate me on my good taste."

"Stop joking, Rose."

The thin gold rim around the edge of Elliot's plate was beginning to lose its luster. I dried it carefully; Elliot worried about things like china and cutlery. "What do you want me to say?"

The violence with which he gripped my arm made me drop the plate. It split neatly in two. "For god's sake, Elliot. What's the matter with you?"

"It's just a colossal joke to you, isn't it? You're never going to choose, are you?

"Choose?"

"Well, you can't keep your life in this state of suspended animation forever, can you? I mean surely it's obvious I want you for myself?"

I didn't stay with him that night. Was Elliot issuing me an ultimatum? How had things reached this point? Life with Paul had achieved a balance; I recognized the problems a divorce and acknowledging a relationship with Elliot would create for my family. Though I believed what I'd said about Aunt Helen, she would never approve of adultery. She may not even have wanted me to go out with Elliot previously, seeing him merely as a suitable friend.

That was the problem with life in Hong Kong. Everything was about what we speculated and guessed, not what we knew. Reality mattered more than truth, and the reality was that there was simply no need to choose between Elliot and Paul. Why should I? My husband offered me a better life than I ever dreamed of, and a kind of intimacy that stemmed from our long time together. Elliot was about adventure, physical pleasure and a kind of love. I had the best of all worlds. What more did I want?

At work the next morning. "It's Gordie, doll. Remember me?"

His voice on the other end of the line resounded. "Plastic or wooden?" I replied.

"Hello?"

"'Doll'. Plastic or wooden?"

"Just a figure of speech. Listen, can we have a drink? I want to proposition you."

Kenton stuck his head round just at that moment. "I told Ashberry to call you. We're doing something with him and maybe you can help."

At least work made sense, I thought, as I went to meet Gordie at the Mandarin that evening. Entering the hotel lobby, I wondered where Gordie got his money to stay at the likes of this place. There was a muted grandeur about the Mandarin. The narrow coffee shop off on its east side was a good breakfast place. And the golden horses on the mural that graced the high marble wall at the base of the stairs in the lobby swept your eye up towards the mezzanine space where society wives congregated for tea, and business people met for drinks after work. Elliot had first drawn my attention to that painting, which, he said was the work of some mad artist who designed wall paper for Cathay Pacific's planes.

Gordie did not stand up when I arrived at his table. "I ordered you a scotch," he said. "It's what you drink, right?"

"Kenton told you." I sat down opposite, ignoring the proffered seat next to him.

"No. Your father did."

I wanted to ask more about his relationship with Dad, but he seemed disinclined to talk about it this time. Instead, he launched straight into business. Kenton was apparently setting up an executive jet leasing business separately with Gordie.

"So the bottom line is that Kenton wants you in KL for about three to six months, after which I'd like you to come work for me in New York."

I digested this. The KL stint was just a last project at Pan Asian, but would give me a lot of time to do some of the set up work they needed for the new company, after which I could simply quit.

"Did you tell my father all this?"

"No. This is strictly between you and me."

"Why me?"

"Because you're tough enough for this shit."

"And what makes you think that?"

"Just instinct."

He saw me hesitate. It was a rather preposterous proposal. Finally, I said, "I'm married, Gordie. You know that."

"What's that got to do with anything?"

It was like David's statement – I hear your husband swings both ways. Elliot's words from the night before also bounced around my brain. There was something suspect about Gordie, just as there was about Kenton and my father. But all this seemed natural, as if my fate followed the same path as theirs.

"I need to think about it."

"So take your time. It doesn't have to happen this year if you don't want. The point is, I'm going to do this with Kenton. But we're not in a hurry. You are going to KL for a bit though, I understand."

It was true that Kenton brought it up from time to time. Nothing concrete had happened, but I was accustomed to my boss' way of doing things. When the time came, everything would move quickly, and I would be expected to respond. In his own way, he had given me fair warning. My life was going to change and it was up to me to decide its direction. This was definitely an unfamiliar sensation.

Paul left for Singapore that Sunday. He was scheduled to be away all the next week. I accompanied him in our car to the airport so that he wouldn't have to take a taxi. On the way, he mentioned something about Albert joining him the next day.

"You know, Albert's asked me to go to the States this year," he said. "To Provincetown in Massachusetts. Have you heard of it?"

I shook my head. "Are you going to go?"

"Maybe we could go together," he began, "at least to New York," he added hurriedly. "Gordon Ashberry wants me to do some work for him, so it would be a chance to see his company there. You could stay with Regina for a few days. Wouldn't you like that?"

I hadn't said anything about Gordie's job offer, although I had brought up the possibility of KL. He had been indifferent to it, the way he usually was when I'd brought it up in the past. "When is all this supposed to happen?"

"Sometime later this year. Maybe in the autumn. It would be a good holiday."

I left him at the airport, wondering about this turn of events. Nothing was surprising these days. Before he left, I promised to pick him up the following Saturday when he returned, since, as he put it, "Albert's coming back earlier and I won't be able to share his car pickup."

On Tuesday, Gordie rang to say he'd bug me on a regular basis until I agreed to work for him, but that it was all right if I kept saying no for awhile.

By Wednesday, Kenton made it clear that I had to let him know whether or not I was going to do the KL stint, regardless of Gordie.

That Thursday, I told Elliot about the increased possibility of being in KL for a few months. He was delighted.

"I'll work out of there, and just travel back to Hong Kong. We could even live together if you want. It'll be great."

He didn't bring up the conversation of the previous week.

Saturday afternoon rolled round. I went to the airport to pick Paul up. On the way, a taxi brushed next to me, scratching the passenger door. Paul was furious when he saw it.

"When will you learn to drive properly, Rose?"

I was taken aback by his tone of voice. "It wasn't my fault."

"Wasn't it? Here, you'd better let me drive."

I handed him the keys, thinking he was just tired from his trip. Back at home, he shut the door to the flat hard. "You're a bitch, you know that?"

Completely unprepared for this outburst, I took refuge in the armchair. He sat on the footstool directly in front of me. "You're a sly bitch." He glared at me with such hatred I wanted to run away.

"What are you talking about?"

"You and Man Yee, screwing each other."

I stared at him, horrified. "What makes you think that? I haven't done that."

"Are you denying you meet him," he pulled out a notebook, "at the ABC on Waterloo Road?"

"Have you been spying on me?"

"Are you denying it?"

"What's it to you?" I was shaking, genuinely frightened by him. "For god's sake Paul, he's your lover. What makes you think he'd be sleeping with me?"

"Because he told me."

"And you believe him?"

"Why shouldn't I?"

"Because it's ridiculous, that's why!"

Paul's face was contorted. And then, almost under his breath, he added, "It's the kind of thing he's capable of."

He tossed the notebook at me. It was from a private detective. I think at that moment whatever love I felt for Paul vanished forever. As he continued to glare at me, his anger at this imagined betrayal between us, I saw only a man whose loyalties had left me. Man Yee controlled him, manipulated him, and he gave in to it all because he couldn't let him go. So he chose to believe Man Yee's outrageous lie. I wanted to shout at him — but I'm your wife! — appealing to his sense of family, which he held over me with such vigilance. But I couldn't. It suddenly became clear that our idea of family was at the root of all our problems.

"I think," he said getting up, "that I'd better move into the study." And then, before I could protest or defend myself, he added, "I'm going out in a few minutes and won't be home tonight. I'll start the divorce proceedings Monday."

I called Man Yee as soon as Paul left. "What the devil are you getting up to? I thought you were my friend."

"It's not what you imagine. I owe you an apology I know, but it's

not at all what you think. I think I'd better not see you anymore."
He hung up on me.

I wanted to scream and cry, but couldn't. There was still dinner at my parents to go to that evening. From feeling in control earlier that week, suddenly, my life was exploding into senseless bits again.

When I arrived alone at my parents for dinner that night, my mother was in a frenzy. She didn't even comment on Paul's absence.

"Your father is going to invest money in some silly venture with a stranger."

Dad was trying to calm her. "Please, I've explained to you. He's the son of a long time friend and business associate."

"Some strange *gwailo!*"

It transpired that Gordie had been to see him. I didn't know what to say. Dad's eyes spoke to our silent conspiracy. He opened his newspaper and prepared to ignore Mum.

"I'm going to tell your sister, and she'll stop you. She knows you have no head for business. What do you think of that?" she continued, almost shouting.

"You will no matter what I think."

"That's because you can't be bothered to think!" Her voice had risen to a higher pitch than usual.

"Calm down, Mum. It's not such a big deal."

"What do you know? You have your head in the sand, just like your father."

And she picked up her handbag and walked towards the door.

I watched her, surprised. "Where're you going?"

"To church! Sometimes I just don't understand this family of mine. Where did I go wrong?"

The dining table was still set for dinner. I brought the food out and served it, my head spinning. Dad shook his head and continued to read.

We had a quiet dinner.

I went home to an empty flat.

Around ten, I called Elliot, asking if he would meet me at the Peninsula bar.

"You? Risk being seen with me? And on a socially important Saturday night?" Elliot liked the privacy of his weekends, and his sarcasm was more than simply teasing.

"I have something to tell you."

"Can't you do it over the phone? Or come over to my place? You know I don't like it when you drink just for the sake of it."

I thought about the first lunch we had, and was about to make a smart remark. But all I said was, "Please Elliot, I need to see you."

"Rose, what's the matter?"

"Please, just meet me."

He agreed, and I wandered into the dimly lit mezzanine level piano bar forty five minutes later. Elliot was already there, hidden in a corner.

He stood as I approached. "I didn't want to be conspicuous." He gestured to the chosen seat. After he ordered me a Glenfiddich, he said, "now, what's up?"

I edged next to him and put his arm around my shoulder. He drew back slightly, startled. "It's okay," I said, "it doesn't matter anymore." And then, taking a deep breath, I said. "It's Paul. He wants a divorce." I told him that Paul set a detective on me, and had reported on my having an affair. The lie slipped out so easily that I hardly believed myself. But I couldn't tell Elliot, even now, that my husband kept a male concubine and would sacrifice me for him.

"So leave him, Rose. Let him go. He's letting you go."

"And do what?"

"Marry me of course. I'm tired of being invisible. Besides, Paul knows now, doesn't he?"

The problem of my deception was already entangling me. "And when you grow tired of being visible?"

He drew me towards him and caressed my face with the back of his hand. "I'll love you forever, Rose."

I backed away, suddenly conscious of the glare on our public stage. "I don't need love forever. It's only marriage that exacts such an unreasonable demand."

"Okay, so don't marry me, I don't care. Just love me."

"But it's not that simple, there're ten thousand details . . ."

Elliot took both my hands and lifted them to his lips. "You know what the ancients say about the ten thousand things. Let me help you make them one. Go on, go home and get some clothes and stay with me for a few days."

I was tempted to go with him that night. But all I could think of was the truth I kept from him. Why had I lied? I had fully intended to tell him all about Man Yee, about what had really happened. Yet when I saw him and felt his touch, as I started speaking to him, warmed by the malt whiskey, I had lied. And so I couldn't go with him, because I couldn't bear the thought of beginning our life on such a blatant untruth.

When he kissed me goodnight and sent me off in a taxi, I don't think he even slightly suspected my dishonesty. He waved goodbye to me, and I pretended not to see his gesture. An awful feeling welled up in me — that I was slowly and surely destroying our love. Or was it simply the unravelling of our bond, a bond founded at best on a precarious kind of intimacy? I didn't know. I just didn't know.

I went home and called Man Yee, waking him.

"I want to see you." My voice was angry, distraught.

"Don't come here, Rose."

"Give me the address. I have to see for myself."

At three in the morning, it's remarkably easy to get a taxi in Hong Kong. I found one almost as soon as I stepped out my door and arrived at Man Yee's flat a few minutes later. The entrance was on a side street at the corner of the main road. As I stepped out of the taxi, I could see the lights of Kai Tak airport across the road.

He was waiting for me.

"Want some tea?" he offered.

I nodded.

The flat was, as he had described, in an old Chinese building. It contained only a few pieces of Chinese furniture — the hard, rosewood sofa was beautiful but uncomfortable, designed for discipline, not living. But I liked its stark severity: the floor made of roughly hewn pale pink and grey granite tiles, the cool feeling of the high ceilings and bare walls, the square simplicity of the room. It was a space to smoke an opium pipe in peace.

As he returned from the kitchen with my glass of tea, I heard a deep cough from the bedroom.

Man Yee shook his head. "It's okay, it isn't Paul." He set the tea down next to me, leaving the metal lid on the glass. Pulling up a footstool, he sat opposite me. "I didn't tell him, you know. He assumed our affair, even though I told him otherwise."

"How long ago?"

"From the time of that New Year's party where you danced with me. I mean, do you believe it?"

"So he's been harboring it for over a year?"

"Yes. And his private detective's been trailing me for at least three months."

"Trailing you?" I was incredulous.

He nodded and looked away, showing me his understanding of my humiliation as the wife unseated by the concubine.

I picked up the glass by its rim and lifted the lid. The fragrance of jasmine warmed my nostrils. Blowing lightly on the tea, I raised the glass to my lips.

"He can't help it, you know," Man Yee continued, "he's the jealous type. Also, Albert might have set him up to it. I think Albert's in love with Paul."

"He's only jealous of you." I couldn't hold back the rising envy. It sickened me, while exposing what I disliked in myself.

"Of you too, Rose, otherwise he wouldn't have been angry at you. He loves you ."

"You forgive him everything."

"And don't you?"

I looked away.

"You do, admit it. Why else aren't you with Elliot tonight?"

"I was."

"So why don't you leave Paul?"

I held onto the glass and stared at the tea. A sprinkling of leaves settled at the bottom.

"Doesn't Elliot love you?"

"Yes, but . . ." I couldn't look at him.

Man Yee leaned forward and gently stroked my cheek. *"Gwai dou haih yan —* gwai are people too. You should know, Paul's *jaahp jung."*

I snapped at him. "It's not that. I don't think I'm so narrow minded. Or racist."

"But you are, aren't you? Just a little bit. Paul does try so hard to be Chinese."

"Elliot's wonderful. He makes me feel like a woman."

"But you don't love him?"

"Maybe, I'm not sure I know."

He picked up my glass and replaced it on the table. He stood me up and took me in his arms. "Why must we love Paul so much?" he whispered. And I began to cry. The peculiar familiarity of my husband's lover was more reassuring, and honest, than any other intimacy.

I didn't sleep at all that night. Wandering around my empty home, I rearranged pictures, reorganized the china cabinet, polished our silver, cleaned my jewellery. In Paul's study, his reference books needed straightening. My brain wouldn't stop reeling through the movie of my life with Paul, sometimes speeding up to erase large chunks of time, sometimes decelerating into slower than slow motion so that every remembered conversation, action, gesture or even a single facial expression forced its way onto a centre stage larger than a cinema screen.

Like Marion's face, the night she told me Paul was "not like other men." She pleaded with a look of desperation. It was not in her nature to beg, and that moment must have been extremely difficult for her. And then, with an almost blinding clarity, I saw Paul's face, the night he told me I owed him the life he'd given me. After my return from KL, he had at first been desperate to hold onto me, to keep what we had. Yet, so quickly, just like his mother, he retreated back into a hard shell of safety formed by a lie. Because that was the night he told me he believed I'd never been pregnant. It was a way of not having to acknowledge his own infertility, which, in some complex fashion, was tied up with his bisexual identity. Likewise Marion, as long as she believed that her son could live a "normal" life in society, she could pretend that nothing was wrong.

How alike they were!

"We're Chinese, Rose." Paul's words, from way back in our teenage life, spoke to me again. "We can't get away from it." He had made it matter to me, the way I knew it mattered to my father, despite what he wouldn't articulate. Something about being our brand of overseas Chinese, mongrel Chinese — desperate on the one hand for the all important *deih waih*, "position," equal status actually with the supposedly "real" Chinese of Hong Kong — made

227

us hard, but a brittle kind of hard. Paul and I were walking on the beach when he said that to me. I had been collecting shells, and had filled a plastic bag with several small and delicate ones. That was when I found the large cone-shaped one which I thought was a great treasure. But Paul had said I should throw it away, because it was ugly and marred by dirt that looked too ingrained to clean. Like damaged goods, he said. I protested, because I liked it, because it was a solid and heavy one, unlike the other pretty shells. So I kept it, which made Paul smile, because in those days he always called me his "special angel," after the song, the one whom he would indulge in all her whims.

In the late afternoon, before we went home, he led me behind a rock where we sat down together, away from all our friends. That was when he stretched me out on the ground and lay close to me in an embrace. It had been a long summer that year; the air was still warm and humid even though it was already early October. We kissed passionately but hurriedly, so that our friends wouldn't find us, and, in our eagerness, the bag of shells crunched loudly beneath me. I had almost cried when I saw my whole pretty collection crushed, and Paul was sympathetic and sweet. But my cone shaped shell remained intact, and I waved it at him happily, saying, see, it wasn't delicate and beautiful, but at least it survived.

That ABC moves like a gwai, *despite his Chinese face.*

A long time ago, some slick Englishman translated gwai *as "foreign devil." But it isn't that simple, is it? In the world I came from, there were Chinese, the* yan, *meaning people or humans, and then there were all the rest, the* gwais.

Yet sometimes I think it was we the yan *who were inhuman.*

Was the truth of my life simply what Gordie says life's about — where devils are angels and angels are devils and all are just yan? *Gordie wonders about his half sister, his father's secret. I've encouraged him to find her, and perhaps one day he will. It's important to make the connection, the way I did with Man Yee, however painful. It exposed a truth about Paul that I didn't want to face but that I was, in the end, better off knowing.*

13

The sun shone brilliantly on Monday morning. Just as I was about to leave home for work, Stan called from New York to say Regina had almost succeeded in killing herself again. Tristan had left her for good. I talked to him a little longer, and promised to try visit, since he seemed to think that was what she needed.

After I hung up, I set off for work. Mixed fractions are a nuisance, I kept hearing over and over in my head, the voice of Sister Martha Gerard looming from a long way back in my childhood. I tried to think about Regina, but all I could remember was our primary three arithmetic class.

Mixed fractions, with their jarringly incomplete shapes, daunted Regina to tears. She simply never understood how their inherent puzzles could yield solutions if you tried. I remember Sister Martha showing us how to arrive at 1963, the year we first learned mixed fractions. Let's say, she began, shoving the wisps of grey hair back into her habit, that you had to solve this problem:

5 2/19 - 1 15/19 = ?

As she wrote across the blackboard, Regina cringed at the sound of screeching chalk.

Well girls, said our East Coast nun, isn't that a nuisance?

Regina made a face at me, but I was smiling, happy, because the whole exercise felt like a wonderful game and made perfect sense to me. "Wouldn't you rather be at the beach?" my sister whispered to me, but my hand waved her comment aside and I refused to look at her.

Now let's solve this, continued Sister Martha, and she wrote in her firm hand a second line of large numbers underneath the first:

97/19 - 34/19 =?

Since both fractions now have a nineteen underneath, you can ignore it, she said, and suddenly it's just a simple sum of ninety-seven minus thirty-four that even a child in primary one can solve!

And the answer of course was 63/19 or, as she put it, the year of

Our Lord nineteen hundred and sixty three.

For weeks after that I'd try to show Regina how to solve the problem, but she refused to listen, refused to understand. Mixed fractions, she claimed, weren't a "nuisance" — that was just Sister Martha being silly to make babies like me believe her. Numbers, like all things, had to be whole, not mixed, to make sense, she insisted. But, I argued, can't you see that you can solve the problem if you try, to which she'd laugh in my face, saying problems were for cry babies like me who would rather cry than laugh. In time, I gave up although that year, I began to resent Regina copying my homework and answers on tests, because it struck me that she was playing the wrong game. More important, I felt she was unfair because she'd never even tried to understand.

Later, I called Paul at his office. "So what happens?"

"I can't talk about it right now."

A strange realization dawned. "You're not going to file for divorce."

He hesitated. Finally, "no."

"Then I'll tell my boss I'll move to KL for a few months, the way he wants me to. It might be the best thing."

"Do that, Rose. Maybe that would be best for now. We'll leave each other alone for awhile. No one need know."

That was it. In less than five minutes, my life changed into something completely different from what I'd known. I could live away from Paul with impunity. He had uttered "divorce," even though he couldn't go through with it, which frightened yet freed me. We had an "understanding," the way our marriage was always about an understanding. And, most of all, no one need know.

"You can have him," I told Man Yee that evening.

He gazed mournfully at me. We were at the ABC, having earlier decided that it made no difference now that the private investigator's report had disclosed our rendezvous. "I don't think so. He's 'divorcing' both of us."

I sipped on my iced coffee. It was too bitter. I added more syrup. "Do you really think he'll go through with it?" I wasn't ready to admit what I already knew about Paul's inclinations.

"What do you think? You've known him longer than me."

That was when I told him about the pregnancy in Plattsburgh, and how Paul had not come through in the end.

"Was it his child?"

"Probably not." Saying that had a strangely exhilarating effect. I had released my secrets to the wind.

"And the second time? Before your wedding? I know it was a false pregnancy, but was it his?"

Secrets were meaningless, I realized, as I looked into Man Yee's eyes. The intimacy he shared with my husband meant that assorted pieces of my life no longer belonged to me. "No. There was this other guy. I don't think I could get pregnant with Paul. He must have a low sperm count, or something, or maybe he's just infertile."

That idea appeared to give him pause. "Do you want a child?"

"No." It had come out so definitely, the answer to a question no one ever posed. All my friends and family, even Regina, assumed I wanted children. They simply thought we were waiting, or, in my mother's case, that I was barren. Part of that had to do with Paul, who invested such a lot in presenting our model marriage to the world. But a greater part had to do with me, because I didn't express opinions either loudly or at all the way, for instance, my sister would. I did what made sense to me, regardless of what anyone else thought. I just didn't bother talking about my private life. Even now, when I was in such a confessional mood, I knew I still held back. Elliot would go crazy over this aspect of me. I couldn't help it; it was just the way I was.

"So why should you be afraid of divorce?"

"I don't know, but I am."

There was a comfort in talking to Man Yee that didn't happen with anyone else. The shared absurdity of our situation, the knowledge we had of each other that we were each invested in keeping away from others in our lives, the private yet public lives we both led — all this contributed to a collision of sensibilities, harboring both concealment and disclosure. It was like looking into a funhouse mirror at myself, where distortion was normal. Earlier, Elliot had called to make sure I was okay. And I had assured him — yes, I'd be okay, everything would be okay. Yet if he could see me now, what would he feel? Anger? Betrayal? With Man Yee, there was nothing to betray.

So, perhaps Paul was right to be angry with us, because what we knew and understood about him left him defenceless. Paul needed to wield so much power and control, yet, right now, Man Yee and I were the ones with the real power. Would he leave us? As he'd told me before, we needed each other. Talking to Man Yee made me realize I wasn't ready to give Paul up, not yet, perhaps not ever, but that it was up to me, not him, to make the real decisions about our marriage.

The next day, Teresa told me she planned to take vacation while I was away.

I had told Kenton I was thinking seriously about going to Kuala Lumpur, but hadn't yet committed to doing it. "Everyone assumes I'm just going to go."

"Why not? Won't Elliot be pleased? He's always asking you to go there."

I made a face. She laughed and left my office. It had been some time since I'd stopped denying to Teresa that Elliot and I weren't having an affair. Even though I'd never admitted it to her, she took it for granted, and was quite nonchalant about it. She was funny that way. What she didn't know, but felt she could speculate about, seemed to meet with her approval. Had I told her, she would probably have felt compelled to disapprove. But I hadn't told her the truth about Paul; she thought he had a mistress.

On Wednesday morning, Kenton called me into his office. "Ashberry says you'll go to KL."

He was issuing my orders to go. I knew there wasn't any point stalling. "I will if you really want me to." I looked at him defiantly, adding, "For the company. Gordon Ashberry may know my father, but I'll reserve judgment about him."

"Forget Ashberry, Rose. If things materializes, we can always talk then. Okay?"

"Okay." Everything moved fast, easily, as if this all made sense. Kenton I could trust. He wouldn't do anything to really cause me problems. Besides, he knew something about my father, about where my roots began, about who I really was. In a work context, I found his authority an acceptable compromise.

Thursday night rolled round and I told Elliot over dinner. He wasn't just pleased: he was ecstatic. "I'll take time off and move in with you."

"You can't do that. It's not like I'll be on holiday. What about the magazine?"

"I'll make a lot of sales calls in KL and Singapore. Besides, the circulation in both those cities is already growing past Hong Kong's. Maybe I'll move the HQ to Singapore. It'll be fun."

"But . . ."

"If you're thinking about Paul, forget him. He's leaving you. He won't care. Think about not having to spend time only in my place. We can even go away on weekends. You don't work all the time, right?"

No, I assured him, I didn't work all the time — it was only an illusion I fostered to keep my life sane. Then, he kissed me, swearing quietly that if he couldn't take me away from Paul now, he never would.

In the weeks leading up to my departure, everyone seemed equally delighted. Paul told my mother this was an extremely important step in my career, which made him an even greater hero in her eyes because he was such a "progressive" husband. Aunt Helen and Uncle Chong were thrilled, and kept giving me names of people they knew in Malaysia to look up. Regina, in her post-suicidal phase, told me that separating from Paul was the best thing I'd done since I'd met him, pointing to her own miserable experience with Tristan whom she "should have dumped ages ago." I wanted to point out that Paul and Tristan were hardly comparable, since the latter never made a commitment to her the way Paul had to me, but I decided to keep quiet instead.

My in-laws were sanguine but supportive. Marion congratulated me on my courage to be different, to do something most married women wouldn't dare do. She even hinted confidentially that her own marriage would have benefitted by such a possibility. Paul Sr., one night at dinner, glared at me with malicious glee. Later, during a private moment, he murmured something about how I'd now have the freedom for my *affaires de la coeur,* although he said it so quickly, and in such a vague whisper, I couldn't be sure I heard right. I shuddered a little, and as he kissed me goodnight he said in my ear, "be a good girl now; I'm still your father-in-law after all."

Gordie never stopped bugging me with his ideas — from starting an executive jet service for VIP's in Asia headed to the west, to offering pilot training for Asian nationals through a cooperative effort with one of the aircraft manufacturing corporations, to starting a flying club in South East Asia. I suppose he was hoping I'd find one of them appealing and agree to work for him.

Even Man Yee approved, saying it was courageous of me to "accept power," something he claimed he was now learning how to do.

And Elliot, dear Elliot, couldn't keep away from me, especially since Paul gave me lots of space, which meant that for a time in my little universe I was quite the queen.

About a week before I left, I went looking for my father at the Tsimshatsui off-track betting shop he frequented on Saturday afternoons. We had this unspoken arrangement. If I wanted to find him in private away from home, here was where I generally met him. He suggested a cup of tea. I glanced around us on Cameron Road.

"There's the pizza place," he offered.

I had never been in Joe's Place during the day, only in the evenings for dinner. The darkened atmosphere surprised me. There was a bar on one side where a handful of Brits were getting sloshed. My father had discovered this place when I was about twelve, and Regina and I had loved their huge, rectangular, thin-crust pizzas, the first of their kind in Hong Kong then.

We sat at a table and ordered our tea.

"So why are you going, Rose?" He knew exactly why I'd come. My uncertainty was not evident to anyone except him.

I didn't reply right away.

"What's wrong? Are things . . . difficult with Paul?"

"We're okay."

"So why are you doing this?"

"It's just work, Dad."

"No it's not." His tone was emphatic. "I can tell it's not. No work is that important as to separate a wife from her husband. Besides, I know Mr. Kenton thinks highly of you, and he wouldn't insist if you refused."

"And if I had been a man? Could I have left my wife for two months?" It was my way of reminding him when he had gone to the States for that long on a special assignment.

"That was different."

I dropped that tack, knowing it would be a waste of time with my father, since he deplored anything that echoed of what he called "that liberation woman thing." Yet the truth of what he said bothered me. Kenton never made me do anything I didn't really want to. He sipped his tea as we sat facing each other in silence for a long while.

"You don't need Paul anymore, do you?"

"No." My reply was automatic.

"That's too bad."

There was an even longer silence, shattered finally by the sound of breaking glasses when a tray full of tumblers fell off the shelf at the waiters station.

"Let's go," my father said. At the doorway, he stopped before heading off in the opposite direction. There was a strange look of understanding in his eyes. "Maybe," he began slowly, "it's a good thing you have an education. After all, I won't always be here to look after you."

Three o'clock.

Saamgang bunyeh or as Dad preferred to say in Mandarin, banye-sanggeng. Dead of night, middle of the night, ancient Chinese division of the night. My "gang" or "geng," my night watch. Less, yet more precise than three o'clock, an hour that's neither here nor there.

Gordie looks beat. I've seldom seen him fatigued. All this must be taking more of a toll than he's admitted. How much longer can those Feds question him?

Dad warned him. I overheard them talking one night before I moved to the US. Even when I'd agreed to go, Dad still didn't take me into his confidence. Doesn't matter a whole lot now. I knew about the arms running. Gordie even hinted as much about his dad and mine doing more or less the same thing years ago. I guess if you gamble like Dad, you have to cover your debts somehow. But he did eventually learn

235

to curb his gambling appetite. I know he did.

So now I'm about to lose my last bit of respectability. In the meantime, Regina's made a reputation for herself in the art world, and is actually quite "respectable." When she goes home she'll do all right. The Arts Centre wants to do an exhibit of her paintings, since she's "avant garde and angry, but frustrated at her powerlessness" which one critic described as the spirit of Hong Kong's youth today. How funny. Paul's going to have a coronary for sure, although . . .

I wish morning would come. Bunyeh — *Midnight or half darkness — depending on your point of view.*

"Leanna wants us over for dinner tonight."

My first weekend in KL. "Elliot, is that a good idea?" In from a swim, I had stripped off my bathing suit in the bathroom, and had just emerged wrapped in a towel.

"Is what a good idea?" He dragged the towel off me and wrestled me to the bed. "We have time. She's not coming to pick us up for another twenty minutes." Whatever misgivings I felt at this unexpected dinner date were overcome during the next quarter of an hour, and, afterwards, I showered and dressed in five minutes flat.

My hair was drip drying as we waited in the hotel lobby. I wanted to ask Elliot about this sudden appointment, but, before I could, Leanna was walking towards us.

"Rose, I'm so delighted to see you again!" She greeted me with air kisses on both cheeks. She was wearing a low cut tightly fitting batik dress which flattered her figure. Her long hair was tied in a French braid, with a matching batik ribbon running through it. She had on three inch heeled sandals, and stood as tall as Elliot. When he leaned over to kiss her, she insinuated her body against his, in a movement that reminded me of Regina.

"So you're here for, two months, is it?" She said over her shoulder as she drove. Leanna had insisted Elliot sit in front because of his longer legs, even though he had protested, saying I should be up there to see the view. I hadn't made a fuss.

"Yes, maybe longer."

She spoke in an affected British accent. "It'll be simply awful staying in an hotel all that time. You know, I have plenty of room.

You're quite welcome to stay with me. Ask Elliot, he knows it's no bother. In fact," she carried on without waiting for my response, "you're being awfully bad, Elliot, staying at an hotel."

She was the type of woman who actually said "an hotel" and made me dizzy with her chatter.

We arrived at her house. I was struck again by how beautiful everything was, how beautiful she was. Leanna whirled into the kitchen, dragging Elliot with her "because he's my sous-chef" while exhorting me to "make myself at home, everyone else does." Elliot gave me an apologetic grin, but followed her. Alone in the living room, I wandered over to the piano. On it was a photo of Leanna and another woman who resembled her. It had to be her sister, Elliot's ex-wife.

I felt a rising tide of jealousy. Aunt Helen was right, she was cheap looking and wore too much makeup and much too short and revealing a dress, the kind hookers wore. But she was sensual, with thick lips that men liked, and provocative eyes. Next to her, Leanna had an elegant simplicity. But earlier, I had caught myself thinking that had her dress been any tighter, her panty lines would show.

"Who are you?"

I turned around and saw a young girl, about nine, glaring at me. She had the angriest eyes I'd ever seen in a child.

Leanna emerged from the kitchen, followed by Elliot. "Anita, Darling. Say hello to Auntie Rosie," Leanna crooned.

I looked at Anita and then back at Elliot. The resemblance was uncanny. I stuck my hand out. "Hi, I'm Rose, not Rosie," I said, pointedly.

"Hi Rose." She shook my hand — her rather iron grip surprised me — and flashed a smile that seemed to come from the heart. As quickly as she smiled, her expression turned sullen again as she disappeared into the kitchen behind her aunt. Elliot watched them go ruefully. He rubbed his nose and blinked. "My daughter's not being very sociable, I'm afraid."

Leanna flounced out a few minutes later. She was barefoot. Her braid had come undone, and she shook it out, tossing her thick, sleek hair over her shoulders. Flinging herself on the sofa, she crossed her long tanned legs. Her tight skirt rode up, showing off a lot of thigh. She seemed quite oblivious to her body. "I'm exhausted!" she exclaimed. "That niece of mine is absolutely impossible and it's all your fault, Elliot. Rose, I'm sorry to bore you with all this family business. Thank god she's leaving in a couple of weeks. And it's about time you got here to straighten her out."

She made me feel even more of an intruder, and I wished Elliot had told me his daughter was there. But I didn't have time to think much more about it, because Leanna swept us all to the table for dinner.

Anita asked. "So where did you come from?"

"Hong Kong."

"Oh." She carried on eating her soup. "I was born there, you know, but I don't remember much about the place because I left when I was four."

"Would you like to come visit?" Elliot asked.

Anita considered this. "Maybe. Do you have a 'swimmy-pool' like Auntie Lee-anni?" Her tone was slightly mocking, slightly condescending, as she imitated Leanna.

"I'm afraid not. Hong Kong's more like New York, only smaller."

I didn't say much during the meal. It was unnerving, this family and life of Elliot's that I hadn't encountered in its entirety. It was his life away from me, a life I didn't share, and didn't know if I wanted to share.

After dinner, Anita asked Elliot to take her for a walk. "Don't worry," Leanna said, "I'll look after Rosie while you're out." I resented her tone, her manner of treating me as if I were a child. But that seemed to be the way she treated everyone.

She directed me to the rattan sofa on the porch behind the mosquito screen. The evening air was comfortable. Leanna seated herself on the rattan swing; her movements were slow and graceful, like a dancer. But every move was suggestive and deliberate, from the way she stretched her legs, to the way she lifted the hair out of her eyes.

"Here," she said, handing me a glass of iced cold chendol. "It's good."

I sipped my drink through the straw, trying to stir away the pieces of chendol at the bottom.

"Elliot's told me a lot about you. He wants to marry you." She looked ahead into the open space as she spoke.

I wasn't quite ready to discuss my lover with her, so I said nothing.

She seemed unfazed by my silence. "He's a wonderful man, you know. I've never forgiven my sister for leaving him. They're getting their divorce, by the way. He's probably told you about our relationship, but let me assure you I only want what's best for Elliot. I'm not here to fight with you, Rosie. I want to be your friend because Elliot loves you, and I care deeply about him. Goodness knows, I've tried to help him as much as I could, especially with Anita."

She looked as if she were about to burst into tears. It was difficult to accept this display of martyrdom, so I said nothing.

"Besides, Anita needs a mother," she added, more calmly now.

"Anita has a mother," I remarked curtly.

Leanna barrelled on. "My sister, bless her, is hopeless. What I mean is, she's marvellous at jetsetting around the world and getting glamorous modelling assignments. But she has no time for a child."

"So why doesn't Elliot take custody?"

She looked shocked. "But a girl needs a mother. That would be impossible. I've taken Anita for long stretches when my sister runs off with some new lover, but there are limits. The poor child spends more time with her French governess. She's beginning to speak English with a funny accent. She doesn't know a word of Chinese. You and Elliot could help her with that."

I contemplated this new role thrust upon me. Could I really be a good mother? I didn't even know what it meant to be a wife, and especially not Elliot's wife. I needed to get off this uncomfortable subject quickly. "Don't you find the constant heat here oppressive?"

"I love it. I was born here and the sun's wonderful. Besides, the trick is not to wear too many clothes." She winked conspiratorially. "I only wear dresses and no panties. It's just the old sarong tradition, as I'm sure you know being part Indonesian yourself." She gave me an innocent look. "You should try it. Elliot likes that. Unfortunately," and she gave my body a sidelong glance, "I do need a bra."

Bitch, I thought, but she did have an enviable cleavage for a Chinese woman — at least a 35B, I reckoned — while I had trouble finding bras small enough. I'd get my own back for that remark. But that solved the panty line problem. I watched Elliot and Anita ambling back towards the house, hand in hand. He suddenly looked much older, as old as he really was, and I was reminded of the ten-year age gap between us.

"You don't like children, do you?" Leanna's voice, challenging and slightly defiant, startled me. She had been so exuberant and gushy previously, oozing warmth and friendship.

Determined not to let her intimidate me, I replied in the same challenging tone. "Why do you say that?"

She backed off and adopted her sweet voice again. "Oh I was just wondering, since I know you don't have any children. Doesn't your husband want children?"

I wondered what, if anything, Elliot had told her about Paul. I hoped not much. "Yes and no," I lied.

"Oh, I see."

I could tell she was reserving her questions for a later time.

"You should have told me more about Leanna. And Anita."

I was moving into a service flat with Elliot's help over the weekend, having decided that would be more comfortable than "an hotel," and also because I was tired of Leanna ringing every day to invite me to stay at her house. Paul had been indifferent when I rang to give him my new contact. "Enjoy it," was all he said.

"What's to tell?" Elliot had commandeered a corner of the closet for his own clothes and was hanging shirts neatly in place.

"They're family. I mean let's face it. If I get divorced, you and I are going to have to deal with family."

"When are you getting divorced? Elliot could be annoyingly cool when he chose. He continued straightening up the closet and barely glanced at me.

"I don't know, but we need to talk about the family side of things."

"Oh, so you are getting divorced?"

"I didn't say that."

"So what are you saying, Rose?" He had finally turned around to face me. "Quit being so Chinese. Why does family matter or anything matter until you decide, once and for all, that you want to be with me? When you do, then we'll have something to talk about."

Elliot was like that at times. I dropped the subject. We were going to dinner at Lars'. Myrna was making satay. It was funny about those two. They seemed to understand, without my explaining, that Elliot and I were together, regardless of my husband. They didn't judge or pry. I liked them for that.

We picked up Anita. She seemed in a good mood that evening and chattered away about school. Leanna was right. The child had a slight French accent. On the way over, she asked about Kristin.

"She's only five, and she's sad sometimes because her mother died," I told her.

"Leanna said I can be her big sister because they're friends of yours."

"Why don't you meet them first, and then decide whether you want to be friends with them yourself?"

Anita seemed pleased about that. Leanna probably didn't deal well with the girl's innate sense of independence and self reliance. I suddenly felt a little sorry for her. Elliot and his wife couldn't be much good as parents; they were still too busy being children themselves.

Lars was happy to see me again. Elliot seemed to enjoy himself. And Anita and Kristin took to each other. It was a relaxed and easy evening.

That night Elliot was unusually recalcitrant. He looked worried. Anita would be leaving the next day. When we dropped her off at Leanna's home after dinner, she had given him a big kiss and said, quite out of the blue, "I love you, pop." It was funny hearing her French accent against that very American expression. Earlier, she had called him "hey, you" or nothing at all.

Just as we were about to get into bed, Elliot remarked, "I used to call my father 'pop', you know." He kissed me lightly on the cheek, and turned his back to me, but I knew he wasn't ready to sleep. I ran my finger down his back.

"I've been thinking about Regina," I said softly into his ear.

He turned back to face me. Elliot didn't talk about himself or his family much. But he always responded if I talked about mine. "How's she doing?"

"Better. I talked to Stan before I left Hong Kong, and he says she's going through a manic high right now, which means she's writing and painting up a storm."

"I'd like to meet her sometime. Could I? In New York?"

He'd asked me increasingly often as of late. I hadn't told him she didn't know about us. "Let me tell you a story," I began. "When we were both thirteen, Regina kissed a guy for the first time. She told me how they went to a movie together and sat in the back row. He French kissed her and touched her breasts. We were in bed when she told me. It was summer and hot. I started to stroke my thighs while she described how he took her hand and placed it on his penis, which was stiff. He pushed her hand away when he got over excited. I imagined him ejaculating in his pants in the cinema, and that it was my hand pushing into his pants. Regina kept talking in a flat voice, describing how he closed his eyes, sweating, trying to control himself. When he calmed down, he started kissing her again, pushing his hand between her legs until his fingertips touched her underpants. I pushed my fingers into my panties and began rubbing myself. My sister continued talking in a monotone from her bed, saying that her date buried his face into her shoulder as his penis stiffened again. I felt myself get wet, and rubbed harder, the friction of my legs against each other making me more and more excited. I didn't want to let Regina know what was happening, so I tried not to make too much movement. 'Did you like it?' I asked her, my body aching with pleasure. 'No,' she replied.' It felt like nothing, nothing at all.' And as she said this, I felt the deep rising flush of my first orgasm."

"Your sister is not like you, is she?" Elliot was already aroused.

"No, she's not."

He was sliding his fingers against my side, his prelude to our lovemaking. There was an easy rhythm about everything here in Malaysia.

"I don't think she derives any pleasure at all from sex. It's strange."

He climbed on top of me. "While it's your principle pleasure, right?"

"Probably," I agreed.

More than a month after my arrival in KL, Paul called for the first time.

"Auden asked about you the other night. He said to send his regards." He paused, and then added, "he says he looks forward to seeing you at the annual ball."

It was as if he had never mentioned divorce. "Are we going?"

"Of course. Don't we every year?" He could have been talking about a routine business appointment.

"I don't know about that."

"Don't be silly, Rose. There's nothing to discuss."

"But there is." By now, I had begun to think about my divorcing Paul, although I didn't yet admit it to Elliot.

"Well there's plenty of time. When you get back I mean. The ball isn't till November."

The stupid ball again. As if our whole world should revolve around Auden, Rose, Wang & Lie. I felt a flush of anger at his obtuseness.

That evening after work, I told Elliot Paul didn't seem to want a divorce anymore.

"So you divorce him, Rose." It was the first time I'd even mentioned Paul since the night we had dinner at Lars and Myrna's. "Look, he finally calls, and all he cares about is that you're back in time for some society ball. Did he even ask how you were? Does he even care?" An impatience crept into his voice. "Honestly Rose, he probably brings his lovers into your home. Think about it."

"I have," I replied flatly. What I didn't like to tell Elliot was that I regularly dreamed about it, and that sometimes in those dreams, he was one of Paul's lovers. Strangely though, I never dreamt about Man Yee.

"What are you keeping from me, Rose? Leanna . . ." He stopped.

"So you discuss us?"

"Come on, Rose. It's not quite like that." He was trying to embrace me, but I eluded his grasp.

"Talk to me, not Leanna. I don't need another relationship like the one with Paul. Besides, she wants you for herself despite what she says." I'd finally said it, the feeling I'd harbored since my arrival. "Remember that night at the 4A's party?"

Elliot had disappeared for over an hour that evening, leaving me with one of Leanna's advertising friends to entertain me. I had found the man tiresome and boring, and had gone in search of Elliot. He was on the balcony with Leanna, dancing, and had had more than his usual share to drink. I watched them for a few minutes. She had her arms wrapped tightly around his neck and appeared to be crying into his shoulder, although not enough to smear her mascara. They pulled apart the minute I stepped out, and Elliot later apologized, saying she had flung herself at him, saying she was still very much in love with him. I didn't stay angry for too long after that, in part because I interpreted it as a kind of victory. But what I kept seeing over and over again was Elliot's hand, close to her breast, while his other hand slid up and down her back as they danced, sliding lower each time to where no panty line showed.

"That's history, Rose. I was drunk and she was horny. What do you want me to say? Besides, I want you, not her. It's just that she and I go back a long way. We share a past, and she knows me quite well."

I couldn't argue with that, but I despised her pretensions. I would rather she not try to be nice to me. As long as she did, Elliot would still be in her thrall, whether or not he would admit it. Also, confronting Elliot's past wasn't easy. He seemed less energetic, less romantic, less the special lover who seduced me over wine and roses. His life was messy; his family chaotic and troubled despite the insistence on familial bliss. The chaos of my family life, led as privately as possible, suddenly appeared to me saner than what Elliot went through. If nothing else, my parents had been responsible as parents, just as I had been socially responsible to Paul as his wife. From where I came, that counted for something.

"Don't you want a child?" Paul's question caught me off guard. "You could get pregnant by someone else and we could still be married," he continued. "I wouldn't mind. That way, we wouldn't have to get divorced."

I'd been in Malaysia for almost four months, yet this was only the third time we'd spoken. It was about a fortnight before I was due to return to Hong Kong, enough time to know that I didn't need to keep up the marriage. The last couple of times he called, he indicated our respective parents thought he visited me three times in Malaysia. I had no idea where he'd gone instead. If nothing else, I admired the way he kept the stories to our families consistent.

"After all, you do have a lover or two, don't you Rose? I don't mean Man Yee. I'm sorry about all that."

"Paul, I . . ."

His voice became gentle, and he was again the Paul I first fell in love with. "It's okay, my love. *San shi er li,* at thirty I took my stand. It's from Confucius. I've been reading him lately. He's easier to digest than the bible."

My husband was beginning to sound like my father. At least, they were both quoting at me from the same analect. I didn't know whether to feel relief or frustration at this turn of events.

"Incidentally, if you get pregnant by a *gwailo,* try to pick one with dark hair."

"Paul! This is ridiculous." Small bombs were exploding all around, but the fact of Elliot's dark hair and relatively trim and small stature was not lost on me in this context. A child of ours, given Paul's Eurasian heritage, could pass.

"Think about it, Rose. It's quite sensible really. We're both sexual creatures. In fact, our lives are defined by our sexuality. We just can't satisfy each other in that regard. But we fit well together socially, even intellectually. Your mother adores me and my father adores you. We both manage quite well in Hong Kong. As our careers progress, we'll be able to travel independently of each other and do what we want out of sight of anyone that matters. And even if there is a little talk, it only helps our image. If you have a child and decide you don't want to work, that would be equally fine. Think about it, Rose. We have all the choices in the world because we have the money, the education, the right social standing. We even love each other in our own way. What more can one demand from life?" He was calm, rational, quite at peace with the world in his manner.

"Don't respond, Rose. Not yet. Just come back to me and let's work something out. You do want a child, don't you? Remember when we got married, how sad you were when you realized you weren't pregnant?" He ambled on pleasantly. I listened to his soothing, lulling tone. We could have been sixteen again, talking about our future. Paul had known, from the beginning, that I was the one he wanted for life. After his call, I sat and stared at the empty wall in my office for a long, long time, trying to determine what to say to Elliot that night.

"Just what do you think I am? Your stud?"

I had never seen Elliot so angry. I had tried to make a joke of things and told him that Paul had a long term plan for us. Bad mistake. "Why are you yelling at me?"

"Because you're going back to him, that's why! I can see that if you can't. You're trying to rationalize your life with him. How can you let that man have such power over you? He's gay, for god's sake."

"Calm down. Look at it from his standpoint. Homosexuality is still illegal in Hong Kong."

"No it's not."

"Buggery is. Besides, he is a lawyer."

"Dammit Rose, hasn't our time together meant anything to you? What more do I have to do to prove that I love you? And you're not going to talk me into getting you pregnant. Good thing I've had a vasectomy!" He left the flat, slamming the door as he went.

I spoke to the door of the flat, stunned. "But I wouldn't do that. I wouldn't ever do that."

He didn't come home that night. The next morning, a Saturday, Leanna called. "Is he back yet?"

I wanted to slam the phone down on her syrupy voice. Instead, I said, "You know he isn't. That's why you called, right Leanna?"

"Oh Rosie," and she sounded genuinely hurt, "it's just a lover's quarrel. I understand how hard it must be to leave your husband. Elliot said you fell in love with him young. I know how that feels. I was heartbroken when my first boyfriend left for England to study."

She really was trying to be nice, trying to squelch her jealousy.

"You needn't worry," she continued, "that Elliot tells me anything personal about you. He has too much dignity for that. We're like brother and sister. He did tell me you're private. I think that's something he likes about you. My problem is that I'm terribly extroverted and always will be. It's just my nature."

"Look, Leanna, I'd rather not talk about all this."

"Whatever you want, dear. But anytime you need a girlfriend,

I'm there. I know it must get lonely for you sometimes here, away from all your family and friends."

Elliot walked in five minutes later laden with a dozen white roses. "Truce?"

I rushed to hug him, almost squashing the flowers.

"Careful." He placed the flowers on a chair and then we embraced and I cried, the first time in ages, promising him I'd find a way to leave Paul and that it was just a matter of courage. He told me he loved me no matter what and said he could wait. I promised him I would sort things out with Paul and leave him by Christmas. He said he wanted to get me pregnant because he wanted our child, and that vasectomies were easily reversible, and that it wasn't my fault if my husband had crazy ideas. I told him I didn't know about marriage, and that I'd make a terrible mother and perhaps I'd just been married too long to Paul to distinguish between right and wrong anymore. He kissed me and asked didn't I know Anita adored me and what a good influence I'd be on her? I said I thought he needed someone like Leanna who could run things beautifully and was artistic and already family, as well as being far more sexy and beautiful than me, and wasn't that why he couldn't stay away, even when Anita wasn't there? He exclaimed that Leanna was like a sister to him and how could I imagine he could prefer her to me, and didn't I realize Anita thought she was silly? I asked if I left Paul would he stop seeing her, even as a sister, especially if we kept Anita, and he replied, Absolutely.

With Elliot, life made sense when we made love. And we did make love, all the time, as much as we could, because our time together in KL was coming to an end, because, for all Paul's ready definition of how life should be, Elliot proved that if I chose, I had the power to change my life and make it whatever I wanted it to be.

Elliot loved me unconditionally, the way a concubine could.

14

Shortly after my return, Paul asked if I was ready to go to New York. He reminded me of Albert's invitation to Provincetown.

"Together?" I was dubious. A new kind of cautiousness had entered our relationship, and I had begun to distance myself mentally from him. He hadn't raised the question of pregnancy again, or divorce. I hadn't raised the issue of leaving him, although I found myself thinking about it daily.

"It's business. Gordon Ashberry and Albert Ho. I thought it might be helpful if we could entertain together, since your dad knows Gordon well."

"I'll think about it," I said.

Man Yee was jealous when I told him. He had recently been reinstated as Paul's first choice lover.

"And you say he doesn't love you? At least you share his life." He looked mournfully at me from across our table at the ABC.

"You share what's important, what's real in his life," I responded.

He gazed thoughtfully into his iced coffee. "Paul cries after sex with me, did you know that?"

I thought about Paul's alternating moods of anger and joy over our sexual encounters, although these days he had stopped making love to me. "Always?"

"Always. He becomes like a child. I try to tell him not to be afraid, but he cries until he can't anymore, and then he becomes his usual mean self."

Between Man Yee and my husband, there appeared to be little tenderness. Paul must have reserved all of that for me, because he still treated me with gentle and generous care, as if I were fragile and precious. And I relished that feeling, even after everything that had happened. Now, I was ready to face who he really was, even if I had to do it through his lover. "Tell me how you and Paul met."

"Oh that was years ago." His face dissolved into a happy smile.

"You know the Ambassador Hotel in Tsimshatsui? There's a bar in the basement which is a gay hangout. He was still at Hong Kong U and I picked him up there one night."

"When exactly was it?"

"1972. January 8, precisely. Over eight years ago."

The day after I left for college! I swallowed a large gulp of my drink. Confronting Paul's reality was going to be harder that I expected.

"Take it easy." Man Yee laid his hand on my arm. "I know it's difficult, but you better know and then decide what he means to you. Look, he started as a young boy, in South Africa, with his cousin Robert. They were just playing around as kids, but one time Robert masturbated him, and, well, it kind of went on from there. It stopped abruptly though, when his mother found out. But Paul's real problem is that he's ACDC, you know about that?"

I nodded. Alternating and direct current. Standard slang from my teenage life. Yet back then I had giggled along with my friends, never dreaming how it would one day apply to me.

"Anyway, at the beginning, I was boss. Until I took him home with me that night, he hadn't touched another man since Robert. He used to be such a sweet boy. And then he grew up, became more sure of himself, became mean. After the first few years, especially after you came back, he would be absolutely cruel to me, because he knew he wielded the power."

I took it all in. Was this why Paul finally let both of us off the hook over our friendship? He knew we continued to meet and didn't object.

"How long will you be away? Paul didn't tell me, you know."

"Three weeks."

His face turned sour. "Lucky you."

I let him believe what he wanted, but it wasn't the complete truth. Paul and I would only be together three or four days, after which I'd spend time with Regina while he headed off to Provincetown to Albert's house. Albert was Robert's replacement, that was becoming clearer to me all the time. Man Yee appeared to envy Albert, but did not harbor the kind of jealousy he leveled at me, or, for that matter, I at him. So perhaps Paul had been telling me the truth when he said Albert was just a friend.

Man Yee left a few minutes later. I wanted to sit for awhile, which I did over a second iced coffee. My mind was muddled from what I'd just learned. From some place in my brain, Kenton's voice saying "fifteen words or less, Rose, bottom line." He said that whenever he wanted to make me tell him the crux of an issue. A good habit, because business problems often got clouded by loads of irrelevant details. Wasn't it the same with life? As confused as my life seemed, with bits and pieces floating all through space, crash landing in scattered places everywhere, assuming problematic shapes that appeared insoluble — I had to get to my bottom line. Which boiled down to this: I was going to New York with Paul to reassert my rights as his wife.

"You aren't going, are you?" Elliot's response, predictable enough, was caustic. "I mean, Provincetown, really. Are he and Albert also planning a *tete à tete* on Fire Island?"

We were lying in bed after making love. The funny thing about being Elliot's lover was that it was inextricably tied to my being Paul's wife. My desire, if not my affection for Elliot seemed to grow with my new found resolution to assert certain marital, if not conjugal, rights with Paul.

"What do you mean?"

"You really don't know?"

I made an impatient sound. "Would I ask if I did know?"

"Okay, sorry. I keep forgetting you don't really know much about America. I meant gay life. Provincetown and Fire Island are popular gay hangouts."

"Oh." Elliot's earlier sarcasm made no impact. "Well, that's just his life, isn't it? Anyway, it'll give me time with Regina. What's wrong with that?"

"He's using you."

"It's business too."

"So that makes everything all right? Sometimes, Rose, your slavish attitude to convention amazes me. Hong Kong convention I mean. You're better than that."

Talking to Elliot was always easier in a horizontal position. It struck me that he was slavishly susceptible to sexual conventions. "But, Elliot, I'm a Hong Kong girl."

He suddenly got out of bed and pulled me roughly up by my arms. "Stand up," he commanded. I obliged. "Now, Rose Kho, Rose Lie, whoever you are, listen to me. You're special to me. For someone so competent, you can be such a coward. For whatever reason, you insist on remaining married to — what is it Regina calls him? — that stuffed penguin? And putting up with incredible hypocrisy from your family, his family and god knows what else you haven't told me about.

"It's got nothing to do with being a Hong Kong girl. You're a liar, plain and simple, and the worst part is when you lie to yourself. It's bad enough when you lie to me — don't put on that innocent expression, I've always known you do — but I don't care. I love you, Rose. But be honest with yourself, that's all I'm asking you to do. I'm willing to pledge all of me to you. Let go and love me. Can't you do that?"

He stopped abruptly and let go of my arms. His grip had been rough, and my arms hurt. I looked at him, trying to read his expression, but was confronted by his slightly myopic gaze. It was disconcerting looking at Elliot without his glasses.

"I'm sorry," he said. "That was uncalled for."

I put a finger to his lips. "Don't apologize." I kissed him, feeling at last as if I were in control, willing myself to love him for the moment as deeply as I could. I felt the heady rush of emotion which so elated me whenever Paul used to declare his love for me. It was a feeling I wanted to hold onto, because it stabilized my emotional state. What did it matter if I'd already decided to go, regardless of what he thought? By now, I knew I didn't really look to Elliot for decisions regarding my marriage. Unfair? Perhaps. But life wasn't really about playing fair.

We made love again that night, and I didn't leave his flat until the early morning hours.

"Let's meet in New York." Elliot's proposition, two days before my trip, threw me. "Why not?" he continued. "It's not like Paul will be around, and your sister will cover for you, won't she?"

I hadn't bargained for this. Elliot was the secret I deliberately kept from Regina.

"In fact, I'd like to meet her."

"No!" The violence of my response shook me. Suddenly, the playing field had tilted in his favor, and I didn't like it. I saw Teresa looking at me and realized I had spoken more loudly than I intended. I got up and shut my office door.

"Okay, Rose. Relax."

The silence on the other end lasted several minutes. I was trying to control the tears. The foundation upon which I'd built my life was swallowing me like quicksand. The trouble with Elliot was that he was now almost as dominant a force as Paul, with the power to upset my balance too often. In fact, Paul was now the calmer force.

He was the first to speak. "I want you to find me exciting enough."

"Is that what you think I want? Excitement?"

"Sometimes."

"How little you know me." How little, I repeated to myself, we all know ourselves.

"I didn't hear . . ."

"It was nothing."

Another pause. And then, right on the beat, "Maybe New York's not such a good idea."

How well he did know me! Elliot made me reach into parts of myself I never ventured to on my own, and then I would be irresistibly drawn to him again. It was becoming a recognizable pattern. "Of course I'll see you, Elliot. I can't bear to be without you. You know that."

I could hear the smile in his voice. "Oh Rose, I'm sorry I've hurt you. I didn't mean to. You can stay with me once Paul leaves, as much or as little as you want. And you spend as much time with Regina as you want. It'll be wonderful . . . "

He rambled on happily, making plans to take me all over New York. I listened to him, swept up by his excitement. The tense anticipation of the past two weeks, as Paul and I trod warily around each other in preparation for the trip, began to dissipate at the sound of Elliot's voice. But a small part of me retreated inside its shell, safe in the world I understood about Paul and Man Yee and me, where Elliot never arrived.

Over the last couple of years, I've wanted to apologize to Elliot for lying to him. I articulated this thought to Gordie earlier this year.

"No apologies needed," Gordie declared. "He's a big boy. Besides, truth is fiction and fiction truth — didn't someone Chinese say that?"

It's difficult to argue with Gordie's logic. He understands me. What Elliot didn't understand was that my need for privacy surpassed any compunction I might have felt about lying. It was the way my father was, the way Paul was — people with obsessions and familial incongruities to hide. Gordie would know.

Wouldn't you know, it was Elliot who first quoted me that truth-fiction couplet, the one from Red Chamber? *He'd read it of course, in Chinese. I never even made it through the English translation.*

Scotch and my night watch. A safe enough place for the moment.

"I'm taking you to Frank's," Gordie declared when he picked Paul and I up our first evening in New York.

"It should be the other way around," Paul remarked.

"Wait till I'm in Hong Kong again."

Frank's the perfect place for carnivores like me. Gordie drove us down to the lower West side in his Jaguar to the meat market on twelfth street. In the dank and rough neighborhood, we walked into a steak house with sawdust on the floor.

"It's unpretentious," Gordie declared. "And you'll love the food. Rose, your dad tells me you 'adore' steaks. These are the best in town, only in my humble opinion, of course."

A portly and exceedingly polite maitre d' showed us to our table.

Gordie never stopped talking. "You both look like you metabolize fast," he said as we sat down. "I'll bet you can eat a lot. Wait, don't say it. I'm being far too personal, right? Here I am, setting back Sino-American relations a century right after our peanut farmer's done his thing."

I suppressed a smile. "Peanuts are a remarkably universal crop."

"Yes they are. Paul, take note and draw up an offer to purchase every peanut farm south of the Yangtze."

It was impossible not to like Gordie. Even Paul relaxed around him and drank more than he normally would in a business cum social context. He had a quick mind, and flitted from topic to topic like a moth drawn to the centre of light. It was intriguing, how frivolous he seemed. But every now and then, he'd make a shrewd observation I wasn't expecting. It was easy to see why Kenton liked him.

But all through dinner I caught myself staring at his mouth a lot, thinking, he has the nicest lips. When he smiled, which he did often, I smiled back.

"He talks a lot," I remarked to Paul that night. "And he seems young to have done as much as he claims."

"Whatever he is, he has the financial backing."

"Really? Where from?"

"Family, I think. East Coast old money. He went to Yale."

"So he's genuinely going to open offices in Hong Kong and Beijing?"

"Looks like it. You'd be surprised; he speaks fluent Mandarin."

I lay awake long after Paul fell asleep that night. Paul had been behaving like such a perfect husband. Even before the trip, he had come home one day with a lovely lightweight jacket for me to "wear in New York's summer evening chill." On the long flight out, he had been solicitous, getting a blanket for me and making sure I was comfortable. And he had talked, trapped together as we were during those hours, about why he really wanted to go on this trip. It was the way we used to talk a long time ago, as teenage lovers, as a young courting couple, planning the perfect life ahead, being, as we strived so hard to be, perfect. False hopes and comforts. Good for their time.

"I need to know, Rose, who I am. Albert said I'd find out in Provincetown. I think I know what he means, but I won't know until I try. It's difficult to explain. I know I've been cruel to you, Rose. Albert helps me, the way . . . Robert used to. Believe me, Rose, I'll always love you, no matter who I am."

His words came back to me, as I sat next to his sleeping form. Maybe it was the wine and the altitude, but he opened his heart to me, the way I used to with him when we had first met. I believed in his love. It wasn't about what was right or wrong, but simply what was. If our life did not become what I once envisaged, that didn't make it wrong. The same was true of our love.

I thought about Elliot, who awaited my summoning. And about Teresa, whose daughter was entering kindergarten. And about Lars, Myrna and Kristin. Lars had recently sent me a photo of the three of them. They looked so happy together, like a family at peace with life. The note in his card had said, "Kristin asks when you'll have a little girl she can play with!"

I thought about all these people who had what I couldn't have, because no matter how I looked at my life, when I pushed aside the clouds that blurred my vision, the only thing I knew with absolute clarity was that I still didn't understand very much about myself at all.

Paul and I stuck to our original plan and went our separate ways for the rest of our trip. I arrived at Regina's doorstep somewhat apprehensively, promising myself I would call up Elliot right away if her place proved more than I could stand.

Regina wasn't home. The Stan that opened the door was shorter and tougher than the Stan I imagined. His complexion and features were very southern European, probably Italian. I had been unprepared for that, having never even known his last name. On the phone, his voice was blandly American, but with a slight lisp, and I had pictured an effete, probably blond, artistic looking Mid-Westerner. Stan could almost have been a jock.

"Oh hi, Rose," he said. "Long time no see. Good thing you arrived when you did — I was on my way out. Make yourself at home."

I wondered what I would have done if he had left before I arrived. But this casualness about everything was typical of Regina and her friends. "You must be Stan. I recognize your voice. We haven't met."

He frowned slightly, but did not seem particularly disconcerted. "No, I suppose not. Guess I've seen enough pictures of you though. Seems like we have met because we've had the kind of conversations we've had, and Regina talks about you often."

"Does she?"

"All the time. She adores you. Anyway, make yourself at home," he repeated. "I'll see you later."

Regina's place was less messy than I expected. She lived in a loft on Greene Street, half of which Stan used as his studio. From what I could piece together over the years, Stan lived there as well half the year. The other half he spent elsewhere, although where Regina never said.

The loft was enormous. Five thousand square feet of raw industrial space confronted me. It was on the second floor of an old garment factory. Stacked in the north corner were several old sewing machines, black workhorses, the likes of which I'd never seen before. There were windows along only two of the walls opposite each other, rows of tall oblongs each made up of smaller, square panes. And the ceilings were high, at least fifteen feet.

Near one of the windows, there was a large painting on an easel in the section which appeared to be Regina's studio and living area. I stared at the picture of the reclining naked woman for several minutes, uncertain what to make of it. There was something familiar about the face, the lips, the teeth. With a start, I suddenly realized I was looking at a portrait of myself.

The contours of my body were exactly right, even the slight arch of my left hip which Mum called my crooked hip. On my right thigh was the scar that never completely faded from the time a neighbor's dog bit me when I was eight. And she had painted my unmatching breasts — my left nipple smaller than the right. Only the hair was different. It was long like hers. I had never worn it that way. I felt strange looking at it, as if something had been stolen from inside me.

The door opened and Regina entered loaded with two full grocery bags.

"Hey, you made it!" She dropped everything she was holding on the floor, ran towards me and gave me a big hug.

"Regina, you haven't even closed the door."

"Fuck the door. You're more important than some silly door."

It had been over two years since I'd seen her. I was unprepared for the sight of her, so thin and undernourished. Her skin was dry and flaky, and her hands and skin felt rough to my touch. But Regina was still beautiful, a radiant glow on her face that came from somewhere deep inside, despite the wear and tear of life. I wondered if she would always be that way.

"Let's do everything!" she declared. "The museums, restaurants, even shopping, a trip upstate to Plattsburgh — whatever you want you name it. I'm not working one bit while you're here."

"Can we talk? Can I brush you hair?" I wanted to know.

She kissed me on my forehead, the way she used to when we were kids. "Anything the princess wants."

I thought about Elliot, patiently waiting until I was ready to call, and put him out of my mind for the moment. He knew not to expect me for at least a couple of days.

We spent the first afternoon and evening talking and eating. Regina cooked me one of her amazingly delicious fried noodle dishes.

"Whatever happened to Tristan?" I asked while we ate.

She frowned, as if trying to recollect who I meant.

"You know, the love of your life? The one you came to New York for?"

"Oh him! He never made it. Naah, he was a washout."

"So you're not in love?"

"Only with art." She stretched, flinging her long arms back behind her chair. "What's love anyway?"

"You should know, you're the poet."

She lit a cigarette. "I don't know a thing, Rose. Nobody does. We just think we do during the illusion of being alive."

"You and your philosophizing. You don't change."

I polished off the rest of my noodles. It was easy being with Regina. I actually enjoyed not being neat, now that Regina wasn't as much of a slob as she used to be. She confessed that it was Stan's condition of her living there, since it was his loft.

"Stan's a good friend, isn't he?" I asked.

"He keeps me going. When I've been low on funds, he's subsidized me."

I pondered that a moment. "Doesn't sound like you."

"It's different with Stan."

"How come?"

"He's gay."

I wanted to shoot back a rejoinder about Paul, but thought better of it. As far as Regina was concerned, Paul would always be a stuffed penguin.

"You know, Aunt Helen thinks you and David Ho should get together. He's back in Hong Kong now."

"Yeah, I know." She made a funny face, sucking in both her cheeks and pulling wide her eyes. "He only likes white bread, know what I mean?"

"You're wrong, you know. Helen says he's sweet on some local girl, a recent graduate from Hong Kong U. One of Chong's protégés. You know how Uncle is, always 'adopting' people. I think she worked at the hotel to get through school."

She registered this. Her expression didn't change for a few seconds. And then, she picked up her wine glass and sent it flying across the room. It smashed against the base of the easel on which rested the painting of me. "Damn the man," she said calmly, never raising her voice. And then, as if she'd only just realized what she'd done, "oh shit, I'll have to replace another of Stan's wine glasses."

I always thought David was just a friend. Perhaps that was the problem.

Regina cleaned up the mess from the wine glass. She swept the shattered pieces into a dustpan and dried the floor with a towel. Her long hair hung round her shoulders as she stooped down. She looked pathetic and frail. That image took me aback.

"What made you paint me?"

She spun her head round from her stooping posture and stared at me. "It was that recognizable, huh?"

"Of course. I felt like I was looking in the mirror."

"Memory, I suppose. Didn't want to forget." She turned back and continued cleaning up.

"Why's it so important to remember?"

"I'm not sure."

We slept together that night on her large, queen size futon. Regina fought battles in her sleep, her grinding teeth loud enough to wake the dead. And her arms flailed, warring with imaginary monsters. I tried to still the arms of my warrior maiden sister. She grunted whenever I touched her, and then rolled over for awhile in peace.

The grinding lasted all through the night.

"I haven't told her yet."

It was three days later, and Regina had gone out to the store. I called Elliot, feeling guilty for the lapse.

"God, Rose, it's good to hear your voice." He paused and continued in a low, persuasive tone. "No pressure, you know, but it's hard sleeping nights knowing you're here in New York."

Early signs of desire. Elliot had an irresistible phone sex manner.

"I'll tell her today."

"If that's what you want. Otherwise, I do understand. I have to be here anyway. It's just that I'd rather not sleep alone."

Spending several nights with Elliot held a magnetic attraction. I had avoided calling, because I knew the sound of his voice would make me abandon Regina, which she would hate. I hadn't promised Elliot anything before I came, but implicit in my non-commitment was a promise good enough for him. Besides, as he said, he was going to be here anyway. That mitigated my guilt a little.

I heard the sound of a key in the door, and quickly ended the call.

Regina came in loaded with groceries. "Who were you talking to?"

"How did you know?" She had found me out, the way she'd always find me when we played hide and seek as children.

"Intuition."

"Come on, Regina, tell me. I hate it when you do that."

She gave me a sly smile. "You make a prominent shadow in the window."

I gave her my best offended look.

"Okay, so I've told you. Now tell me. No secrets, remember?"

Of course I remembered. Once, when we were seven or so, we had run away from home together. We had gotten as far as three blocks away and stopped at the bus stop where Regina had said we should wait for the bus. It was on Prince Edward Road, and a number nine bus stopped in front of us. I looked at it, not knowing where it would take us, and panicked, saying I couldn't go, I was afraid. Regina had comforted me and said she would take me home. "You can't tell Mum," I begged her, because I was terrified our mother would ask Dad to spank us for doing this. "You can't let her find out. And you can't tell anyone else."

Regina had promised me, "it's our secret, and I won't tell a soul. But you have to promise me you'll never have any secrets from me." And then Regina threatened that she would tell Mum and also all our friends what a coward I was and I cried and begged Regina not to do that, and promised her I would never keep any secrets from her.

Until Elliot, I had told Regina everything.

I looked her straight in the eye. "I'm not staying with you the rest of my trip."

She dumped the grocery bags on the floor. "So who're you staying with?"

"No one you know."

Regina appeared relatively calm. "Okay. You want to take off after we go to the MOMA this afternoon?"

"That would be," I hesitated, "convenient."

She kicked off her shoes, and brought the groceries into the kitchen. "Well, life should be that way, shouldn't it?"

I cringed at her sarcasm, but was relieved by her otherwise ready acceptance. Before we left for the MOMA, she said that if Paul called she'd say I was out. I promised to check in with her daily.

At the MOMA, Regina dragged me to see the Munch. I didn't particularly like the painting — it was gloomy and dismal, and depressed me. Regina had insisted, saying it was time I learned what real art was about instead of boxing myself into Escher.

"I love Munch," she said, looking straight ahead at the painting. "He keeps me from killing myself."

"That's morbid of you."

Her eyes flashed. "It's what your type would say, isn't it?"

I started a little at her sudden change of tone. "What do you mean, 'my type'?"

"Oh, you and Paul, Mum and Dad. You know, the bourgeois compromise."

"Honestly, Regina. You make us sound like something out of a French novel."

"Oh go away and leave me alone!"

Her words came out in a sort of shriek, and I saw several people turn and look at us. I was embarrassed at my sister's strange behavior. At the same time, a warning signal in my brain made me realize that something was extremely wrong. This wasn't the Regina I understood.

"You come here," she went on, "with your fancy clothes and money and self satisfied life, even though your marriage is a complete farce. What makes you think you've got a right to live like that? What gives anyone the right to live like that?"

"Calm down, Regina. I didn't mean anything." I put my hand on her arm. She shoved it off and began to walk away towards the exit.

"Regina, wait," I called after her. But she strode off, at such a rapid pace I could barely keep up with her. "I'm not like you and Paul. I don't understand make believe love. You needn't have stayed with me at all, you know," she called back through the crowds. I tried to keep sight of her, but she marched off into the streets towards the subway. Before I knew it, she had disappeared.

There I was, a block or so away from the MOMA, quite baffled. Her outburst had been unexpected. We had had a wonderful time, or so I thought, eating in Chinatown and the Village, shopping, sightseeing everywhere, nattering all night and not getting enough sleep. I stood there in midtown, trying to figure out what had gone wrong, and what to do next. My first thought had been to follow her into the subway. But the subways intimidated me, since I didn't know my way around the system. During my stay so far, I'd only taken taxis and had always been with Regina. On my own, with no map or reference point, I felt slightly marooned.

I went to the nearest phone and called Elliot.

"I'll be right there."

And he was, and I kissed him on the streets in full daylight, unafraid. It was a wonderful feeling, being anonymous in a strange city and knowing Paul was miles away in Massachusetts. He hadn't called once since I'd been with Regina. He probably wouldn't.

Elliot took my bag, and we walked away from the museum, his arm around my shoulder.

"I love this," he exclaimed. "I'm on home turf for a change."

I laughed. "God, I've missed you, Elliot."

"It's Thursday."

"So it is."

Elliot drank that afternoon. I watched him become silly, very different from his cool, business-like self in Hong Kong. "You're not home," I said to him at some point, "you're on vacation!" to which he responded, "New York will always be home."

We had nine, glorious days. Elliot commandeered all the

arrangements, right down to choosing what I should wear, which was baffling. Normally, he never paid attention to my clothes. We were staying in an apartment on East 96th which belonged to some friends of his who lived in Athens. "He's been posted there for a couple of years, but they bought this place cheap and didn't want to let it go," he told me. "Now, they lend it to itinerant wanderers like me." I finally remembered to call Regina three days after I left her, and she sounded fine. She told me Paul hadn't called, and asked if I was getting enough to last me till I had to go to "prison with the penguin" again, but I ignored that remark, knowing that at least I got more than she did, and was happy that she had forgiven me enough to talk to me.

He took me to a concert in Saratoga. We spent the night there where the air was still chilly after sunset. It reminded me of Plattsburgh with its open outdoor space.

"You can breathe here," Elliot said, as we checked into our cabin motel room. "I used to come here in the summers when I was in high school, and worked my summers here in college."

"College," I repeated.

He closed the door of the cabin and placed our bags by the dresser. "Yeah. College. Somethin' wrong with that?"

Most of the time, Elliot spoke generic American English, sounding almost like a Mid-Westerner. Only a slight East Coast inflection crept into his accent. On extremely rare occasions, he sounded very New York. This was one of those times. "I guess I never stop to think about you in college."

He laughed. "Or that I had a life before Rose. I know I know, I only exist because of you."

We went for a walk before the concert that evening. Elliot had insisted on getting up at five in the morning to "beat the traffic," although as far as I was concerned, upstate New York didn't know the meaning of traffic compared to Hong Kong. I realized how little I thought of the American side of Elliot, so used was I to seeing him in Asia.

"So where do your parents live?" I asked.

"Saratoga," he replied. "Don't worry," he added, seeing my surprised look, "they're in Israel."

"Israel?"

"You have a penchant for repeating what I say lately."

"I can't go to Israel on my Indonesian passport."

He smiled. "I know. But my family is Jewish, you know."

I knew that, but it hadn't ever registered. I supposed there was no reason it should, especially in Hong Kong. But my political and racial background clearly had registered with Elliot. It struck me, as it often did when I was around him, how ignorant I was.

I found myself kissing Elliot a lot during those nine days. Whether we were on a subway together, on in a restaurant or in Lincoln Centre, I would turn to him and kiss his cheek, his hands, his lips. It was almost as if I wanted to reassure myself he was tangible, really there. It was almost as if I wanted to reassure myself how much I loved him.

On the afternoon of the tenth day, he said, "Would you like a steak tonight?"

"Steak?" I stared at him in amazement. Elliot hardly ever touched red meat.

"There you go with the echo effect again." He laughed at my surprise. "There's a lot you still don't know about me. So, what about Sparks?" he continued. "And wear something really really really sexy because red meat makes me positively horny."

"Elliot!" I gave him a look of amused indignation.

He looked faintly, but not believably, sheepish. "Sorry."

This wasn't the Elliot I knew in Hong Kong, restrained and overly formal for the most part, and almost shy in his politeness. "Anyway, Sparks is the best steak place in New York."

"I thought Frank's was."

"Frank's?" His eyes widened in disbelief. "Someone's been feeding you a pack of lies. Did you go there with Paul?"

"His client took us."

He shook his head disparagingly. "No class. Doll, with me, it's only the best."

No, I definitely didn't recognize this Elliot, I thought as I got dressed. He never called me "doll" or carried on in this manner. He was starting to sound like Gordie. I actually liked it, because it was unexpected. But I had a nagging feeling it was out of character, that it was a show for my benefit because he suspected I thought of him as weak. I suppose I did, because he too readily took a back seat for my affections, patiently accepting the few crumbs I threw him.

As we pulled up to Sparks in our taxi I caught a glimpse of the valet parking attendant driving a sleek Jaguar away. Had I been more alert, I would have recognized it and avoided what happened next.

The man in front of us inside the restaurant was upset at the *maitre d'*. "What do you mean my reservation's for eight thirty? I made it for seven thirty."

"I'm sorry, Mr. Ashberry. We must have made a mistake because I show your party of six at eight thirty. I'm afraid . . ."

I knew immediately, but there was nothing I could do.

"That's it, we're out of here! I'm taking my group elsewhere." He turned around and crashed right into us. "Why the . . don't you watch where . . . oh goodness," and he stared with the shock of recognition, "Rose Lie! I'm terribly sorry, I didn't mean. . ." He stopped as he caught sight of Elliot, who had his arm around me.

I could feel my face turning bright red as I tried to disengage myself from Elliot. He kept his arm firmly planted on my shoulder. A desperately sinking feeling assailed me. "Gordon, Gordie. What a coincidence." I held out my hand, which he raised to his lips, a mischievous glint in his eye.

He turned to Elliot. "I'm at a disadvantage since you know who I am. You are?" His look of polite inquiry held the faintest mockery of a smile.

I quickly interjected. "Gordon Ashberry, Elliot Cohen. Elliot's a friend of my family's."

"An old friend," Elliot added, trying to stare him down, unsuccessfully, since Gordie stood almost a head above him. Elliot gave the small of my back a sharp poke. "In fact, you might say we're extraordinarily well acquainted." There was a defiant edge in his tone. "So, how do you two know each other?" His tone became distinctly New York as he said it.

Gordie winked at me. "Rose and I go back a long way, right doll? You could say she came to New York to meet me, with her father's approval of course."

Elliot drew me lightly towards him.

Gordie's eyes laughed. "You look even more ravishing tonight, by

264

the way. Of course, you always do." His eyes took in my low neckline. I felt goose bumps on my breasts.

This was how a cornered animal felt! I wanted to brazen my way out the way the two of them were doing, but couldn't. I felt naked in the "really really really sexy" crimson wisp of a dress I was wearing, the same one my mother-in-law bought me years ago.

"But, mustn't hold you up. I still have to find another restaurant tonight. Good to have met you, Cohen. I'm sure we'll be running into each other again." He pumped Elliot's hand in a hearty handshake. "And Rose," he leaned over and kissed my cheek, his hand lightly brushing my arm as he did so, "I'll see you in Hong Kong." He whisked off, and I breathed a quiet sigh of relief. "By the way, Elliot," he called out as we entered the doorway, "she likes hers rare."

Elliot was chuckling all the way to our table. I was furious.

In our booth, he leaned against me and gently kissed my neck. "So it's 'Gordie' huh? Don't say it, he prefers to be called that, right? What was that remark about your father all about? Who the hell is he?"

"Family friend. Also a business connection for Paul."

"Did I catch you with your panties down, doll?" he whispered in my ear.

"Shut up!" I was trembling slightly.

"Well well well, so even the unflappable Rose does get shaken. That's so unlike you. Maybe you've met your match?" He pulled away and opened the menu. "I'm starved."

"Elliot, it's not what you think."

He was calmly perusing the wine list. "You don't have to explain. Want to get absolutely smashed? That's what you like to do, right?"

I gritted my teeth. "He's Paul client and a long time friend of my father's."

"So we've both been caught with our pants down, right doll?"

"Why do you keep calling me that?"

"What?"

"Doll. I don't like it."

He closed the menu and looked at me. "Why? Because Gor-die," and he stretched out his name in a silly, schoolboy voice, "calls you that? And what else doesn't my delicate little Rose like, hmmm?"

"Why are you being like this?" I was off balance and despairing of regaining control. It was such an unaccustomed feeling around Elliot.

He reopened the menu and trained his eyes on the page. "I'm jealous. So sue me. Even if you did leave Paul there'd always be some other, younger guy lusting. Do you really like your steaks rare?"

The deliberate calm of his voice was so comical that I began to giggle. Elliot shot a sidelong glance at me.

"First she's almost hysterical, and then she laughs. What's with you anyway?"

I put my hand over my mouth to stop the giggles. They turned into hiccups.

"Elliot, I . . . this . . . is just too silly . . . for words." I said in between hics and sips of water.

"You sound ridiculous."

"I . . . know."

"We're both ridiculous, aren't we?" His voice had softened into the Elliot I knew. I gulped down the last of my hiccups. "I'm just as bad as you," he went on, "trying to be the lover I think you want."

I rested my elbows on the table and leaned towards him. "You are."

"What?"

"The lover I want."

We gazed at each other for a moment.

"Don't need the red meat," we said in unison.

"Or the wine," I added.

We didn't eat dinner that night.

I flew home with a reticent and sullen husband, the complete opposite of the man who had accompanied me on the trip out. Once during the long flight, he abruptly said, "I wish we could live in America."

"You don't like America."

"We could be free there, Rose." He looked pleadingly at me.

"You mean, you could be."

"I wouldn't be as jealous there."

"Wouldn't you?"

"I don't think so."

"Wouldn't it be simpler if we just stopped pretending, and give up what we have?"

"No!" He was emphatic. And then, gentler. "No, it would destroy my parents."

"Your parents or you?"

"What about your family Rose? Your father?"

I didn't reply. Paul knew he had pushed the right button and turned smugly away. He resumed reading and we didn't speak again the rest of the flight.

Except for the first night, when we both collapsed gratefully into bed, Paul didn't spend any nights at home all the next week.

Marion called me once, at four in the morning, apologizing for the hour but saying she couldn't sleep. It was a Thursday night. Paul wasn't home. Without her even telling me, I knew Paul Sr. wasn't home either.

It was mid winter and cold. She picked me up in her car half an hour later, and we drove out, far out, to the furthest beach on Castle Peak Road, marked on the road at nineteen and a half miles. And then we walked on the sand, just talking, until the sun rose.

This was what family meant, she said, the privilege to share a private moment, a moment that no one else would ever know about. She put her arm around me; it was one of the rare times she displayed any emotion. You're as dear as a daughter to me, Rose, she said. You understand about Paul, about us. I had put my arm around my mother-in-law's waist and said, very softly, you mean the world to me, Marion. I'll never do anything to hurt you.

In a perfect world, Marion would have been my mother, and my father would be happily married. Even now, when none of this really matters anymore, I look back and see a kind of happiness and peace in the midst of the turmoil of my life back then. Family. What would my life have been without family?

I talk to Gordie about many things in my life, but not about Marion, never about Marion.

15

Over yam chah, I showed Aunt Helen all my photos of Regina. "So thin!" she exclaimed and exhorted me to tell her everything that was upsetting my sister. The fact of my deserting Regina for Elliot jarred me, and I was fretful as I tried to talk about my sister until Aunt Helen finally asked, "what's the matter, Rose, are you ill?"

Mum harangued me over Regina's illegal status. When Paul and I came to dinner, she turned her anxiety on him, demanding to know why he couldn't help fix things for her. It got so I almost wanted to blurt out that my sister's real problems were far more serious than her visa status. Afterwards, Paul said, puzzled, "but Rose, you know what your mother's like. Why let it upset you so much still?"

We were driving back to our flat when he asked. At this point, two weeks after we had returned, he had been home once. "It's all going to come out eventually, about Regina's depressions and suicide attempts, I mean. I can't hide them forever."

Paul pulled the car into our driveway. "Only if you tell her," he declared, as he pulled up the hand brake. "You don't have to do that."

"And what happens when she really kills herself?"

"Don't be melodramatic, Rose. It's not like you. You know your sister only does those things to get attention."

I wanted to talk to him some more that evening, but he left abruptly, without even saying good night.

The next evening, Regina called. "So you're fucking Elliot Cohen." The shock waves of my silence must have transmitted because she continued, "he came to see me, you know. Offered to buy your painting. I told him he had to fuck me first to get it, and he did. But I still didn't let him buy it." And then, she gave off a harsh, long laugh, and hung up.

Elliot had remained in New York another ten days after I left. I hadn't seen him since he returned, although he'd called to say he was back. I went over to his place immediately, without any prior warning.

"Okay, so I did. I just wanted to get a little closer to you, Rose," he said, after I'd demanded to know whether or not he had been to see her.

"But why didn't you tell me?"

"Because you'd have stopped me."

"You told her about us."

"I didn't. She guessed."

"You fucked her."

"Don't be ridiculous."

"That's what she says."

"And you believe that?"

I asked him about the painting, which he admitted he would have liked to have, but denied the conversation Regina described ever took place. My head was reeling. Everything with Elliot had always been straightforward, except for Leanna. And now, except for Regina.

I was shaking. "You didn't have any right to do this." I shouted at him. I couldn't stop myself from crying. How could I explain that this was the one secret I wanted to keep from Regina, and now it was gone. Elliot took me in his arms and began to kiss me gently. He held me tightly as I struggled to break loose, angered by his betrayal.

"Rose, she's your sister. She loves you. All she said were good things about you. But she is a very troubled woman."

His words calmed me. "How could you tell?"

"Experience. My brother's been in and out of mental institutions since he was fourteen."

"Brother?" I looked at him, surprised.

He had released me now, and sat me down on his sofa. "Like I've said, there's a lot you don't know about me, Rose. I went to see him after you left."

I dried my eyes, feeling foolish about my outburst. "Why haven't you told me about your brother before?"

He shrugged. "Nothing to tell. Just another New York manic depressive. My family takes it in stride. He's a good kid. Likes playing with Anita."

Again, the spectre of Elliot's past wavered. "By the way, how did you find Regina?"

"I asked Helen. Told her I was headed to New York and could I look up her niece. Don't worry," he added, seeing my anxious expression, "I made the timing of my trip sound like it was after yours. She did tell me you were going, by the way."

That relieved me. Elliot went quiet a moment. And then, with a startling abruptness, he said, "it's okay Rose, we can just be lovers if you prefer."

I looked curiously at him, but as quickly as he had said it, the slightly unhappy expression on his face that had been there a moment ago disappeared, and he was Elliot again, my dependable lover.

"I thought Regina loved me."

"She does."

"Then why this?"

"Maybe she's jealous. You have something she hasn't got, even though she might not admit what you have is important to her. Who knows for sure? We all have our secrets, Rose."

He hugged me and it was soothing. It was hard for me to imagine Regina jealous of me. All through our girlhood, and even through college, I envied her her freedom. She never seemed bound by the strictures of our Hong Kong society, choosing to turn her back on all of it — her background, friends and even family. That night, I slept through turbulent dreams of Regina in the lighthouse. It was my storm dream, with rains that drenched me to the skin. Regina in the lighthouse window. This time, she was naked in between Paul and Elliot, both of whom were touching her, trying to make love to her.

I awoke with a start, the sound of Elliot in his shower at the edge of my consciousness.

When we were fourteen, Regina tried to kill me. She didn't mean to do it; she was sleepwalking. I woke up one night and found her standing over me with the kitchen knife in her hand, raised above her head. Some instinct told me not to scream. Very carefully, I led her back to bed, removed the knife and put it back in the kitchen. When my mother was looking around for the knife the next day, I realized I'd put it in the wrong place. But she found it, and thought nothing further of its temporary misplacement.

After New York, my life appeared to go on as usual. Paul and I readjusted ourselves to a pattern of our marriage, as did Elliot and I to the rhythm of our affair. But Paul was home a lot less, and I was with Elliot a little more. The undertow of change tugged, even though on the surface, life simply rolled on, and nothing really changed.

The November day my father called to say Regina and Mum were both being hospitalized, I dropped everything I was doing and moved home temporarily. Paul drove me there. "Your mother needs a rest," Dad told me while I prepared him tea. He was in a state of semi-shock. "It's just for a little while," he added, gazing at me pleadingly. "Your mother will be better after a little while." He looked blank and utterly helpless. There was a pathetic appeal in his inability to cope.

"Of course she will be," I reassured him.

"Your sister was too much of a shock for her, for us. Why would she want to kill herself?" He was muttering to himself more than to me.

"Here dad, drink some tea."

He smiled weakly at me. "Thank you Rose. You're a good daughter."

I called Stan late that night, after Dad was asleep. His voice was weary. "Regina's recuperating. She was pretty far gone this time, and she'd lost a lot of blood."

"What did she do?"

"Slashed her wrists. I didn't find her until it was almost too late."

I pictured my sister lying on blood soaked sheets in that huge loft, the life ebbing out of her little by little. It had always been pills before. "Did she leave a note this time?"

"Same as the last. 'Declassé, deraciné, deflowered and destroyed.' It's so melodramatic. She just won't give it up. You know, Rose, I think she needs to go home."

"What do you mean, 'home'?"

"I mean, I think she needs to get out of New York for a bit and go back to family. She won't say so, but that's what she needs."

"What triggered it this time?"

"Her exhibition got cancelled. She ran out of money. I found two hundred dollars next to her with 'TRICK' scrawled across one of the bills. You can guess the rest." He made an impatient sound. "It's not like she needs to worry about money. I cover the rent here and let her paint. There's always food in the fridge — whoever can afford to fills it up, and our friends who use the studio contribute. What more does she want?"

I tried to imagine explaining this aspect of Regina's life to my parents. How could they begin to understand? Even I didn't, but at least with me nothing about her shocked me anymore.

"Listen, you know I didn't tell your parents everything, but I figured they ought to know the truth about her suicide attempt. Someone ought to know and do something. She's still your family after all. It'll help if you come over, Rose."

"I doubt it." I related to Stan the last, manic phone call, down to the gory details. There seemed no reason to hide anything from him. "She hates me," I finished.

He remained unflappable. "No she doesn't, not really. It's just jealousy. She hates herself more than you. Regina's suffering from a kind of wilful schizophrenia, or something." He said it calmly, as if it were a perfectly ordinary thing to say about someone. But as I thought about my sister, I knew that what he said was close to the mark. Once again, the impossibility of telling my father flitted through my head. Would I ever be able to say to him, face it Dad, half our family's stark raving mad, or, at least, somewhat touched in the head. I might as well have driven a dagger into his heart.

Yet surely Dad knew! Was it simply that he only knew how to deal with it by not dealing with it? Confrontation wasn't his style, yet things always went his way in the end. It was like when he left Pacific American, a forced retirement, and finally took the Golden Phoenix job. Mum nagged and nagged, complaining that he didn't have the guts to face his boss and demand his right. He countered that an easy job in the cargo subsidiary was enough. But there had been truth in what my mother said. My father didn't demand rights, not as a husband, or father or even as a brother — when he needed to borrow money from Helen he wouldn't do it, and only took what was forced upon him because Mum insisted, or asked

Helen herself.

So here I was, confronting for him, however unwillingly, because there was no one else in the family who could.

I stayed with my father at home. Mum had collapsed from shock when Stan called with the news. During my mother's first week in the hospital, Dad sat with her every day while she railed at him, blaming him for not loving Regina, blaming him for the life he hadn't given her. I went with him twice, and watched him take it all, never arguing back. He didn't play the horses that week.

The day it happened, a Thursday, I had asked Teresa to tell Elliot that my mother was in hospital, because I didn't have time to reach him. My mother's stay had stretched into a second week. The strain of living at home with my dad, watching him brood silently each night, was starting to wear on me.

"And what about you?" Teresa was kind, motherly. "You need some rest too. Tell Mr. Kenton, or I will if you won't."

"It's too personal." I replied. Teresa only knew Mum was hospitalized with a serious illness and that I was living at home. I hadn't said anything about Regina. "Besides, you know how he is at separating work from private life."

"You needn't tell him everything. Just say your mother's ill and your family needs your help. Even he'll understand. You think just because you do it, that everyone else suffers in silence. Take time off. You work too hard anyway. Look how much weight you've lost."

She was right. I had lost weight, quickly, unintentionally. She was so commonsensical about things. Why couldn't I be like that? "I'll be okay."

Teresa picked up the pile for Kenton and headed towards her desk. "By the way, Elliot called a couple of times. I told him you'd try to call when things settled down a little."

"Thanks." I smiled at her.

"You might as well marry him. He's crazy about you."

"Is that what you think?"

"Not really. But at least it's practical." She walked out and shut my door.

I rang Elliot. "Teresa's given her stamp of approval."

"Come on, Rose. That's not why you called."

"I can't take this anymore."

"Calm down. Tell me all about it."

"Regina's . . ."

"Tried again?"

"It's at least the fourth time I know of. Only this time, my parents know."

"You couldn't hide it forever. Nor should you."

"Don't you know the Chinese drown their mentally ill babies and hide away the adults? You don't understand Elliot. They can't take it."

"And can you? Should you take it all by yourself? You're not in China."

"I can't see you for awhile."

"Rose, I'm the least of your worries."

I wished it were true, I thought as I hung up. I left work early and went to the hospital. My mother was awake. Dad sat beside her, reading a paper.

"Oh Rose, Rose. You're my good girl. What lovely flowers you brought me. Thank you."

I kissed her cheek. "How are you, Mum? Feeling any better?"

"The doctor says I've made a marvellous recovery. It's like a miracle, Rose, that I should recover from such a difficult operation. Isn't it remarkable? I hardly feel a thing." She smiled at me, acting as if I were visiting her for the first time.

I glanced at my father, puzzled. He shook his head discreetly. "Regina's well," I began.

"Did Regina call to wish me well?" She turned to my father. "I am the luckiest mother in the world with such wonderful daughters!"

She chattered on happily. It was frightening how changed she was today, not arguing with my father and blaming him for what had happened. I caught my father's eye. He shrugged helplessly, a look of resignation on his face. As I listened to her chattering, my thoughts drifted to Elliot, wishing I could show him this, wishing I could make him see what Paul understood completely. But it was easier for Paul to see. In his family, as in mine, denial was a way of life.

There was a knock at the door.

"Paul!" My mother was radiant with delight. "Such a thoughtful son-in-law! Look, he's brought me a lovely fruit basket. How kind of you to come. Do you know, my doctors say you will hardly be able to see a scar from my operation."

Paul glanced at me. I discreetly shook my head. "My parents send their best wishes." He leaned over and kissed her. "I'll tell them you're making a fine recovery." He caught on instinctively, even without being told. Paul was good in the crisis of others. I knew he hadn't told his parents everything.

"Rose," my mother waved at me. "You tell Regina to come home soon. I spoke to Helen last week and she tells me David Ho is definitely staying in Hong Kong for the time being, and that he said Regina was terribly attractive. You see," she nodded proudly. "I always knew someone important would pay attention to my Regina." It was as if the last week had vanished from her life.

Paul and I left the hospital together; he promised my father he'd come over to my parents' place later with me. In the car, he touched my cheek, and I felt the comfort of his kindness. "I'm sorry, Rose," he said. "I wish I could make it go away."

I leaned my face into his shoulder and began to cry uncontrollably. "It's okay, Darling," he repeated over and over. "I'm here. I'll be here . . . forever." I calmed down enough for him to drive us home, where he walked me into our bedroom, sat me down and kissed me, tenderly at first and then passionately and we ended up making love that afternoon, the first time in months, releasing all the pent up sorrow we'd both harbored, bringing me back to our first time, recalling, if only for an hour, the love I once felt for him.

"Come live with me, Rose." Regina's matter-of-fact request struck me as almost making sense. "If Elliot really loves you, he'll come to New York for you."

"You make it sound easy."

"Anything you want badly enough is easy. You take . . ."

"What's hard and make it easy." I finished her dogma. I had asked her, earlier in our conversation, why she had said what she had about Elliot and her response had been a curt "I don't know what you're talking about."

"By the way, do you know a Gordon Ashberry?"

"Yes," I responded warily.

"He's absolutely crazy. Madder than a hatter."

She should talk, I thought. "Did he look you up?"

"He made a studio appointment and then offered to buy all my work. He seemed particularly fond of the one of you, but I told him it wasn't for sale. By the way, he says you're coming to work for him. Are you?"

Somehow, what she said about Gordie rang true. An image of him as a giant octopus conjured itself in my mind. I saw him sitting on the banks of Manhattan, his tentacles reaching out simultaneously across the Atlantic, all of the United States and the Pacific Ocean, meeting in Hong Kong where I struggled in his clutches. "Wishful thinking."

"I liked him, for a businessman that is." High praise from Regina. "One of the braves."

"I'd have thought he'd be on the other side. You know, blankets with measles and all," I said, recalling the story Regina once told me about Lord Amherst giving measles-infected blankets to the Indians in Massachusetts.

"You're wrong." Regina could be certain with the barest of facts. "He's one of the originals who'll ultimately be destroyed."

It wasn't worth enlightening her.

"You know," she continued, "I think he likes me."

Stan had warned me about this, that Regina was increasingly suffering from delusions about men wanting her. Tired of being an artist, had been his prognosis.

"I didn't think you had time for men," I ventured cautiously.

"Why not?" The flash of anger in her voice. "Do you think you're the only one who deserves lovers?"

Regina was fragile. Helen was right about that. Despite her beauty and talents, Regina had never been loved by a man. I thought back to the loss of her virginity, one Saturday afternoon on our living room floor with the sports captain of the neighboring boy's school. She hadn't even liked him. She had done it for the benefit of everyone else, because she bragged to all our friends about her "conquest." It had been bravado, all bravado. The real reason, the one she'd never admit, was because Paul had asked me out. Had there been all that much about her I should have envied? It didn't seem so now. My life, which she called directionless, struck me as infinitely preferable to her ups and downs. I knew my denial; she didn't. In that, at least I was more honest than she was.

I was suddenly certain of one thing. Should I decide the preposterous, meaning to leave Paul, go to New York, and work for Gordie, I knew I wouldn't live with Regina unless I had to. No more unconditional love for my warrior maiden. It saddened me, that knowledge, because it meant that I'd finally accepted she and I were severed for good.

As rapidly as the crisis began, it was over, all within the space of eleven days. My mother came home. I went home also, now that my father no longer needed my company and a cook. Paul stopped being my husband since I no longer needed one. And Elliot reinstated his position as lover and confidante.

Over dinner the next Thursday, Elliot brought up the issue we had suspended for the past eleven days. "It's going to be difficult for you to leave him before Christmas, isn't it?"

It was early December, and we were both in a less than amorous mood. "It will be," I agreed, cautiously.

"I understand, you know. The thing is, I'd like to have Anita come to Hong Kong for Christmas." He paused, and I knew he was about to tell me something I wouldn't like. "It means Leanna will also come visit."

"I see," I said.

"Rose, it isn't anything. Okay, I know you may be right and she maybe has the hots for me, as you put it. But I'm partly to blame, although," he added quickly, "you know there's nothing between us. Besides, if you're with Paul, it's not like you'll have time for me when the Christmas season rolls round."

I chose my words carefully. "And do you want me to see Anita?"

He bit his lower lip. "Yes. I mean of course. We'll have dinner here together one night. I'll even send Leanna out that evening."

Things were shaping up to be a difficult Christmas.

That weekend, Paul said, "This isn't right."

"What's 'this'?"

"Our marriage."

I thought back to his cool offer to father my yet unconceived child by a lover, any lover. "I should have thought that was obvious."

"Let's get through Christmas and talk about us after that. We need to make some changes."

It was impossible not to be sarcastic. "'We'? You mean you, don't you?"

He was completely unperturbed. "Please, Rose, it's hard enough for me."

I didn't see him for the next three nights. Man Yee called on the morning of the third day and asked me to let go of my husband. I hung up on him.

Twelve days before Christmas, the family gathered for dinner at Spring Deer restaurant at my father's invitation. He wanted, he claimed, to celebrate longevity.

It was an odd evening. Paul and I were on good behavior, but there was a tension between us that was evident. Paul's parents sat at the table looking uncomfortable. Helen and Chong looked tired; it was a busy time of year for my uncle. My mother was lost on her plane of amnesia, chattering away about her "operation." When Marion asked at one point what exactly had been wrong, my mother simply stared blankly and replied that she had been terribly, terribly ill.

Only my father seemed to enjoy himself. He smiled at everyone in his amiable manner. At the end of the meal, he actually clinked his glass with a chopstick for silence. He needn't have bothered. There was hardly any conversation.

"It's wonderful of all of you to come this evening," he declared.

My mother nodded happily.

"This is a good time of year," he continued. "As one year comes to an end, we may as well put aside the past and look forward to a new year, don't you think?"

Everyone murmured a polite assent.

Encouraged, he carried on. "What pleases me most is that we are all family together, even if we don't see each other very often. But then, that's just life in Hong Kong after all."

I was beginning to wonder about Dad. He could be expansive

sometimes, but this was a bit much, even for him. I tried to catch his eye, but he seemed to be looking at everyone except me.

Later, at the car park on Middle Road, Helen and Chong waited at the entrance with me for Paul to emerge with our car.

"Sometimes, I don't understand that brother of mine," Helen said. "He is the most baffling man. "Out of the blue, for no reason at all, he invites us all to dinner. Even your in-laws, which is really stretching it for him. For longevity, he says. What does he mean?"

I smiled. "You know how Dad is. He probably got a windfall from the horses." But I thought about his desire of achieving a Confucian seventy. He was six and a half years away.

"Honestly, Rose. You're the only sensible one left. Has your father said a word about the suicide attempt?"

"Not exactly." I was uncomfortable, knowing what would ensue.

"You know I wouldn't say this to anyone but you, but both your sister and mother need the services of a good psychiatrist!"

"Helen . . ." Uncle Chong began.

"Chong, Rose can take plain truths, can't you dear? You know I love Regina dearly, but she simply can't go on like this. She'll self destruct."

"Stan says she's remorseful in private."

"He isn't family though. He doesn't have any real responsibility for her."

And did I, I wondered as Paul drove out. I said my goodbyes and climbed into our car, thinking that Stan was better than family for her. At least she occasionally told him the truth, which was more than she would do with the rest of us, Helen included.

"Father says you're looking pale, Rose," Paul said.

"Did he?"

"He thought perhaps Hong Kong life was too tiring after your idyll in Malaysia. Those were his words," he added hastily.

"Is that what you think too?"

"No."

We drove on in silence. Paul switched on the radio to a classical music program. I hummed along to the end of the Rachmaninoff piece.

"That's impressive."

"I've heard it somewhere before." It was the variation of

Paganini's theme, one of Elliot's favorites.

"Good memory. That's what my father says you have."

"Does he?" I couldn't place Paul's meaning.

"Yes. He says you know Dr. Ng's number by heart in case you had to call him in an emergency since he lives next door. I didn't know that."

I said cautiously, "he must be mistaken. I have the number written down, but I'd need to refer to it."

Paul chewed his thumb, keeping his eyes on the road. "There haven't been any, uh, emergencies, have there? I mean when I wasn't around?"

What had Paul Sr. implied to Paul? Would I ever know? "Oh no," I said calmly. "I'd have told you if there were."

"I'd hope you would, Rose." There was relief in his voice.

"Of course, Paul."

Once we got back, he parked and walked me to the door. He was about to turn around and leave — Paul always took a taxi to Man Yee's, leaving the car in the space for appearance's sake — when something made me take his arm. "At least come in for a moment, can't you?" I asked, more sharply than I intended.

He pulled his arm rather roughly away.

"Is my touch so abhorrent?" My voice almost loud.

"Rose, please. Is this necessary . . . ?"

That was when I struck at him. He was so startled he didn't have time to react, and I hit him hard across the face. He looked at me in bewilderment. I recoiled, horrified. "Paul, I didn't mean to . . ."

"It's okay, Darling," he took me in his arms and opened the door to our flat. "Come on, let's go in."

Standing by the front door, I found our living room strangely empty. I closed the door behind me, but didn't go into the flat. It felt barren. The place was clean, the way we both liked it. Everything was in order. That was when I said, "You haven't sent me flowers for over a year."

Paul had his back to me, headed as he was towards the armchair. He stopped. Without turning around he said, "has it really been that long?"

"It's felt like much longer."

"I'm sorry, Rose. I wish it could have been different."

"I know." I could feel the tears beginning.

He still did not turn around. "I can't make love to you anymore, Rose." He paused, waiting to let his words sink in. "I can't be the kind of husband you want."

"But you just did, not so long ago."

"That was different. Your family was going through something difficult."

"And what should I do?" I hadn't moved from the doorway.

"If you want to leave me, I'd understand."

Tears were streaming down my face. "Do you want me to?"

He faced me now from across the room. "No!" Almost a shout, almost angry, but his eyes were wet. He lowered his voice. "I'm sorry, Rose . . . oh, these useless apologies! But I do still love you."

We both stood for a long time, crying, looking at each other without saying a word. There was no need for words. I understood what my husband was trying to say. There had been no jealousy or rancor in his voice. I could walk out of his life right at that moment, and he would have let me go. Otherwise, I could remain his wife in name only. It was no longer about power, or money, or even social convention, although our marriage would provide a convenient front. Even before he'd said it, I knew. He did love me, he always had in his own way, just as I had in mine. Love wasn't about what either of us did or didn't do; it was about a bond we couldn't deny.

Finally, he said, "I'll live with Man Yee. It's only fair you have this place. But I'll continue to park here, if that's all right with you."

When I didn't respond, he continued, "Your parents needn't know if you don't want them to. As you probably realize, my parents . . . know, in a manner of speaking. They just don't talk about it."

The tears simply wouldn't stop. My body felt extremely heavy, and I sank to the floor. Paul came over and knelt beside me. "Please, Rose, it'll be fine. I'll still look after you. You do what you want, go where you want. I don't anymore have a right to demand anything of you. If you choose to remain with me, I know you'll be discreet."

Gordie called me at work the next day to say he definitely needed someone in the new year, and was I still interested? I said what I always did, that I'd think about it, only this time I added that my life was complicated, as he obviously knew. He replied what I did with my life was my business. After he hung up, Kenton stuck his head in and told me that it was time to start thinking about the future. I stared at him quizzically. He said I'd find out in the new year, but that he'd always give it to me straight. I said I knew that.

At least work was sane.

16

Three days before Christmas, I was out shopping with Marion. The pre-Christmas season around her was much more fun than around my mother. Mum only cared about church, gifts for the priests and arranging special flowers for the midnight Mass. For Marion, Christmas was the time of year she unbent and had fun.

We were at Lane Crawford's. Marion shopped at few other places. I had asked her once why she didn't go to some of the Japanese or local department stores. But she had looked at me in unfeigned surprise and said, "But my dear, what could they possibly have there that I'd want?"

A saleslady was showing Marion a perfectly hideous velvet evening dress. Marion looked at me and raised her eyebrows slightly. Her mouth twitched.

"Thank you, no. I'll just look for a moment." She turned away and said under her breath, "honestly, have you ever?" and I suppressed a laugh.

Marion loved evening dresses. She bought me more than I could wear, and every one was expensive, sexy and pleasing to Paul. By now, I'd learned not to protest. She handed me a pale pink cashmere sweater. "What do you think? For your mother?"

I pictured the pale yellow sweater she'd given my mother last year, which still sat, unopened, in Mum's closet. "I don't think so, Marion. She doesn't wear sweaters much."

"Not unless they come from Granville Road."

It was rude of her to insinuate Mum only liked cheap things, but I couldn't help smiling. The trouble was, it was true.

A voice sounded behind me. "Rose, how lovely to see you. Where have you been? Elliot's been missing you dreadfully."

I froze.

Marion looked at me questioningly. I turned around and tried to say something but Leanna gushed right on. "It's been bad of me, I know, to take up all his time, but you know how it is with

Christmas and everything. He's invited to so many functions, and I try to accompany him as much as possible. But I know he'd rather be with you." She flashed a sickly sweet smile at me. I felt like slapping her mouth.

"After all," she continued, "you two make such a lovely couple."

And then, Leanna looked at Marion, and then at me, and despite my mounting anger, I felt this terrible sorrow, this awful despair. She stood there, like some rough beast, stalking me, holding me captive in one spot, so that I couldn't speak, couldn't move, couldn't run away.

"Oh, I . . ." Leanna began.

I glanced at Marion. Her face accused me. Without a word, she walked away and left the two of us standing there.

"That," I said, "was my mother-in-law." I left Leanna, and tried to follow Marion. But when I reached the outside of the store, she was already being driven away in a taxi.

Hours later, I stormed over to Elliot's. He stood at the door and stared, and I heard, "Darling, who's that?" and pushed my way in. Leanna was standing at his bedroom door wearing only a thin kimono. She turned red when she saw me, and rushed across the hall into the spare room where she was staying.

Elliot was fully clothed. He closed the front door. "It's not what you think, Rose," he began quietly. "I was giving her a massage. We're family."

I glared coldly at him "I don't care if you were fucking her all day."

"Rose . . ."

"Don't patronize me. I take it Anita's out."

Leanna emerged, dressed, from her room. "Rose, please don't get the wrong idea. We're very close, and always have been."

"You know perfectly well why I'm here, you hypocritical bitch."

She edged away from me towards Elliot.

"Rose! How dare you talk to Leanna that way."

"She didn't tell you, did she Elliot? No, I can tell she didn't. Well, guess who I saw today while I was shopping with my mother-in-law?"

"Rose," Leanna said quickly, "I didn't know who she was,

284

honestly I didn't."

Elliot looked at her. She avoided his eyes.

Leanna rushed away in tears to her room. "I didn't mean it, Elliot," she said as she closed the door.

Elliot put his arms around me. I was shaking. I don't think I'd ever been as angry in my life.

"She really didn't tell you, did she?"

"No. What happened?"

I recounted the incident, adding, "Marion will tell Paul's father."

He led me to the kitchen and poured me a glass of water. "Here, calm down. It was going to come out sooner or later, Rose. I'm not sorry."

"Of course not! What do you have to lose?"

He looked away. "That's not fair." His tone was even but cold.

"I wanted to do it my way, at the right time."

"And when would that have been? Never? How long did you expect me to wait?" He had raised his voice.

"Do you think that just because it's all okay in bed that that's my whole life? What do you think I do all the hours we're not together? I have my family, and a life."

"You and your family! You're such a hypocrite Rose. When you're with me, all your Chinese family responsibilities vanish. The minute you walk out of my place, you're suddenly a different person. Is that it? Maybe Leanna's right. All I am is a convenience between your legs!" He was shouting at me. "You've never loved me, have you? While I've been wearing my heart on my sleeve for you. I haven't been near another woman since you and I started up. Not that it matters to you."

"And all these women are falling over themselves in pursuit?" I couldn't stop myself. "Like dear Leanna? Who pretends to be so sweet to me, but finds every excuse under the sun to call you all the time so that you'll come visit her."

"Leave Leanna out of this."

"Why should I?"

"You're just using her as an excuse because you'll never had the guts to leave Paul!"

"And so she goes out of her way to help me, right?"

"It was a mistake. You heard her."

"She's destroyed my life." I felt the tears welling up, and choked them back angrily. "My father will never forgive me."

Elliot looked at me in shocked silence. I couldn't help crying now, the truth of what I'd just said stunned me. It wasn't Paul who kept me from loving Elliot. My mother would probably welcome a break up; she could say "I told you so" smugly. And Regina? What difference did she make anymore?

Elliot relented and embraced me. "Oh Rose, you do love someone after all."

I wanted to tell Elliot I loved him, but the words stuck in my throat. I realized I had never said that, never dared fully commit myself to him. And, maybe, deep inside, I knew I didn't love him, but hung onto him because I needed him for what he could give me. He was right. Around him, I didn't have to be responsible, didn't have to confront the reality of what I'd allowed my life to become while being able to unload all my feelings to him. Because I had allowed it, all because I wanted a pretty picture of life — family, marriage, social standing, a good job. All in the best asexual Hong Kong way, where the ugly side got buried beneath the facade of ritual behavior.

I calmed down eventually, and prepared to leave.

He walked me out of his flat to catch a taxi. "Let me take you home," he asked. I refused, saying I wanted to be alone. "Call me, Rose, please," was the last thing he said to me as I shut the taxi door.

The phone was ringing as I came into my home. It was my father-in-law.

"Marion told me," he said.

He was the last person I needed to hear from at this point. "I don't have anything to say to you."

"Now Rose, there's no need to be like that, is there? Marion will get over it. Paul doesn't have to know, does he?"

"He does anyway. Besides, he wouldn't want me telling the world about him. I'd do that, you know."

"Now that would kill Marion. You wouldn't do that to her, would you?"

I relented. Marion mattered to me and always would. If I cared at all about face, it was face for her, to prove that I deserved her kindness and concern over the years, that I deserved the right to be her daughter-in-law. In some ways, I wanted that role even more than that of Paul's wife. "What do you want?" I repeated.

"Just to see you."

"I'm surprised you're not over here. Isn't that usually your style? Oh wait, I forgot. You're afraid I'll call Dr. Ng, whose number I've memorized?"

"He's out of town. Seriously, Rose, I just want to see you."

I hadn't been alone with him once since the incident, and wasn't going to start now.

"Isn't Marion there? What will she think?"

"I'm not at home. Come out and meet me. We'll have a drink."

He wouldn't try anything in public, I reasoned. He repeated again his wish that I meet him, naming the bar at the Peninsula where he was at. For Marion's sake, I agreed, and also because I didn't want him to come over.

When I arrived, he moved away from the bar and led me to a table, because "ladies don't sit at bars."

Perhaps because I had studiously avoided him, he now seemed unfamiliar to me. As he lit a cigarette, the flame from the lighter illuminated his face. He was pale, like Paul, but there the resemblance ended. Paul was his mother's son.

"Say what you have to say," I told him, "and then I'm leaving and you're not following me. I intend to call Marion from here before I leave, and let her know we've had a talk in case you want to try anything."

He waved his hand dismissively. "Don't be silly, Rose. This is a public place. By the way, you shouldn't meet your lover in your father-in-law's drinking hole."

My mind flashed back to the night Elliot and I had been here. "I didn't know this was where you drank. So you've known all along?"

"Yes. I even had Elliot Cohen checked out." He said his name in a malicious tone, as if to say, you see, I really do know.

"I don't believe you."

"My dear Rose, when you're as old as I am, and have been frequenting the same establishment for years, you'd know that the bartenders are the soul of discretion, and can be bought for a small tip. All I did was ask him to tell me the name of the gentleman with you, and he showed me his credit card slip. The rest was easy. Your lover has quite a checkered past, you know. Why aren't you with him tonight?"

Paul Sr. had a hypnotic stare. I imagined him in front of a jury. Paul had told me once that his father could persuade anyone round to his point of view, if he wanted to. I broke his gaze and sipped my scotch. "So what do you want?" I demanded.

"Rose, Rose, you pretty little thing. Stop trying to be so tough. Do you know, I liked you the first time I met you, when you were what, seventeen? You seemed so fragile and awkward, but there was a resolute toughness about you that appealed to me. And you were rather old fashioned. I remembered your clothes weren't trendy at all. You were absolutely charming, trying so hard to impress your boyfriend's parents. I told Paul afterwards he would be a fool not to do everything in his power to hold onto you. You know, I was the one who told him to go see you in the States. Paul always needed a little prodding."

As I listened to him, I found myself wishing that the surface of my collective life, which embraced my family and in-laws, could be real. I wished that this conversation, in its seeming innocence, didn't have to be marred by reality. "I didn't come to hear you extol my virtues," I declared. "Tell me what you want, or I'm leaving. And calling Marion," I added.

He reached his hand over and brushed a hair away from my mouth. I backed away, chilled by his touch. "Marion," he said, "and you get along, don't you?"

"What is it to you?" But the memory of that afternoon plagued me. I was afraid I'd lost Marion's approval forever.

"Please Rose," and suddenly his expression became gentle and even kindly. "I promise I won't bother you. It's just that I find you . . . attractive."

"I'm leaving." I picked up my purse and began to edge out of my seat. He placed his hand on my arm, and his grip was firm but not painful.

"He's not my son."

"What?" I sat still and stared at him.

"Paul's not my son."

I waited, not sure what to believe.

"I married Marion because she was pregnant."

"Then who . . . ?"

"Robert's father. My brother Alex."

He allowed the shock of understanding to permeate. I knew he was telling the truth.

"Does Paul know?"

He lit another cigarette, and gulped down the rest of his drink. "No. Want another?" He pointed to my almost empty glass. I nodded.

"She continued the affair even after we were married. It didn't end until he moved to Canada."

"But Robert was . . ." I stopped myself. I meant to say that Robert was fourteen before his family moved, which Paul had told me, because, shortly afterwards, Paul and his family had moved to Hong Kong.

He understood my meaning. "Yes, it was a long time. She's never stopped loving him, you know. He gave it up after he moved, for his own family's sake." His face changed, and it became cold and sad. "She used to say his name at night for months afterwards. 'Alexander, Alexander, come back.' I would hear her moaning. Do you have any idea what that's like? Living with someone who cries for her lover in your bed?" He was not looking at me, and in his eyes was the resignation of a long accepted pain.

"So why did you marry her?"

"Need you ask? Family, of course. Alex begged me. She wouldn't have an abortion, and I was the only single male left in the family. Alex meant the world to me, so I did it for him."

My husband and Robert. Like father, like son, or was it brotherly love? It dawned on me that Paul Sr. had probably never told anyone about this.

"Besides, she was an intelligent woman, brilliant in her love for my brother. I thought some of that brilliance might be left for me. There weren't many Chinese families in South Africa then," he added. "And my sister-in-law is a hopeless fool. Like me."

Despite my dislike for him, I said, "I'm sorry," and reached out to grip his hand.

He held my hand with both of his. "So that's my secret, Rose. Don't feel bad I know yours. It's very small by comparison."

I withdrew my hand. He had broken the hold Marion had on me by his revelation. It didn't matter what she thought anymore. "What do you want me to do?"

He chuckled in reply, and put his hand to my cheek. "Whatever you want, my dear girl. Whatever you want."

Christmas came and went.

The first Thursday in January, Gordie flashed into town. "Can I see you for dinner, alone, Doll?"

Leanna hadn't left, having extended her stay because, according to Elliot, there were some "family matters" to work out. "Why not? Everyone else does."

"What, for dinner?"

"No, alone."

Even in those early years of our acquaintance, Gordie lightened me up, brought out a refreshing flippancy. We met for dinner at 3-6-9 in Wanchai, the best Shanghainese hole-in-the-wall I knew, which was what he had asked for. For appetizers, I ordered him a huge bamboo steamer of steamed pork dumplings, and *hoi jit*. I watched in mild surprise as he devoured two dishes of the latter. Despite all his years in Hong Kong and his very Chinese manner, Elliot still couldn't bring himself to like jellyfish. As for Paul, he called it nutritionally valueless, and wouldn't eat it at all.

"Uncle Jimmy loved Shanghai food," Gordie said between bites.

I laughed. "I still can't get used to hearing you call him that. But you know, he wouldn't take us to a Shanghai restaurant, because Mum doesn't like the food."

"Met your sister, by the way."

"I know. Why did you?"

"It was accidental. Someone I knew had seen her work and told me about her and I rang her up. It didn't take long for me to figure out who she was."

"Mmm."

"She's jealous of you, isn't she?" When I didn't respond, he continued, "Guess I'm not surprised. You know, your dad hardly ever mentioned her? In fact, the only way I found out she existed was because I asked him once if Rose had any brothers and sisters."

Bits and pieces of Rose. He was making me uncomfortable.

"Okay, so why are we having dinner?"

"That's what I like about you. You don't waste time." He wiped his mouth with his handkerchief. "Kenton can't tell you this yet, so I will. Cathay Pacific's going to buy Pan Asian and take over your air rights. You guys are finished."

"Pity. It was fun while it lasted." I was dancing my fingers nervously over the teacup.

He took hold of my hand. "I guess your job's the least of your worries, huh?"

"Mmm." I withdrew my hand and took a sip of tea.

"All right, I won't come on to you." He grinned. "But I still want you to come work with me."

"Why? Whatever for?"

"You'll have fun."

"I'm sure of that."

"I'll be better for you than your husband. Or Cohen."

I chuckled. "I'm sure of that too."

"So. Say yes."

"I'll have to talk to Dad." I looked into his eyes, wondering if he really understood, wondering how much our connection really meant. Perhaps, I wondered too much. Life was easier when I just did what I felt like doing.

"Then you'll have to say yes." He took my hand again, only this time, he held me by my wrist, his fingers circled firmly round it like a manacle. "Uncle Jimmy promised you to me, years ago. You're my picture bride, Rose." With that, he twisted my hand round and touched my palm to his lips. "Come on, Doll, let's split."

Gordie's picture bride! When I first came to New York, that's how he introduced me to everyone. Yet despite his flippant manner, he's really quite serious underneath. Conversations with Gordie, even the nonsensical ones, are always memorable. He's only asked of me what he knew I could give.

And he's still the only man who can get away with calling me "Doll."

It'll be sunrise in less than a couple of hours.

Looks like they're winding up out there. Some of them are leaving anyway. The ABC keeps looking back through the glass at me. So I've had too much to drink. He would too if he were in my shoes.

I'll miss this office, and my conversations with Lady Liberty. I don't know when I started talking to her, but she's such a comfortable, familiar face, and her blank eyes aren't haunting. I don't remember what I say to her, just silly pleasantries in my head when the working day makes me look out the window. And she's far enough away, out there on her island, never to impinge on my freedom.

Remembered conversations can't be accurate. Words can be recorded, but not the person who speaks the words. Technology, mercifully, hasn't come that far.

At the end of January, I finally saw Elliot again. Our interim phone conversations had been short, abrupt. Leanna, he claimed, simply had refused to leave. I didn't feel compelled to object.

"Let's go out," he said as soon as I arrived.

I walked into his flat, closed the door and stared at him. "Why?"

"I don't know. I need to be around people."

"Shouldn't we talk about it first?"

"Why? We talk about 'it' all the time. We just never act." He kept biting his lip as he spoke. "Come on, let's go to that place in Sai Kung. No one will see us there."

I thought about Paul's barrister friend who lived out that way. "It's a long way."

"So?"

"Okay."

He didn't say a word the entire ride out in the taxi. Nor did he touch me. The place was empty when we walked in except for two English couples at another table. They glanced up as we walked by. Elliot stopped at the booth behind theirs.

"Can't we sit further away?" I didn't like the idea of them hearing our conversation. "There are plenty of places."

"If you insist." He was impatient. "I'm not hungry," he said, as soon as we sat down in the corner booth.

"Elliot, what are we doing here?"

"Leanna didn't insist on staying. I asked her to." He waited expectantly.

"And . . .?"

"We're used to each other. I guess it's just that we go back such a long way. She understands about Anita's anger, and about the way her sister is. Even my brother. She understands about him . . . In fact, I offered to give her the massage, I asked her to come stay in the first place. She resisted for the longest time, but finally agreed to come stay, for Anita's sake."

"Elliot, what are you trying to tell me?'

He kept looking at me and turning away. "I haven't been completely honest with you, about Leanna, I mean. That time you saw us at the party in Malaysia, it was my fault, not hers. She was more than just my occasional mistress before. I asked her to marry me, and then finked out because I couldn't take the responsibility." The revelation seemed to calm him, and he remained silent for several minutes. "I slept with her again," he blurted out. "Just before Christmas, the day you left my place after the row with her. I couldn't help it." He looked guilty and relieved all at the same time. "I've been wanting to tell you."

"And that's why you brought us here?"

"Yes." He nodded sheepishly. "It was only once, though, and it wasn't her fault. It was just that she was crying after you left, and looked so helpless . . ." his words trailed off. "Well, it just happened. She feels dreadful about it too. But because she's totally honest, she asked me to tell you."

His eyes were so earnest, and he seemed in such need of reassurance. "Elliot, it's not a crime."

"You're not angry?"

"I don't have that right."

"Of course you do!" His voice rose in a slight frenzy, and he caught himself. "Sorry. I didn't mean to yell."

Elliot continued nervously. "You don't know Leanna well, but she comes across much more confidently than she really is. She's actually quite shy and conservative. After that one incident, she only agreed to stay on if I wouldn't touch her. Even before, she had apprehensions about our relationship because I was her sister's husband . . ."

As he chattered on, I caught myself only half listening to what he said. It didn't seem important, all this confessing he seemed compelled to do. Funny, but after all this time, he was still a stranger to me. I looked at his neatly proportioned features, and somehow tonight, they looked wrong, as if some bits were askew.

Part of Elliot's attraction was his attractiveness to other women, women he appeared oblivious to. Whenever I pointed out some woman had the hots for him, and there always was gossip about him, he would be surprised, having not noticed her at all. But he was naive about Leanna, who was obviously heightening her value by playing hard to get, biding her time until the timing was right. After all, she had no reason to stay on almost a month in Hong Kong, especially since Anita had left to go back to school. I believed him when he said she was conservative. Despite her flamboyance, exaggerated and provocative, I suspected she might be frigid, the way Regina was. What most women didn't know about Elliot was that they, not he, had to make the first move, that they, not he, would have to make desire evident. But then, most women didn't like confronting their own lust.

And then I wondered about us. Despite all his protestations, and my stalling, had he ever really fallen in love with me? After all, he'd once said it himself, was there anything deeper to our relationship than excellent sex and his desire to teach me about his passions in the arts, and my desire to learn? Could we sustain ourselves on our brand of erotica? Or would that eventually fizzle out because it had no place to go?

That night, we didn't go back to his flat at all. He drank, I didn't. We talked shop, much more than we normally did. He'd heard rumors about the Cathay Pacific buyout of my company, and said it would be a shame if it happened. That night, I looked at Elliot and didn't see my lover. I wondered how long the lover would stay away.

"You must try to understand about Paul." Marion's voice trembled slightly. She had summoned me to tea. It was almost two months after the encounter with Leanna and the first time she'd spoken to me since.

"I do understand."

"Discretion is all he needs. Who was that dreadful woman anyway?"

I gave a minimal explanation, adding that she would be harmless in Malaysia.

She picked up her cup, and her hand seemed to shake. I

suddenly felt sorry for her, for her wasted life, her wasted love. Marion wasn't a cold person, but marriage and conformity had made her cold. Her love for Paul was the last spark of love she could kindle.

She raised the cup to her lips, and as she lowered it back on the saucer, it came down too hard and some tea spilled onto her skirt. I dipped my napkin into her water glass and rubbed at the spot. It was an off white gabardine skirt, and would have stained.

"Thank you, dear." She took the napkin from me and rubbed vigorously. As she replaced the napkin on the table, re-folding it neatly, she said, "You're such a perfect daughter-in-law. Please don't leave him. You know we all love you dearly, Rose, don't you?"

"He's already left me, you know." And I told her that he hardly lived at home.

"Oh," she uttered. "I didn't know." She thought for a moment. "Paul won't leave the marriage though. You know that, don't you?" Her face flushed as she spoke. She continued speaking, almost too rapidly, "You must know that? He loves you in his own way. He just isn't like other men. Remember the first time I told you? It doesn't mean he won't take care of you or . . ." She stopped abruptly and stared at me helplessly.

"Please, Marion, let's just leave things for now."

It was eight in the evening when I finally returned home in a peevish mood. I'd eaten dinner alone, after walking for over two hours around Tsimshatsui window shopping aimlessly, although I'd hardly had any appetite. Elliot rang around nine.

"I need to go back to New York for about a month, maybe longer. It's Anita. She doesn't want to stay with her mother. I have to face this. It's like Leanna says, I can't keep running away from things."

"What about your business?"

"It'll survive. I can keep in touch from New York."

"So what are you going to do, about your daughter I mean?"

"Maybe move her to Malaysia, and myself as well. She likes it there."

I waited to see if he would ask me to go, but even as I thought it, I knew he wouldn't. Elliot was beginning to divest me from his

295

life, whether or not he realized it. Perhaps that wasn't the worst thing.

"Look, Leanna's going. I'm sorry about that Rose, but I can't handle Anita for that long on my own. There won't be anything between us. I promise. I don't want to be another Paul to you. This is just . . ."

And on he went for the next fifteen minutes, describing in detail all their arrangements, as if he wanted to assure me of the physical barrier he would go out of his way to erect between himself and Leanna. It all seemed so unnecessary somehow. If he wanted badly enough to sleep with her, because he felt intimate towards her, or needed her, or was just plain horny, what real difference did it make? Love and sex were not as inextricably entwined as he thought. Paul was proof enough.

The door to the flat opened, and I turned around, startled.

"Paul's back," I said to Elliot. He had gotten into the habit of ringing me at home because I'd told him it was all right.

"Oh, I'm sorry Rose," and he hung up abruptly.

Paul ambled over. "Hello." He didn't kiss or touch me. These days, he reserved displays of affection for when we were around other people. He looked relaxed, reasonably at peace with himself. "I spoke to mother," he explained.

"What a coincidence, or was it?" I frowned, perturbed.

"It was coincidental. I didn't know you were having tea."

I was still holding the phone, and replaced it.

"Who were you talking to?"

"No one important. What did your mother tell you?"

He paused before replying. "That she didn't want us to get a divorce. I told her it was up to you. It had to be."

"Paul, why are you here? Do you expect me to tell you one way or another? Because I won't, you know. I need more time to think about all this."

"Oh, there's no hurry. I promised I wouldn't pressure you and I meant it. I . . . I had a fight with Man Yee." He pulled a long face as he said it.

I closed my eyes for a few seconds. A nagging headache was forming. My stomach tightened into many knots, while bits of me imploded. Yet I couldn't shout, couldn't get angry. The whole situation was almost comic, but with Paul I couldn't laugh about these kinds of things. He took himself too seriously for that. "What did you fight about?" I asked as I opened my eyes again.

His relief was evident. Paul had always been sensitive to my unspoken feelings, and worried about them. "He wants me to divorce you."

"What did you say?"

"Same thing I told my mother. Not unless you wanted it."

"It'll pass. He's just being temperamental."

Paul smiled weakly. "I know."

"Go on," I said. "Call him. He'll like it that you're doing it while I'm here."

His reaction gave away that he'd already contemplated it, but hadn't quite the gall to do it. "Do you really think so?"

"Yes."

He needed no further prompting after that. I went into my room to give him privacy. Within a few minutes, they had made up as I knew they would, and he was ready to go back to his lover's. He knocked on my door to say goodbye. As he left he kissed my cheek, "Thank you, Rose. Albert was right about you. He said you'd understand." And he left.

What the hell was wrong with my life?

I wanted to talk to someone, to connect with another human being who could understand this, and unload some of my frustrations. I thought of my dad, but conversations with him were about what wasn't said. Tonight, I wanted not only to confront the paradox of my life, but accept it as well. What prompted my next act I still don't fully understand. I called Paul Sr.

As the phone rang, I hoped Marion wouldn't answer. If she did, I would hang up.

"Is Marion there?" I asked when he answered the phone.

"Rose! Oh no, she's asleep. She isn't well."

"Come meet me. Buy me a drink."

He hesitated. "Are you sure about this?"

"Positive."

Paul Sr. was already at the Peninsula Bar when I arrived. This is my father-in-law, I reminded myself as he seated me. I wanted to hold onto that notion, to make our connection as real as I could, to make him family and therefore someone I could trust, despite everything.

"So what's this all about?" he asked.

"Paul doesn't live with me anymore."

He barely glanced at me. "So you have what's known as an 'arrangement'. What's the problem with that?"

I stirred the ice in my drink, trying to find the right words. "Everything's going to change."

"Why? Is Paul, what's the term these days, 'coming out'?"

"Something like that."

"It had to happen eventually. Marion just wouldn't accept it."

He was so cool, so unruffled. I felt like throwing my drink in his face. "Then why did you try to keep up all these appearances?" My voice was edgy, hostile.

He seemed surprised. "Really, Rose, don't be naive. You're your own mistress. You could have left him. Besides, it was Marion, not me. I never insisted you accept such an untenable situation."

"But you didn't do anything to stop it."

"Didn't I?" His mouth curled in a cruel smile.

I shuddered, but persisted. "So, it's justifiable, what you did to me?"

"Momentary lapse. You're making too much of it. I am a man, after all. What about your precious Elliot? You still have him, don't you? Divorce isn't such a terrible thing these days."

It wasn't what I wanted to hear. Paul Sr. had accepted a far more untenable situation than my own without initiating change. I wanted to daunt his unflappable manner. "Do you know, Paul expected me to get pregnant by Elliot and pass the child off as his own?"

He chuckled maliciously. "Like mother like son, eh Rose?"

And then, I couldn't hold back any longer and a tear slid down my cheek. I wiped it away quickly. Paul Sr.'s expression softened. He stretched his palm forward and laid it against my face. I didn't recoil.

"Dear Rose," he said. "I suppose I should have been kinder, shouldn't I? But there we are, life that is. Sometimes, things aren't a question of choice."

His voice was so resigned. I cradled my father-in-law's hand against my face, warmed by his touch. He'd said it for me. Things weren't always a question of choice. It's how my own father and he had lived their lives, and they saw no reason why anyone would want to behave otherwise. It was partly to do with being Chinese, behaving like a "gentleman" as prescribed by Confucius. My womanhood didn't count, couldn't count, not if I didn't want to upset the social order into which I was born. Mum both fought it and conformed to it, and Regina fought it all the way. But were either of them happier than me? I didn't think so. Neither of them had found answers. There were no rights and wrongs in all that had come to be my life. There were no great moral dilemmas or ethical principles in the Western sense that could guide my actions, or the actions of those closest to me. My greatest "wrong" was wanting to be a part of this Hong Kong Chinese social order I called home. In this home territory, this emotional landscape to which I was inextricably tied, Paul Sr. was just another fallible human being. Like Mum, Dad and Marion. And Regina and Paul. And Elliot.

And me.

I left Paul Sr. that night and stopped by the Star Ferry to look out at the harbor. I stood there alone till the early morning hours, when the neon lights of the island no longer illuminated the buildings. My heart cried for hours, although my eyes were dry. Something changed inside me that night. Time is forgetful, but I remembered that moment accurately, because it wasn't about what someone said, or some event that occurred. It was about me, and who I was. And that was something I knew deeply, completely, which no person or event could ever take away.

Almost morning. Death of the dark.

17

March to June were quiet months.

In July, the Pan Asian sale became public news.

Kenton called me into his office the day before the news broke. "You could go work for Cathay Pacific."

I made a face. "No thanks. Too big. And," I added, "too British."

He chuckled. So are you coming with us?" Kenton planned to remain in Hong Kong to run the Asian end of the operation with Gordie.

"Let me think about it."

That afternoon, Teresa answered the phone and said "New York," signalling *chi sin* crazy so I knew right away who she meant.

"Ready to dump those two yet?" This had become Gordie's standard opening line.

"Not yet."

"At least now you're saying 'yet'. How are you?"

"Miserable, my love." It rolled off easily, that little endearment I didn't mean. But Gordie loosened my speech, thanks to his outrageous manner. I wanted a love, any love, to replace the emptiness in my heart.

"Then come to Gordie. I'll take care of you any way you want. What do you say, Doll?"

I smiled into the handset. "Last time, it was gigantic Chinese fans for the Soho galleries, and before that satellite factories in Xiamen and what was the one before that? Oh yes, mail order adoptions of Chinese babies. What's next?"

"I'll buy your boyfriend's magazine, what's it called, *AsiaMonth*, right? It's enough of a money maker. Got a good mailing list. Then you can be your lover's boss. How d'you like that?"

An appealing passing thought. That was what Gordie always seemed to be about. "And what about Paul?"

"I'll open Hong Kong's first gay bar in Central, then you can be your husband's mama san."

I laughed.

"Take it from a man — we're not worth the heartache. Come work for me instead."

It wasn't a job any sane and rational person would take, but I didn't feel sane and rational. Like Gordie said, as long as he paid me well, and he would, and I worked hard for him, what did it matter why I did it? Any job was just a job; what mattered was life. Besides, I knew perfectly well why. There wasn't much of a life left for me where I was.

The following week, Stan checked Regina into a sanatorium.

"I couldn't take it anymore, Rose," Stan's voice was tired, and a little defensive. "I figured since none of you were going to take responsibility for her, I would. I'll even pay for it, but I'd like some help."

I thought about Aunt Helen's remark, that Stan wasn't family. What good, I wondered, was Regina's family? None of us had the courage Stan had in dealing with her. We swept her under the rug of distance, and, in my mother's case, pretended her problems didn't exist.

"I'll pay, Stan." How quickly I responded! But then, money was always an easy solution, a typically Hong Kong solution.

"She needs to see one of you, you know?"

"I'll be there."

Stan would never have any problem from me, ever. I owed him, more than he'd ever understand or even demand. It was time I took some real responsibility, even if no one in my family would. That day, I told my parents that I intended to go look after Regina. My mother approved, because she felt I was being a good sister, although she maintained the fiction that Regina was seriously ill with some mysterious disease. Dad pulled me aside and asked what Paul thought about all this. I said I hadn't told him.

A few days later, I called Gordie and told him I was coming to work for him. About time, was his reply.

"You're going where?" Teresa was incredulous.

"New York. I can't stand working for institutions, only lunatics."

"But what about Elliot?"

I tossed my head back and laughed. "My god, Teresa. You didn't even ask me about my husband."

She blinked. "You're right," and then she began laughing too. "What about your husband? You can't be serious."

"Dead serious."

"But how soon?"

"Oh, I don't know. Soon, I think. Moving to New York will take a lot of effort."

"Why not? You need a rest. With Mr. Kenton leaving, why should you stay? You don't need the money."

"Yes I do, if I'm going to leave Paul." It startled me, how readily I knew that.

Her eyes widened. "Are you really going to divorce him?"

"I don't know." Her saying "divorce" brought home the reality which was harder to be brave about. "Perhaps I'll just go on short term assignments. Like I did to Kuala Lumpur."

"With Elliot again, huh? I know you saw him in New York. You can't keep doing that, Rose."

There were times that my secretary had a better grip on my life than I did. "Why not?"

"Do you think life is a storybook? That you and he can run away into the heavens like the princess and the cowherd?" The Milky Way festival was only a few days away. Teresa actually taught her daughter to observe it. I had found that amusing when she first told me some years back. It was incongruous for this modern woman to pay heed to such an old ritual.

"You do that every year."

"Silly. That's just for tradition, so my daughter will remember the old Chinese legends deeply. Besides, she still young, and it's okay for her to dream about her future husband."

"And I'm not? Young, that is?"

"You're both too old, you and Elliot, to be playing with fire."

I was going to say it was becoming a dying flame, but thought otherwise. Teresa made her own assumptions about Elliot, and I wasn't going to enlighten her.

"Besides," she continued, "what will you say to your father?"

I ruminated on that for a long time afterward. Teresa didn't know the whole truth about my mother or Regina — those weren't the kinds of things I shared with her. But a kind of unspoken intimacy had sprung up between us, and she had instinctively known, somehow, what was truly important in my life.

"What is it between you and Gordie?" Elliot was irritated when I told him I was moving to New York. "And why didn't you talk to me first?"

Things had been strained between us since he came back from New York. The situation with Anita hadn't been resolved. Leanna had come to Hong Kong and stayed a week. I suspected he had been sleeping with her, but wouldn't admit it.

"It's a job. I'm going because of Regina." We were sitting at his dining table, the dishes from dinner piled in front of me.

"And are you leaving Paul?"

"I haven't told him about this move yet."

"You're not answering my question."

That was when I looked Elliot squarely in the face. Where was the man I thought I fell in love with? We hadn't talked about music or poetry or art in months. Our meetings were fraught with unfinished discussions about whether or not I was leaving Paul. Leanna called without fail each time I was at his place, which led me to suspect their affair, or at least that they were in more constant contact than he acknowledged. He had taken three extremely short "business" trips, on weekends, which were untypical, always to KL, and didn't explain. I never accused him, never questioned.

And our lovemaking? Hurried, infrequent and short.

I moved aside the pile of dishes and stretched my arms out across the table to take his hands. "You know what you told me once about improvisation?"

"Come on, Rose, don't change the subject."

His hands warmed mine, which were perpetually cold, even in summer. I put a finger to his lips and made him bite it gently, the way he often did, and ignored his appeal. "You said that sometimes, musicians didn't know when to end an improvisation, that they did what amounted to the equivalent of treading water."

"So?"

"I don't want us to tread water."

The irritation that had been hovering around him for too long finally relented. He played with my fingers, bringing them to his lips and biting them gently. "Is that what we've been doing?"

"I'm afraid so." I could feel desire, something I hadn't felt in awhile with Elliot.

He tugged at my arms and made me stand up. "Come on," he said.

"What about the dishes?'

"Later."

He didn't answer the phone when Leanna called. Before we fell asleep, he thanked me for letting him go. I told him it was my pleasure. He admitted that he'd probably wind up marrying Leanna. I replied if he didn't mind I'd rather not come to the wedding, but said I'd send "Olivia" if he liked. He laughed and asked if he could still visit me in New York. I said, if he wished. We didn't sleep till much later. And I never did the dishes.

At least we parted friends.

Telling Paul was easier than I thought. I had asked him to see me at home, and my request had been almost hostile.

"I like Ashberry," he declared. "Will he arrange a green card?"

It was typical of Paul to bring something like that up. 1997 was still seventeen years away.

"He's offered."

"Take it." He grinned. "I am your best legal counsel, aren't I?"

He was handsome. The smooth skin and well groomed look he bore still impressed me, made me proud of him. I watched him tilt the Escher; it had gone slightly askew. Without him around the house, I realized I hadn't been as neat as we used to be. How much of that picky meticulousness was Paul, and how much me? It was hard to say.

"So do you think you'll come back? I'd come visit, well, you know what I mean."

Talking to Paul was about not saying what either of us meant. He hadn't once asked me in all the last months whether or not I would divorce him. He wasn't going to ask now.

"I don't know."

And then, Paul stretched his hand out to me, and some of my hostility faded.

"Come here." He tried to sit me on his lap, something he hadn't done since we were teenagers making out in the park. I tensed, unaccustomed by now to physical contact with him. "Come on, it's okay," he said to my hesitation. "I want to tell you something." It was comforting, being in his arms, being a teenager again. "Rose, do you know one of the reasons I was first attracted to you? It's because you look like a boy." He said it lovingly, holding me close to him. His touch was affectionate, like a brother's. "A pretty boy," he added.

"But Paul . . ."

"Shh, I know, I know, it's ridiculous. But Rose, you are a bit like a boy. You've always cut your hair short, and you're a bit of Peter Pan who hasn't grown up. If you had been a boy, you'd probably have become a pilot, like your father."

He had something there. Perhaps I was my father's son, the one he'd never had. Part of my running off to work for Gordie was to embark on a new adventure. It had something to do with the denial in my family, except that I chose not to self destruct or head down the path of amnesia.

"After all," Paul continued, "your wanting to be near Regina is to take care of her, isn't it? She's the fragile girl, not you, despite your opposite outward demeanor. I know she was the 'tough' one when you were kids, but you've grown up to be responsible and level headed and not overly subject to your emotions. It's all rather male, don't you think?"

"She's my sister. I can't bear to see her suffer."

He kissed me on the lips, and gave me what I sometimes thought of as his "big brother" look. "I do care about you, you know. And we do belong together, forever, regardless of what's happened to our lives."

I giggled. Life had been fun necking with Paul in the park; that long ago connection, however silly, bound us. The absurdity of our marriage was farcical, but I still couldn't help feeling devoted to him. I had thought a great deal about divorce, but it seemed drastic and frightening. The best thing about Paul was that we didn't really have to talk about a lot of what he called the "administrative details" of marriage. We were alike in day-to-day things — we planned and set schedules and stuck to them for the most part. In many ways, we were both entirely predictable and even boring. But we understood each other. We knew the intimate problems of our families. And above all, we could generally count on each other to do the right thing for each other in what mattered.

He whispered, "Run away with me from your parents," which brought me back to our early days and the conversations we used to have. "Let's," I replied. "When?" "Tomorrow." "Can't." "Why not?" "Math test." And we both collapsed into a spasm of laughter.

On Saturday afternoon, I went looking for Dad on Cameron Road. We sat down for tea in Joe's Place.

"Are you going to work for Cathay Pacific?"

"I don't know if I want to." There, it was out at last. I knew it had been on his mind.

He nodded. "I think I understand."

That was when I told him I was going to work for Gordie, and that I'd be in New York for awhile because Gordie would arrange for a green card.

"Are you leaving your husband?"

My father had never challenged me so directly before. A small part of me squirmed, still did not want to answer, since, even with Paul, things were left unsaid. But I knew there was no escaping it now. Dad was demanding I make a decision.

My head was bowed and I wasn't looking at him when he asked. I took a deep breath and faced him. "We won't disturb our present arrangement."

The radio broadcast announced the winner of the last race. My father showed me his ticket. "Look," he said. "My longshot won."

18

The next month was a frenzy of closing up my life in Hong Kong. I called Regina once a week, who talked non stop, sometimes babbling almost incoherently. Stan kept telling her I would be coming to New York, and she was always happy about that. I still went to work mornings at Pan Asian, to help complete the handover.

About two weeks before my departure for New York, Dad collapsed at his desk. Mum wasn't home when it happened, so his secretary rang me. They're taking him to St. Teresa's, she kept repeating, as if that somehow made it all right.

I panicked and rang Aunt Helen. "I don't know what to do," I said.

"Now calm down. Get over there right away and I'll meet you. I'll have Chong try to reach your mother."

Her brisk and efficient manner steadied me. "Okay."

In my mind, ten thousand things swirled. I tried to reach Paul but he wasn't in. Somehow, it became imperative I reach him and I almost shouted at his secretary that she must find him as quickly as possible. I knew I should simply go right away, but I remained in my seat. Teresa kept glancing at me; she could see there was a problem. And then I rang Man Yee, whom I woke and he said Paul wasn't there and asked why was I ringing, but I hung up without replying. I sat a few minutes longer and rang Marion. She was out. Finally, I rang Paul Sr.

"It's Dad," I blurted out as soon as my father-in-law came to the phone. "It's my dad."

"Rose?"

"He's going to die. He's going to die." I was trembling, suddenly very afraid. "He's going to die."

It took some moments, but Paul Sr. eventually calmed me down and got the story out of me. He told me to hold on. Then he rang my secretary Teresa, explained what happened, and asked her to take me in a taxi to the hospital. And that was how I got there, where Helen was already taking charge of communicating with the medical staff.

Paul Sr. arrived next, and it was several hours before Uncle Chong and my mother showed up. Mum and Aunt Helen hovered around me, as did Paul Sr. Marion arrived a few minutes later. At nine, the doctor emerged and spoke in low tones to my aunt. My mother had gone through the last hours in something of a trance.

Helen gathered us in a circle. "He's in a coma. The doctors simply don't know whether he'll regain consciousness. . ."

She continued to speak, but something in me just couldn't hold together anymore and I started to cry. Paul Sr. put his arm around me, and I continued to cry into his shoulder, shaking.

My mother stared at Helen. "A coma? A coma? It can't be."

"Now now, don't worry," Chong began.

"Worry? How can I not worry? He could be in a coma for years."

I stopped sobbing and stared at my mother, trying to decipher her meaning.

"He's always been healthy," she continued, "while I was weak. I always expected he would be fine and could take care of me. How can he be in a coma?"

"Dad's not all that healthy," I said.

"Of course he is!" She looked almost angry.

I disengaged myself from Paul Sr., and tried to collect myself "Mum, you're in shock. Let me take you home."

"I must tell Regina," was all she said as I led her out of the hospital.

My aunt stayed with Mum that night, and told me to go home. I called Man Yee again, but Paul still wasn't there. That was when I called Elliot. I was crying, wishing I were in his arms. "Listen, I'm sorry to bother you but could I come over?"

He didn't respond. And then it dawned. "Leanna's there, isn't she?"

The apology in his voice told me all I needed to know. I rang off hurriedly, embarrassed by my emotional plea.

"You should have tried harder to reach me," Paul said when he called.

"I called Man Yee, and spoke to your secretary several times."

"Well you know how it is. Sometimes, Man Yee and I . . ." his voice trailed off

"No Paul, I don't know." He had no right to reprimand me when it was his private life that was at fault. The truth was that I simply didn't know, and frankly, didn't want to know.

"Your family must have wondered where I was."

"Well, I'm sure your parents knew."

"They were there?"

"Yes, Paul."

The next afternoon, I went to the hospital and sat by my father's bed for hours. Mum told me she was too upset to come. Helen stopped by while I was there. He looked frail. I came back every day for the next two weeks and sat by him, willing him into consciousness. Somehow, I knew he might never wake up again.

Almost dawn. The sky's beginning to lighten. What a gorgeous red glow.

Gordie's showing the Feds the door.

And the sun's just coming up. On my back, not in my eyes. About time.

Once my mother accepted that Dad might never regain consciousness, she had a good story to tell her acquaintances. "Just like that, imagine. I thank God every day that He let him live, because maybe one day he'll get better." But she cleaned our home, eradicating every sign of my father's possessions. "No point keeping all this stuff, is there Rose? If your father gets better and comes home, he'll like everything nice and neat."

Should I have objected? I remember my sense of despair as I watched her sweep through the rooms, finally taking all his clothes out of the bedroom and moving them into the spare room, which was Regina's and my old bedroom. He was already dead to her, I realized, and perhaps had been for a long time. I wanted to get angry at her, to stop her from this senseless rampage. But it seemed to keep her balanced, to help her through what must have also been a difficult time for her. So I busied myself instead with the numerous arrangements involved in setting up my life in New York.

A few days before I was finally due to leave, I stopped in to visit my mother. She was calmer these days, and almost happy in her new life without my father. Whatever I felt about her behavior I kept to myself. There seemed no point now. In fact, when I suggested postponing my move because of Dad she became quite indignant and declared that my father would have wanted me to go. Mum wholly approved of my going, because Paul confirmed that Gordie would be a substantial business connection, and also would help me get immigrant status. To her, this was a supreme wifely sacrifice. Since I was unable to produce a child, the least I could do was get my husband and I a green card. I didn't even try to set her straight.

Before I left that evening, I caught sight of my father's chair in the living room on which his most recent pile of Newsweek magazines were bundled for disposal. As I stared at them, I kept waiting to hear the click of his key in the front door, the sound I listened for as a child every evening around six. On top of the bundle sat his Flying Tigers model plane. My mother had grumbled about it over the years, calling it an eyesore that cluttered up the decor. But she never dared touch it, until now. I picked up the plane and held it up to the light. The blue and red insignia on the tail, on what Dad used to call the tiger's tail. And then I remembered, once when I was quite young, my father told me that the famous American, Mr. Walt Disney, had personally designed the Flying Tigers trademark. Now, I wondered if this logo was the one he meant. I wrapped the plane carefully in a newspaper, and placed it in a large plastic bag. There'd be a place for it in my New York office.

The night before I left, I woke up with a start from another lighthouse dream. Regina had been replaced by Leanna, who wore a tight, see-through dress. She had on a bra but no panties. She pressed herself against the window, calling Elliot's name. The rain poured, but I didn't get wet. From the opposite distance, Elliot and Paul appeared and began walking towards me. Slowly, the two of them merged into one figure. Sometimes it looked like Paul, sometimes Elliot. Finally the figure disappeared completely, fading slowly like a ghost. Leanna turned into Regina, only she didn't look young and beautiful the way she always appeared in the dream, but thin and worn, like the last time I saw her. I tried to run towards her, but my feet remained in the same spot no matter how hard I ran. When I awoke completely, I saw that I had kicked all the covers off the bed.

October 1987

Enough scotch.

Six years in New York. The first two living with Regina were hell. But I coped. I had to do it to get her out of the sanatorium. She's better now and lives with Stan again. She's almost bearable these days. Still patronizes me and complains that I have no soul, but at least she doesn't try to kill herself anymore.

Radio's playing Grieg's "Morning." Elliot loved that piece. I wonder where he is now. He called once, about four years ago when he was in New York, but we didn't meet. Leanna was with him

Dad's still asleep. I guess it was his way of making it to seventy.

Don't suppose I'll ever find out about him, Kenton, CAT and all that. He was right; it doesn't matter. At least I have his "souvenir" 707. Dad said modern vendors didn't make model planes like they made this one. The doors open and the roller staircase hooks up to a latch in the doorway. It's made of metal, not plastic, and is heavy. The rubber tires grip firmly onto the shelf.

Life feels real in the mornings. Dad used to tell me that when I cried at night, scared of the dark, scared of feelings I didn't understand as a child. Mornings, he said, meant the cycle hadn't ended so I needn't despair.

He was right. Life could be worse than having to go back for awhile. I got my MBA, thanks to Gordie who encouraged me, so it'll be easy enough to get a job if I need to. Better than a passport, he said. Or, if I don't want to work, Paul will take care of me. Marriage in Hong Kong has its advantages. I'll have the old flat, which is probably worth a fortune by now. Besides, I may even get to keep the green card.

Gordie's headed my way. He's making eating signs. Life, Gordie says, only becomes civilized after breakfast.

It's going to be a beautiful day. Even the East River's sparkling.

1st edition *Hong Kong Rose* (Asia 2000 Ltd., Hong Kong, 1997)